GROUP HEX
Vol. 2

The Great Lakes Horror Company

The Great Lakes Horror Company
presents

Group Hex
Vol. 2

New and Previously Published Works
Collected by Andrew Robertson
Art Editor: Brad Middleton

Illustrated Edition

Published by the Great Lakes Horror Company

Kelley Armstrong, Suzanne Church, Brian F. H. Clement,
Derek Clendening, Alessia Giacomi, Sephera Giron, Danann
Hawes, Repo Kempt, Nancy Kilpatrick, Monica S. Kuebler,
Shebat Legion, John R. Little, D. J. Adadjii, Stephen B. Pearl,
Mary Rajotte, Lou Rera, Andrew Robertson, Douglas Smith,
Robert Smith, Julianne Snow, Jessie Turk, Jason White

GROUP HEX VOL. 2

A GREAT LAKES HORROR COMPANY BOOK

Group Hex Vol. 2 copyright © Great Lakes Horror Company, 2017

"Amautlik" copyright © 2017 Repo Kempt
"Base of a Triangle" copyright © 1998, 2001 Nancy Kilpatrick
"Bone Drum" and "Pen" copyright © 2017 Monica S. Kuebler
"Curtain Call" copyright © 2017 Derek Clendening
"Dead Flowers by a Roadside" copyright © 2012 Kelley Armstrong
"Death Over Easy" copyright © 2012 Suzanne Church
"End Game" copyright © 2017 Alessia Giacomi
"Evidence" copyright © 2017 Jessie Turk
"Fiddleheads" copyright © 2013 Douglas Smith
"Garlic Steamed Mussels" copyright © 2017 Robert Smith
"Gratitude" copyright © 2017 Danann Hawes
"Hiss Click" copyright © 2017 Stephen B. Pearl
"House of Dandridge" copyright © 2017 Jason White
"Husks" copyright © 2017 Mary Rajotte
"It's Never Over Easy" copyright © 2017 Julianne Snow
"Memories" copyright © 2017 Sephera Giron
"Shells" copyright © 2017 Andrew Robertson
"Subdermal" copyright © 2017 Brian F. H. Clement
"The Cast Iron Skillet" © 2017 Shebat Legion
"The Last Straw" copyright © 2017 Lou Rera
"The Soul Broker" copyright © 2017 D. J. Adadjii
"The Slow Haunting" copyright © 2009 John R. Little

Cover Design © Dinis Freitas

Art Editor: Brad Middleton.

All artwork is copyright © the artists, used by permission.
Previous publication information appears in the About the Authors section

Interior Formatted by Julianne Snow — www.juliannesnow.com

FIRST GREAT LAKES HORROR COMPANY EDITION, OCTOBER 2017

ISBN-13: 978-1976581472
ISBN-10: 1976581478

GROUP HEX
VOL 2

THE STORIES

THE ARTWORK

HUSKS

Mary Rajotte

The incessant beeping of a full computer system failure was the last thing David Powell needed when he started his shift at the Avalon Publishing House.

The other copy editors were running around like a herd of spooked cattle when he set foot in the office that morning. Janet, with her dishwater gray complexion, looked like she'd swallowed a glass of sour milk. She winced at David over the top of her horn-rimmed glasses. Her mouth hung open like she was about to speak but she made nothing more than a pathetic little peep.

"What the hell happened?" David asked.

"The writers," she squawked. "They lost everything."

The words pinged around David's brain like a hyperactive pinball, giving him an instant migraine.

The fluorescent lights overhead flickered a few times before they buzzed back to life. The sound made David's teeth ache.

"Where the hell's Alex?" David asked, spinning in his spot. "He isn't supervising, that's for sure!"

Janet cowered into the folds of her turtleneck and skittered away.

David turned to his other co-workers, hoping for a response. Experience told him that was as futile as expecting stimulating conversation from the fake plastic tree in the corner.

Jesse, an ancient relic of a man, paused in front of David and jabbed his skeletal finger up in the air at the pockmarked ceiling a few times. "They called him upstairs."

David did a double-take. "What do you mean... upstairs? Like..."

"He's one of *them* now."

Jesse couldn't shuffle his decrepit ass away from David any slower. Fists clenched at his sides, David's neck burned. That Neanderthal got called upstairs? He could barely string two sentences together. When he did, they were monosyllabic and with the education level of a kindergartener.

"So, who's doing Alex's job?"

Everyone scattered, heading back to their white cookie cutter workstations at David's question, leaving him to seethe alone. Overhead, the alarm continued to screech from the intercom. Seeing his fellow employees hunched over their keyboards as though they had the tiniest hint of initiative in attempting to fix the problem made David clench his molars together.

"Well, *someone* has to do something."

He snatched the white plastic key card from Alex's desk on his way to the elevator. A quick tap to the keypad with the card activated the doors. As soon as they slid open, David rushed inside and jabbed the button for the top floor.

"B-b-but, David," Janet called out from behind the fake plastic tree with the authority of a church mouse. "You're not cleared to go up there."

David arched an eyebrow in her direction. "I am now."

The door closed between them. Soppy, milquetoast elevator music whined from a speaker in the ceiling. There was a quick rush of stale, recycled air before the floor numbers started to ping off one-by-one. One floor for each of the years he'd spent mired in wishful thinking. One for each year he'd forgone life without any distraction other than his writing.

David massaged his aching hands together. A couple of practically crippled claws and weekly injections to keep his joints from seizing were all he had to show for the hours spent fixing other people's mistakes. He was only a handful of years from retirement. It was time to make management pay attention before his hands gave out completely and he was nothing more than a useless husk.

The suits who'd written the corporate policy frowned upon those of the lower echelon barging into other divisions. David didn't care. It was obvious someone upstairs was slacking on the job. Opportunity was knocking and he was more than ready to answer.

A double-chime signaled his arrival at the top floor. The doors slid open.

The Writer's Floor was nothing like David imagined. There were no over-sized leather chairs arranged in a semi-circle around a fireplace; no small groups of authors swirling bourbon in highball glasses while they chatted about their latest brilliant works.

Instead, he found himself standing in a long sterile corridor. Ignoring the series of uniformly-fashioned doors lining either side of the hallway, David proceeded. He stopped in front of an over-sized window that offered a glimpse into the darkness beyond. He stepped up to the glass and cupped his hands around his eyes.

It took a few moments, but when his eyes adjusted, David could make out half a dozen translucent caterpillar-like shapes as tall as him. They hung from large meat hooks bolted to metal grating along the ceiling. Overhead lightbulbs cast each one in an eerie red glow.

Next to the door, David noticed a red phone bolted above an entry panel. He raised his hand and pressed the key card to the panel before he even thought about it. A sharp buzz-click sounded. The vacuum-seal released and the door popped open. David nudged it with his boot. He wasn't sure why but he held his breath as he crossed the threshold and edged forward.

It was stifling inside. His heart hammered so loud it drowned out the voice in his head that told him to go back where he came from. But curiosity had him under its spell and it lured him closer. He reached out to the larger pod in the group and grazed it with his fingertips.

Its skin was warm and supple, and yielded to his touch, but there was something rigid inside. It poked against the thin membrane, giving it the look of the distended belly of a snake that had devoured something twice its size.

He pressed his fingers into the soft tissue. The figure inside jolted to life. The pod lurched from side to side. David shoved it when it veered toward him. It swung away then careened back, hitting him with such force that it sent him crashing to the floor.

David skidded away until his back slammed against the open door. He clung to the doorframe, unable to fathom what he was witnessing. A distinct trill sounded from inside the larger cocoon. The sound sent the other pods twisting and writhing like worms impaled on fishing hooks, yet somehow they remained tethered to the rattling metal framework.

Something prodded against the translucent sheath of the large pod, stretching out until a long, spindly limb pierced the membrane. The creature within plummeted to the floor, landing with a distinct *splosh*. Immediately, a harsh alarm sounded from overhead and the red lights overhead started to blink intermittently.

The pungent tang of sour sweat prickled David's nostrils. The thing on the floor let out an eardrum-shattering screech. The remaining cocoons careened from side-to-side until they too broke free from their tethers and crashed onto the tiles.

Pruned misshapen bodies writhed in gelatinous goop. Their skin was pallid beneath the sheen of mucous, slicking sparse patches of stringy hair to their faces like tangled spiderwebs. With their arms bent at awkward angles, they hunched like newborn calves yet they were the size of full-grown adults. Somehow, they were able to contort their backs into impossible poses and pop their abdomens in and out of joint. Yet these things were impossibly human.

Behind David, the quick patter of boot-steps grew nearer, but he was too engrossed in the grotesque scene in front of him to look away.

"Powell! What the hell's going on?"

Mr. Channing, his boss, rushed through the doorway and skidded to a stop when he saw the gruesome creatures. He scraped his fingernails across his bald head a few times, revealing a prominent pit-stain under each arm. "Jesus H..."

The sound of Channing's voice only caught the attention of the beings. They froze, jutting their jaws into elongated yawns. Their heads, misshapen by clusters of oozing lesions, looked like putrefying melons caving in on themselves. Hunched together, the things clicked that strange language back-and-forth.

"This was never supposed to happen," Channing said. "We have fail-safes in place to avoid this kind of nightmare!"

"So, you know all about this?" David said, clutching at his stomach. "What the hell *are* those things?"

Channing glared at him. "This doesn't concern you, Powell. What the hell are you doing up here anyway? This area's off limits. You don't belong here."

But David didn't give a crap about any kind of reprimand. He only cared that one of the mutated creatures had pushed itself up onto its haunches and was watching them.

When David locked gazes with the thing, it threw its head back. It emitted a shrill cry then started cleaving a path across the floor with one arm. The other arm was meager and malformed, and hung from its body like a limp chicken wing. The skin across its scalp was so translucent David could see its pulsating brain.

He backed away and made it out to the hallway just as the thing launched at them in a sudden burst of energy. Its legs flailed behind it, making a distinct squelching on the tiled floor. Channing managed to slip through the doorway just before the creature caught up to him. David hauled the door closed, not daring to breathe until the suction-seal was secured.

Channing pushed past him and reached for the red phone bolted to the wall. He propped it to his ear with a shaking hand.

"Yes, sir. It's me," Channing said into the receiver with a wavering voice. "They got cut off from their oxygen supply when the power went out. The pods have been compromised."

They? David thought. *The pods? What the hell's going on here?*

"I realize that, sir. A month too early. Even two." Channing scrubbed at the back of his neck. "Protocol to follow, yes. I know that. But... are you sure you want to me do that? We'll lose months here, sir. And with the state of the others—"

There are others?

A sudden thumping on the other side of the window punctuated the debate. The creatures flung themselves against it, leaving splatters of bloody mucous on the glass. The one that chased them had managed to drag itself upright. It pawed at the observation window with sticky fingertips, staring out at them from behind bulbous, opalescent eyes.

Channing moved toward the control pad and punched in a series of numbers before responding with a strained, "Yes, sir."

As if sensing Channing's intentions, the creatures thrashed harder against the window, leaving oozing imprints. David edged a few steps back, fully expecting them to come crashing through the glass at any moment.

Channing replaced the handset and stood unmoving with his arm in the air and his fingers poised over the control pad. His entire arm shook. His chest heaved in and out and his brow glowed moist with sweat.

David watched the freakish creatures but he couldn't make sense of any of them. *Whatever* they were, *whatever* they were doing here, it was wrong. *They* were wrong.

But Channing wasn't going to go through with it. David could tell by the way his hand wavered over the blinking button. It was the same as those idiots downstairs. He didn't have the balls. David knew deep in his gut if he didn't do something about these things *himself*, no one else would.

So, he lunged forward, reached over Channing's hand and punched down the button with the full weight of his body.

The intercom let out a forlorn *buzz-buzz-buzz*, which signaled a rush of water through the pipes overhead. Within seconds, a valve had opened in the ceiling of the lab and a torrent rained down on the creatures. They erupted in a chaotic frenzy on the other side of the window.

David recoiled to the opposite side of the hall, and watched the things thrash and tear at one another in a desperate attempt to get away from the deluge. But the force of the water was so intense, it sent their bodies thudding against the glass. In mere moments, the room had filled, and diluted their wails into nothing more than choked gurgles.

Adrenaline shock-waved across David's scalp. He knew exactly what he'd set off inside that room yet he couldn't look away, not even when the bedlam finally stopped and a body floated in front of the window. It pirouetted to reveal its pale pink belly distended with water. Its mouth hadn't completely formed yet. There was a gaping hole in its face where its lips should be. Bile scorched the back of David's throat.

Without a sound, Channing pressed a switch on the control panel. The water level started to recede and the bodies fell from view. Unable to stop himself, David stepped up to the window to peer inside. It was silent. Still. The creatures lay lifeless on the floor like water-logged driftwood.

David jumped at the sound of a door buzzing open at the end of the hall. A tall man in a grey suit came striding toward them. His lips were clamped together in a taut slash. Two men in blue work jumpsuits scurried behind him, rolling a half dozen over-sized bins to the door. One prodded at the keypad while the other kept his hand poised on the door handle.

"Mr. Avalon, sir." Channing greeted him.

"Is it done?" Avalon said, propping one arm up to knead the muscles in back of his neck.

"Yes, sir. It is."

"Quick thinking there, Channing. Bravo."

No way, David thought, stepping between Avalon and Channing. "Actually, it was me, sir. I flushed the system."

"Oh?" Mr. Avalon tore his gaze away from the blue-suited men as they entered the room and glanced at David's name tag. "Powell is it?"

David steeled his jaw. "Yes sir. David Powell."

Avalon pulled a small tablet from inside his jacket pocket. He jabbed at the screen a few times, and then raised one eyebrow. "Copy editor. You don't have clearance for this floor."

David swallowed. "No, sir. I don't."

"And you discovered this little problem... how?"

Avalon turned his attention back to the workmen. With white masks secured over their noses and mouths, they slipped thick goggles over their eyes. David expected them to jump back from the gruesome scene but they got right to work.

"The alarm was going off when I walked into the office today." David side-eyed the workmen, thankful he wasn't one of them. "I didn't see anyone else doing anything."

"So, you stepped in?" Avalon turned back to him, his eyebrows jutted upward like two lightning bolts.

"*Someone* had to."

Avalon gave a satisfied head-nod before glancing up at the activity in the lab. Stepping carefully over the pale, bloated bodies, one of the workmen unfurled a plastic sheet and then waited for the other to stoop and shovel one of the creatures onto it. After wrapping the body, they repeated the process with the others. When they finished, they hauled each of the bodies one-by-one toward the door, depositing each into a separate bin before shoving the bins in the direction of the elevator. There was no conversation between the two; no hesitation in their actions. The fact that they simply went about their business like this was just another day at the office made David's skin prickle with gooseflesh.

Avalon turned his attention back to his tablet. He swiped at the screen, nodding and making a satisfied face as he read.

"I like you, Powell," he finally said. "We need someone with your drive up here."

"Here?" David's stomach lurched at the thought. Maybe getting on that elevator this morning wasn't such a good idea after all.

"No. I'm talking about a promotion."

"A promotion, sir?" David squeezed his fists together but tried to keep his cool.

Avalon broke into a smile. He turned on his heel and started down the corridor. "Follow me, Powell."

David needed no further invitation. He bounded away from Channing, and away from the workmen and their grotesque cargo-laden bins without looking back. He caught up to Avalon, who buzzed himself through the big white door at the end of the hall.

Stepping over the threshold, David was plunged into another world. An orderly regiment of freestanding walls separated each workstation from the next. A scattering of vintage desk lamps gave the room a cozy glow. It was so dimly lit that David couldn't make out any of his fellow writers, but the clickety-clack of their keyboards sent a flush of relief across David's shoulders. *This* was how he'd always imagined the Writer's Floor.

Avalon turned to David and nudged him with his elbow. "How does in-house writer sound?"

Before David could answer, a woman in a white lab coat came striding toward them.

"Sir, this loss of our assets couldn't come at a worse time, just as we're about to—"

Avalon held up one hand to silence her.

"We'll deal with that once the system has had time to recover. For now, we continue with the status quo."

The woman wrinkled her brow, paused a beat, and then said, "Continue with the old system?"

Avalon nodded. "We have Powell here to thank for taking initiative and ridding us of a costly mistake. As a reward, I'm making him our latest author-in-residence. He'll be a welcome addition to our roster, don't you think, Susan?"

Susan cast a wary gaze in David's direction. "But sir. With everything we've lost today, is this really the time to—"

Avalon took Susan by the elbow and pulled her to one side. "That is exactly why I'm doing this. Those things in the lab? You didn't see them. You don't know."

"But sir. That's to be expected," she whispered. "They weren't ready yet."

"They weren't just premature, Susan. They were *deformed*. Every last one of them," Avalon said, not exactly keeping his voice low. "We're just lucky the quality control system kicked in before we reached the point of no return. Now, until we can figure out what the hell went wrong, we'll continue the old fashioned way. Got it?"

Susan pinched her lips together and gave a curt nod.

"We've lost a hell of a lot today, Susan. I want you to do whatever it takes to make up for that loss. Even if that means we run 24-7. Is that understood?"

Without waiting for a response, Avalon patted her on the shoulder before he turned and flashed David a paper-thin smile.

"Right. As I've said, Powell deserves a seat in our roster of writers. Please set him up at a workstation. I want him to start immediately. Unless you have any objections, Powell?"

David squeezed his shoulder blades together and held his head high. "Not at all, sir. I've wanted this from the moment I started working here. This is where I belong."

Avalon smiled and slapped David on the back. "You see, this is why I like you, Powell. You're not afraid to go after what you want. You'll do very well up here for us. Of this, I'm sure."

David felt light-headed. Everything was happening so fast. But with Avalon watching him, David kept his expression neutral. "Thank you for this opportunity, Mr. Avalon. I won't let you down."

"Don't thank me yet, Powell. Soon you'll be a slave to the grind like the rest of our writers. But as you can hear..." he cupped his hand to his ear and tilted his head to one side, "no one's complaining."

David's heart raced. That alarm today was no accident. It was fate stepping in, handing him what was rightfully his. All those mind-numbing hours fixing other people's mistakes had finally paid off. After 25 years of loyalty to Avalon Publishing, he'd finally earned the recognition he deserved.

Reminders of those things on the other side of the door quick-flashed in David's mind. Their misshapen bodies. Their haunting gazes. Their gut-curdling screams silenced in a watery deluge. The unceremonious disposal of their bodies in those over-sized bins. Was this promotion really worth it? Was the cost too much?

"Mr. Powell," Susan said.

When David snapped back to reality, he found Susan standing in front of him, jabbing at her portable tablet. Other than looking a little over-worked, she didn't seem to have a problem with what was going on around Avalon Publishing. Those guys in the blue jumpsuits didn't seem to either. David sure as hell wasn't going to be the one to say anything, not when he'd finally made it to the top floor.

"Please verify your information and sign here." She held out the tablet and a stylus pen to him.

David instinctively rubbed the tops of his hands. She'd been reading his personnel file. David took the tablet from her and pulled it against his chest. He hoped to hell she wouldn't notice he could barely keep his grip on it.

He scanned the information. Everything looked correct. His address—check. Marital status—single. His next of kin—both parents deceased, no siblings. Medical information—only the arthritis. David swallowed hard before signing it and handing it back to her. If she wasn't going to mention it, neither was he.

She gave the info one last scan before she motioned to the empty cubicle on her right. "This will be your workstation. Have a seat."

David drew in a sharp breath before moving inside. In the center of the cubicle sat a black leather ergonomic chair. It had a long scooped seat. Affixed to the back, a nylon harness left a tangled mass of straps and buckles hanging at either side.

It looked like it belonged in a dentist's office but David didn't care. He looked up the aisle. From the continued patter of keystrokes in the cubicles around him, it didn't seem to bother any of the other writers. They'd obviously gotten the memo that being called up to the top floor was a golden opportunity. Now that David had been handed the same chance, he wasn't going to blow it by questioning Avalon's quirky set-up.

He sat down on the edge of the seat and then swung his legs around onto the elevated leg rest. As he settled in, two men in lab coats stepped out of the shadows and appeared beside him. One attended to a large monitor affixed to the side wall. The other wheeled a rolling table complete with keyboard into the cubicle.

"Relax now, Mr. Powell," the first tech said as he maneuvered David's head back against the chair's small headrest. "I'm James. This is Scotty. We're here to get you set up."

Scotty moved in front of David. He slid the straps over David's shoulders and then secured the buckles across his chest with a decisive tug.

When David tilted his head back, he discovered an elaborate rigging system secured to a steel rod from the ceiling. The sight of it made him shiver but when he looked from one of the attendees to the other, they showed no hint of apprehension. Maybe this was just how they did things here. Who was he to question their methods?

James leaned over him and reached for one of the cables, which he yanked down and held in position in front of David. There was a black harness affixed to the end. James lifted David's left arm from the armrest and slid the harness around his bicep. Once the strap was buckled into place, James repeated the procedure with David's other arm. When he finished, James stepped back, leaving both of David's arms suspended in mid-air.

"Uh, wait a minute. What is this?" David's carotid pulsated when he found he couldn't move either arm more than an inch or two.

"It, uh... keeps you secure while you work," James said.

He exchanged glances with Susan, who was supervising the proceedings. As she looked on, both James and Scotty slipped an armor-like glove onto each of David's hands. Segmented joints of black plastic snapped together to form robotic-looking fingers. Before David could react, Scotty maneuvered the rolling table into position under David's hands.

"Try it," he said.

When David looked up at him, he realized he was talking to James, who stood with his fingers poised over his tablet. After a few quick taps to the screen, David's fingers started to move across the keyboard.

"Hey! Wait a minute!" he said, watching as his hands flew over the keys of their own volition.

"Looks good," James said clearing his throat. "You're all set, Mr. Powell."

"Set for *what*? What are these things? I thought I'd be writing my own stories." He held up his hands and wriggled his fingers at them. "*You're* the ones controlling things."

David tried to pull off the gloves but the cables kept him propped up like a helpless puppet.

Scotty rolled his eyes at David before exiting the cubicle.

"Mr. Powell, please," James said. "The gloves are just a tool to help you. Given your condition, that is."

David's face burned. Someone had been paying attention to his file after all.

"All of our writers wear them," James continued. "The words will still be yours. These just... help to keep your productivity up with Mr. Avalon's standards. Alright?"

David nodded, feeling the hot pulse of panic on the back of his neck diminish to a dull throb. The last thing he wanted to do was blow this chance by asking too many questions. Maybe he could talk to Avalon about it later.

"Good. You'll do great. Just relax now, huh? You've made it to the top floor, Mr. Powell. Enjoy it."

James moved out of the cubicle just as Susan approached David with a medical kit in hand.

The quick, cold swipe of a cotton swab on the side of his neck was a prelude to what came next. The pinprick of a syringe made David jolt in his seat. A sharp torrent of adrenaline flushed his system, making everything in the room seem to move at hyper-speed. His muscles pulled taut against the restraints, but the harness kept him from getting very far. After a few moments, every fiber in his body slackened like pulled taffy, and his thoughts started to run together, slow and syrupy like globs of paint on a palette. Susan unbuttoned David's shirt and pressed a sticky electrode pad to his chest. When she finished, she pulled a length of clear tubing from her kit. She held it up to his nose, then looped it around his ear and extended it down his front side. She snipped it off before pulling out a small bottle and smearing its contents on one end.

When she moved toward David, his eyes bulged and his body went rigid, but the combination of the harness and the drugs proved too much to overcome.

With one hand on David's forehead, Susan inserted the end of the tube into his left nostril and with the other hand, fed the tubing down his throat.

"Swallow please, David. Swallow a few times for me," she directed when he started to gag.

David complied, with each swallow massaging the tubing further until his inclination to retch subsided.

"Good. Very good. Relax now."

"B-but..." David sputtered.

"You agreed to this, didn't you? To be one of our writers?" Her voice cracked as she spoke.

David nodded and tried to respond but his tongue felt as heavy as a dead slug in his mouth.

"Then *this* is what it takes," she said quickly, before squeezing her eyes closed and taking in a deep breath. "Please. Just... relax now. You're in good—"

Before she could finish, an alarm sounded from somewhere beside them. Susan jumped and cursed under her breath then bolted from the cubicle.

"I'll be right back," she snapped at the men as she brushed past. "Deal with this."

David made a weak attempt to free himself but they'd secured him too well. His body felt gangly. He could barely keep his head upright. His eyelids fluttered and threatened to close. He sat there defenseless, unable to do anything other than watch the scene play out before him.

Both James and Scotty crowded into the workstation across the aisle. A man sat harnessed in the same manner as David. He was completely unresponsive to the blaring alarm on the monitor above his head.

Armed with his tablet, James prodded at the screen a few times. After a few moments, the man let out an airy gasp. His joints lurched slowly at first, then moved in a stilted rhythm that made him look like a disjointed marionette.

That's when David realized. It was Alex.

David tried to quell the surge of panic that cobwebbed across his scalp. Alex's face looked hard as stone and his eyes stared ahead blankly as his hands fell into a mechanical rhythm across the keyboard.

"Looks like his blood's flowing again," Scotty said. "Luckily he wasn't down long enough for a complete circulatory breakdown."

James went into one of the other cubicles and grunted. "Don't pat yourself on the back yet."

David fought his fatigue and directed his wary gaze to the woman in the next workstation. Something was wrong with her. She looked like a comatose mannequin blanched of all color.

When Scotty joined James, he tilted his head back and drew his breath in sharply. "No, no, no, no, no!"

A plastic feeding tube dripped a steady stream of water onto the floor. James reached for the tube and pinched it off to stop the leakage.

"Who the hell left her like this anyway?" James asked.

"I did," Scotty said. "They told us to start phasing this group out for the new ones. That's it! No other direction. Nothing. You know they're always keeping us in the dark in here. How the hell was I supposed to know what to do?"

"What, so you were just going to let them wither away to nothing?" James shook his head at him.

"Come on, man! They're basically just mindless shells now anyway," Scotty whispered just loud enough for David to hear. "There's no life left in 'em. Not really."

"If that's how you feel then why are you still working here?"

Scotty held out one hand and rubbed his fingers together. "Dollar dollar bills, y'all."

"Seriously? The pittance they pay us to keep these husks pumping out bestsellers? That justifies treating these people like they're expendable?"

"Aren't they though?"

James recoiled, holding both hands up and backing away from Scotty.

"Oh, please," Scotty said. "Don't tell me you care about them. You've hooked as many of 'em up to the system as I have. I'll bet you're not so welcoming when they roll out those things they're incubating under heat lamps back there and hook them up like the rest of Avalon's little puppets."

"Enough!" James said, lunging for him. "I can't stand to listen to you anymore. Let's just check the rest of 'em before Susan gets back."

James jumped into action and leaned over the woman to press the button on the monitor. When the alarm stopped, he lifted the feeding tube and tried to direct it back into the woman's mouth this time.

"Please drink this, please, please."

But when the plastic touched her mouth, the woman's jaw crumbled in on itself and fell into her lap.

"Fuck!" James started into the darkness but stopped himself, then spun around and threw his hands up.

The movement caused the dried out husk of the woman to disintegrate like ash. Her remains wafted upward and illuminated like stardust in the dim lamplight for a moment. But in the next, all traces of her were gone, save for her clothing, which fell into a defeated heap on the floor.

A door closed out of view. Hurried footsteps sounded on the tiled floor and then Susan appeared off to David's side.

Scotty moved in front of her. "Look, Susan, I—"

She held up a hand to stop him. "I don't want to hear it. There's just way too much going on right now for me to listen to your excuses. All I want is for you to do your job. Check *every one* of these workstations. You'll do whatever it takes to save the ones you can, got it? Before Avalon comes in here and fires all of us."

Both James and Scotty nodded before pushing past her and getting to work. She stood there for a moment, wringing her hands in front of her before smoothing down the front of her lab coat.

When Susan turned toward him, a wave of nausea flooded David's system. He willed his body to move, to get up, to do *something*, but nothing happened. Instead, he sat there like a rag doll at the mercy of his own ambition.

She took a few steps in David's direction then stopped halfway. She spun back as if to say something to the techs but stopped herself. She shook her head abruptly, and then strode toward David, stopping in the entryway to his cubicle. She looked up at his monitor before moving beside him.

"At least we have you, isn't that right?"

She leaned over him, pried one of his eyes open and shone a small light into it. David could feel his body trying to recoil from her touch, but it responded with only the tiniest twitch from his smallest finger.

"Everything looks good, Mr. Powell. Are you ready to start a new chapter in your career here at Avalon?"

She stood upright and smiled down at him but her lips wavered. Her gaze ping-ponged from David, then up to the monitor, and then back to him again.

"Everything will be alright. You can relax now, okay? I promise you we'll take good care of you as long as you produce. All you have to do is let the words come to you. If you get tired, the gloves will do the heavy lifting." When she leaned down to whisper in David's ear, her toneless voice made David's nerves twang with dread. "This is your dream job. Remember?"

At first, there was nothing. David couldn't will his hands to move. His thoughts percolated one torturous moment at a time. Then, just as any last fragment of self-confidence he possessed threatened to shatter completely, his fingers sprung to life.

One word appeared on the screen above him. Then another. Soon, David had written his first sentence. And then a full paragraph. When he finally relaxed and gave in, he could barely keep up with the unending torrent of thoughts all vying for his attention. His fingers flittered across the keyboard and soon, he fell into rhythm with the other writers around him. The sound of their typing rose to a lively din. Just like that, he was living the dream.

He'd finally made it to the top floor at Avalon Publishing. It wasn't exactly what he expected, and it sure as hell wasn't the way he'd dreamed it would be all these years. But how could he complain?

He was one of them now.

AMAUTALIK

Repo Kempt

When the first child disappeared from the village that winter, the elders blamed his parents. The father was a drunk and the mother had a history of neglect. Their six-year-old boy had been playing alone near the shoreline when he vanished. Winter tides caused the thick sea ice to split and heave, creating dark crevasses into the depths beneath. Gossiping locals in the remote Arctic community agreed that the unsupervised toddler had likely slipped into one of those fissures, but his little body was never found.

Three weeks later, when a girl of similar age went missing while crossing the frozen bay with her friends, it was considered a tragic coincidence. But when a third child disappeared that winter, the Inuit elders whispered a long-forgotten word, a name not spoken for a generation. And that name was *amautalik.*

The left jab struck Killiktee in the nose, snapping her head back. White lights flared behind her eyes before her world went dark. The second blow missed her chin by a finger-width as she stumbled backward from the impact of the first. She struggled to regain her footing on the icy ground, the extra weight of her unborn baby making it all the more difficult.

Joanasie lunged at her again with his fists raised, his long black hair swirling in the rising wind. Killiktee's arms flew up instinctively to shield her face. But this time, her attacker kicked. The sole of his winter boot landed hard on her swollen abdomen and she fell on the frozen snowbank, the wind knocked from her lungs. She curled into a fetal position, clutching her belly, gasping for air. Joanasie loomed over her with his fists clenched.

"I'm not the father," he told the gathering crowd in Inuktitut. He pointed at Killiktee on the ground. "She's a whore."

Most of the onlookers knew it was Joanasie's child inside her. They knew he had taken the girl by force as he had taken others. They knew all of this, yet no one stepped forward to confront him.

Killiktee took several long and laboured breaths, counting each in her mind, before she opened her eyes. Joanasie was gone. She pushed herself to her feet, bowing her battered head and sweeping the snow from her dirty parka with trembling hands. The crowd had dwindled considerably, but those who remained beneath the streetlamp outside the local store stared hard from under clouds of cigarette smoke and ice crystals. Killiktee's icy fingertips found the fresh bruises on her face. Heat and nausea washed over her with each touch. Her belly ached from the blow, but Killiktee felt the baby kick before she even took a step. An unclean feeling swept over her. Hateful thoughts toward the child had plagued her for months, as did the overwhelming guilt that came with them. She wanted the child to disappear. She wanted to run to Maata's house, and throw herself back into her arms, back into the warmth of their bed. But the realization struck her, as it always did, that Maata was gone. Six weeks and counting. Humiliated and exhausted, Killiktee stumbled away from the lights of the storefront.

The derelict community health centre had seen better days. Harsh antiseptic and the odour of old books permeated the patient assessment room and paint peeled from the water-stained ceiling. Sitting on the examination table, Killiktee shifted her weight continually to relieve the nagging pain in her lower back. The faded-red vinyl squeaked beneath her when she moved.

When the nurse returned, she held out two white pills and a paper cup filled with warm water. Killiktee swallowed the medicine without question.

"The *good* news is the baby survived the ordeal," said the nurse. "It helps that you're so young and healthy. But we don't want to take any chances. Especially given that your due date is already past." She licked her thumb and forefinger, flipped back through her clipboard chart to search for something specific and marked it with her pen once she found it. After the nurse finished reviewing her notes, she offered a matter-of-fact smile to Killiktee. "We're putting you on the next flight to Iqaluit. Medical evacuation. You'll be induced once we get you settled over there."

The nearest hospital was in the capital city, Iqaluit, fifteen-hundred kilometres away as the raven flies. Killiktee nodded, considering all at once the many things and people involved in such a trip. She rubbed both hands over the surface of her midriff and clenched her teeth in discomfort. "Induced?"

"The doctors will help make the baby come out," said the nurse. Killiktee raised her eyebrows high, indicating she understood.

"They're calling for a blizzard this evening," the nurse continued, looking out at the blowing snow through her own reflection in the dark glass of the window. "So we'll have to move fast to get you out before it hits."

Killiktee momentarily considered telling the nurse that moving quickly wasn't an option in her current condition, but instead scooted forward on the examination table until her bare feet hit the floor. She flashed a reasonable facsimile of a smile and gathered her belongings from the floor by the door. When she picked up her parka, a medium-sized kitchen knife fell out of the front pouch and clattered across the tiles. The nurse looked at the blade on the floor and then at Killiktee with a mix of surprise and confusion. Killiktee bent over cautiously, aware of the potential pain in her back, and picked up the knife.

"For protection," she said, holding up the blade flat across her open palm, so as to be non-threatening as possible. When the nurse's expression didn't change, Killiktee continued while staring at the knife, as if contemplating the power it held: "Next time, I'm going to fight back."

The nurse's face relaxed as if she suddenly understood. "You can leave that here. You won't need that on the flight." She smiled sheepishly, feeling foolish for her sarcastic tone and added: "No one is going to hurt you anymore."

Killiktee pulled her coat over her head. The nurse spun around to place her clipboard on the countertop and Killiktee quickly tucked the knife back into her pouch.

"Do you have someone who can bring you your things?" asked the nurse as Killiktee opened the door toward the waiting room. "Or at least get them together so we can pick them up on the way to the airport?"

"What things?"

"Toiletries, change of clothes, your ID cards."

"What are toilet-rees?"

"Things you'll need to travel with," said the nurse. "Just call someone and have them bring whatever you need for the trip over here before the police arrive."

"I don't want it," said Killiktee.

"The knife? I'm sure if you leave it here, someone from your house can pick it up later."

"The baby," Killiktee clarified.

The nurse frowned, disappointment flooding her features. "Well, have you thought about adoption?"

Killiktee nodded, grimacing as a spark of pain flashed in her right jawline. "*You* could adopt it."

The nurse chuckled at the absurdity of the statement and then lifted the back of her hand to her mouth as she realized the inappropriateness of her reaction.

"I'm too old to have a child to look after," said the nurse. "But I'm sure someone in this town would love to have your child. To love and care for as their own."

"Everyone hates Joanasie," said Killiktee. "No one would want to take his baby."

"I'm sure not *everyone* hates him."

"Everyone," Killiktee said, staring at the floor of the room. "I hate him." She noticed the puddle of melted snow that had formed around her winter boots. Then she realized she was crying.

The nurse laid a hand on Killiktee's shoulder and ducked her head to eye level.

"What about those three families who lost their children this winter? I bet they would love to have a baby to care for."

Killiktee raised her head, tears flowing. "The *amautalik* will take more."

"Everyone keeps saying that word. What does it mean?"

"She has a pouch on her back. A parka like mine, but with a hood for the baby, an *amauti*. Only filled with rotten seaweed, made from walrus hide. She stuffs the children inside it when they play on her ice."

"Oh, it's like a boogeyman."

Killiktee shook her head. "My grandmother said it came when she was a child. It took five kids."

"So you think we'll lose two more kids before this winter is through." A patronizing tone slipped into her voice and the apparent concern in her features suddenly seemed excessive.

"Maybe," said Killiktee.

The nurse smiled, her eyes sympathetic.

"Have you ever thought about leaving this town? Is there any place you'd like to go, even for a while?"

"I've never been anywhere," said Killiktee, pausing to take stock of her short life. "All my relatives are here. This is home."

The nurse slumped her shoulders, nodding almost imperceptibly, and clasped her hands in front of her. "I've already notified the police of the beating. It's your choice what you decide to do about it. You can speak with them when they arrive."

"I don't want to talk to the police."

"They will be coming soon to drive you to the airport for the med-evac. You should make that call home now so you can get your things ready. The police can pick them up on the way."

Killiktee shuffled out into the waiting area holding her belongings. Every movement hurt somewhere different. She would be thankful when the time came to lie down. A woman near the desk held a newborn with another small child clinging to her leg. Perhaps a baby wouldn't be so bad, even the child of a monster. Maybe in time people would forget the child's history and love the little girl as Killiktee would learn to love her. She reached for the public telephone on the wall near the front door and raised a finger to dial her mother's number. As she did so, a damp cough drew her attention to the waiting area. An older woman with a metal cane propped against her leg leaned in to whisper in the ear of a younger man seated next to her. They looked away when Killiktee's eyes met theirs. Killiktee hung up the phone and left the building.

Standing outside on the steps of the health centre in the frigid wind, she cursed her unborn child, cursed the bastard who had put it there. She thought of the life her baby would have in this little town. The same life that Killiktee had suffered through. The same life that Maata had chosen to end rather than endure. Regardless of its sex, the baby would be a constant reminder of a man Killiktee hated. She took one last look toward the nurse, who was occupied with another patient, and trudged away from the health centre into the surrounding night.

An hour later, Killiktee brought her cigarette to her chapped lips. Standing at the edge of the frozen ocean with her back to the lights of the community, she looked out across a thousand miles of barren landscape, shrouded in the perpetual darkness of winter. Pulling her hood down, the fur trim tightened against her face. She knew the police would be looking for her. She knew the pilots and the nurses would be waiting.

Her grandmother had told her stories of the *amautalik* when Killiktee was a child. The hideous ogress kept the children alive in her lair, feeding them on the black milk of her breasts, in order to eat them later during the long, cold winter when food was scarce. As a little girl, these terrible stories kept Killiktee from roaming near the shoreline, and haunted her dreams.

The cherry of her cigarette glowed with each inhale, smoke mingling with the icy crystals of her exhale. Her back ached from the earlier fall and the pain from the kick had not subsided. Killiktee grimaced as a spasm rippled through her. She pulled off her dog-fur mitten with her teeth and slipped her bare hand into pocket of her parka, resting it on her abdomen. She took one last drag and flicked the smouldering remains of the filter into the darkness. Maybe she should do what she was told, get on the plane, and have the baby. Perhaps she could make a life here for them both, even without Maata. From the corner of her eye, she saw someone on the edge of the shore, perhaps a hundred metres away. They yelled to her, a few words lost on the fleeting wind. Their arms waved over their head, as if trying to get her attention. Killiktee glanced back at lights of the town, glimmering in the swirling snow, then she spun back around to face the barren landscape. The baby kicked at her mother's sudden movement and Killiktee grimaced when a cramp erupted in her lower back.

It was then that she decided. She would no longer be shamed or burdened. She would be redeemed, loved by everyone around her. One child, a tender newborn, a sacrifice to save the others. An offering the greedy beast could not resist.

Without knowing where she was going, she walked out into the darkness on the sea ice, looking for the *amautalik*.

The crisp snow crunched beneath the soles of Killiktee's sealskin boots. The meagre light from the twinkling stars and the full moon reflected off the ice and snow around her. There was barely enough illumination for her to maneuver through the rough pack ice heaved up by the tide as she marched further from the safety of her little town. In the distance on her left, the Inuit sled dogs were chained in rows to steel pins driven into the surface of the thick ice. The dogs, sensing her presence, howled in unison. She knew from the stories that the *amautalik* despised the canines who would bark at its presence and alert the children.

The baying of the dogs intertwined with the sound of the gusting wind. Powerful cramping seized her lower body again. For a moment, she felt as if her pelvis might have broken. Killiktee paused, standing in the dark, breathing deeply until the pain passed. The hair on her neck rose sharply, her face tingled with anticipation. Every laboured breath of icy Arctic air burned her nose and throat. Then, as quickly as the pain intensified, it subsided. For the first time since she left town, she noticed the bitter cold had slipped beneath her parka and seeped into her very bones. She had to keep moving.

Killiktee walked for what she felt was a lifetime, pausing only to catch her breath or when the pain overwhelmed her. She squinted all the while, trying to discern anything around her in the dim light. She looked back at the distant lights of her community, which drifted in and out of view with the blowing snow until she reached her last chance to turn back, before the town disappeared from view.

The rising hummocks of ice had made traveling more difficult, especially with her distended belly. She had not eaten in hours, and she was not dressed properly for this unplanned trek. But she could not go back to town. She could not face the shaming eyes of the locals, or the wrath of Joanasie again. The foolishness of her decision crept into her mind, but she blew it out with a deep exhale, resting on one knee in the hard-packed snow. It would be better to die, she told herself, to join Maata in the afterlife. If she died, the baby would die, and the three of them would live together in the heaven her grandmother had so often talked about. She pushed herself to her feet and walked faster, trying to get the sluggish blood circulating in her tired legs. An Inuit girl on the ice at night should have been armed with a shotgun to deter lurking polar bears. But there were much worse things than simple bears.

Killiktee trudged around a mound of ice that was too large for her to climb. Her calves ached and the cold sapped the strength from her body. As she rounded the side, a deep crevasse appeared in the thick ice. A foul odour drifted from the hole toward her on the wind. The spasms overtook her again, queasiness accompanying the pain. She bent over, her hands on her knees, breathing slow and deep. The cramps were coming faster now, with more intensity. She knew she could not go much further. Before she could take another step, a noise erupted in the darkness.

Killiktee stood transfixed as the horrible creature dragged itself out of the blackness of the chasm with its bony arms and ragged talons. Even at twenty steps away, its breath reeked of rotten meat. Killiktee cringed at the overwhelming odour, stumbling away from the opening in the ice. The wicked creature bared its teeth, a crooked row of bony shards. Its eyelids were tightly closed, blinded by the light of the full moon. The *amautalik's* eyes were clearly better suited for living deep beneath the ice in the darkness below. Its nostrils flared, inhaling the scent of the young girl and her unborn child.

The *amautalik's* bulbous head was covered with a black mass of tangled, greasy hair with tiny bones woven into its locks. A necklace of baby skulls on a string of sinewy flesh wrapped around its neck. The gruesome jewelry rattled as the beast shambled out of the icy fissure. The ogresses' gelatinous body shifted beneath the layers of animal pelts, creatures she had likely eaten in times when no children were available.

Killiktee's face trembled as the beast approached her. She bit hard into her lower lip to keep from screaming as the creature opened its mouth wider than Killiktee thought possible, revealing the full set of its jagged fangs. It belched, unleashing a icy cloud of decaying stench toward her. The ugly beast stopped in its tracks and reached out with its spindly arms, curling and flexing its talons toward the baby inside her.

Killiktee retreated, gripping her midsection. The razor-sharp fingernails of the *amautalik* gleamed in the moonlight and Killiktee reached up with one hand to touch her neck, imagining the blood pouring out over her fingers should the creature decide to slash it. The beast rotated its hands and flashed it claws, clicking the bony nails together rapidly, creating an unholy rhythm.

It lumbered forward again, its nose twitching as it sniffed like a hungry dog. Killiktee kept pace, stepping backward to keep the distance between them. The long claws of the creature dug into the thick surface of the ice, dragging its body behind them, its stubby legs somewhere beneath its fur garments. The smell of rotten fish and old blood swirled on the wind. Killiktee collapsed on one knee. A stabbing pain ripped through her as if the baby was trying to claw its way out.

She pushed herself up and turned to run, but the legs of her pants were weighted down with ice. Her muscles failed her. Killiktee staggered, toppling head first toward the ground. Twisting at the last second to shield the child, she landed on her side with a crunch on the top layer of snow. Tears streamed, freezing even as they fell. Warm fluid released from somewhere within her, flooding her snowpants and running down her frostburned thighs. The searing pain in her lower spine intensified as she rolled onto her back. Her child was coming. She reached down into her pants and found a slick wetness. Withdrawing her hand, the blood on her fingers shone black in the light of the moon. Slipping in and out of consciousness, she bit down hard on the lower trim of her parka, threw her head back in agony and pushed as the hungry creature watched and waited.

The baby was born, slipping out of her womb onto the frozen ground, steam rising from its fragile body in the moonlight. Strangely, the creature did not advance. It slouched down behind a hummock of ice, watching from the shadows. Killiktee's snow pants were down around her ankles, her lower half exposed to the elements. With the baby out, she pulled them up in anguish. The gelid wind had ravaged her bare thighs during the birth, the cold searing her legs. She rubbed them aggressively with her free hand to ease the pain. When it proved futile, Killiktee gathered what little strength she had left strength and scooped up the child, clutching it to her chest with both arms, looking upward at the repugnant beast. Still, it did not move. The *amautalik* slumped further downward, hunching its back, claws resting on the ice at its feet, and closed its eyes.

It was several minutes before Killiktee dared take her eyes off the *amautalik* and look down at her child. The baby had yet to make a sound. Even in the dim light, her mother knew that something was wrong. She raised the newborn heavenward to get a better look. Feeling with her hands, she found a girl's organs between the infant's legs. The child's lips were dark, purple around the edges. Her misshapen head lolled back as Killiktee supported her neck. Its eyes were closed and its mouth gaped wide. There was no life in its tiny frame. Spittle dripped from Killiktee's chin, her nose ran. Teardrops fell from her cheeks, glittering like diamonds in the moonlight on the baby's bluish, flaking skin. Killiktee lifted her head and let out an anguished moan into the sky above. At the heartbreaking sound, the creature opened its eyes and howled along with her.

Trembling with grief, exhausted, Killiktee held the child out to the creature. An offering to spare the community more suffering. Killiktee shut her eyes and longed for the warmth of her home. She pined for the bed she had once shared with Maata. Instinctively, her eyes snapped open and she pulled the child close as she heard the beast trundled toward her, the hard-packed snow crunching beneath the weight of the creature. The *amautalik* extended a spindly arm and touched the child's fragile skull with a bony outstretched finger. As the dirty fingernail stroked the child's head, Killiktee felt that same gnarled hand gripping around her heart. The creature slipped her claw gently around the baby and Killiktee, knowing the child was already gone, let her daughter slip from her grasp. The *amautalik* brought the child toward it and lifted the matted pelt that covered its breast. It brought the baby lips to its swollen nipple.

Killiktee watched in silence as the creature tried in vain to get the child to feed. An abrupt gust of wind sent the dark hair of the *amautalik* swirling in the wind. Memories of Joanasie rushed in. Images of the beating flickered her mind. Smells and sounds flooded her head—his fetid breath as he pinned her to the bedroom floor, his taunting laughter at Maata's funeral, the harsh whispers of the locals as she passed them in the frozen streets. Fixating on her frail dead child at the hideous creature's breast, a hot gush of blood filled Killiktee's tired, frozen limbs. Rage surged up through her at the grotesque sight. She drew the kitchen knife from her parka and lunged at the beast with a cry that came from deep within her, rivalling even the howl of the wind around them. The blade sank deep into the beast's corpulent neck. Before the ogress could react, Killiktee pulled out the blade, dark with the *amautalik's* blood in the light of the moon. Hot fluid sprayed across Killiktee's face. The creature's horrendous screeching filled the air as it realized what had happened, clutching its free hand to the gush of black blood from its open wound. It lashed out at Killiktee, who pulled back as the hooked talon sliced toward her face. The claw tore down across her chest, ripping through the fabric of her parka to the tender flesh beneath. The baby fell to the ground as the beast clutched both hands to the growing fountain from its neck. As the pain of the slash set in, Killiktee lunged and stabbed the creature in the neck and face. Again, and again and again.

The beast fell backward, squealing. Killiktee stumbled back as well, exhausted from her attack, and collapsed. The creature's cries morphed from high-pitched shrieks to low moans of agony, rolling onto its front and dragging its body back toward the crevasse in the ice, leaving a wide trail of blood on the snow. Within seconds, the *amautalik* slumped down into the darkness as ungracefully as it had appeared. Killiktee crawled, scooping up the minute fallen corpse. Once she had her baby in her grasp, she turned onto her side, clenching the child to her blood-soaked chest with one arm. She flailed the knife in the direction of the retreating beast until she was sure it would not return to kill her.

Once she was certain the beast had fled, she held the child away from her to get a better look. In the moonlight, the child's eyes were as black as the spaces between the stars. Killiktee planted a tender kiss on the little girl's forehead. The infant gazed up at her mother, mouth open wide, black milk still dripping from her crimson lips. A faint sound escaped Killiktee's daughter's throat; not a baby's cry, but a whistling hiss of air escaping. Killiktee never took her eyes from her child, marveling at her apparent resurrection.

Killiktee felt as if a heavy blanket had been draped over her, weighing her down. A sudden warmth seeped into her torso and the feeling in her limbs had gone completely. She looked skyward, realizing how far from home she was. The smell of blood filled her sinuses and the night seemed to grow darker as if the moon had slipped behind a rare cloud. She kissed the child again on the crown of its head.

Killiktee smiled, stroking the little girl's bluish cheek, pulling her to her breast as she watched her own frozen exhale lifting upward in the moonlight. Hot blood flowed from between her legs and from the wound on her chest, pooling on the sea ice beneath her. She closed her eyes and lay her head back on the snow. She would rest here for a short while before their journey home. A moment, no longer. Killiktee would bring her daughter back to town and show them all her beauty. But first, the child would need a name. A girl's name. She slumped further down onto the ice, letting everything go.

"Maata," she whispered.

IT'S NEVER OVER EASY

Julianne Snow

Hearing the platter clatter down on to the table top in front of him, Mark refolded the day's paper and looked up, "Thanks Peg. Do you know where the ketchup's at?"

Mark sat at his usual table, expectantly looking to Peg, the habitually disgruntled waitress, for an answer. Ketchup was the *coup de grâce* on his regular order: coffee, black and as thick as mud, and the heart attack special—three eggs over easy, two thick slices of white bread slathered in butter, four rashers of crispy bacon, six links of sausage, and a mountain of home fries. A normal person might look at the amount of food and balk, but not Mark. Each day he sat down at one of *Phil's* tables and clogged his arteries with all the saturated fat they could hold.

He got no response as Peg hurried away to serve the other customers sitting in the small diner. Spying a bottle on the next table, Mark scooted to the edge of bench of his booth and stretched his arm across the space between the two tables. Coming up short, he snorted before heaving his bulk off the cracked vinyl. Reaching out to grab the bottle—

"Get outta the way already! These plates aren't gonna serve 'emselves!"

Mark stepped back, pressing himself against the edge of the other table, embarrassed his stomach still blocked her path. Deciding instead to slip quietly into his booth he answered with, "Sorry Peg."

"Makes no difference to me. I'll just let the other diners know why their food is cold."

Mark's face burned. He wanted to say something to her, stick up for himself in some way, but the words didn't come when he opened his mouth. Besides, Peg was already gone; she hadn't waited to see if Mark would offer a retort. Looking down at his cooling plate, he filled his open mouth with food.

His morning continued much the same way as they always did—he'd eat his food, read his paper and surreptitiously stare at the others in the diner. He liked to make up stories as he people-watched—carrying on inane and funny little conversations with himself as he saw their mouths move. It was a silly little habit, but one he couldn't shake.

It harkened back to his days as a child when his mother had always insisted he sit still and not cause a scene while they were out. In fact, talking aloud was reason enough for a beating. His mother, the epitome of class despite having been raised on the wrong side of the tracks, had managed to wrangle herself a good man for a husband. A banker and a deacon at the local church, Mark's father was strict and pious. He wanted his family to reflect his values and many a night was spent reading the Bible and praying.

Somewhere along the way, Mark had rebelled as many young men do. He wanted to be himself and for some reason, he didn't think he could be that person in the shadow of his father or a God who didn't appear to want him to experience life. His young mind couldn't see past the religion of his parents to the message actually contained within the words.

Once he was old enough, Mark moved out. He'd found a job in an adult store on the other side of town and worked on his embarrassment each and every day. At the time, it had seemed like a good idea, a way for him to strike back at his parents, but the truth was he had no idea what he was doing when he started. Most of the items in the store were utterly foreign to him and he'd never really watched television let alone had any exposure to pornography. But he soon learned.

Working in the shop meant his parents disowned him, but in truth, Mark wasn't sure he really minded. He was tired of being told what to do and what to think, and he liked the self-importance of the position. People asked him questions. They wanted to know his opinion on which videos had the best story lines, and what lubricant was most popular. He relished his job, even though he'd never actually had sex in his life.

Some rules were too hard to break and Mark was saving himself for marriage. Not that any girl was ever going to look at his fat-covered frame and pornography-hocking job and think to herself he was a great catch. Not in his small town anyway.

A loud noise from behind the counter drew Mark out of his own thoughts. He looked toward its source and saw Manuel backed up against the front counter. Thinking it might have been a fire, Mark looked past the cook, expecting to see flames radiating off the grill.

Nothing.

Manuel looked out toward the restaurant, his face contorted in fear. He screamed, "*Esta vivo!! Sálvese quien pueda!*"

The forcefulness of his scream got the attention of everyone in the diner. Most couldn't understand him, but as Peg ran back toward the kitchen, many figured out there was a problem, abandoning their breakfasts and their bills for the brisk morning air.

"Lo que está vivo Manuel? Es otra rata?" Mark saw Peg scan the floor for evidence of the rodent, broom clutched in her hand just in case.

"*No! No! Los huevos! Están vivos!*" Manuel looked terrified, his eyes not leaving the flattop as he bent himself back over the counter.

"The eggs? Alive? No Manuel, los huevos no están vivos," Peg put down the broom, and turned to Manuel, her face a dichotomous mask of calm and concern.

Manuel was having none it though. He was petrified. Something had certainly scared the man. Mark, one of the only remaining patrons still in the diner, made his way over to the counter, thinking to offer some sort of help to Peg and Manuel should it be needed. Once he got to the counter, he got his first look at the eggs sizzling on the flattop.

They looked normal. Until one of them moved.

"What the heck was that?"

Peg spun around to Mark, her face a mask of startled surprise, "What are you talking about?"

"The eggs. One of them moved!"

"For fucksake! Not you too!" Peg hit him with a look of disdain, turning back to Manuel before saying, "Can't you see I've got bigger fish to fry without you helping make things worse! Go back to your seat and let me handle this, okay?"

Mark looked back to the eggs, his attention riveted on the whites as they twitched. "Peg, just look at them!"

Peg's eyes turned away from Manuel to focus on the flattop. As the egg whites expanded so did the whites of her eyes. Backing up slowly, she reached for the broom again. Finding the handle, she clasped it to her chest, which heaved in her nervousness.

"What the hell is happening?"

"*Los huevos! Los huevos!*" Manuel had slunk to his knees, his hands together in supplication as his face rose to the heavens. "*Dios, por favor, sálvanos!*"

One of the older men who hadn't retreated outside spoke for the first time, his voice gravelled with age and tobacco abuse. "There is no God."

In response, the skin around the yolks burst open, releasing the creamy orange fluid. It expanded across the hot surface, seeming to search for the cool edges of the nearby cutting surfaces. As it moved forward, it dragged the whites behind it, hastily trying to get off the heat.

Mark stared at what was unfolding. Five eggs were making their way off the flattop while four other eggs bubbled and burned.

"What do we do? Should we call someone?" Peg's voice rose a few octaves while watching the show and her distress was palpable.

"Who would we call? It's not like there's a number on the carton that says 'In Case of Mutant Eggs Call'." Humour was one of Mark's coping mechanisms. "Wait, is there a number?"

Before anyone could think of checking the carton, a shriek rang out through the room.

All their eyes turned back to look at the kitchen, scared for what they might see. The shriek wasn't human and for that simple fact alone, the blood chilled in Mark's veins.

Five eyes stared at the patrons from the countertop. Five mouths, with rows of sharp teeth, opened in unison. Five identical otherworldly shrieks filled the air with terror.

The first one flew at Manuel, landing on his chest. Manuel screamed in both panic and pain as the razor-sharp teeth tore into his chest. Blood sprayed outward, painting Peg in crimson. She screamed, backing away and bringing the broom she still had clutched in her hands upward.

She swatted at the thing on Manuel's chest, beating it and him further into the ground, her screams becoming sobs as the reverberation travelled up her arms. Manuel stopped screaming but the inhuman sound of tearing flesh and slurping blood didn't.

No one knew what to do. Peg was valiantly trying to save a dead Manuel, but there was no point in beating a dead horse. Mark moved his bulk around the counter, his eyes never leaving the four remaining mutant eggs on the countertop, putting up his hands in an attempt to calm Peg. She looked at him with glazed eyes, her face showing the blue mascara lines of her tears.

"What do we do?" she sobbed, the broom coming to rest of the floor.

"We get the fuck out of here and call the authorities," Mark tried to speak calmly, but he heard his own voice rise in panic at the end.

"You guys had better move now!" The warning came just as two of the mutants launched themselves into the air. Mark and Peg clasped each other tightly, each one trying to shield the other while moving away from the incoming onslaught. It was a strange dance; one that would have been comical had the situation not been so dire. Skirting the counter, the two managed to evade them, but only just.

"Where do we go?" Mark asked as two remaining egg-liens popped off the counter and into the air. Landing swiftly on Manuel's body, they began to feast, the cacophony of mastication rising to an almost deafening level. The two who had made their move on Peg and Mark, only to be thwarted, had already slithered over to the dead body for their share.

"Outside?" The elderly man pointed toward the door as he spoke. Turning to look, they could see the faces of the other patrons plastered against the glass. None of them could really see what was going on, but it was obvious their fear kept the window between them and the horror unfolding inside.

"If we go outside and these things escape, there's no telling the damage they'll do. I don't want the deaths of all kinds of people on my mind..." Mark, the practical type who wasn't one to place himself in danger, tried to reason aloud what the next steps should be. "Maybe we should try to catch them? Or corral them until the authorities arrive?"

"Son, if you think I'm staying here to catch these abominations, you're crazy! I'm going out that door and I am not looking back!" Striding down the aisle between the booths of the diner, he stopped when Mark spoke again.

"I know who you are," he said. "I remember you from church. Deacon Wright, isn't it?"

"So what if that's who I am? I lost my faith a long time ago..." as he spoke, his head dropped and his shoulders slumped. "I'm no longer the man I once was."

"How can you just turn tail and run? Especially knowing many more people could get hurt?"

"Listen son, I'm one guy. And I'm an old one at that. I can't help you." He turned on his heel and made his way toward the door again.

With his hand on the doorknob, Wright stopped again when he heard the next words out of Mark's mouth.

"Ecclesiastes 3:8"

Wright looked back at him, puzzled. "'A time to love, and a time to hate; a time of war, and a time of peace.' What does that have to do with anything?"

Mark didn't want to admit it was the only verse that sprang to mind as his mind raced to find a reason to make Wright stay. "It's time to fight."

"Are you kidding me? How about 'For God hath not appointed us to wrath, but to obtain salvation by our Lord Jesus Christ.' We can trade scripture all day, and those things will still exist. And they'd likely have killed us!"

Mark stared at the deacon, a man who had once given a promise to protect the town from evil. He searched his mind for something to say before he left, something that would make him change his mind.

Peg let out a scream. With their attention solely focused on the battle of wills over leaving, none of them realized the feeding frenzy had stopped. Mark's head whipped around to look at Peg, her body now covered with larger, bloodier versions of the entities cracked from the eggs.

Stepping back, he tripped over his own feet, coming down hard on the worn linoleum. Lying still for a moment, he sought to find the words to convince Wright to stay.

He found none.

But the truth was he didn't need them. Feeling a hand on his shoulder, he looked up into the wrinkled visage of the older man. Helping him to his feet he said, "You're right son. Neither of us can leave until we've seen this through."

Peg's screams still punctuated the tension in the air, but they were lessening as the seconds ticked forward. She fought against the egg-liens, her hands macerated pulp from the action of their teeth. But still she worked against them, buying the rest of the group time.

A strangled command burst from her throat. "There's a rat trap by the backdoor! Get it and we can try to shove these things inside it."

Wright hurried to the back of the kitchen as Mark tried to catch his breath. The fall had knocked the wind out of him and he struggled to calm his heartbeat as he filled his lungs. Passing out now wouldn't do them any favours.

Peg struggled, her body losing some of its strength and fight the deeper the mutants bit into her. She focused on them, but with only two badly injured hands, they were making a bloody mess of her body very quickly.

Mark had no idea how she was still able to fight. Looking at her, all he could see was blood. Everywhere. Most of her body was torn ragged.

Wright returned with the wire contraption—a veritable mind cube for the uninitiated. Coming up close to Peg, he stood there, poised for action but unable to figure out how to help. He bent down onto one knee, placing the trap on its end and reached out for one of the damned things.

It let out a shriek when he touched it, causing Wright to jerk his hand back quickly. "What the hell?"

Mark moved a little closer, wanting to help but not knowing how. He grabbed onto the counter with one of his hands and lowered himself to his knees which creaked and burned in protest. "You hold the cage, I'll grab them."

Wright looked at him and nodded. The two of them were going to have to work together if they were going to get through this. Looking at Peg, they could both see the last sparks of life in her dying eyes. Soon, she wouldn't be able to fight the egg-liens off any longer.

Mark steeled himself against the noise it was sure to make and placed both hands on the egg-lien. It shrieked and bucked, the slimy mass trying to wriggle around so it could shred his hands. He held on firmly, digging his thick fingers into the meat of it.

Working sloppily, as there really was no other way to do it, he shoved the nipping mass into the rat trap and focused on the next one. Their attention was still on Peg's flesh for the most part, but there was no way to know when they would turn their ravenous attention to Mark and Wright.

"Hurry!" It was Wright. He seemed nervous, frightened and who could really blame him? Peg's eyes were no longer open and her arms had fallen to her sides. Almost stripped completely of flesh, her body wouldn't hold their attention for long.

Laying his hands on another, Mark worked quickly but not without sustaining some injury. Their teeth were razor sharp and they had no qualms about using them. Fairly soon the palms of his hands were slick with blood and the lacerations burned like nothing he'd ever felt before.

And they were going numb.

As his right hand slipped again, a thought sprung to mind: was there something in their saliva that acted as a poison or a paralytic? Was he about to become their next victim?

With three of the five egg-liens in the rat trap, Mark felt the panic rising from deep within him. Not the same sort of panic he'd felt earlier when he's first seen the creatures. No, this was different. Like a wave, it was taking over everything within him. All he wanted to do was get up and run. Run like he hadn't been able to run in years. Run so far away these things would become a distant memory. It overwhelmed him. Made his brain fogged but clear all at the same time. His body was telling him to retreat.

Mark looked at Wright, his eyes betraying his thoughts. Scrambling to gain his feet, he heard a voice. Quickly turning his head side to side he couldn't figure out who was talking to him. Wright knelt on the ground next to Peg's body with a look of bewilderment on his face.

Be calm my Son. Be calm.

"Who said that?"

"Who said what?"

All will be well my Son. Just finish what you started.

"What? Finish what?"

"Who are you talking to?"

Son, you must collect these beings so they cannot kill again.

"Are you kidding me? I'm getting out of here!"

"Mark! Don't leave yet, we've almost got them all!"

Trust in me my Son and all will be well.

Mark looked at Wright, studying the creased lines of his face dotted with crimson. It felt like long minutes passed as he stood there, trying to reconcile his desire to take flight with the plea to stay and fight.

In the end it came down to his father. What would his father have done?

Fight.

Mark wholeheartedly believed that. And it wasn't that he was going to stay for his father. Or his mother even. He was going to stay because it was the right thing to do and his father had taught him to do the right thing.

Struggling back to his knees beside the still body of Peg, he took hold of the second to last creature, grasping it tightly despite the odd numbing pain he felt. Swinging his arms toward Wright, he thrust it into the trap and removed his hands, allowing the deacon to slam the lid shut again.

The noise coming from the trap was unnerving. Shrieks and screams polluted the air around them along with the coppery tang of blood.

With both of them shaking, Mark turned to grab the last one.

It was waiting for him, its mouth in the parody of a snarl, grinding its sharp little teeth together. It was ready to fight.

The egg-lien launched itself at Mark's chest, just as he brought his hands up to defend himself. By the grace of God, his fingers found some purchase on the slick surface of its skin. He held on tight as the creature squirmed and spit at him.

Mark could see the anger in its eye. The desire to strip the flesh from his bones. But he didn't care. Turning his body sideways, he motioned to Wright he was ready.

In a few blinks of an eye, Mark had shoved the creature into the trap, roughly reuniting it with its kin as Wright slammed the door of the trap shut and firmly latched it. Both Wright and Mark took deep breaths, trying to calm their racing hearts.

They shared a look, one that spoke of the horror they'd ensured. One that bonded them together forever. No one would be able to understand what they'd gone through—heck they had no idea what had truly transpired—but for some reason, these two men had been chosen to save a small town from disaster.

The authorities hailed them as heroes while no one could understand or explain the presence of the egg-liens. Whether they were an anomaly of nature or a supernatural attack, one thing was for certain: Mark and Deacon Wright never ate an egg ever again.

BASE OF A TRIANGLE

Nancy Kilpatrick

Y ou scan the empty subway platform, uneasy. A glance at your watch, then at the digital time overhead reveals the late hour. The trains do not run often this time of night. I can see you wondering why a man like yourself is standing here now when you could have been home earlier, safe in your bed. Wondering why do you do this so frequently. Why you feel so disconnected.

Your hands jam deep into your pockets. You jerk your head to the right and stare down the track into the black oblivion of the tunnel. In my direction. This sudden movement causes your body to weave. You do not see what you hope to and, as you turn away, I hear a prayer mumbled, *Please let the train arrive soon.* I suspected you would come here again at night, alone. You're my age now, although I have been here five years already. It's nice to have company. I get lonely. It's as if I am one part of a triangle and cannot exist on my own. You must know how that feels.

I balance on one of the rails and lean into the platform but can feel neither surface, and stare up at you. Because you're drunk, your perceptions are heightened but blurred, and your intuition soars; you look down, squinting, almost as if you can see me. I know, though, that you cannot. Few see beyond the concrete to the intangible, but many sense this nebulous realm. I am like a negative image, white on black, your opposite. All that is solid about you is ethereal in me. I emit no female scents. I can no longer be touched or caressed. And yet we are separated by only a crease in time.

You experience a mild air current pass over you as I edge along the track, closer; for a split second you imagine the train might be coming after all.

I see you often, you know. Here, during other hours, requisite brown briefcase in hand, reading a newspaper, checking your phone, your harried face mingled with thousands of other harried faces, looking hungry, not prepared to confront your fate. During the day you are gregarious and it feels abnormal to you now being here by yourself, except for the memories that have a life all their own. You glance around the long platform again, peering at the dark corners, trying to see through pillars, wrinkling your nose at an offensive odor, afraid you are not as alone as you believe.

All at once you sense me. The hairs on the back of your neck prickle. Fear makes your movements frenetic. You stagger past the newspaper box but the lurid headline—a fatal accident—cannot catch your eye. It is the tracks that draw you; as you near the platform's edge, caution becomes automatic. You wobble a foot from the rim, examining the cold steel in the pit below, and the dangerous third rail. You find the bleakness of the metal strangely uplifting. My dark world of base metals is so foreign to your own. There are no plastic cases here, pregnant with the latest micro-chips, already obsolete. All ties are finite connections, like a family with a long ancestry and the certainty of no progeny. For a moment you long to meld the iron in your blood with the iron rails and embrace immortality. I cannot be replaced by the latest model.

Your ambivalence is touching. I know you so well I can almost empathize. You feel my struggle for emotional life ride the air and imbed itself into your lungs like a dense wet fog. Your eyes flash the horror you experience: I am a disease, a virus digging in, becoming part of you as you will forever be a part of me.

Panic is overwhelming. You cannot breath. You gasp for air.

In the distance, train wheels grind against the metal tracks. Their shriek causes you to reel back slightly from the platform's edge. Your hand claws at your throat. Your body, off kilter, threatens to catapult into my waiting arms.

I know what it is like to pitch forward, alone, crashing onto the icy steel rails only to be crushed and severed beneath the sharp wheels of an oncoming train, flesh singed beyond recognition when a hand touches the high voltage rail. I know the screech of metal against metal and bone. Human screams multiply. Faces blur. Warmth seeps from the flesh. Lack of oxygen strangles the fetus within, so dependent. And all the while aware that the clumsiness of a drunken stranger tore me from the living. Yes, I know this and more. That's why when you fall into my arms I will catch you. Believe me.

The powerful train barrels toward the station, too fast. You clutch your coat collar tight to your throat. Your muscles tense. Sweat streaks your forehead and trickles down your temples to your flushed cheeks. Tears gush from your wounded eyes.

You stare at me, pleading for forgiveness. I beckon you to join me, but you must hurry. You shake your head and at the same time lurch forward like a walking corpse.

The train whistle blasts a warning. The air rumbles. The concrete beneath your feet vibrates, or are you trembling? I grasp your ankle, forcing your foot to the edge again. You open your mouth to scream, but the sound is crushed by the whistle's extended shriek.

Only seconds remain. Take the step. Join me. Forever.

You teeter on the edge.

Leap into my world!

Now!

Wheels screech, but the brakes cannot quickly halt so many tons of steel. A pale face presses against the conductor's window of the lead car. The expression is haunted, fast frozen in déjà vu.

Metal passes through me. Devoid of a physical body, I cannot feel it, yet the lingering memory reminds me of the night our triangle formed, when, in an eternal moment, we three connected.

I examine your distorted features as you stumble onto the train. The doors slam closed. The conductor is rattled but manages to throw the correct switch and the train moves forward like a silver entity at home in the bleak tunnels. Soon it abandons the station as you have both abandoned me.

It is always quiet here after the last train passes. I fall back onto the tracks, onto a familiar spot, although I cannot rest here, or anywhere. I know you will return to this station again and again at this time, because you must. For the same reason, the conductor drives through here nightly, always at this hour. I will wait for you. For both of you. I know some day you will join me. I will make sure of that.

CURTAIN CALL

Derek Clendening

September 15, 2016

Ms. Gloria Robbins
670 Main Street
Buffalo, New York
United States 14202

Mr. Glen Thibodeau
Doral Corporation
550 Park Avenue
New York, New York
10154

Dear Mr. Thibodeau,

The purpose of my letter is to advise you of my resignation as president of the McGovern Theatre effective immediately. Forgive the abruptness of this letter and please do not contact me to try and change my mind. My decision is final and I will thank you to respect it.

You deserve an explanation and I will provide one. After all, I signed a new contract three months ago. I have worked at the McGovern Theatre for fifteen years of unwavering commitment and a decision like this one must come as a shock.

Problems coincided with the start of theatre renovations. There was no shortage of them, let me tell you. Theatres like the McGovern are steeped in history, tradition, and character, not necessarily in that order. Its character trumped its history and tradition, but the latter two will always hold a special place in my heart.

Because of the theatre's rich character, I have been determined to maintain it. Your theatre possesses a unique beauty that should be preserved forever and that was what I was doing. You will remember I made those very same points in my renovation proposal to you three years ago. Oh, but I didn't call it a renovation then. A facelift was what I had in mind.

Sometimes I wonder if I would be as fond of the McGovern if not for its grand staircase, art deco ceilings, or red carpeting. Still, I have found a home here I have not found anywhere else in my professional life. To leave like this puts a real strain on me, please be assured of that.

Public backlash I hadn't counted on, though. Buffalo's numerous historic spots have been given facelifts inside and out to preserve their beauty. City Hall, Lafayette High School, and Central Terminal have all done more than I have done to the McGovern and that's to say nothing of the abundance of historic homes.

So, what's the big deal, you may ask?

All I wanted was for the McGovern to stay among their ranks and to never regress. That meant some changes must be made, but we would never change the theatre's spirit. You said it yourself when you gave me your blessing to move forward with renovations.

Your blessing came with handsome funding and for that I will always be thankful. Planning was needed to send renovations into full tilt and meant the actual work did not begin until six months ago. We agreed the theatre should stay open during renovations and my plan should reflect it.

My first move was exterior renovation, which was done at low tide for theatre attendance. When people see the McGovern from the outside, I want them to be enticed to see its inner beauty as well. The first real backlash was over my plan to remove the concrete 'McGovern Theatre' sign from atop the building.

I assured the local media this would be the only significant change to the building. The Western New York Historic Building Preservation Society made a stink about how that sign is part of the original building and is therefore part of Buffalo's heritage. I rebutted that the sign was not significant because of the gorgeous marquee that'd been in place for decades. That didn't stop them from trying—and failing—to obtain an injunction to stop the procedure.

My predecessors are responsible for the marquee, but I left that out. Professionals don't throw others under the bus, no matter who made the move.

A three man team came to work on a sign and only one was up on the scaffolding when the accident happened. For the record, what remains on paper anyway, is that several faulty beams in the scaffolding gave way or were not assembled properly and that caused the man to fall.

No, he didn't take a forty foot drop to the concrete, but his limited drop will give him nightmares for life. He fell a quarter-way down the scaffolding, but had the presence of mind to latch onto a sturdy beam. His only injury was a broken wrist. Even still, he held on admirably until the fire department got him down.

I already explained all that to you when you phoned me immediately after you received the news. I won't waste any more time on it.

Then stories began to swirl. I don't mean rumors. God knows there will always be plenty of those. No, I'm talking about the stories that have been told in variations about the McGovern for decades. They were as unwelcome with me as criticism in the media about removing the sign, one that still hasn't been removed incidentally.

There's the story about the Lady in White who floats through the front of the house late at night. Staff and even some of the actors claim to have seen her, but I can't substantiate that. I think she's the oldest legend, but there are also accounts of a faceless figure—a mist supposedly—that sits in the box closest to the stage.

You might not be aware I've made every effort to squash any publicity of the theatre as a haunted location. Every fine old place should have a ghost, some would say, but I do not believe that. I might not have killed the legends, but I have used my office to prevent any effort to legitimize the stories.

That included forbidding haunted hayrides from stopping at the McGovern to spin their yarns to customers. My predecessors might have been more permissive or more 'fun' to some, but I see the theatre as a place of business and there just isn't time for campfire stories.

I can't stop employees from thinking what they will about the stories, though. If I catch one of them loafing while telling some tale about it, I may tell them to get back to work. I may do worse. I don't really go that far, though. Usually I just give them the look and I find that says more than words anyway.

Rumors don't mean much—someone in my position ought to know that—but a prevailing opinion among the McGovern staff was that the scaffold incident wasn't really an accident at all. The spirits and bogeys and hobgoblins in the theatre were to blame for faulty beams or negligence.

How do I know what the staff thought? I don't spend my whole day in my office, but it is still hard to know exactly what my people are thinking. As you know, at least one employee can always be depended on to talk, which gives me a handle on what's going on. My talker was a young man named Bennett who apparently was the only one that didn't believe the scaffolding accident was caused by some sort of haunting or curse.

There was no need to squash those ideas, though. People will think what they're going to think and I would just shake my head about it. There are just so many hours in the day and I wouldn't waste time stopping anyone from thinking those things. After all, I can't be the thought police.

Things took a sharp turn after that, though. The men who were to remove the concrete sign refused to go back up there and finish the job. Even though they were told there was nothing more to the scaffold problems, they simply wouldn't do it. I didn't pursue the matter beyond that. At the very least I could say I had done something to appease the people who were bent out of shape about the sign.

The problems that followed had to do with the McGovern staff. I don't pretend to be a popular or sympathetic figure around our theatre. Names like 'Ice Bitch' may seem well earned, but the people who so cleverly assign them have no idea what it's like to be in my shoes.

I would bet they don't know I'm very much aware of what they think of me. I'm comfortable with the name and the reputation. That is because I have always taken my role as president of the McGovern seriously and I have always reached for the highest level of excellence.

The last six months have taught me one thing: not everything comes as you would expect it to. In fact, you can be assured of curve balls here and there. So far, I had dealt with no insubordination as the myths were concerned. That changed about a month after the scaffold incident.

I decided to re-carpet the theatre. For most of its history, the McGovern's carpeting had been red, but I thought a gold-colored carpet would look beautiful. The job started with the front of the house. Most of that would be easy enough since very little area within the theatre was carpeted anyway. The work to re-carpet the theatre took just one day and then the workers would continue working on the hall by the balcony entrance.

The re-carpeting was finished just before a production of *RENT* began its run at the McGovern. They told me it was the toughest job they've ever completed, but they didn't specify the reason except to say the floors were 'stubborn'. Maybe they thought inanimate things were supposed to just cooperate with them. I don't know. Otherwise it seemed like they simply wouldn't talk about it.

Since a rejuvenated theatre is only as good as its cleanliness, the theatre was thoroughly cleaned between performances. Charmaine, my most trusted employee, was assigned the task. Don't get me wrong. I don't feel about my employees the way they seem to feel about me, and I really do value hardworking people.

After the first post re-carpeting cleaning, she came to me with a cracked voice and wandering eyes. She spoke to me so softly, so timidly.

She might have known how to keep her head down and her mouth shut, but I had never thought of her as timid.

"What is it? I asked.

"I was wondering…"

"Wondering what? Use words, Charmaine."

"I was thinking that maybe I can have some help to clean the theatre. Just a little help."

"If I had enough staff for that sort of thing, I would assign someone to help you. As it is, you're doing what you're doing because there are so few hands, and you're the only one I can count on to make this a one-woman job."

"Just one person, so I don't have to be in there alone."

I placed my hands on my hips, hoping to intimidate her, but doubt I succeeded.

"The auditorium," she said. "It…"

"It what?"

"I don't know. When I'm in there, sometimes when I'm alone, but not always… it's like it breathes. Like it breathes… and it eats. Don't you understand?"

I did. Sometimes when I was in the theatre, alone or not, I thought the proscenium arch was a gaping mouth that could swallow me whole. Silly, yes, but there was a stark difference here. I knew it was like saying a cloud looked like an elephant or a race car. I certainly wouldn't let it stand in the way of doing my job. What she called breathing might have been the heating vents for goodness sake. I couldn't account for the eating part, but I didn't feel the need to.

"Charmaine," I said. "Listen to me. I'm talking to you as your employer now. I need you to put your hang ups aside and go in and finish all of the work required. If you don't… I will have no choice but to cite you for insubordination." I looked down at my watch. "And you've now wasted five minutes you should have spent cleaning the theatre for the evening performance."

She stared at me for a moment before turning away and inching toward the theatre door. Yes, she might have been defiant for a moment, but she still had mouths to feed at home. Whatever her hang ups were, I thought she was smart enough to set them aside to avoid discipline for insubordination. Honestly, I would have hated to do it to someone as obedient as Charmaine and that was why I gave her a second chance. With a large staff, you can't make exceptions.

After that, she went back to work and so did I. Because I was in my office, I didn't hear her scream, but I did hear the commotion coming from the theatre. My door was always cracked open, but I doubt I would have missed such a ruckus. I dashed out the door and found a crowd around the auditorium door. I pushed my way through to see what had happened.

When I reached the front of the crowd, I found Charmaine on the floor with a gash torn out of her leg. Our dress code requires all employees to wear black dress pants regardless of their position or, quite frankly, the weather. Her shredded pant leg looked like someone had taken hedge clippers to them. Gouts of blood poured from her leg.

As theatre president, problem solving is my duty and that includes health and safety issues. My gut forbid me to move her. This was a situation for paramedics and I called for an ambulance from my cell phone. The ambulance arrived in less than ten minutes and I cleared everyone out while they did their work.

Charmaine was taken to Erie County Medical Center and released later that night after more than ten staples closed her wound. I cancelled that night's performance. It was the right thing to do and there was no way the theatre would be ready for guests in time anyway.

In the meantime, I needed answers. Stupid accidents happen. People trip on carpets and break their noses, but an accident like this should not have happened in a safe environment.

When the scaffold incident hit, I asked Bennett for the dirt, but he wasn't immediately available after Charmaine's accident. A girl named Theresa, who worked mostly as an usher, told me what happened... or what she thought had happened.

"She was carrying on about teeth," Theresa said. "That was after the screams. It was like I couldn't calm her down for anything, but once I did, she babbled about teeth. I didn't actually see what happened to her, though."

"Are you sure that's what she said?"

"Yes, ma'am, I'm very sure. People were crowding us and it was getting loud… and the moment was just so stressful. I'm sure she said something about teeth."

"That *is* odd."

"She said something bit her, something with really sharp teeth. Like a dog or animal had done it or something. I really don't get it."

"Neither do I."

"That's all I really got from her before too many people crowded around us… that something in the auditorium had teeth and bit her."

"Thank you for the information."

And I left it at that. Protocol was crucial and I felt the first thing to do when Charmaine returned to work was to get fill out an accident report. Charmaine never returned to work.

Let's not confuse that with Charmaine tendering her notice. When people leave the McGovern, they give us two weeks' notice. The employees that want any kind of reference, I mean. We called Charmaine the first day when we only thought she was late for work or didn't realize she supposed to work.

When she didn't answer, we realized she didn't mean to come in. Second day, ditto. Even if she had come in on the third day, she would have faced serious discipline. Even the most reliable employees cannot be given a free pass after something like that.

It was a moot point, though. Charmaine would never return to the McGovern and I knew why. The incident report form was filled out without her participation and my comfort waned. Maybe it was because I hadn't heard the usual story about the lady in white or the mist in the auditorium for that matter. Hearing the theatre breathed was bad enough. That it had teeth made me wring my hands.

That legitimized the idea. It gave it a body, made it real. To be honest, my own comfort level about the theatre had dropped. I told you I did not hear Charmaine's scream, but I didn't have to. I can hear it in my mind. I replay it over and over and imagine teeth sinking into Charmaine's flesh.

All was quiet for a few weeks, at least in terms of accidents. Re-carpeting of the entrance to the upper balcony had continued and the work slugged along just like it had when they had done the same to the theatre proper. There was just this resistance to having a fresh carpet laid down. Or maybe it was the color? The worst part was I was starting to believe it.

Then it happened: the first casualty.

I say it like this because, up until then, we'd only had accidents. No one involved in one wanted to come back, but there had been nothing fatal about them.

This was no accident, though.

After Charmaine's incident, I waited before tapping anyone else for information. It was a matter of sensitivity, which most certainly is part of business. We were not talking about contractors here. Charmaine was one of their own and I respected that. A few weeks passed before I stopped Bennett in the hall. He nearly blew right past me.

"In a hurry?" I asked.

"No. I guess not."

He twitched and his eyes scanned the perimeter enough to convince me he didn't want to have any conversation with me.

"I was hoping you could help me," I said.

"Okay."

"I need to know something. Charmaine's accident... did you see anything."

"No."

"Did you hear anything, something that came after?"

He wouldn't look me in the face.

"Bennett," I said. "Listen to me. This is very important. I need to know what others are saying about the accident."

"I don't know."

The sentence came out as a whisper. I knew he was lying and I wasn't mad at him for doing it. In a way, I understood his need to lie given how he was acting.

I wanted to grab Bennett and shake him, which was unthinkable for me. Desperate times begot desperate actions and I wasn't exempt from that. Thank God I kept my composure as well as my hands to myself. I thanked Bennett and let him go, which felt like the only right thing to do. He didn't want to talk and I couldn't force him.

I wanted to forget Bennett's expression, his feeble speech, but I just couldn't. Something was wrong and I couldn't push myself to ask him what it was. Sometimes it's better to let things go, but I felt like it wasn't one of those times. Regret would consume me later.

As with Charmaine's accident, I was in my office and was almost tuned out to everything. My door was still cracked open, which meant I would notice any commotion that could erupt. This time, there was no scream. Even the commotion was lesser than last time. As it turned out, that was because the incident occurred much farther away from my office than Charmaine's accident had.

I charged down the hall and found a crowd at the front door. I remember pushing my way through a smaller crowd when Charmaine was injured, but there was no way I could do it this time. I was helpless for information and that made matters much worse.

You would be surprised at how fast news moves when you're in your office. A camera man bearing the logo of the local NBC affiliate on his coat was part of the crowd. That was when I knew things had spiraled out of control. Even the thought of that made my heart race and my lungs heave.

Because I had been left so helpless, I did something I normally would never do. I grabbed people, gripping their sleeves and arms, and shoved them out of the way. I all but bulldozed my way through the crowd.

I saw nothing, but I heard competing voices shout that someone had jumped from a third storey window. You would think my heart would have pounded harder, but it didn't. It made me sweat. Unusual happenings had become commonplace at the McGovern and that instilled more fear in me than shock.

I tried once more to squeeze my way to the front of the crowd when the police pushed us back and cordoned off the scene with yellow tape. Being theatre president meant nothing in a crowd like this one and I was left in the dark like everyone else, at least temporarily.

Police later told me Bennett was the jumper. I froze, speechless. I realize I have told you little about Bennett O'Brien, the person. He was a part-time employee studying library science at SUNY Buffalo. Unmarried, he had a live-in girlfriend, and occupied a lower apartment on the West Side.

In the following days, the police interviewed every employee in the building at the time of the jump, including yours truly. Buffalo's finest showed me professionalism and respect. They knew each one of us had been through a very traumatic experience, and gave us our space and didn't push us to talk.

Before they spoke to me, Annette, a semi-retired woman who has worked in the theatre gift shop for a year told me Bennett had jumped out of desperation. He'd babbled about how something in the theatre—or even the theatre itself—was trying to eat him and no one could make sense of it. More like no one *wanted* to make sense of it.

Deep down, we all knew. I remembered thinking the proscenium arch looked like a mouth that could swallow me whole. He might have seen something so awful he never wanted to face it again. Or he didn't believe he had truly escaped whatever had tried to eat him. Annette said she had personally seen him run out of the theatre, so that came first hand.

She admitted the part about something trying to eat him had come second hand.

Annette was not one of those reliable talkers like Bennett had been, but I wasn't looking for that now. Part of me didn't want to know what had driven him to jump even if ignorance solved nothing.

Buffalo P.D. detectives spoke to me last. When they asked me if I had any idea why Bennett would have taken his own life, I told them no. I felt horrible about lying, but what was I supposed to tell them? Then they asked if he had ever shown signs of depression or given me any reason to believe he was suicidal or anything else to add. Again, answered no.

I wished I could have told the truth about something. To be honest, I just wanted to get out of there. The McGovern closed for three days and I must say those were the worst three days of my life.

I *want* to say that, but it wouldn't be true. The lies I'd told the Buffalo P.D. should be the end of all lies from me, as far as I was concerned. What followed was worse than the three days of theatre closure and police interviews.

When things go wrong, you fix them. It's business as usual after that and I've always thought it was a good policy. This was so much different from anything I'd ever faced. It's like I became stuck in the moment the commotion began and have been unable to come out of it.

More became clear to me, though. The McGovern was slipping through my fingers. I'd lost control. Since I've been president, autonomy over the theatre has been mine. I've done the hiring and firing and have reported only to you. That is because I have only felt truly accountable to you.

I have come to realize I am also accountable to the people that work for me. I wouldn't call it a conscious thought. I've shared it with no one else, but I was forced to acknowledge it thanks to the changes that occurred in me almost instantly after Bennett's jump.

Unlike Charmaine's scream, Bennett's jump replays itself in my bad dreams. I might not have seen it happen, but I don't have to. My mind is powerful enough to construct a scene in which Bennett doesn't walk to the window, but runs. And here's the thing: he doesn't hesitate at the window. He's not one of those people that stand on the ledge, staring down at the pavement below. That's for people who have second thoughts.

Bennett had no second thoughts. I didn't have to hear theories from the gossip mill. I only had to close my eyes and I could see him doing it. He jumped not only because of what happened to him in the theatre, but because he never wanted to see it again. His action was the only way to ensure that.

The theatre reopened, and when I went home, I went to my room and shut the door. I didn't come out until morning. That was the first day. I hadn't planned to be so idle, to shut out the world, but that was what I did. Maybe I couldn't have stopped the jump, but that meant nothing when a deluge of shame devours you. All you can do is think about what you could have done differently, how you could have acted to prevent the desperation that led to the jump.

Now Bennett's girlfriend was alone in their West Side lower unit and I spent my nights in a room with a bottle that didn't leave my hands. Before, I only drank wine when at a restaurant or a party. Even then I kept it to one glass or, at the most, a second. In the weeks that followed Bennett's jump, my full bottle found itself half-empty each night.

When I took this job, I felt powerful, like nothing could stop me. Yes, I have much to be proud of, but the events of the last month have taught me I overestimated myself. I still take pride in my accomplishments, but I am a long way from unstoppable. It isn't just because of guilt. It is because the theatre says it should be so.

Sometimes I wonder when I will see whatever there is to see in the McGovern. When will my number be called? I can say with all honesty I would rather be gobbled up in the theatre than for it to be one more person under my watch. With all my effort to make sure everything at the McGovern is done to the highest standard, I couldn't save my employees from the building itself.

I have always held myself accountable for everything that happens here and that includes the failings of my employees. It also includes the fate of my employees. If I cannot do that, I cannot carry out business as usual.

That is why I have determined that my time at the McGovern Theatre has run its course. No job is waiting for me in case you are wondering. I have no job prospects and no hope at all when you get right down to it. Still, I need to be in a place where I can conduct business as usual and that is clearly not the case here. Like the resistance to new carpeting, the McGovern will have business conducted on its own terms.

Before I leave this place for the last time, I need to know what really lives in the McGovern. I need to see what it is that caused such harm to people under my watch. It isn't morbid curiosity. A sense of moral duty burns in me and I will not have satisfied it until I have faced the music. I can never start a new job with such lingering guilt on my mind. Worse, I will never enjoy a good night's sleep again.

Maybe nothing will be there. That's how these things work, right? You never actually hear the breathing sounds or see the theatre's teeth unless it wants you to.

A watched pot never boils.

Still, I have to go and face it for myself, to look it right in the face and accept whatever comes.

And so I will now take the opportunity to thank you, not just for fifteen years of generous employment, but for taking me on in the first place. Lord knows you have many qualified candidates to choose from. I hope we can meet again someday under far happier circumstances.

Kindest Regards
Gloria Robbins

Ms. Robbins' letter was found undelivered in her office, signed and in a sealed envelope addressed to Mr. Thibodeau, the day after her disappearance.

FIDDLEHEADS

Douglas Smith

The fiddleheads were back.

Andy Pembleton saw the ferns as he walked in the wooded ravine behind the house where he lived with his Mom. It was the same day that he had his idea.

His idea to find his little brother.

Nothing had been growing in the ravine yesterday. But now the ferns had already pushed their curled heads two inches above the forest floor, peeking bright green through the gray corpses of last fall's dead leaves.

Andy stared at the patch of new life at his feet. The fiddleheads always meant spring was finally back. But they also meant the anniversary of losing his little brother.

Ever since Martin had gone missing nearly two years ago, not a day went by in which Andy didn't want him back the way that only a twelve-year old boy can want something. But lately, his longing for the only friend he'd ever known had grown into an almost physical pain.

Walking in the ravine helped him feel better. The town kept talking about putting paved walking trails in back here, but they never had.

He was glad because it kept the woods his private place, a place of secret paths and hidden glades that only he knew. A place where he could be alone.

He sat on the ground in front of the patch of new fern heads, ignoring the damp that seeped through the butt of his jeans. The days were getting warmer, and the wet earth smelled of new life and old rot. Life and death were all mixed up together in here.

Of all things in the ravine, he liked the fiddleheads best. The ferns fascinated him in a way he could never figure out. Maybe it was how fast they grew. They'd be fully grown in less than a week and would stand taller than Andy, and he was big for his age.

Maybe that was it. The fiddleheads showed how fast things could change. How fast things could come into this world.

How fast they could disappear from it, too.

Reaching down, he snapped off the head of one of the ferns. He pulled it, unwinding it, then let it curl back into the shape that gave the fern its name. He remembered when Dad first showed the ferns to him and Martin.

But Martin was gone now, and Dad didn't live with them anymore. Just the fiddleheads were left from that memory.

He heard Mom calling him for lunch, from the patio door of their house. He sighed and got up, reluctant to leave his special place, but feeling a little better. He stuck the fiddlehead he'd broken off into his pocket, and turned to leave the ravine.

Then he saw the little mound where Patches, the family cat, was buried. His stomach tightened. Fiddleheads were growing on top of the mound, death and life mixing there as well. He'd be glad when the fiddleheads were high enough to hide the spot.

Turning his back on the grave, he walked home.

That evening, sitting at the cluttered kitchen table, over a supper of hamburger stew and Kraft Dinner, Andy decided he'd try to tell Mom how he was feeling lately.

He could still talk to her sometimes, though not the same way as before Martin disappeared. She didn't spend as much time with him, either. Since Dad left them, she had to work in the day and at night, and often weekends too. But sometimes Andy wondered if being around him reminded her too much of Martin.

"Mom?"

"Uh huh?" Mom said, not looking up as she shook some pepper on her stew.

"I..." he began, wondering if he should tell her. "I still miss Martin," he finished, all in a rush.

Mom put the pepper shaker down and sat very still.

He wished he hadn't said anything, but he couldn't stop now. "I mean, I mean I miss him more than ever lately. Even more than when he... when he went away."

Mom looked out the window, and for a moment, he didn't think she was going to answer him. Then she turned back and even smiled in a sad kind of way. "We'll always miss him," she said. "But what you're feeling, it'll get better."

He thought he knew what she meant, and it made him angry. "Because we'll forget him, you mean."

Mom shook her head. "No. We'll never forget. Not ever."

He believed that Mom wished that she *could* forget Martin, and that made him even angrier. He felt as if he was going to cry.

Mom tried smiling again. "We won't forget. It just... it just won't hurt so much."

He didn't want it to stop hurting. He just wanted Martin back. "Why am I even sadder now?"

Mom stopped smiling and got up from the table. She started to clear the dishes. "Because when Dad... when your father left, it made us remember all over again when Martin left us too."

Dad had left last fall. Mom blamed a lot of things on Dad since then. He shook his head. "I think it's because this is when Martin went away. Next week."

Mom was silent for a moment. "Yes," she said finally. "Yes, it was." He knew that she was trying to forget, not remember. But he'd never forget May 2. It was only three days after Martin's birthday. Or what would be his birthday if Martin were still here to celebrate it.

Mom scraped what was left on her plate into the garbage. "He would have been nine years old," she said, as if she was talking to herself.

"He's *going to be* nine years old," he almost shouted, and his voice broke a bit.

Mom put her plate in the sink. She stared at him, and he could feel his heart pounding. Finally, she turned on the water. "Yes," she said softly. "You're right. Martin's going to be nine."

He finished his dinner in silence. Martin had disappeared on his birthday outing, and he knew that Mom didn't like to talk about that day. His real birthday had fallen on a Wednesday that year, and Martin had wanted his party on the following weekend instead, so that they could all go to *Canada's Wonderland*. The family had just moved to Toronto from Vancouver, and Martin had never been to the theme park.

Thinking about that day always confused him. It held both some of his favourite memories, along with the worst thing that had ever happened to him. And it had started the changes between Mom and Dad. He knew they both blamed each other for not watching Martin more closely, for not seeing him wander off. For losing him. Sometimes he blamed them both, too.

But mostly, he blamed himself.

After dinner, he went up to the little bedroom that he used to share with Martin. He still thought of it as "their" room—his and Martin's. Pulling out his memory box from underneath their bunk bed, he sat down on the worn brown rug and opened the cardboard shoebox.

A picture lay on top. In it, he and Martin were on a roller coaster at Wonderland, their arms raised over their heads as the coaster began a long drop. They were laughing. They were happy.

That had been before he and Martin had argued. He didn't know for sure if that had made Martin run off, but he always blamed himself.

Other kids made fun of Andy, for being behind a grade and in a special class. Martin had never done that. But that day at Wonderland, he and Martin had stood watching a play with some characters from TV in it.

"They look different than on TV," Andy said.

Martin looked up at him. "They're just actors in costumes, Andy. Not even the real ones from the show."

Andy liked that show and was happy to actually get to see the characters. What Martin was saying spoiled everything.

"No, they aren't. They're real," he said.

Some kids around them snickered, and Andy felt his face get hot. Then, for the first time ever, Martin looked at Andy the way kids at school did.

"Andy," Martin said, "don't be so *stupid*!"

He spun around and stepped toward Martin, towering over him, his fists clenched. "Don't you ever call me that!" he yelled. "I'm not stupid. Don't say that!"

Eyes wide, Martin backed up a step, bumping into another kid. All of the kids had become really quiet, then a little girl started to cry.

He grabbed Martin's hand. "C'mon. Let's go."

Martin pulled his hand away, but followed Andy back to where Mom and Dad were waiting. The adults just smiled, unaware of the argument. He didn't speak to Martin, didn't even look at him again, for the rest of the day.

So he hadn't noticed when or how Martin disappeared. He just knew that he had yelled at Martin that day, and later his brother was gone...

He jumped as he felt a hand on his shoulder. Mom knelt beside him on the floor. He hadn't heard her come in. She gave him a hug, something she didn't do that much anymore, then she took the picture out of his hand and stared at it.

"I wonder what he'd look like today?" she said.

He shifted so that her arm came off his shoulder. "You mean what he *looks* like."

"Yes. Yes, that's what I meant," Mom said, but he knew it wasn't.

Suddenly, thinking about her question, he felt confused. "What do you mean? Martin will look like Martin."

Mom shook her head. "Look at you in this picture. See how much you've grown? How different you look? It's been two years..." Mom's voice trailed off, then she tossed the picture in the box, face down. She stood up. "Martin would... *will* have grown and changed too, Andy." She went back downstairs.

He picked up the picture again, staring at himself in it, not at Martin as he usually did. He had to admit that he did look different now—taller, wider shoulders, hair darker and longer. And a face that was, well, different.

He reached into his pocket and pulled out the fiddlehead from the ravine. He thought about how fast they grew, how fast they changed.

That's when he got his idea.

The next morning, walking in the ravine, thinking about his idea, he noticed that the fiddleheads had grown even taller. They were now at least six inches high and had already unfurled rows of feathery arms below their curled tips. He swore he could see them growing, moving, like people rising and stretching from an earthy sleep.

Sunlight sneaking through the trees high overhead painted the fiddleheads in ever shifting shapes of sun and shade, making the new ferns look as if they were dancing. He stared at the patterns of light and dark.

Light and dark. Light and dark.

Life and death. Light and dark.

Andy reached into his pocket and pulled out the Child Find flyer that the police had distributed when Martin disappeared. Andy stared at the face on the flyer, taken from a photograph that Dad had snapped that fateful day. A picture of Martin then.

But not the way he would look *now*, Mom had said.

He stared at the fiddleheads.

Things grew. Things changed.

The police and the missing child agencies were looking for the *wrong* Martin. If they were still looking for him at all—the police detective never returned Andy's phone calls, and Mom wouldn't even call them to follow-up anymore.

At first, he had wondered why Martin didn't come home himself. He didn't think that Martin would still be angry with him. Martin must miss him as much as he missed Martin. He figured that Martin had run off and gotten lost that day and was still lost, or had bumped his head and forgotten things, like on TV shows.

So he would search for Martin, for a kid around town who looked like how Martin might look now—taller, darker hair, thinner, and well, different. He just felt sure that he'd know Martin when he saw him again. He'd bring the kid here, where no one else came, and show him their house from the ravine. If the kid recognized it, then he'd be Martin, and he and Andy could march up to the front door and surprise Mom.

It would be great. Everything would be good again. Maybe Dad would even come home.

Feeling better than he had in a long time, he turned to leave the ravine, to go over to the mall and start looking.

Something moved off to the right. He turned. The fiddleheads swayed in a breeze he couldn't feel. They parted, and he saw Patches' grave again.

He swallowed. Yeah, things grew, things changed.

But things died too.

The sunlight flickered through the trees, playing over the fiddleheads dancing beside the grave. Light and dark. Life and death. He stared at the little grave. Soon the fiddleheads would hide it, and he wouldn't have to think about it anymore.

He walked out of the ravine. The fiddleheads seemed higher already.

Things weren't going like Andy had figured. The kid looked around the ravine, acting scared now.

"Where are your games?" the kid repeated, his voice even louder this time.

"Quiet," Andy said in a loud whisper.

"No!" yelled the kid. He looked like he was going to cry.

It had been easy to get this kid to come here. Andy had seen him sitting on a bench in the mall, playing with his handheld game player, and had told the kid that he had lots of game cartridges he was giving away. Finding a boy who fit what Martin might look like now had been harder. Andy had thought this kid did, but he wasn't so sure anymore. The kid said his name was Billy not Martin, and he hadn't recognized Andy or the house. He didn't know any of the things that Martin should know.

Billy began trying to edge past him, toward the path they'd come in on. "I don't think you have any games."

"Yes, I do," Andy said, stepping in front of him.

Billy shoved at him. "Let me go. I'm going home."

"No. You can't," Andy said, standing his ground.

Billy was crying now. "I'm telling my parents. I want to go home. Let me go." Billy tried to push by him again.

Trying to leave him. Like Martin. Like Dad.

Andy, bigger and stronger, grabbed Billy and threw him to the ground, landing on top of him. Billy started to scream, so he shoved a hand over Billy's mouth and another hand around Billy's neck. The screams turned to gurgling sounds. Billy started to punch at his face.

Trying to hurt him. Like Martin. Like Dad.

Andy started to cry. This had all gone wrong. He just wanted to find Martin. He just wanted to have his family back. He just wanted to stop feeling all alone.

He twisted his face away from Billy's punches, and something moving to his right caught his eye.

The fiddleheads swayed in the breeze, back and forth, back and forth. They parted. He saw Patches' grave.

It had been late October that day. Dad had just left, and Andy was missing him and Martin really badly, missing the family he once had. He had sat in the ravine surrounded by fiddleheads that stood brown and withered like tiny skeletons. Dead and gone.

Gone like Dad. Gone like Martin.

Patches, a black and white stray, had followed him and crawled into his lap. Andy had sat there that day, stroking its fur, tracing the white and black patches with his finger.

White and black. Light and dark. Life and death.

It had felt good to have Patches with him, something warm and alive, something that hadn't wanted to leave him.

Like Martin had left. Like Dad had left. Leaving him. Hurting him.

Andy had started to cry that day. He was tired of being hurt. No one would hurt him again. No one would leave him again.

Patches squirmed in his lap. Trying to leave him. Andy grabbed him and pushed him down. The cat hissed, trying to claw Andy. Trying to hurt him, trying to leave him.

Sobbing, Andy squeezed his hands hard. Something cracked, and Patches lay still in his lap.

After a while, Andy's sobs stopped. Billy's noises had stopped too. Beneath him, Billy lay really still.

He stood up, shaking. He stared at the body but didn't really feel anything except being scared and wanting to puke. He looked around.

The fiddleheads still stood parted, showing where he'd buried the cat. Putting his hands under Billy's arms, he dragged the boy through the ferns, away from the path, and dropped him there. Then he fell to his knees and threw up, retching and coughing. Wiping his mouth on his sleeve, he got up and stumbled out of the ferns on shaky legs. He looked back.

The fiddleheads were slowly rising back into place. They seemed even taller now, thicker too, like they were trying to help him hide the...

Like they were trying to help him.

Broad and full, the ferns reached out to touch each other, forming a feathery green wall, hiding his secrets for him. Andy couldn't see anything behind them. Not Patches' grave. Not Billy.

The fiddleheads whispered on the wind, telling him that it was okay, that he was only trying to do something good, that he was just trying to find Martin.

Things die, Andy, they said, but things come back, too. We die each fall, but each spring, we come back. Martin will come back too. You just have to keep looking, they whispered, just have to keep looking.

The fiddleheads swayed, back and forth, back and forth, and Andy stood watching, swaying with them, listening as they whispered to him. After a while, he turned his back on the ferns and walked home.

The fiddleheads were right. He would just have to keep looking.

EVIDENCE

Jessie Turk

❝My name is Sarah, and to whomever finds this tape… this is my account of the disappearance of Jaime Walker."

Detective Wayne Barnett leaned back in his home office chair, his expression thoughtful. After a long pause his thick callused hands reached out and reset the video to frame one, and hit play. The first few seconds of the digital video began to roll. Detective Barnett leaned in close to the speaker of his laptop and listened carefully to the sound of the recorded voice, paying careful attention to the pitch and speech patterns.

"Definitely a kid's voice," the detective murmured aloud to himself. He made a note of his findings in the spiral notepad on the desk beside him. This case was getting stranger and stranger by the hour.

On the evening of June 3rd 2017, the Detective had been called to a residential area in the western end of Toronto. Earlier that afternoon, neighbors had phoned 911 reporting smoke and the keening of a fire alarm coming through the open kitchen window. Police and fire department arrived at the scene expecting to deal with a kitchen fire, but instead found a slaughter house. Upon entering the home, first responders found the body of a woman in her late sixties. She was found in the front hallway, not three feet from the front door, and had sustained severe lacerations to her arms and face to the point where a visual confirmation of identity was impossible. They found a second body in the kitchen, a woman in her early thirties, with nearly identical lacerations. The burner on the kitchen stove was still lit when first responders arrived at the scene. They'd discovered that the cause of the smoke had been a slice of flesh that had fallen on the hot stovetop and begun to blacken.

The victims, identified by their dental records, were Iona Duncan and her daughter Marie Walker-Duncan. Neighbors interviewed by police at the scene of the crime stated that the mother and daughter had moved into the area a couple of weeks prior to the incident. They'd come with Marie's young son Jaime to prepare the new house while Marie's husband Paul stayed behind to sell their old house in Saint John's, Newfoundland.

Barnett gazed intently at the image now frozen in the media player on his computer screen. The first video file on the memory card was of the missing boy, Jaime Walker, sitting alone on the swings at a park located only two blocks over from the scene of the crime. This was just one in a series of dated video clips, all located in a folder simply marked "Jaime Walker". The folder was contained on a memory card, the sort used in a modern DSLR camera, which had been taped to front of the basement door at the scene of the crime.

At first, Wayne expected that he would find some sick and twisted confessional video made by the killer. Sadly, it would not have been the first time Barnett found such a thing at a crime scene. What he did not expect to find was a series of videos, each labeled with dates going back as far as two weeks before the murders.

Detective Barnett hit play and the video resumed. Jaime Walker rocked lazily back and forth on the swing, using his toes on the sand to anchor himself. The video, obviously taken at a distance, tightened in on the boy, cutting out most of the playground from view. Little details about the boy came into focus as his picture enlarged on the screen. He was skinny, though that was a poor word to describe his appearance. Sickly was a far more appropriate term. Most kids were thin and wiry, but even skinny children possessed the plump round cheeks of youth. Jaime, with his sunken eyes, sharp brow and protruding cheekbones looked more like a tiny old man.

"My little sister pointed him out to me at the playground yesterday. She said that there was something wrong with him, but she couldn't explain what," Sarah explained from behind the camera. The fact that the voice clearly belonged to a young girl explained how she could walk around a park recording children without raising any suspicion from the surrounding adults.

"I didn't understand why at first. He looks normal enough to me, but then I started looking, and I mean *really* looking, and I started to notice something weird. I have to get this on camera, otherwise nobody will ever believe me."

The camera bobbed ever so slightly as she naturally shifted her weight, but stayed focused in on the boy across the playground.

"Watch the kid on the trike," Sarah instructed her unknown viewer.

Behind Jaime, a small boy on a tricycle entered the right-hand side of the screen. He followed the concrete track that circled the border of the playground until he exited on screen left. Barnett watched the clip the first time through without noticing anything out of place, so he rewound and watched the boy on the trike a second time.

Like a light turning on in the night, what he was supposed to be noticing was suddenly glaringly obvious. As the boy passed behind Jaime, he went out of his way to be as far away from the swing set as possible. The small child was biking as far to the outside of the concrete track as he could manage without biking across on the grass.

"...and the dog," Sarah angled the camera more to the right as a jogger loped past with a big yellow lab on the leash beside him.

Once again, nothing seemed out of place, until the jogger entered on screen right with a yellow lab loping along beside him. The dog seemed content at first with its ears up and its tail wagging. It seemed to be enjoying its run alongside its master, at least until it got close to the swing set. The moment it locked eyes on Jaime, the dog spooked and tried to bolt in the opposite direction, nearly dragging the jogger from his feet. No matter how much the man tried to calm the animal, he refused to go back toward the playground.

The video continued like this for several minutes, and Detective Barnet noticed a distinct pattern forming.

"None of the animals or young kids will go near him," Sarah murmured, giving voice to what Barnett had already concluded. "I've been sitting here for an hour, and it's the same every time. Even the older kids don't want anything to do with him. He makes them uncomfortable."

For reasons Barnett could not explain, what Sarah was saying in her video was undoubtedly true. She demonstrated the phenomena on camera more than half a dozen times. There was no denying that the vacant expression and dead eyes of Jaime Walker put the people around him on edge. Unfortunately, Detective Barnett could not see how these videos connected to the murders.

The next successive videos on the memory card were much the same as the first. Jaime sitting at a picnic table, Jaime walking to school, Jaime sitting on the front porch... In another video, Jaime was crouched over an abandoned game of marbles, meticulously counting each one. A handful of children, presumably the owners of said marbles, stood forlorn at the edge of the playground. Like in every other video, every single child went out of their way not to stand near Jaime.

"He did the exact same thing a day or two ago. He ran across the playground when he saw a bunch of the other kids playing jacks," explained Sarah. "I don't think he can help himself. Any time he sees a bunch of small objects he has to count them."

Detective Barnett made a note of Sarah's observation in his notepad. While Jaime's behavior was unusual, obsessively counting objects did not mean there was anything wrong with the boy. Still, if Sarah thought it was significant, then Barnett made sure to write it down. It would help him better understand Sarah's thought process, and why she felt the need to follow around a complete stranger with a camera.

Barnett hit play on the next video.

"This next video may contain graphic content," warned Sarah's voice from behind her camera.

The camera's lens careened violently from side to side, making it difficult to decipher what was happening on screen. Occasionally, the camera would stay still just long enough for Barnett to make out a line of garbage bins and an old wooden backyard fence. The wannabe investigator's hands appeared along the edges of the shot as the camera swung low, bouncing off a metal trash bin with a jarring *clang*. Evidently, Sarah decided to go hands-free and leave the camera recording while dangling precariously from a strap around her neck. She needed both of her hands available so that she could implicate herself on camera using one of the garbage pales to scale the fence and trespass into someone's backyard. To her credit, she managed to pull herself to the top of the fence without falling or breaking her camera, but the dipping and bobbing motion of the video betrayed her precarious balance.

In an annoyed voice, so low the camera's microphone barely caught the words, Sarah muttered, "This looks so much easier in crime shows..."

The corners of Detective Barnett's mouth turned up slightly despite himself. In real life, police officers rarely had need to sneak into people's backyards. That was the purpose of a warrant.

Sarah was heard taking a deep breath to gather her courage, then hopped down from the top of the fence. Wayne could hear the air leaving her lungs as she landed on the lawn below. Her hands wind milled wildly along the peripherals of the shot as she tried to maintain her balance, but she ultimately lost her footing and toppled backward onto the lawn.

The camera settled in Sarah's lap, revealing a pair of navy blue slacks and child-sized dress shoes. Barnett immediately reached for his notepad beside the laptop. He recognized the pants as part of a middle school uniform. The same school that his own daughter, Beth, attended.

With a groan, Sarah pulled herself to her feet, allowing the camera to dangle from the neck strap and swing wildly from side to side. Barnett paused the footage and began to slowly tap the right directional key on his laptop. He scrubbed through the video frame by frame until he found a moderately still image of the back of the house. Barnett recognized the old green patio furniture sitting on the back porch. Sarah had been standing in the Walker's backyard not two days before the murder of Marie Walker and Iona Duncan.

"Jaime's mom hasn't come home from work yet, so they haven't had a chance to see," Sarah said between short breaths, still recovering from her fall, "but one of the kids next door was home sick and said the Walker's dog stopped barking. They said it was weird because the stupid thing hardly ever shuts up. I thought I'd come look myself, and this is what I saw through the fence."

Sarah picked up the camera and turned to face the reason she'd risked being caught trespassing. Barnett's stomach lurched. Some small part of him had expected the dog to be dead, but there was dead, and then there was butchered. The mangled corpse lay spread out among Marie Walker's upturned lavender bush, in a manner eerily like the crime scene photos sitting on Barnett's desk.

Little was left of the dog's throat but a mass of matted blood and fur. One of the forepaws was torn clean from the body, and sitting in a puddle of blood in the middle of the overgrown lawn.

Behind the camera, Sarah coughed, disturbing a swarm of flies which were already feasting on the corpse. The unseasonably hot and humid weather had turned the dog's corpse rancid quickly, and the smell had attracted a massive cloud of insects.

"Poor thing." Despite the obvious revolting smell, Sarah leaned in closer to the body capturing every bit of the gory detail on camera. "Looks like it got in a fight with a rabid animal."

"Oi you! Come away from there, now!" A voice called out from off screen. It sounded like a woman, and Wayne caught a hint of an East Coast accent.

The camera spun to face the back porch of the house where Iona Duncan stood, arms folded over her breasts in a picture of disapproval. Barnett recognized her from what few photos had been unpacked around the Walker household.

"Best leave that be, girl," Iona shook her head severely. "Now, you'll be telling me what you're doing in my backyard, and with a camera no less.

Why would a pretty young thing like you be coming 'round to take pictures of a dead dog?"

"I, uh, well you see the neighbors heard…" Sarah mumbled, but could not come up with a reasonable explanation for why she had not simply gone to the front door.

"You've been sniffing around this neighborhood a lot these past few days," Iona accused.

Sarah paused, and croaked as if she were about to speak, but then thought better of it, and stayed silent.

Something in the older woman's face softened, making her look more curious than upset about finding a strange girl in her backyard, "Stop fretting girl. I'm not going to bite you. Now, why don't you tell me what you're about? I know you've been keeping tabs on Jaime."

"I've been…" Sarah took a deep breath to calm her nerves, and to give herself a moment to consider her next words, "I've been gathering evidence. Ma'am, I think there is something wrong with your grandson."

"Aye, he is sick. My daughter moved him all the way here to be closer to the best doctors." Iona cocked an eyebrow, "Unless you think differently?"

Sarah swallowed a lump in her throat, "I don't think a doctor is what he needs. I can show you what I have on my camera. All the dogs in the park, the other children, the strange way he has been acting… I don't think the boy in the videos in Jaime."

"So, what you're saying," Iona paused, eyeing the camera as though she were to deliver the twist in a scary campfire story, "is that the boy sitting inside the house right now is not my grandson? You're saying he is something altogether different? An imposter?"

Sarah's response was weary, "Yes, Ma'am."

"Now, let's pretend for a moment that what you say is true. Say young Jaime is not what he appears to be. That would make him something out of the old stories, now wouldn't it? It would be old, and something dangerous. Not the type of thing a little girl should be poking her nose into, right? The dog knew, and look at what happened to him," Iona eyed Sarah first, and then the camera, clearly illustrating her point.

"Wait, but, if you know, then why would you-?"

"Let it live in my house? Well, if the stories were true, and I am not saying that they are," Iona reached a hand into her apron pocket and pulled out an object made of dull grey metal. "Let's just say I have designs to drive the little beast out."

Carefully, as though she suspected the thing that looked like Jaime but was not Jaime, was eavesdropping on their conversation, Iona Duncan pulled an object made of dull grey metal from her deep apron pocket. The camera's lens narrowed in on a pair of scissors made of thick, heavy metal. They were not the kind with flimsy plastic handles sold in most department stores. From handle to tip, the scissors were the length of Iona's rail thin forearm, and looked like they had a considerable weight to them. Detective Barnett's grandmother had an almost identical pair from the fifties. He recalled that they could cut through damn near anything so long as they were routinely sharpened.

"Purest lump of iron I could find in the house," explained Iona, "My mother always told me that a piece iron under the pillow is enough to drive most undesirable things from a home. Your elders will always know a trick or two like this, which is why smart young girls such as yourself should leave these matters to adults. In fact, I think you should run home and put something iron under your own pillow. We wouldn't want something nasty following you home, now would we?"

Detective Barnett could imagine Sarah's expression behind the camera when she realized that Iona was dismissing her like a misbehaving child. She was a plucky girl who would risk being caught trespassing on private property with a camera, all because she knew the adults would never believe the truth about Jaime otherwise. Barnett got the impression that standing idly by was not something she was apt to do, but when faced with Iona and her imposing maternal authority, what else could Sarah say?

"Yes Ma'am," the young woman finally conceded. Detective Barnett didn't believe for a second that Sarah was being truthful, and it wasn't just because he knew he had one more video to watch. The harsh frown lines of Iona Duncan's face said that she didn't believe Sarah either.

"Now," Iona snapped, "why don't you put that bloody camera down and head on home."

The footage cut off abruptly as Sarah stopped recording.

Detective Barnett sat staring at the blank screen of his laptop. One thing he had not expected to find in this case was a delusion shared by an old woman and a little girl. They thought a sick little boy was an imposter? Were they both insane? The child he could believe falling into superstition, but surely Iona must have known better! Detective Barnett was glad that at least Marie knew the right of it, and brought the boy to Toronto seeking medical professionals instead of chasing old folk tales.

For all his trouble, Barnett had learned one useful piece of information about the days leading up to the murders- it was possible that whoever killed the dog also murdered Marie and Iona. The attack pattern was too similar to be a coincidence.

Detective Barnett took a long slow sip of the cold coffee in the mug on his desk, and then settled back into his office chair. It was time to watch the last video on the memory card.

The beginning of the video contained ten seconds of black frames before anything appeared on screen. The only indication that the video had even started was the sound of muffled breathing being picked up by the microphone. Clearly, Sarah's camera did not have a low-light function.

A small square of light flashed across the screen as the camera swayed back and forth on its strap. The camera recorded a thud and a rattle as it smacked against something wooden sounding. Barnett suspected it was the Walker's backyard fence. Ignoring Iona Duncan's warnings, Sarah was using the same trash bin to scale the fence for a second time. The only source of light, the kitchen window, shone bright hot white and yellow in a grainy sea of black. Sarah hit the ground running and scurried toward the shining beacon in the distance.

"I came by the house to keep an eye on things. Then I heard something inside. It sounded like a scream," Sarah's hoarse whisper was made almost inaudible by the way the camera's microphone was being jostled around. "I'm going to check the back window to make sure everything is okay."

Treading carefully along the back porch so she would not make too much noise, Sarah made her way to the back window. She needed to use one of the lawn chairs to climb up and get a proper view inside the kitchen window.

Detective Barnett's stomach lurched in dread. He already knew what Sarah would see through that kitchen window. He'd witnessed it himself not hours before, and it was not the sort of thing any child should have to witness.

Sarah let loose a string of profanities not suitable for any child as she hoisted the camera to place it on the window ledge. The view was partially obscured by the lace curtains on the window, but Barnett could make out distinct splashes of red all over the kitchen counter and stove top.

Through the poor audio quality picked up by the camera, Barnett could hear the distinct sounds of a struggle from somewhere inside the house. The video blurred as Sarah bounded off the lawn chair and ran for the back door of the house, which had apparently been left unlocked. She was no longer bothering to hold up the camera by hand, instead opting to let the heavy camera bounce against her chest, turning the following thirty or so seconds into a dizzying smear of shapes and colour. If Barnett paused video, and scrolled through it frame by frame, he could vaguely make out the kitchen and a dark shape on the floor which he knew to be Marie Walker, but not much else. Sarah seemed to know it was too late for the woman, and instead made a bee line for the front hallway where Iona was caught in a life or death struggle with her attacker. A fight she would inevitably lose.

Barnett leaned forward in his chair and adopted the posture a sports fan would assume during the last few seconds of overtime. This could be the last piece of the puzzle that Barnett had been waiting for. If Sarah had managed to get the attacker on camera it could blow the case wide open. Part of him still had a gut feeling that he would see the absent father, Paul Walker, on the video viciously attacking his mother-in-law with a knife.

Sarah lurched to a halt at the end of the hallway. The camera bounced against her chest where it eventually settled and gave an unobstructed view of Iona's bloodied body. There was no man in the hallway, but Barnett did see something dash into the living room. Barnett tried to scroll through the video frame by frame, but it was no good. Whoever it had been moved too quickly for the camera to catch anything meaningful. It was just a dark shape, nothing conclusive.

Sarah tip-toed cautiously down the blood-soaked hallway one step at a time. Her fearful trembling caused the camera to shake against her chest and turn the hallway into a haze of colour. Behind the camcorder, Sarah could be heard fumbling with the zipper on her backpack until her hands found something that rattled softly. When her hands remerged on the edge of the frame she was carrying a small mason jar filled to the brim with an assortment of shiny plastic beads; the kind of thing a kid might keep on hand for crafting supplies.

Detective Barnett blinked at his computer screen in bewilderment. In the face of a possible murderer, why would Sarah immediately think to reach for a jar of beads?

"Iona," Sarah hissed as she approached the unmoving body. Her body and the camera stayed angled toward the open doorway where the dark form had disappeared. "Iona please tell me you're still alive…"

Moving cautiously, the camera lowered as Sarah knelt beside Iona and her trembling hand could be seen as it reached out to check for a pulse, or at least that is what was intended. It was obvious from looking at the woman that there was not much of a neck left for Sarah to find an artery. Barnett knew that, even if Iona had still been alive, it would not have made any difference. In her condition, Iona would have bled out long before an ambulance ever arrived.

The hallway light glinted off something clutched in Iona's pale ashy hands; the iron scissors.

The sound of footsteps skittering across the wooden floor made Sarah and the camera jump with fright. Whatever was in the house did not sound like any human- the footsteps were moving far too rapidly for it to be a full-grown man, and Barnett could swear he could hear claws scraping against the hardwood.

The camera lurched forward as Sarah's hands scrambled desperately for the abandoned scissors along the far edges of the screen. Her arm slid across the pool of slick blood, splashing tiny dots of crimson all over the camera lens. Just as her fingers closed around the handle of the heavy metal scissors, the hallway echoed with the sound of talons.

With an ear-splitting scream, Sarah was dragged backward, the camera yanked along the floor after her. The scissors, slick with Iona's blood, slipped from Sarah's grasp. She tried desperately to claw her way back to her only weapon, but her fingers could not find purchase on the hallway floor. Whatever had hold of Sarah, human or not, was still strong enough to drag the struggling girl nearly all the way back to the kitchen.

In an act of desperation, Sarah hurled the jar of shiny beads into the open doorway of the basement cellar as she was dragged past. The glass jar clipped the doorframe as it sailed through the air, shattering the glass into a thousand tiny pieces. The air in front of the camera filled with falling beads shining like stars against the open black doorway to the cellar. They sounded like rain as they clattered across the hallway floor and down the cellar stairs.

Whoever, or whatever, had been dragging Sarah immediately lost interest in its prey in favour of chasing the beads. A bony foot covered in leathery black skin stepped past the camera, which had settled upside down on the runner carpet. The murderer's foot was roughly the same size as a child, but the skin had the tone and pallor of a corpse. It's long yellow toenails scraped across the blood covered floor, causing the distinct clicking sound Barnett heard when the creature ran. The thing followed the sound of bouncing beads through the basement door, where the darkness swallowed it like a great gaping maw.

Sarah's breath came in short panicked gasps as she crawled on hands and knees back to where the scissors dropped in the scuffle. With trembling fingers, she picked up the blood slick metal and got to her feet. She paused only for a moment to take a deep breath, before descending into the cellar.

The metal scissors, which seemed exceptionally massive in Sarah's tiny fingers, were held out in front of her in a closed fist.

The final moments of the video were pitch black. Sarah dared not turn on the basement lights, perhaps because she feared drawing the creature's attention. Barnett could only hold his breath and listen to the muffled sounds of footsteps, followed by a dull thud.

Out of the darkness of the cellar, Sarah ended her video with one final warning, "To whomever finds this video. I've trapped the thing posing as Jaime Walker in the basement using scissors made of iron. Whatever you do, don't go into the basement. It's not dead, that much I am sure of, so no matter what don't move the scissors."

Here, the video ends.

Blood running cold in his veins, Detective Barnett's eyes slowly traveled across his desk to where a pair of heavy metal scissors sat wrapped carefully in an evidence bag. It had been Barnett himself who had pried the old scissors from the work table after they had been found with the sharp end planted deep in the tabletop. Barnett himself had been the one to process and catalogue them, but as far as he could tell there was nothing special about them. The only blood evidence on them belonged to Iona. If Sarah used them against the creature on camera, she hadn't managed to land a hit. Barnett had brought them back to his home office, along with the memory card and the iron lock, so he could continue working after his family had gone to sleep.

"Just the ramblings of a scared little girl," Detective Barnett assured himself. "Nothing to get all worked up about."

Knock. Knock.

The two sharp knocks at the door cut through the silence like a knife and made Barnett jump so high off his seat that he overturned his coffee mug.

"Daddy," Beth murmured in a drowsy tone as she peeked her face through the gap in the door. "Can you come tuck me in? I don't feel well."

Barnett let out a relieved sigh, "Just a moment sweetheart, I will be right there."

Without thinking, Barnett began to gather up the case files and shove them into his desk drawer. The last thing he needed was his daughter getting nightmares from seeing bloody crime scene photos all over his desk. Sitting on top of the case file, wrapped in plastic, and nearly forgotten, were the Iona's iron scissors.

Beth's big brown eyes followed her father's hands as he fumbled with the evidence bag. Detective Barnett supposed that, to a child, the scissors could look like a frightening weapon a wicked witch might use to harm naughty children. The mistrust in Beth's eyes when she saw him holding the sharp metal object was understandable.

As he turned, the Detective let his elbow purposely brush against a box of paper clips sitting among the clutter on the desk. The container fell to the carpeted floor soundlessly, scattering dozens tiny pieces of wire in front of his feet.

When Barnett looked up from the mess he'd made of his office floor, Beth was standing in the room with him. She crouched on the balls of her feet gazing in rapt attention at the paperclips as she counted them one by one.

BONE DRUM

Monica S. Kuebler

If you cut me open from

chin to pelvis,

crack my skull,

slice wide my arms

and legs.

If you snip out my

organs one by one

so my heart could no longer pound for you

so my lungs could no longer breathe and gasp for you

so my stomach could no longer hunger for you

so my brain could no longer love and lust for you

so my muscles could no longer tense and thrust for you.

If you boiled down what was left.

Boiled my body

'til the last of the tendons

and tissue and earthly flesh

were worn from the bone

smooth

then I'd be the sum of everyone

and the sum of none at all.

However, if you picked up one of those bones

and struck it against a drum.

You would see that even then

I would create music,

art, a beat that can entrance

the living to dance to it.

It was born in my bones.

If you cut me open from

chin to pelvis,

crack my skull,

slice wide my arms

and legs.

If you snip out

my organs one by one,

you would see that

you would feel that

you would know that too.

HISS CLICK

Stephen B. Pearl

The hiss click of my regulator echoes off the stone walls of my tomb. The bubbles ascend, following along the rocky slope into a narrow crack of light too small to fit both my dwindling tank of precious air and my body. A taunting promise, a siren's call. Only a few meters and there is air to breathe, sunlight to warm me. A few meters and there is hope, there is life.

Hiss Click

The stories all say the dying go into the light. Is that the promise the chimney holds? Is it my personal pathway to the beyond? I smile around the regulator in my mouth.

"But that I am forbid to tell the secrets of my prison-house, I could a tale unfold whose lightest word would harrow up thy soul, freeze thy young blood, make thy two eyes, like stars, start from their spheres, thy knotted and combined locks to part and each particular hair to stand on end, like quills upon the fretful porpentine."

Could old William have foreseen this death, pinned by earth staring up at sweet air and salvation?

Hiss Click

I take another breath, each hiss click of my regulator counting down to the inevitable. I have a little time. A little time to wonder, to think. Is the passage wide enough to fit me if I drop my gear? Would the free ascent be short enough for me to survive? Would I catch on a snag and be pinned in that narrow crack of rock? Would I find my escape route, cut by nature millennia before I was born, to be a false promise that will end my life in the most horrible of ways?

Hiss Click

Fear clutches me like an icy claw closing around my heart. In a panic, the animal within screams for me to cram myself into the narrow gap above and ascend. A slightly more reasoned part of me demands that I dive into the churning murk below and scramble blind and ignorant for the passage out. I have to master those urges before I can begin. In panic lies death.

Hiss Click

I check my depth gauge again. I have the best equipment. Double tanks, buoyancy compensator, depth gauge, pressure sensor. Hell, I even have a compass on my wrist, not that it does me any good. I take off the compass, a gift from my Mother, who passed into the beyond ten years ago this March. If she had known my fate, would she still have sat through all those swimming lessons? Would she have given me my first wetsuit? The box had been huge under the tree, my only gift that year, aside from the obligatory stocking stuffers, but it had been more than enough. I drop the compass.

Hiss Click

I remember the joy of opening that box. How I caressed that black Neoprene. The suit opened a world of chill waters and glories to me that most people never see. The suit I now wear is far in advance of that relic from my teens, but you always love your first. I check my depth gauge. I'm only three meters down, well within the depth for a free ascent and no worries about the bends. That was one set of fears dealt with.

Hiss Click

I check my J valve. The fact that I still have one will shock many divers in this day of pressure warnings and gadgets. While tough! I've heard all the mockery. The reserve that the J valve holds back is useful. It means I don't have to stress checking my tank's level all the time. I still check, but it is a comfort knowing that if I get distracted by the wonder of the dive, I will have the inescapable reminder of running out of air to bring me back to the here and now while I have enough air to surface by pulling on a simple leaver.

Hiss Click

Now the J valve serves as a reminder for when my time is up. When all hope of rescue is gone, and my choice is the insane risk of the chimney, or death. I fear drowning. The agony of those last minutes when the lungs burn for air sits in my imagination like a hungry wolf. The final gasp where water enters the lungs triggering the gag reflex and exploding the alveoli in the chest. How long will my brain continue to work, forcing me to endure the pain? How many seconds will my body be racked with coughing as I try to expel the water and take in air? But there will be no air to take in. How long before the creeping blackness, as my brain shuts down amidst the agony.

Hiss Click

I push down on the growing terror, forcing myself to calm. The crazy part is I would do it all again. Not this particular dive, of course, but the diving. The world of water is like a drug to me. The glory of caves seen only by a handful of human eyes is as close to the divine as a man can come. Even this cave, that may well be my tomb, is a wonder never before seen by humans. I know that will change with the coming mutilation of this watery labyrinth. I can't blame the company. As long as people use electronics the copper has to come from somewhere, and the mine supplies the jobs that keep the town alive. It makes fiscal sense to pump out the aquifer and keep working the deposit. Draining the caves is an unfortunate consequence.

Hiss Click

My death will be the first of many. The creatures evolved to live in this watery labyrinth will succumb to man's needs. In years, when the copper has been extracted, the mine will stop the pumps. The caves will slowly re-flood, but so much of what they are, what makes them great, will be lost. When the caverns are dry, someone will likely find my body. A neoprene-clad skeleton to remind them of the waters that once here flowed.

Hiss Click

Today's outing was supposed to be a simple cave dive. A last chance to experience the cave system the way nature intended flooded and beautiful in its unsullied majesty. We took all the precautions. Safety lines, known route. It was a pleasure trip. No point in mapping when everything was going to change and you already had the maps you'd need. I hope Claudia made it. She probably did. I'll miss you, beloved.

Hiss Click

She would have loved this chamber. Where my flashlight's beam pierces the eternal dark of the earth I see bands of colour running along the uneven walls of an arched, natural cathedral. I hover inside a temple to the gods and goddesses of the deep earth. Geb, Hecate, Hades, Kali. So many I couldn't possibly know them all by name. I pray to you all, named and unnamed, let me go and I will be a better man.

Hiss Click

It won't be long now. I take off my wrist watch. It is a small thing, but it could still snag on a rock. It drifts to the cavern's floor some three meters below where I rest against the cave's ceiling. I've always loved the weightlessness that water granted. Water the element of emotions. Add fire to water and you generate passion, creating steam that drives so many of man's creations.

Hiss Click

I turn my attention to the safety reel clipped to my equipment and undo the snaps holding it. I pause to examine the frayed end of the cable. I am a victim of a perfect storm of circumstance. One minute I was swimming across the mouth of an unexplored side cavern. Claudia had stopped to examine some banding in the rock of the cavern's wall. The next minute a current, like nothing I've ever felt before, sucked me into the side passage. I can only guess what caused the current, but I would think that the mine broke through a layer of porous rock connected to the cave system. Tonnes of water were sucked down that side passage, catching me in the flow like driftwood.

Hiss Click

Panic had taken me. I was helpless, driven by forces I couldn't control. Silt blocked my vision and then I jerked up tight on my safety line. In the confusion hope had glimmered. I flipped to face into the current and dragged myself back along the line.

Hiss Click

The edge of the cavern must have been sharp. The water kept flowing as the line pulled back and forth. I heard the break as a loud ping that echoed off the cave's walls. I was sucked blind and helpless along the cavern. An eddy threw me up into the hollow of my tomb above the current's flow. In the calmer waters I managed to wedge myself into a crevice in the rock. The water below me is still clogged with silt, making it imposable to see through or navigate in. I could be ten meters from the main cavern or a hundred. Either way, in that silt I could never find my way.

Hiss Click

I bite down on a surge of panic. Is it kindness or cruel irony that the silt didn't penetrate up to the stagnant water at the top of the chamber? Sunlight glimmers down the chimney, piercing the roof. Looking up, I see the ripples above. So near but yet… I sigh

Hiss Click

I re-examine my life, all the chould-have-beens. So many missed opportunities, some I'm glad I passed on. Tracy would have been fun for a week or two, but I couldn't hurt Claudia. I love you, my mermaid, although your taste in friends leaves something to be desired. Was I right not to mention Tracy's offer? Who knows? The job in the Caribbean? Maybe that one would have been worth taking, but Mom had just died, and Dad needed someone.

Hiss Click

Dad will take it hard. Maybe, just maybe, Amanda will shift her ass and try to be there for him. At least my will is explicit. My dear sister cannot snake my savings. I'm glad I paid extra so my life insurance covered diving accidents. Claudia will at least have that. Gods, John, I swear if you come sniffing around Claudia I'll haunt you. She deserves better than a philandering poser with delusions of adequacy and a fake Rolex.

Hiss Click

I hope Claudia is safe. The current might have snatched her too. I... I just can't think of that right now. If it took her we'll be together. If the chimney pans out, we'll be together. If not... It's sick but I catch myself thinking that if Claudia isn't safe maybe I don't want the chimney to pan out. Maybe I'd rather not face the world. I'm sure Tracy would be willing to console me. That thought is enough to send a shudder up my spine. The looks are there, but what's between the ears... Burrrr. Another kind of panic begins to rise. I push it aside. Horror wears many faces.

Hiss Click

Who will attend my funeral? Dad, of course. Amanda, because it wouldn't look good if she didn't. Claudia. Maybe she'll wear that little black dress that shows off her legs. Gods, she has the most beautiful legs! A swimmer's body, with a backside that can still make teenaged boys walk into trees. I close my eyes and remember the best parts. Her long, black hair, now streaked with silver. Her beautiful face. Those eyes, striking blue with a starburst pattern with the little laugh wrinkles that had grown at the edge of her eyes over the years.

Hiss Click

Who else? Walter. Yea Walter would come. Funny how you drift apart, but the people who are really in your life never change. No matter how much time passes between visits, a cold beer and a couple of jokes and Walter fit. Now Walter and Claudia... If she has to lean on someone, let it be Walter. He'd look after her. Probably kick John's ass. That thought makes me smile.

Hiss Click

The gang from the dive club will pay their respects, if they don't have anything else to do. Marcy and Kevin from work. Bernie and Ellen, but only to support Claudia. After all, she is their daughter. Funny how much money matters to them.

Hiss Clap!

The regulator catches and the walls close in. My time is up. There will be no rescue rising from the billowing silt below. There will be no sudden drop in the water level drawing precious air down to me. The gods of the deep will grant me no miracle that is not of my making. Perhaps that's for the best.

I pull down my J valve. The spring releases the last 250 pounds per square inch of air in my tanks.

Hiss Click

I start undoing buckles, dropping every piece of extraneous equipment. Somebody is going to get some nice swag if they happen down the tunnel. Maybe the Gods will consider it an offering and shift their butts to help me. No, I'm sure Gods have more important issues to deal with than a single mortal life. I've never understood why humans are so egocentric. Oh, I am a man of faith, but my gods administer the natural order. They keep the sun burning evenly, the pressure of the mantel in the sweet zone so that super volcanoes don't destroy the world. They are a consequence of, and the administrators of, the natural world. All powerful, all knowing, all loving. I'll leave that to the advertisers.

Hiss Click

My weight belt drifts down. Now the buoyancy compensator around my tank holds me against the ceiling like a turtle on its back, only I'm facing down into a void. I shine my light around one last time. As tombs go the chamber is beautiful. I focus on the inconsequentiality to keep the horror at bay.

Hiss Click

A deep breath and I turn off the light and let it drift away. It was a gift from Claudia for our twenty-fifth. I'd give it away a thousand times for a slim chance to hold her once more. Now the cavern is black, like the dawn of time before a single star had graced the cosmos. The primal animal fear of that darkness, where anything might lurk, threatens to shatter my hard-won calm. Only, the distant glow at the top of the chimney can be seen. Only, that faint hope holds back the terror. The rocks that line the chimney form a negative image, threatening to grab me and pin me to die alone as I strive for that light.

Hiss Click

I slip out of my harness. The tanks float against the cave's roof as I take some last desperate breaths. Breaking all the rules, I hyperventilate hoping to trick my body into not wanting to breathe for a few extra seconds.

Hiss Click

Hiss Click

Hiss Click

It's becoming harder to pull air out of the tank.

Hiss Click

I'm gone. Dropping the regulator I pull myself into the chimney. My wetsuit helps me float and I release air as I rise so I don't pop a lung. The passage narrows I continue to rise until—

The End?

THE SOUL BROKER

D. J. Adadjii

C hristopher Frizer thrust a twenty-dollar bill at the taxi driver, then angrily pushed open the door and stepped out. Rush hour was over, yet they had barely moved a half a block over the past five minutes. A bicyclist, who had just veered onto the sidewalk to avoid the open car door, swore at him repeatedly. But his attention was focused on his iPhone as he caught up on the state of his investments now that the markets had closed for the day. He weaved through the tightly-packed crowd on University Avenue until it was too congested to go any further, all the time wondering why there were so many people about. Car horns began to blare from all directions, and he stood on his toes to peer over the crowd. The entire intersection and beyond was packed with revellers who were shuffling along like old-school zombies, and many were holding up homemade signs. *Great*, he thought. *Another bloody protest. Fucking apocaholics.*

He read an article once where "apocaholics" was used to describe investors who repeatedly fell victim to media-generated frenzies about the financial markets. Christopher thought it literally applied to these numbskulls who feared that a cataclysmic event of biblical proportion was on the horizon, and that governments across the globe were downplaying the scare in order to prevent mass hysteria and anarchy. They believed a gigantic meteor, dubbed "2016 WF9," was on a collision course with the Earth. Hundreds of thousands could die if it hit a major centre, or landed in the ocean to generate a devastating tsunami. With either outcome, the likelihood of a worldwide event akin to a nuclear winter was highly probable. NASA had completely dismissed the predictions, claiming the object would only come within fifty million kilometres of Earth's orbit. This should have occurred over four months ago, in February, yet the trajectory had somehow changed, and now the mysterious celestial object was not expected until December. According to a self-proclaimed prophet overseas, this was a sign from God that the human race was being given a few more months to prepare for nothing less than the End of Days. The doomsayer had seemingly appeared out of nowhere with the declaration, and soon had a small entourage in tow. Initially her tale had been relegated to conspiracy websites that ran exposés on UFO sightings, the Illuminati, and cryptids like Bigfoot and the Loch Ness Monster. That changed after FOX News aired a contrived story that practically celebrated her message of impending doom, and thanks to social media, it wasn't long before she was trending worldwide. Now her true believers were becoming more vocal, and opportunists such as the alt-right movement were using this simmering chaos to spread their own agenda of fear and hate.

As he forced his way through the crowd, an older woman directly in front of him prompted a double take. Her silver-streaked hair was fastened back in an impossibly tight, flat braid, and she had a charcoal-grey ponytail that trailed down her back. For a moment he thought it was his mother, which was impossible considering she had committed suicide years ago. Still, seeing the woman gave him chills, and his heart started pounding relentlessly. She seemed to be part of a group that looked as though they had fallen right out of a dystopian novel, and he was hit with the overwhelming stench of fetid body odour. They were half-heartedly chanting about the end of the world, as if they had already given up and just wanted it to be over with. It wasn't until she turned to face him that he was truly convinced his mother had not returned.

The woman looked as though she hadn't slept in months. "Have you repented? Are you ready to be judged?" A flash of recognition crossed her face. In a tone only slightly less confrontational, she added, "Mr. Frizer?"

He prided himself on his knack for remembering faces, at least for those who travelled in the same circles. She obviously knew him, but he couldn't place her at first. Then in his mind's eye he saw an image of a larger woman, her fleshy face coated with makeup in an attempt to hide her spotty complexion. But now the blotching was all too apparent, and her flesh had become taut and molded over the bones of her face. Gone was her spiked platinum blonde hairdo. It was Alice Davey, and she had changed significantly since he last saw her five years ago. He was about to push past her but hesitated. The last thing he wanted was an impromptu chat with a former client, and he wondered what the odds were for this chance meeting to even happen. He should have been on his way, yet couldn't help but stoke the fire just a little.

"Mrs. Davey, so nice to see you again. You're looking well."

"May the Lord have mercy on us. We're all doomed! It will definitely happen this time, I know it to be true."

"Yes, I believe so. Thank God years ago you and your husband prepared for this. Is Paul here?" He managed a passable level of sincerity in his voice.

Alice bit deeply into her bottom lip, almost to the point of drawing blood. "After we liquidated everything, Paul put the money in the bank while we weighed our options. We finally decided to donate it all to St. Gregory's Catholic Parish." Flushed with anger, she emphasized her words like a hen pecking at the dirt. "But none of it ever went to the church! He emptied the account, then left me. Moved to San Diego, where we had planned to take our second honeymoon before… before all this…"

As her words trailed off, a lanky, sallow-looking young man with a threadbare beard put his arm around her and pulled her in tight. There was dried snot caked along the top of his tendril of a moustache, and he repeatedly blinked his bloodshot eyes. He was muttering under his breath, and every third word was "Jesus." The sign he held above his head was barely legible, and read "JUJMENT DAY IS COMMING!!!"

Alice wiped her eyes as she glanced up at her companion, and smiled sweetly. "If it wasn't for my friends, I would have never survived Paul's betrayal. My soul is clean, and his will burn in Hell!" Her sentiment was echoed by the squalid cluster of protesters that sheltered her.

Christopher already knew about Paul Davey's change of heart, and felt no remorse over Alice's predicament; he wouldn't be much of a businessman if he thought otherwise. He had profited tens of thousands of dollars during the two doomsday scares of 1999 and 2012 thanks to a handful of millionaires who found religion once they thought the world was about to end. His clients were all looking for a quick path to redemption, and he sold them on the concept of salvation through donation. He still couldn't help but marvel at the absurdity of it all. They spent a lifetime obsessing over wealth, caring little about the nasty shit they did as they clawed their way to the top of the food chain. Then out of the blue they turned to religion after becoming convinced that their time would soon be up, and the chance of a happy ever afterlife was unlikely—without intervention. He couldn't fathom why they thought that ridding themselves of their worldly possessions would somehow tip the scales in their favour, or why they even believed in the afterlife to begin with in this day and age. Although Christopher presented himself as a God-fearing man devoted to doing his part to cleanse the souls of his clients, he was an atheist at heart. It had been a fun game, and he enjoyed taking advantage of stupidity.

For every desperate client he took on, he had at least three upstarts waiting in the wings, ready to scoop up their property at a discounted rate. The spoils were then donated to charity, or returned to his client in a lump sum—minus his generous take, of course. After all, he was doing the Lord's work! Inevitably, the fateful day would come and go without any sort of catastrophic event, leaving his clients with a very uncertain future. To his surprise, some of them actually continued their selfless ways, helping the less fortunate or some such nonsense. Most, however, simply fell off the grid, but he'd occasionally read about them in the obituaries. Unless, like Paul Davey, they realized their mistake before it was too late. It wasn't his place to pass judgment, and he cared little of the outcome; he still got his cut no matter what.

With a raspy cough, Alice's companion spit a gelatinous, grey mass onto the sidewalk. Christopher figured that most of the pungent smell was coming from him, and could barely stifle a laugh. His frustration over the inconvenience imposed by these apocaholics was mounting, so he decided to move on before he said something truly cruel. Then someone grabbed his shoulder and spun him around. An old man stood there, but his eyes expressed deep sympathy, not anger. He had a thick, white head of hair and looked spry for his age. His only other distinguishing mark was a deep scar that ran across his right cheek. "Mister..." he muttered, and then trailed off as his focus fell elsewhere on the crowd.

Christopher pushed the old man away, and then motioned toward the homemade sign as he moved past Alice's group. "Nice spelling, by the way. Good job with all the exclamation marks, too. Really sells the message." The yellow, emaciated waif scratched his head as he mouthed the words that he had written. Christopher continued toward the restaurant, and a path inexplicably opened up in front of him amid the sea of baseball caps, windswept hairdos, and hand-scrawled warnings of impending doom.

The restaurant's terrace sat two storeys above ground and provided a bird's eye view of the surrounding neighbourhood. Christopher was directed by the *maître d'* to his usual table, and he unbuttoned his navy Dormeuil suit jacket as he sat down. He peered over the glass enclosure to get a better look at the crowd below. Regardless of the masses assembling across the globe, the threat of a potential meteor impact seemed unspectacular compared to the scare over the Mayan Calendar prophecy a few years ago, which involved a major galactic alignment over 5,000 years in the making. He had made a killing then, far more than over Y2K. But with the Doomsday Clock recently set to two minutes to midnight, this non-event—in his mind—may yet prove even more profitable. He decided to have one more kick at the can, just to pad out the nest egg.

He scanned the menu but wasn't very hungry, so he ordered a Spanish Coffee and the *soufflé au chocolat de l'âme*. He watched the waitress intently as she sauntered back into the restaurant. Her name was Jacquelyn, and she was from Montréal or Québec City, or someplace French. He couldn't remember the details, but he did recall that in bed she was as flexible as Nadia Comăneci in her heyday. A strong breeze suddenly picked up, chilling the early evening air. His cell phone rang, but there was no caller ID. Considering only a select few knew his private line, it probably meant business.

"This is CF," he answered, but there was no response. He was about to hang up when a voice came through the other end.

"I am looking for Mr. Frizer. Is... is this the man to whom I am speaking?"

Christopher immediately recognized the caller's voice. It was the same pesky foreigner who had left him a number of rambling voicemail messages over the past week, and he sounded like a drunk Arnold Schwarzenegger. He was usually lucid to start, but then would veer into a fervor about the end of the world and saving souls. Clearly he was losing his mind.

"Mr. Frizer?"

He saw no potential in this fool, who was too far gone—an apocaholic in the worse sense of the word. One of his former clients must have given out his phone number, even though this was prohibited in their contract. He exhaled quickly and then glanced at his watch. "Sorry, you have the wrong number. Goodbye."

"*Bitte*, Mr. Frizer. *Der Teufel!* I... I do not have much time. We must speak. *Sofort!*"

Christopher ended the call, but seconds later the phone rang, again showing no caller ID. He let it go to voicemail. Minutes later, the man was calling again. He engaged the line, and then quickly hung up. By the time Jacquelyn arrived with his order, he was in the mood for something a little stronger.

"Get me a double martini, would you, hon? With four olives."

She leaned toward him and lit the small red candle that adorned the glass-topped table. She blew out the match with a short, quick puff.

"Made your usual way, Chris?"

"Yep. With *La Sarabande*, and as dirty as your mind." As she walked away, he made a mental note to take her home one of these nights.

When his phone rang yet again, he turned on the mute switch then set the device aside. As he sipped the Spanish Coffee, he idly tapped a diamond-studded cufflink against the railing. The crowd below was expanding, and now filled the gaps between cars for at least three blocks. Horns blared as tempers flared. A few beat cops were beginning some semblance of crowd control, and were soon joined by several more officers on bicycles and horseback—but the unruly mob had become so dense that all the police could do was try to prevent others from joining in. Shouts emanated from the ones being corralled, and several sat down in protest. A little farther up the street, two large men were pushing and shoving each other until one was struck from behind. Both fell to the ground as more joined the fray. Christopher smirked at the unfolding commotion below. *If I'm going to make any money this time around, it won't be with these clowns. Clearly they're all from the Other 98%.*

He took a newspaper from the table behind him and rolled his eyes once he realized it was the local daily tabloid. The headline cried: "Satan Spotted in Yonge-Dundas Square." *Seems legit. I've seen Jesus there before, handing out pamphlets.* Greatly amused, he almost spit out his coffee as he scanned the article. One witness was convinced that The Great Deceiver was in Canada because Justin Trudeau was one of his disciples, and the Liberal Party was turning the country into a cesspool of gay sin. Yet most believed it was due to the meteor hurtling toward Earth. The story continued into the back pages, and ended amid a directory of phone-sex ads. He wasn't surprised that the reporter failed to note that all previous doomsday scenarios had come to naught.

He checked his watch again, then tapped on the face before holding it up to his ear. Then a pungent smell washed over him, and he coughed as he looked over the railing to see if Alice Davey's group was nearby. He didn't see them, so he checked the bottom of his shoes, but the soles were clean save for a few scuff marks. The smell soon dissipated, and the shrill sound of police sirens drew his attention back to the street.

"Ahem…"

Christopher was glued to the fights that were breaking out below. "Jacquelyn, can you believe this?" Snapping his fingers, he added, "Grab me a real newspaper, would you? A copy of *The Financial Times* will do."

She cleared her throat again, and he slammed his hand onto the table as he turned to get his martini. But he changed his tune once he realized it wasn't her. The woman standing there was in her mid-thirties, and her angled face was framed by silky, black hair. Her olive skin practically glowed in the early evening light, and her visage was the embodiment of luxury and wealth.

She placed her briefcase next to the chair as she sat down across the table. "May you live in interesting times," she said, with a hint of playfulness.

Christopher couldn't place her accent, but the tailored cut of her Armani suit spoke volumes, so he decided to forgive her bold intrusion. "I wasn't expecting any company," he replied in a smarmy tone. "But I always have time for a pretty face. What can I do for you?"

"I apologize, where are my manners. You are Mr. Frizer, yes?" She motioned her hand toward his. Her pale, sinewy fingers tapered to stubby nails that were coated in a deep red, which made them look like bony matchsticks. Clearly she was due for a manicure.

He hesitated, then nodded, but made no effort to shake her hand. "I'm afraid you have me at a disadvantage, Miss…"

"If I may be so bold, it is *Ingram*, is it not? Ingram Frizer? I have been looking for you for quite some time." She cracked a half smile, and added, "It has taken forever. You are a hard man to track down."

Folding his arms, he straightened up in the chair. His mother had always called him Ingram, which is why he hated anyone else doing so. "I go by *Christopher*, my middle name. My friends, and those using the proper channels, never have trouble finding me."

She seemed unfazed by his rudeness. Leaning in, she whispered, "You are the Soul Broker, yes?"

He immediately shook her hand and winced at the feel of her clammy flesh. "I never liked that nickname, but I *am* in the business of helping others in their time of need. You must understand, however, that consultations are always scheduled, and potential clients are vetted beforehand, Miss…"

She returned his smile. "This is of a most imperative nature, and time is of the essence. We *must* speak tonight."

No beating around the bush with her, he thought, *she's all business*. His first new client seemed to have fallen right into his lap, with no legwork required. He hoped that any others he took on were reeled in just as easily.

"I'll make an exception, just this once."

"Excellent. Now, what I—"

A scream pierced the din of the activity on the street, and he leaned over to take a look. It was chaos below. Several young men, holding tiki torches, were being confronted by anti-racism demonstrators. Police had detained a handful of people, while five lay motionless on the ground. A paramedic was performing CPR on one of them, while a second was trying to stem the flow of blood from another. One of the fallen had his head twisted at an odd angle, and his hair was matted with blood. The woman kneeling beside him screamed as a police officer helped her to her feet and whisked her away. Goosebumps rippled over Christopher's skin when he saw that a small group was looking up at the terrace, directly at him— oblivious to all the hysteria.

He shook away the eerie feeling and refocused on the woman sitting across the table. *She must be loaded. Looks sane. Hopefully she hasn't fallen over the edge.* "Where were we? Ah, yes." He cleared his throat, and began the pitch that he still knew by rote: "Here's the deal: I'll take any asset, from jewelry to real estate and other property, and liquidate it for you. I'll then direct the funds to a charity, or a church of your choice. Or, I can just give you the money. Minus my standard take, of course, which is ten percent. But that may fluctuate, based on—"

"Excuse me, Mr. Frizer, I—"

"Please, call me Christopher. As I was saying, my take will fluctuate based on the market, which can change by the hour. As we approach the, ah, End of Days, I may not be able to get you top dollar. So I suggest you don't hesitate, because—"

"Christopher, you must hear me out."

He wondered if he had misjudged her. But he rarely questioned his instincts, and pushed on. "If you're not here to offload some primary assets then what are you selling? There is a limit to what I can manage. Are we talking foreign holdings? Because overseas transactions will definitely require more effort on my part, and—"

"Enough!" she shouted, her black eyes so full of rage that she gave him a moment's pause. But in a flash, she was all smiles. "Please, I wish to ask you a few questions."

She spun the newspaper toward him, and then jabbed one of her stubby fingernails into the headline. "What do you think of this?"

"Well, if these rumours are true, then the end may in fact be near."

She nodded. "May God have mercy on us all." Then she bowed her head and made the sign of the holy cross.

"Amen," he replied, and then mimicked her reverent gesture, although his half-hearted attempt looked more like an X. "These are troubling times indeed, which is why you must make your decision as soon as possible."

"My mind has been made up for some time now."

He was encouraged by her response. "Then you've come to the right man. I was put on this Earth to help others, to show them the path to redemption, and assist in cleansing their conscience. No matter what happens over the coming months, don't be concerned by what others may think. Only you know what's best for yourself."

"A philosophy similar to my own."

"I had a feeling we'd share a certain connection."

As she cupped his hand in hers, she asked, "Are you a religious man?"

He failed to notice the coldness this time, and motioned toward the newspaper. "Do I actually believe that Satan has come calling? That a meteor may trigger an apocalypse? Well, it is in my best interest to keep appraised of such curious events. So I may help others, of course. Miss…"

"Aimal. My name is Aimal. To be frank, my adherence to religious dogma has lessened over the years. But with everything that is going on now, perhaps a change of heart is in order." She locked her eyes onto his, then added, "Have you heard of The Seven Signs?"

He nodded. "Yeah, I think I saw that film years ago. Demi Moore was in it, right?" She was one of Christopher's favourite actresses back then, but only after she got the boob job and starred in that stripper movie.

"No, you misunderstand. I speak of The Seven Signs of the Apocalypse."

"Right, I remember now. Those predictions by that French guy, Nosferatu something."

"Nostradamus," she corrected. "*L'an mil neuf cens nonante neuf sept mois, du ciel viendra un grand Roy d'effrayeur. Resusciter le grand Roy d'Angolmois, avant après Mars regner par bon heur.*"

"You lost me, Aimal." The French reminded him of Jacquelyn, and he wondered why she was taking so long with his martini.

"Christopher, Nostradamus predicted that in 1999, an unprecedented worldwide revolution would take place, and great conflicts spanning the globe would result in social turmoil and a new world order. However, as you know, the millennium scare turned out to be nothing more than a means for some to capitalize on the foolishness of others."

He cleared his throat. "Yes, but all for a good cause."

"Indeed. However, I am not talking about *his* predictions. I speak of the ones found in the Book of Revelation. The first four signs concern the Riders of the Apocalypse. Upon breaking the first seal, a horseman will ride to conquer many foes, and win many wars. There has been so much conflict lately, especially in the Middle East. Very telling, yes?"

If she has a point, she'd better make it soon. His enthusiasm for this conversation was dwindling. "So you believe that this sign has come true? But they've always been prone to war over there. Some of them practically still live in the Dark Ages."

"But what of the next sign? The second horseman will banish peace and bring anarchy to the world. Many will die as wars break out everywhere—"

"We've been killing each other for centuries. Hell, as soon as mankind climbed down from the trees, it's been pure anarchy."

She playfully bit her lip. "Playing the Devil's Advocate, I see. Well then, what of the third sign? This horseman brings famine to the earth."

"Remember Live Aid? Or Live 8, for that matter? How long has there been famine? Probably as long as there's been war."

Her hands began to tremble as she clasped them together. "Then the fourth horseman, Death, and the fifth, Hell, will be given free rein to slaughter with war, famine, disease, and wild animals!"

"Wild animals?" Christopher rolled his eyes. He was starting to believe that maybe she was already too far gone. "For someone who has fallen away from religion, Aimal, you still seem pretty familiar with the Bible."

She paid no attention to his sarcasm. Her skin was flushed, and she took several short, quick breaths. "The fifth sign! In Heaven, the souls who were martyred for preaching the Word of God will be given white robes, as they await their fellow servants of Jesus who were also martyred on Earth."

By this point he was barely paying any attention to her. Checking his phone, he noticed the voicemail indicator was flashing repeatedly. Four more missed calls. "Listen, why don't we chat about this tomorrow—"

Aimal rose from the chair, and with clenched fists she pounded the table for emphasis. "The sixth sign! The sun will become black as ink, and the moon a blood-red. The stars will fall from Heaven, and the skies will roll up like a scroll. Mountains will shake and shift, and there will be a vast earthquake!"

She was becoming so animated that Christopher was reminded of those late-night Christian evangelists with the 800-numbers, who sold tacky religious trinkets made by Third World children who were probably Buddhists. With a smile, he imagined that she and his voicemail stalker would make great pals. He decided that enough was enough, but when he attempted to stand up, she grabbed both of his wrists and held them firmly on the table. Her grip was a vice, and he couldn't move. Despite his best efforts, he was beginning to panic.

Aimal was now to the point of yelling. "Then four angels stand on the corners of the Earth, to hold back the wind so it can no longer travel over land or sea. The final sign sees God surrounded by seven angels, as an eighth casts down a golden censer that is filled with fire from the altar of Heaven! Sounds like a meteor, does it not? There is a catastrophic earthquake, with thunder and lighting. Then the angels blow their trumpets—"

"Stop it!" shouted Christopher.

She quickly regained her composure but the fire still burned in her eyes. He yanked backward as she released him, and winced as pain shot through his wrists and up his arms. The terrace was empty, save for them, and he couldn't understand why her outburst hadn't drawn any attention from inside the restaurant.

He hesitated, then continued. "If you don't want to do business, then please leave."

She sat down, then calmly picked up her briefcase and set it on the table. "I do, just not in the capacity that you think. You see, I am Satan, and I have come to save your soul."

His eyes widened as the gravity of her words sunk in. Then he let out a huge belly laugh. "Well, the madness is there, but you're dressed too nicely to be with those lunatics on the street. I don't know what the hell you're selling, babe, but I ain't buying."

"I am who I say, Christopher Frizer. You must believe that the end is truly near. God has sent me on a mission, and—"

"God? Honey, apocalypse fever has fried your brain."

"Please, hear me out! In time, you will be convinced that I speak the truth. I am doing God's work, and I need your help."

He looked back at the restaurant and saw Jacquelyn chatting to the bartender. On her serving tray was a single, large martini glass, and he imagined it held three fingers of gin and an abundance of olives. *I'll be ordering another one of those as soon as she gets here.* "You've got about thirty seconds until the waitress arrives. Then it's goodbye, because I only drink alone."

She smiled and glanced out of the corner of her eye. "Agreed. Looking back, you will consider this to be the most important decision you ever made."

He let out a dismissive laugh. "Whatever. The clock is ticking, *Satan.*" He saw Jacquelyn stop at one of the tables inside, then lost her as a flood of new patrons entered the restaurant. *Dammit, her service is shit tonight.*

"Shall we begin with a test of faith? Think of one sin. One bad thing that you have done, something… shameful."

"Shameful? I'm no angel, honey." Thoughts of last Christmas Eve crept into his mind, but he quickly pushed them away. Behind him, Jacquelyn called out his name. "Guess the fun and games are over, Aimal."

With a satisfied look he turned to get his much needed drink, but Jacquelyn wasn't there. To his surprise, it was Nicole Thomas, his former secretary. Her blue eyes welled with tears, and streaks of deep, black mascara ran down her cheeks. He was taken aback by her appearance, and it took a moment to register. Then her hand tore across his face.

"You son of a bitch. All I agreed to was one drink before heading home. You damn well knew I wasn't looking for anything else!"

He quickly stood up to confront her. "Nicole? How… that was forever ago. In case you've forgotten, you were flirting with me all day. I could tell you wanted it." His entire evening was going off the rails, and he spoke without thinking. "You mean you didn't like your *Christmas bonus?*"

"How can you say that? Fuck you!" She buried her face into her hands and started sobbing. Thin streams of blood began running down the length her forearms, which pooled at her elbows and then started dripping onto the terrace.

"Jesus… what the…" With fear in his eyes, he whipped his head toward Aimal. "She's lying. Don't believe a word of it!"

He spun back around and knocked the serving tray right out of Jacquelyn's hand. The martini crashed to the ground in a tumble of broken glass and green olives. Her look of shock was mirrored on Christopher's face.

Nicole was gone.

The two of them just stared at each other, unable to speak, until Aimal broke the stalemate. "Quite an interesting scene. You have been a naughty boy."

Jacquelyn picked up the shattered remains of the drink, then went back inside to retrieve another. Christopher sat down, and rubbed his cheek as thoughts of Nicole raced through his mind. "She… she sure left in a hurry." His eyes drifted to the floor as he added, "I thought she moved away."

Aimal tapped her fingers on the briefcase. "Nicole *is* gone, believe me." As she settled back into the chair, she added, "Office romances can be so complicated. My deepest apologies for the shock, but I was never one to beat around the bush."

"You? Just because I'm having the worst night of my life at coincidence central doesn't make you the Evil Incarnate."

She shrugged, and then sampled what was left of the chocolate *soufflé*, giving him a wink as her tongue flicked along the tip of the fork. "So tasty. This will be such a delicious game."

Storming off of the terrace, Christopher practically knocked over Jacquelyn as he made his way to the exit. "Put it on my tab," he said, spitting his words. Then he flew out of the restaurant and snaked his way through the boisterous crowd, managing to claw his way underground into the subway just as the Toronto Police Emergency Task Force was moving in for the kill.

Dim rays of morning sunshine weaved through the window blinds, which cast a faint orange glow throughout the bedroom. Christopher sat down on his bed and began lightly massaging some *Saphir Medialle D'Or* into the leather of his favourite pair of Stefano Bemer dress shoes. Footwear was the most important part of an ensemble, he believed, next to the tie of course. This reminded him of a line from one of his favourite old movies: *Rudy never asked any questions about your finances. He'd just look at your heels, and know the score.* After several minutes he scrutinized the result under the harsh light of the table lamp, and noticed a small hole had torn through the sole. He cursed as he threw the shoe across the room, then sat in silence for a few minutes. With his head hung low, he got up and went to the walk-in closet to pick out another pair.

Events at the restaurant still weighed heavily on his mind. Upon arriving home last night, he had cracked open a bottle of his favourite Bordeaux, a 2000 Château Beychevelle, and started looking for a distraction. For over an hour he sifted through his tie collection; half a bottle later, he laid out three selections, and then went to bed. Still, it took him almost fifteen minutes this morning to decide which one to wear. He chose a silk Charvet, with traditional red stripes.

He always left the ironing to last, and was never satisfied with the result. His mother had taken over all the domestic chores after moving in with him, and she was a whirlwind at the ironing board. In a few minutes flat, she'd have his dress shirt looking sharper than anything out of *Esquire* magazine. Occasionally he watched her work, and managed to pick up a few pointers. After she died, no housekeeper he employed could ever meet his expectations, nor could any professional dry cleaners, which is why he chose to just do it himself. It was cathartic after a fashion, although today it took him longer than usual to make the shirt presentable. He wished he had spent more time watching over his mother.

As he was buttoning up his shirt, he heard a faint noise coming from outside the bedroom. *Creeeeeak... thump... creeeeeak... thump.* He followed it down the hallway, then stopped in front of the guest room and listened intently. The sound was on a loop, as if something was swaying back and forth like a pendulum. His hand began to tremble as he took hold of the door handle, and then he quickly entered the room. He was met by silence, and the vacated space looked as undisturbed as ever. There was no one there, and he chided himself for being so foolish.

Once outside his condo building, he scanned up and down the street but didn't see any cabs. He was about call for one when he realized that he hadn't yet checked the voicemail messages that his stalker had left him the night before.

"Mr. Frizer..."

An old man stepped out from the side of the building, and he was the same man that Christopher had seen yesterday with Alice Davey.

"What do you want? Don't you have a protest to get to?"

"Mr. Frizer, I fear that I am too late..." He began to stammer, and mumbled a smattering of German before returning to English. "Your soul is in jeopardy. Only I can help you!"

It was then that Christopher noticed the man's accent. "You're the one who's been calling me!" He raised his hands in frustration, and then clasped the sides of his head. "Why me? I seem to be a magnet for you idiots this time around. I don't know who's worse. You, or my new best friend Satan."

The old man was noticeably shocked. "What do you mean?"

"Fuck off," he said pointedly, as he flagged down an approaching cab. He had to forcibly push the old man away before he could free himself enough to close the car door. As the cab turned the corner, he saw him drop to one knee and put his hands together as if in prayer.

Ella, Christopher's new secretary, was surprised to see him since he was rarely at the office on Fridays. Being the top gun at Doré Capital allowed for a lot of flexibility with his day job, so long as he delivered. Working for Toronto's premiere brokerage firm came with many perks, including a means to suss out potential clients for his own doomsday roster. Considering the two loonies he'd already had to deal with over the past twenty-four hours, he felt it was time to go through his files to look for better prospects. He told Ella that in no uncertain terms was he to be disturbed for the rest of the afternoon.

Pacing along the row of windows in his six-figure salary corner office, a glass of Chivas Regal in hand, Christopher watched the human vermin scurrying in the streets far below. He had to push through another pack of protesters on his way in into the building, and wondered how many more of these end-of-the-world scares were going to happen in his lifetime. There had already been at least two major ones, so perhaps the third time *would* be the charm. He gestured as if dropping a bomb on the crowd of naysayers, and made the sound of an explosion. Then he grinned as he imagined himself sitting atop an enormous stack of cloth sacks adorned with dollar signs, as he watched the lemmings topple over a cliff and into oblivion.

Thoughts of his mother this morning had soured his mood, and he took another deep drink. His empty stomach grumbled as he refreshed the glass, then he sat down at his desk. *Maybe I should just skip this apocalypse, I'm sure there will be another one sometime soon. So far it's been pretty underwhelming.* He took another drink, and it wasn't long before he was fast asleep.

"Chris, wake up. Chris..."

As his eyes slowly opened, Christopher wiped the dried spittle that had collected at the corner of his mouth. Through blurred vision he saw Paul Davey hunched over the front of the desk, and unlike his wife, the man had changed very little over the past five years—save for his California tan.

"Hey... I thought you were in San Diego. Talk about a coincidence, I just ran into Alice yesterday. She's been better. I thought you would have left her something before you took off."

Paul stared back at him with soulless eyes, but didn't answer.

"Did the money run out? Is that why you're back?"

He shook his head, then finally responded. "The money lasted for quite some time. In fact, I'd just bought a yacht when it happened."

"What? Did you gamble it all away? I'm not sure I can help, I mean, you'll get as much selling it as I will."

"Why did you tell me to go against her wishes?"

"I didn't tell you to do anything. I merely suggested that you think on it a while, to ensure that you were making the right decision. What was best for you. Ultimately it was your choice to make."

"But you shouldn't have planted that sense of... uncertainty in my head. Look at me now!"

"So you lost a bit of money. It's not the end of the world. Go back to your wife and apologize. You should see the group she's hanging out with nowadays. She'll be more than happy to forgive you."

"Forgive me? I'm past forgiveness. When Judgment Day came, I wasn't *marked*, Chris. Me, and dozens of your other clients, you've damned us all. We can't get in!"

Although Paul was one of Christopher's most rewarding deals, he had always been a borderline apocaholic. Now it seemed he'd completely fallen off the end-of-the-world wagon.

"Paul, there won't be a Judgment Day. Believe me, you have nothing to worry about."

"You're not listening! It happened, and now it's too late for me. There's no end to this eternal misery. No matter how hard I try, I... I can't die. She won't let me." Paul then reached into his jacket pocket and pulled out a Glock 19 handgun. Pointing the barrel at Christopher, his eyes began to glisten in the fading daylight.

"Calm down, man! We can work this out!" There had occasionally been arguments—and even lawsuits—between Christopher and his former clients, but none had ever led to violence. As he fixated on the gun, out of the corner of his eye he searched the desk for something heavy to throw at him.

"How can you live with yourself?" he cried, but then his grip began falter as he turned to the windows as if distracted by something outside. Then he let out a deep sigh. "I've come to realize it's pointless, Chris. But I keep trying, because maybe, just maybe, the next time it'll work."

Calmly placing the tip of the gun into his mouth, Paul closed his eyes then pulled the trigger. Brain tissue and blood exploded in a spray of crimson from the top of his head, which careened off the ceiling above and then fell onto the lush, grey carpet.

"Jesus Christ!" yelled Christopher as he flew around the desk, then fell to his knees at the sight of the bloody mess in front of him. Paul's body twitched as what remained of his life seeped into the carpet.

"Ella! Ella!" he screamed, wiping a spatter of blood as it splashed across his face.

As his secretary pushed open the office door, he tearfully turned away from the carnage.

"Ella! God, Ella! Call 911!"

She rushed toward him but appeared confused. "Mr. Frizer, are you okay?"

In a state of shock, he motioned toward the body. But there was nothing there.

Paul Davey was gone.

By the time Ella managed to coax him into a cab, he had emptied the bottle of scotch. At home, into the early hours of Saturday morning, the drinking continued until he passed out in front of the television.

Christopher was hung over and could barely move. The intense pounding in his head was unbearable, and he desperately wanted some Tylenol. Then he slowly became aware of another sound, far off in the distance. *Creeeeeak... thump... creeeeeak... thump.* He forced himself off of the couch, and the trek along the hallway seemed to go on for an hour. By

128

the time he stood outside of the guest room, the noise had become so intense that he could barely think. *Creeeeeak... thump... creeeeeak... thump.* Without hesitation he opened the door—and saw his mother hanging from a taut rope looped around her neck, her dead white eyes in sharp contrast to her purple, bloated face. She swayed back and forth as her weight pulled on the ceiling fan. *CREEEEEAK... THUMP... CREEEEEAK... THUMP.*

He screamed as he awoke to the jarring voice of a TV evangelist, and then cursed as he felt around the cushions for the remote. As soon as he switched off the television, he saw Aimal standing in the doorway of the den.

Exhaustion had all but zapped his will, and he was too hung over to fight. "I can't take this anymore. I don't care how you got in here. Just get the hell out."

"Is it not yet apparent that I can go wherever I like? Even inside your head?"

He pushed himself up on the couch, then motioned toward the door. Instead of leaving, she walked into the room and sat down next to him.

"Come now, Christopher. Surely you realize that these ghosts from your past have been more than just mere coincidences."

"Leave, Aimal. Please. I'm not in the mood for your silly games."

She shook her head, and feigned disappointment. "After everything I have shown you, still you are not convinced. You are one tough customer. And yes, the third time *is* the charm."

Aimal stared at him with a devilish grin. Then over her shoulder, Christopher saw his mother walk into the room. She looked exactly the same as the last time that he had seen her alive—the morning before he had found her corpse hanging in the guest room. She smiled weakly but showed little emotion when Christopher stumbled over and hugged her tight. He started to cry, but she made no effort to console him. Instead, she gently pushed him away.

"Ingram, my dear. That woman is your only hope. *My* only hope. Join her, or we'll never see each other again." Then his mother was gone, as quickly as she had arrived.

He collapsed onto the floor and wept.

A satisfied smile crossed Aimal's face, and then she took on a more serious tone. "I am sorry, but you left me no other choice."

He couldn't bear to even look at her. "This is a dream. A fucking nightmare."

"One that you cannot escape. Judgment Day *is* coming, which is why I am here."

She raised him up and tenderly wiped away a fresh tear on his cheek. As she led him back to the couch, he was practically speechless.

"My God..."

"*Our* God has shown pity on me—on us—now that Final Judgment is approaching, and has commanded me to collect the souls of those who have embraced a sinful lifestyle. But He will not assist me in my mission, which is why I need a right-hand man. Someone who knows how to play the game. A real people person, like you!"

Her lighthearted approach made his stomach turn. "But why? I mean, I may be paraphrasing, but didn't it say somewhere in the Bible that you and God weren't exactly bosom buddies?"

"True, I was banished from Heaven. But there was no great battle. I was merely too ambitious. And as they say, history is written by the victor. Or, in this case, His followers. Mankind's existence, as you know it, will soon be over. Although I hate to see an end come to such a beautiful creation, it has provided me with an opportunity to get back into Heaven."

"But why would you want to? I thought Hell was your domain."

"Christopher, there is no Hell. Not in a physical sense. There is no fire, no brimstone. No red-skinned caricature poking you with a pitchfork." Aimal cupped his face in her hands, and her tone hinted of loss. "Not to be in Heaven, but able to see those who are, yet unable to feel them, touch them, join them... that is Hell, my friend. It is even worse for me, because I know what Heaven is truly like, which is why I am so eager to get back in."

He reluctantly moved her hands away. They were warm, and so comforting. "But all the stories…"

"You have only heard rumours. Misconceptions. Myths. You have never heard my side. What really happened." She moved in closer, and placed his hands over her heart. "Long ago, there was talk of a new world that would be made in the image of Heaven, and a new creature in the image of God. After I fell, I was desperate. I greatly missed my lost paradise."

"Then you found Adam and Eve."

"Yes. I put every effort into finding this new utopia. It would not be Heaven, but the closest thing to it. I loved their maker, and I soon fell in love with His new creation."

"So your intentions were benevolent?"

"Of course! All I did was try to make friends with these new creatures…with mankind. I feared that God had warned them about me, so I took on another form. I did not want Adam and Eve to be frightened. I just wanted to be with them. I needed love. I needed companionship."

Christopher saw the tears welling up in her eyes, and began to feel a tinge of regret. Had he misjudged her? Could she really be telling the truth? The atheist in him still wanted to believe that this was all a big joke. But everything that had happened since yesterday was starting to convince him otherwise.

"But… wasn't Eden destroyed because of you?"

"That was not my fault! They lacked even the simplest of knowledge. After overhearing Adam question the world around him, I decided to help my new friends. I convinced Eve to eat from the Tree of Knowledge, and he soon followed."

"Which led to their destruction…"

"Hardly! Just think of what they got in return. Knowledge. Inspiration. My actions facilitated the advancement of human thought. I am the mother of science! Of invention! Without me, there would be no merit in seeking the right path. Without suffering, you could not count your blessings. Without death, there would be no religion. In falling from Heaven, I became the most useful servant that God has ever known. That is why He has given me this chance to help mankind once again."

"So you want me to repent?"

She let out a dismissive laugh. "Oh, if it were only that simple. The number of sinners is overwhelming, and I have limited time in which to convince them all. That is where you fit in."

"Me? Believe me, I'm going to pray my ass off. There's no way I'm missing this boat."

"You can pray all you like, but…what is that quaint expression? *You do not have a snowball's chance in Hell.*"

"Can't you be serious? This is my soul we're talking about. I haven't been that bad. I…" He paused as she shook her head. "I mean, what about all the folks I helped in their time of need? All the charities I've given their money to over the years? Surely that must account for something. I may not be first in line, but—"

She offered a sympathetic look. "Not a chance. That is, not without my help."

"Why should I trust you?"

"Because I am desperate to return, and there are so many souls to collect before Judgment Day. I cannot do this without you. In fact, you have already been helping me without even realizing it. The souls of your clientele are already part of my legion, ready to follow me into Heaven."

"What if I—"

"Christopher! After all I have shown you, after everything I have said, still you do not believe me." She shook her head in disappointment, unable to contain her frustration. "The choice is simple. Join me and I will wipe your slate clean of all past transgressions, and you can continue on as normal. Or, you can forget we ever met. Do whatever you wish. Think of all the praying you would have to do, and how your lifestyle would change. Yet it would all be in vain. Trust me, I am your only hope. I am your salvation."

"But you're the mother of lies!"

"As I said, tales about me have been completely blown out of proportion. I always keep my promises, and this contract will guarantee that both of us get what we deserve." Aimal then opened her briefcase. Inside were several sheets of paper bound into a scroll, which she rolled out onto the coffee table.

He peered closely at the handwritten script. "Is that... Latin? Seriously?" A look of desperation crossed his face, and he felt like he was going to throw up.

By this point she was all business. "This contract states that I will cleanse your soul of all sins, and in exchange, you promise to help me in my quest to get back into Heaven."

He had a sinking feeling, as if trapped at the dead end of a dark alley with no visible means of escape. "I don't know... I... There's got to be another way."

"I appreciate your spirited nature. Perhaps my acquaintance, who was once in a similar position, can help you make the right choice."

When Christopher saw the old man—his voicemail stalker—walk into the room, he threw up his hands in disbelief. "You have got to be fucking kidding me."

Aimal struck a pensive look as her eyes darted between the two men. "Oh, we have been friends for years. Doctor, please join us, and fill him in."

The old man bowed slightly, but made no eye contact. "I once was a scientist, and wanted to learn more about the world around me, back when such activities were considered blasphemous." Christopher was surprised that he now seemed quite lucid, and had no difficulties speaking.

"So I kept my activities hidden," he continued, "yet became frustrated after I could find no more answers. Ultimately I studied black magic, and then summoned our... friend." His eyes drifted up to Aimal, until Christopher drew his attention.

"Let me guess, she offered you a contract—"

"Which I accepted. For almost a quarter of a century, she served me and granted my every wish. Afterward, she took possession of my soul, to do with it as she pleased."

With a sneer, Aimal interjected. "Doctor, tell him how grateful you are. Did I not hold up my end of the bargain?"

"Yes indeed. I experienced many wonderful things while I was alive, and I thank you for that." He sat down on the chair across from them, then looked directly at Christopher. "Now it is my turn to help her, as per our contract. I will follow her into Heaven, for I have no other choice... meaning, like you, I have little chance of reaching Heaven without her help. I hope you choose wisely."

"See, Christopher? The Doctor knows first-hand the truth behind all the lies that have been told. I do mean well, and I do keep my promises. Sign the contract. You will be helping me a great deal. Most importantly, you will be helping yourself."

Aimal reached into the inner pocket of the briefcase and retrieved a small, ornate knife. She faced little resistance as she turned Christopher's hand so that his palm faced upward. Her black eyes sparkled as she broke the skin with the edge of the blade, drawing blood as she quickly traced the crease of his lifeline.

"Old habits die hard," she said with an amusing grin, then flipped over his hand and squeezed. Trickles of blood slowly collected in a small pool on the parchment.

Christopher winced and tried to pull his hand away, but she held it firmly in place.

"In triplicate, please."

Upon completing the final binding signature, the dripping blood slowed to a standstill, and the pool darkened into a deep, reddish ochre as it coagulated on the contract.

Outside, the early morning sun shimmered over Lake Ontario, casting hard shadows into the den as it sliced through the venetian blinds. Minutes passed as Christopher sat motionless on the couch, staring at his hand. As he wiped traces of blood from his palm, the wound slowly faded then disappeared.

Aimal stared intently, almost lovingly, into his eyes. "Our business here is done. Remember, your slate is now clean as far as I am concerned. We will see each other again soon, but until then, carry on as you wish." She drew toward him, and then planted a long, seductive kiss on his forehead. "You have made me very happy."

When he looked up, she was no longer in the room. Nor was the Doctor. Defeated and in a state of disbelief, Christopher picked up his iPhone and then laid down on the couch. Three more missed calls had been placed overnight, each from an unknown ID, and he deleted them without bothering to listen. As he turned on the television, a whispered conversation behind him went unnoticed. Aimal and the Doctor were still in the den, intertwined with the deepest shadows that light failed to penetrate.

"Damn you," growled the Doctor, "do not ask me to do that again. Surely my debt has been paid."

"It is far from being fulfilled, Faust. You will do whatever I ask. Rejoice, for we have secured the first of my champions, and our conquest can truly begin."

"I cannot take much more of this torture."

"Do not try my patience. I tire of your attempts to undermine me. In a few months this will all be over, so just be glad you are on the winning side. What will *be* the winning side. They will never see it coming."

"Yes, my…my Lady."

"It seems I must up my game, as I am no longer trending in Canada. There is quite the tinderbox forming in downtown Vancouver as we speak. We simply must go take a look."

"*Ne tradus bestiis,*" he mumbled under his breath, and then followed her into the darkness.

SHELLS

Andrew Robertson

My room smells like an old tent, but that's just what it is. In fact, when we aren't travelling from town to town, and village to hamlet, I spend most of my time reading, repairing costumes, or getting ready for the show in this old canvas tent with wide orange and yellow panels that have mildew and mold growing in the folds. Southern heat covers everything in an oppressive blanket of warm, moist pressure. It feels like breathing moss. But that is fine for me because I spend the rest of my time in a tank filled with cold water that leaves my skin dry and cracked.

Some nights after the crowds leave, I dive deep down to collect the pennies they throw in my enormous fishbowl, and when I surface I can barely move my icy legs enough to take my tail off. Around this place, not many people will offer a helping hand without expecting something in return. Truth be told, not all of them even have hands, at least not in the traditional sense. And if they do, they don't want to touch mine. I'm considered very pretty but my hands are dry like sandpaper, with tiny flakes of papery scales ready to fall off at any time, and my fingers have extra skin between them that gives the appearance of a fish-like web. My physical difference makes wearing gloves to hide it impossible.

When I was younger, the other children in the orphanage called me Scabby Frog Fingers. Children can be cruel, if not creative. My shockingly pale green eyes, like the tender leaves of a fiddlehead, enhanced the frog part of my nickname. This deformity, along with my more desirable and conventional features, made me perfect for adoption into a touring circus and sideshow as Hydra, the Mermaid Girl. The nuns took a bag of sticky coins and handed me over with an old and itchy blanket, a loaf of bread and a worn out bible. The bread was the only useful thing in my pathetic dowry.

I replaced a previous attraction that was actually just a large fish tail, probably a tuna, attached to an orangutan torso floating in formaldehyde. Poseidon the Demon Beast of the Sea drew equal amounts of scowls and screams from the paying public, some decrying it as a fake, while others were certain that the legend they were told by the Showman on the way in was true. Poseidon was said to be caught in the net of a courageous Captain whose crew met their end battling the evil sea ape. The Captain managed to avenge all the sailors lost by stabbing the unholy creature in the gills and then hauled it ashore where the sideshow happened upon him. Some trick lighting and filthy liquid combined with an odour which kept the crowds moving made Poseidon quite the spectacle.

Over time, the Showman decided that living, breathing oddities were the way of the future and while touring the poorhouses and orphanages for the malformed and grotesque he found me; a girl with flakey, fish-like hands that knew how to swim and desperately wanted to leave the sad, grey house filled with the unwanted. The grey house was replaced by Poseidon's stinking tank, barely scrubbed clean, but for me, a step up in the world. Truth be told, most of Poseidon didn't make it out the tank on the first go the formaldehyde was so diluted, and it was up to me to drain the reeking water and scrape the monkey's rotting, milky skin and fur off the green surface of the glass.

Once I had arrived, I found that the same hostilities of my old world would be a part of my new one. Other women in the show were jealous of my looks, choosing to look past my hands and the repulsion they brought to most men's eyes, and instead to focus on my face and body. I soon learned that a yielding and available body was one of the best tools for barter but that wasn't how I conducted myself. Years of abuse taught me to ignore their petty comments and concentrate instead on the work I needed to do to survive.

Julianna was one of the girls who wanted to be the beautiful mermaid instead of the snake charmer or, on other nights, a dancing girl for lonely souls with whiskey-soaked ambitions at half-mast. She had made it clear years before I joined that she was willing to do anything for a cheap necklace and a fifth of scotch, and so she stayed a dancer. A fortnight ago the petty little minx tried to sabotage my tank by filling it with old fish heads and rubbish from the dinner tent right before the show and received a sound beating from the Showman for it. She should have been more careful regardless. The girl can't swim and just a minute could be enough to get tangled in the hidden tubes and fake aquatic weeds in that frigid water and drown.

What Julianna doesn't understand is that with my grotesque hands I have something special, and as the audiences tend to dwindle when there is nothing truly unique, special means you get to stay. You had a home and food. Nobody wanted to be a castoff sideshow performer left to work the streets of Louisiana. It was a sure death, if not by murder or starvation, then a slow, horrible finale from the Great Pox. Pretty girls rapidly became walking, toothless skeletons with fallen noses and milky eyes best suited for the grave, not the boudoir.

Now I am one of the star attractions of our Ten in One. My tail was crafted by one of the fortune telling gypsies and it is the most beautiful thing I have ever owned. Even in my dim quarters, the French sequins and glittering fibres in the material are picking up the candlelight, bringing my scales to life. And underwater, with the big green and blue lights hitting the tank, the effect is like the side of a rainbow trout. My pale eyes shine like a menacing blade. I flutter the tail and splash a bit of water at the curious onlookers with the long frond of fins at the end. I smile at the crowd and then wave, sure to stretch my fingers out as far as I can before placing my hand flat against the glass and baring my fake, wooden fangs. That is when the crowd will gasp or squeal, suddenly certain that I am the real thing. Some women faint and their men sit them down on the benches nearby before returning to lean in over the musty red velvet rope that acts as a barrier. They feign fascination with this 'species' but I can feel their eyes moving all over the very human parts of my body.

I hear a shuffling sound behind me and turn from my reverie.

"Hydra, how are you feeling today?" Dr. Barnaby joined our troupe recently after being chased out of a town for botching an operation on a rich woman, leaving her confined to a wheelchair as she slowly leaked her way to a painful death. It wasn't his fault. He did his best, but the nurses didn't close her up properly or wash the tools in the necessary manner. Now he takes care of all of our medical needs, which for some of us, like the Fattest Boy in the World, the Human Alligator and the Living Torso, is a godsend. Many of the acts suffer from constant sores, rashes and other ailments that cause a stink like death and get infected from the environment we live in, and if one of them dies, everyone suffers the loss on ticket sales. I'll never get used to the variety of perverse curiosities that these presumably normal people need to have satisfied. If we aren't on stage as advertised on the bright and garish canvas paintings outside the fairgrounds, there are roaring crowds to answer to.

The Doctor also helps to craft new and terrifying creatures using old taxidermy or recently deceased beasts from the zoo that accompanies our stage shows. The creepy beasties he creates are always popular at these carnivals. Sometimes he even travels into the towns along our route looking for medical oddities. Some arrive alive and are immediately displayed in a tent of tiny cribs with wire mesh lids. Their tiny heads, extra legs or arms and bisected faces, wailing and neglected, always cause a great commotion with the guests, but very few of these creatures last very long. Most arrive in large jam jars like newborn monsters. I don't like it, but I have no choice in how they conduct business. The coffers don't fill themselves.

"Please Doctor, call me Cascata." I smile at him while I reach for the long wig dyed a deep green to match my persona as Hydra, Mergirl of the Adriatic Sea. The length of the wig helps cover my breasts, which are almost entirely visible given the scant upper half of my costume; two sea shells covered in pearls and backed with spirit gum. Once underwater, the wig only does so much, but it puts my mind at ease. I also have the fake coral and seaweed that hides my breathing tube to work with.

"My skin isn't bleeding as much," I continue smiling as I glance at my hands. "That comfrey ointment you made was excellent thank you. I hardly feel any pain when I pull myself out of my tank, and the burning doesn't last as long afterward."

He stands in the door a while longer, looking a bit uncomfortable as I remove my blouse to apply the shells. I would wait for him to leave but being late for show time makes the Showman angry and I cannot afford to take a chance like that. He didn't feed the Siamese Twins anything but bread and water for a week when they refused to do a song and dance act they thought was degrading... at least that was the story. I think it was more like they didn't want to go on a date he had arranged for them. We all have what the Showman considers side duties. Keeping rich men with varied tastes happy is definitely on the menu, like it or not.

"Well I have to go tend to one of the gorillas. There was a fight while they were trying to get him in the cage after the last show and I'm not sure that this one will survive. They are such a big attraction and things have been slow so hopefully I can stitch him back up." He lets out a long sigh. "Be sure to put the oil I gave you on your skin before you go into the tank, it will help." He nods at me, eyes wandering before he catches himself and turns on a well-worn heel to leave.

It must be awful to go from a respected member of society to stitching together old bones to make a leering group of idiots happy.

I press on the shells to see if the gum has dried, feeling their cold surface against my breasts, and then reach for the fake fangs. I had always thought of mermaids as beautiful princesses that lived in the sea, coming on land for love, giving up their immortality to marry the prince. Here they want mermaids to be beautiful but terrifying demons of the deep.

I pull the tail on over my legs as the smell of cigarette smoke and humanity comes leaking through the flaps. Once the crowd starts to gather, I can't be seen as either woman or mermaid, so each day one of the stagehands and labourers Pablo comes to roll me out in a wheelbarrow between the tents and in the back way. If ever someone did see me at the least I would be in character.

Today he is whistling.

"You seem very happy today," I say smiling at him.

He smiles back and positions the wheelbarrow so I can hoist myself from the chair to the barrow before replying.

"Today is a good day," he responds. "I have finally saved enough to move to New York City and be with my family."

"That is such wonderful news Pablo! How did you manage that?"

"Odds jobs for extra money," he says, his eyes shining with excitement but avoiding mine.

I don't press further because for people like us, there are many ways to make extra money and if he chooses to spend time with a wealthy widow, plantation owner or to assist the doctor with procuring his grotesque catalogue of fiendish stuffed animals and tiny floating bodies, it's none of my business.

Pablo wheels me out of the tent, and once outside I notice that the air is cooler but the noise is tremendous.

"Sounds like a good crowd tonight," I comment.

"Yes," he replies. "The governor's son is getting married and he has brought his friends here to celebrate. Cascata, they aren't gentlemen, so be happy you are in the tank and not in the dancing tents."

I shudder in grim anticipation of their leering grins, but there's nothing to be done. Perhaps they will throw enough pennies at me to buy a new dress. We arrive at the sideshow tent and Pablo deftly rolls the barrow through the canvas flap to the backstage area where my large tank awaits me behind the curtain at the back of the stage.

The strains of a popular song played on accordion die out as the previous act, the Rubber Woman exits the stage. Pablo helps me up the ladder fixed to the back of the glass as I go hand over hand and then slide into the cold, dank water.

Once inside, the sounds of the outside world become meaningless, a muddled murmur aside from the familiar cadence of my introduction before the curtains open and I am to be in character.

I glide backward staying at the bottom of the tank, teasing the audience as I eye them, and sizing up what I am to be subjected to. Many men dressed in southern finery holler at me, waving and motioning at their chests. Yes, I know what they want, but there is an art to all of this, and I want them to be patient for what the Showman calls the 'reveal'.

Coyly, I peek out from behind the fake coral and turn my head toward them then quickly away as if afraid of all these important men and the few women who have wandered in this evening. The wig rises and falls like snakes around my head as the water shifts. I build up the mystery by pushing the green tendrils of hair in front of my face, one arm across the tiny shells covering my breast, then turn to swim with my back to them. Wrapping my arms tightly around my body with my hands low near my waist, I let my fingers slowly climb up my sides, teasing. This move also gives me an opportunity to use my breathing tube while using the old magician's trick of misdirection. The crowd starts to roar with frustrated anticipation. I turn and rush toward the glass. Stretching out my fingers, I slam my webbed hands against the slimy surface of my tank while bearing my fangs.

Even underwater, I can hear the screams from both men and women followed by nervous laughter and a shower of coins. I turn so I am upside down and launch water toward them with my tail as the grand finale.

Each night is similar. Every night ends as the curtain falls to hide me surfacing and struggling out of the water with Pablo to catch me if I fall.

Helping me into the wheelbarrow, Pablo is silent as we leave.

He starts walking toward my tent, then veers sharply right, almost colliding with a few posts and ropes before turning into a different tent. Inside it is dark and smells of garbage.

"Pablo, why are we here?" I stammer, growing fearful and trying to get out of the wheelbarrow. He pushes me back and then picks something off the ground. The tent flap opens and Julianna walks in.

"Oh no, you are like a fish out of water!" she squeals. A cold sweat breaks out over my skin as the lights from the fairgrounds show me the silhouette of a long sledgehammer in Pablo's hands.

"I am sorry for this Cascata. It was my only way out."

I scream at the top of my lungs but no one arrives to help me, my cries drowned out by the introduction of the headlining act and rounds of applause. Pablo raises the hammer and brings it down on my legs again and again.

I start to lose consciousness as they both run out of the tent, the nickel tang of blood in the air. The flap closes leaving me gasping in a stinking darkness as I fall out of the barrow and into piles of old food, rotten meat and horse shit, more a fish out of water than I've ever been.

"Cascata, can you hear me?" The Doctor's voice asks.

The dim light of the medical tent that also serves as the Doctor's personal quarters burns my eyes as they slowly open. Trying to shift under a blanket in the sagging cot, I feel tremendous pain and the attack immediately comes back to me.

"Where's Pablo?" I demand, voice hoarse and halting in my throat. "He attacked me and I'm certain... that Julianna was behind the... whole thing."

"He is gone Cascasta, left the sideshow that night but Julianna is still here. In fact, she told us that she witnessed the attack but didn't come forward at first for fear of Pablo taking revenge. She is very upset for you."

Like hell, I think to myself, another racking pain seizing my body.

"My legs," I gasp, realizing where the pain is coming from.

I reach to remove the blanket and the doctor lays his hand on mine.

"There have been some... changes," he explains. "Your legs were beyond repair, the skin destroyed and the bones smashed to bits... so we did an operation that gave you new skin. There was no other way Cascata."

I slide my hand under the blanket and immediately recoil, feeling fur and a slick, tough surface underneath. My lip begins to quiver with fear and tears well in my eyes.

"What is that?" I nearly scream, my voice breaking.

"Well after the gorilla didn't make it, we had an opportunity to fix you with a graft of his skin. We made you a new tail and now you truly are a mermaid."

The Doctor's voice contains notes of glee as he draws back the blanket, and I feel bile rise in my throat at the hideous sight. There is a gorilla skin tail where my legs once were, covered in fur with deep scars where the animal hide has been stitched together. As I attempt to move, I can feel where the tail is sewn into my own skin, fusing with my own body.

"But I'm supposed to be beautiful!"

The tent rustles as the Showman walks in.

"Cascata you are awake, my dear," he says with a grin. "This is better. You are better than before, and the Doctor saved your life, you must be thankful for that. You are a miracle, and now you will be our featured star. What more could an orphan ask for. Fame, money, a living legend!"

Tears stream down my face as I force my gaze away from the horrific new reality of my body.

"Don't you see how famous you will become?" The Showman bellows. "You combine all the beauty of a mermaid with the fierce qualities that made Poseidon so popular. You will now be known as Poseidon's Mistress, She-Demon of the Depths. There will be line ups right through to the next town to see you, people will pay good money to throw live fish into your tank and watch you rip them apart."

I feel a warm flush rise in my cheeks as the indignity of my life as nothing more than a crippled geek sets in. Then rage takes a hold of my heart.

"Have you ever considered having two She-Demons?" I ask the Showman, wiping the tears from my face. "That would be a true spectacle and Julianna told me she would give anything to be in the main show. And what a great way to repay her for coming forward with the truth so you could save my life."

The Showman's eyes light up with the possibility I've presented to him as my tongue turns to acid.

"But can she swim?" He asks.

"Oh yes, she told me herself she is a great swimmer. You should get her in the tank right away so she can show you."

THE CAST IRON SKILLET

Shebat Legion

L aura Lee slid down the smooth surface of the washing machine; her back pressed against it; crouched in the darkness and anonymity of the laundry room, hiding. Her husband was too drunk to think of looking for her there, and she almost smiled but grimaced instead. Whoever would have thought she would have ended up in a bivouac beside her Maytag?

She could hear her him stumbling in the hall, a crash, and a curse muttered as he walked into a wall. Again, she almost smiled. For, yes, it had come to the point where she found his drunken state almost humorous. Therein lay the horror, that she could somehow find any of this to be funny.

"You don't pay the bills!" he had screamed, face reddened with rage. What had started the argument, Laura Lee could not remember, only that it had escalated, and somehow, she was to blame. There was no way around it now; there was nothing she could say that would be the *right* thing, no magic phrase that could placate her husband. The thing would have to run its course, whatever the cause of this fight was not relevant, staying out of his way, was.

Laura Lee ran the tips of her fingers across the smooth white door of the washing machine almost absently. It was somehow comforting. She patted the machine as if it were a dog and then stiffened as it made a slight sound, its metal frame slightly buckling in response to her ministrations. She listened carefully, her face still and blank. Perhaps her husband had gone outside. Maybe he had gone down to the boat. Maybe she could sneak out of the laundry room, to where she wasn't sure, but her knees were becoming cramped from crouching for so long.

The slightly opened laundry room door allowed her to see into the kitchen. Laura Lee had a view of the pine kitchen island with its pans and pots and hanging lids, those that were left, for he had kicked the island when he called her a "bitch." The island looked intact, thank goodness; it was a present from her mother, as so many of her belongings were. She didn't know what she would say if it were to become broken, rather, she did, she would have to lie.

Rhyming Simons—a childhood memory of running off the edge of the dock, straight into the water as fast as she was able. Where the name of this game had come from, she never could find out, but she had come to borrow it to mean something more than running into the water. To her, it meant running into danger, and she had been thinking to herself, "It's Rhyming Simons time. My god, its Rhyming Simons time," for the better part of three hours now.

Running to, running from. She had run *into* danger, and now, she was enacting 'hiding *from* danger.' On the days that she cursed herself for being a coward, she remembered this one thing, she was doing Rhyming Simons—yes, but she was also saving her own life.

Laura Lee flexed, and the washing machine flexed with her, making a slight sound as it did, almost as if it were perhaps agreeing that, yes, she was right, saving her own life was important.

She stared shock-eyed at the kitchen island, askew where he had left it. It was, in actuality, a medium sized cart, with shelves and on wheels, but very sturdy. It solved the need for counter space quite neatly. She blinked.

She could see one of the wooden spoons and the strainer pot where they had fallen, as she listened for the sound of breathing other than her own. She licked her dry lips. He had made her beg.

"Until I think that you are sincere and when I know that you are really, *really* sorry and that you mean it, don't even think to say you are! Don't you dare! And don't you fucking have a cup of *my* coffee in the morning and have fun with the 'nic cravings!" He had roared, "Don't be smoking any of *my* cigarettes, and don't you dare eat any of *my* food!"

He had gone on and on until she had said that yes, she was sorry, yes, she did mean it, and dammit she *was* sincere. The entire time shaking, and yet, thinking to herself as she begged for forgiveness, *Is he really doing this?*

But of course, he really, really was, and it wasn't the first time. However she may have tried to explain it to herself, she didn't understand how her husband, who could be so nice at times could turn into what? A monster? Yes, a monster, and so quickly after he had a few drinks in him.

It was truly astounding how much he could drink. While it was mostly beer that was his preferred beverage, tonight, he had added whiskey. She knew what that meant. She would have to be especially careful, and even that would probably not be enough.

"I have stress!" he had screamed with spittle across her face as she tried not to cringe, tried not to show fear because to show weakness would have made things worse for her. "Stress!"

Well, yes. He did have stress. Everyone had stress, but best not to think about that because she could hear the front door slam as the monster reentered the house from where it had gone. It. He.

The bottle lay on the floor where he had thrown it, and it was almost empty.

She crouched in the darkness, trembling and willing her cramped legs to just shut up already, enough with the complaints, this was her life, not only her knees that were at stake here.

In Amanda's brighter moments, she thought, *He has never hit me, not really. Pushed, yes. Threatened, yes. Broke things, expensive things. Maybe he will stop, the sun is shining, and he is smiling, and maybe he will see what he is doing, maybe he will.*

But in Amanda's darker moments, when the sun was gone and when her husband was not her husband but the monster instead, she thought only of getting out. Getting away, escaping, somehow, somewhere. And, she sometimes thought about how nice it would be, how convenient, if the monster would just die. A heart attack maybe, or a stroke; either would do just fine. Then he would be gone for good. Yes, she would probably feel bad about it, and she would grieve, but truly, it would be best.

"Where the fuck are you, Laura Lee?"

She heard him calling from the bedroom. There was the sound of something breaking, and it was probably something expensive too. Her lips curled up into an almost smile again, *why couldn't he break cheap things?* They had so many extra cups. The ones with the turkeys on them were not something she would miss, but it was almost as if the more expensive the object, the more satisfying it was for him to break it. It didn't make sense since so much of what the monster complained about was how badly in debt they were.

"His debt," a voice seemed to say, and it was the voice Laura Lee called her inner goddess voice. It was a voice of reason, or rather, a voice that tried to reason with her, even if it was only inside where no one could hear it except for her. "His debt," the voice insisted, and this was mostly true.

Her husband did have a tendency to buy things he could not afford. When she asked for something for herself, out of the money she made, the money he took, the money that he kept, her money, on the bank card that was in his wallet and not hers, it became her fault somehow that they didn't have the money for it.

"Laura Lee!" the monster roared, and she closed her eyes.

"You do not have to live this way," the voice reasoned. "He is in the bedroom, run for the door, and get to a neighbor. Call the police."

"But," she objected. "He is so fast!" And it was true. He could be very fast, and if the police didn't keep him and if she couldn't find somewhere far enough away to hide, she knew that this call for help could cost her dearly. In her dark moments, when that sun did not shine, Laura Lee knew that if she had her husband arrested, he would track her down and kill her like a dog.

A heart attack or a stroke would solve everything.

"Sweetheart," the voice said. "You can hope for him to drop dead all you want, but it's not something you can count on. Go. Go now! Get up and run! You are in trouble, worse than before. Go! Live now, worry about the rest later. This is your life we are talking about here!"

She almost did. The voice was that insistent. She almost uncurled herself from where she crouched with her arms around her knees, but she didn't, and she could hear that voice inside of her give a sigh of exasperation. She could hear the monster in the living room and knew she had lost her window of opportunity. If he found her, he would be angry, and he had drunk a lot of whiskey.

"But," the voice said firmly, that voice, her inner goddess voice. "He is already angry, there is no help for it now. Get out while you still can."

"I can't! He will catch me," Laura Lee mourned. "It isn't like I can fight him, he is so strong!"

And this was true, yes. Her husband was strong, but the monster was stronger, and the sun was not shining tonight, no, not at all.

She couldn't fight him, and that is when her eyes turned to the cast iron skillet that had fallen to the floor with a huge clang when he had kicked the center island, wheeled, cart-thing.

She could hit him with it if she had to. She could tell the police that he had come after her and that she was afraid and had hit him with it out of self-defense. It wouldn't even be a lie. Maybe she could hit him enough times that a heart attack or a stroke would seem like a mercy in comparison.

"Well," Laura Lee's inner goddess argued. "But could you really? Could you really hit him? Let's look at this reasonably. The skillet is heavy, and you are not exactly known for upper body strength."

"Yes!" Laura Lee argued back. "Yes, I could! I could use both arms. Get a good solid grip on it and bash his face in.."

"But what if he died?" the goddess inside of Laura Lee asked. "What if you ended up killing him?"

"What if I did?" Laura Lee shrieked silently.

"Could you live with that?" asked the voice, and it did seem as if the goddess was interested in the answer. So was the washing machine apparently, for it gave another small ding as Laura Lee shifted.

"The monster would be dead," Laura Lee whined. "Dead and gone, and then, and then…"

"Perhaps," the goddess mused. "And yes, perhaps you could live with that today, but what about tomorrow? Could you live with that tomorrow? The day after that? Forever?"

"Yes," Laura Lee answered in a surly tone, even though she knew that the goddess was right. There would be no living with it tomorrow. His death would haunt her forever. Along with the word 'bitch,' came his other word for her, which was 'wuss,' and to Laura Lee, meant 'coward.'

She dug her fingers into her legs; maybe she *was* a coward. Maybe she was.

"No, you are not!" the voice said. "But you must decide because the monster is coming closer."

And dear lord, it was true. She could hear him coming, and soon he would see her, and then what would she say? What? "I was cleaning the laundry room in the dark?" No, of course, she could not say that!

"Then, it's one or the other honey. The skillet or you make a break for it, because sometimes, whatever you do, it's going to be Rhyming Simons whether you like it or not."

Laura Lee jumped to her feet and ran for the skillet, grabbing it as the monster , then rushed toward her. She threw it for all she was worth at the center island wheeled cart thing, and she hit it too. The skillet made a booming, smashing sound, and the monster bellowed in surprise. Laura Lee ran as if her life depended on it because didn't it? Yes, yes it did.

"Rhyming Simons! Rhyming Simons!" Laura Lee screamed as she ran past her husband, out of the door, and down the street, and into the first driveway that she found.

The sun was gone, yes, and maybe it would be gone for a very long time. But maybe, just maybe it would not be gone forever, and the voice gently agreed that this was true.

DEATH OVER EASY

Suzanne Church

I've always figured a heart attack would be my ticket to the next life. My arteries and I have differing opinions on the virtues of steaks, eggs, and bacon. So last Wednesday, at 11:00 am when Death waltzed into my diner, I grabbed my coat, which hung on the hook below my *Classic Cars* calendar, swallowed hard, and said, "How does this work?"

"You take my order," he said.

My coat fell from my hand, making a soft thud as it hit the floor. "I get it. You like to play with your quarry before you eat it."

"I'd rather have eggs."

"Oh."

Death cleared his throat, sounding like he'd had one too many smokes in his lifetime, deathtime, or whatever. "I'll have three, over easy, with bacon and whole wheat toast," he said. "The sign says you're famous for your raspberry jelly."

"Ran out during the morning rush. How about grape?"

"Give me honey, instead. I've never acquired a taste for grape."

The situation could've gone a thousand ways at that point. I could've told him to go to hell, but I didn't want to give the guy any ideas. I could've insisted we cut to the chase, because I'm an impatient person and if I was going to die, I wanted to bite it before the lunch hour rush. But when the bastard settled into the booth like he owned the place, and flashed me the vilest, most crooked set of stained teeth I had ever seen, I decided to do what I do best.

Pulling my order pad from my apron, I said, "Number three, coming up. You want coffee?"

"Black. I'm lactose intolerant."

With a final look over my shoulder at my only customer, I retrieved my coat from the floor, hung it on the hook, and headed into the kitchen to make the dark dude his breakfast.

Death finished the eggs and bacon, but left a half slice of toast. I warmed his coffee a couple of times, and still he lingered at the table, spending his time studying the picture of the *1965 Ford Fairlane* hanging on the wall above his booth. I must have glanced at my coat ten or more times, waiting for my cue to leave, but he didn't seem to be in any hurry.

When my assistant, Betty, arrived, she headed for the kitchen, donned her apron, and set about making fries for the lunch crowd.

"Anything else?" I asked Death.

"The bill."

"Can I get my coat, first?"

He placed his hand on my wrist. His flesh felt cold, not like ice, but cold enough to drive home his job description. As he moved, dust shook free of his grey trench coat and released the stench of attic must and lanolin. I wondered if I would ever get the smell off the vinyl booth seats.

"The cheque, please. I would like to be on my way."

"It's on the house."

Death stood, continuing to hold my wrist with his right hand, and reached in his coat pocket with his left. Bringing out a ten dollar bill, he said, "This ought to more than cover it."

I stared at the money, all the while praying for him to release my wrist from his shiver-grip. Finally, he did.

"See you next Wednesday." And with a tip of his fedora and a swish of his trench coat, he glided out of the diner looking more like a dancer than the ultimate equalizer. A trail of dust motes traced his path like monikers.

"Quite the stranger," Betty called from the kitchen. "You get his name?"

"Nope." I headed into the kitchen so I wouldn't have to yell and added, "Said he'd be back on Wednesday."

"From the look of him, I'd rather he stayed gone."

With a nod, I said, "Couldn't agree more."

I arranged for the town lawyer, Cliff, to make up my will. Like any small town, just about everyone had slept with every eligible partner their own age, and Cliff and I were no exception. I'm sure he'd blabbed the news of my urgent, last-testament request to anyone who would listen by the time he showed up at my door on Sunday morning.

While contemplating the fact that I likely had only three and a half days to live, assuming that Death showed up at eleven on Wednesday, the doorbell rang.

Suddenly the couch seemed more comfortable than it had ever felt before, but I forced myself out of it and headed for the door.

Of course, Cliff, feeling like he owned the place since he'd slept with me all of once back when we were in high school, let himself in. "Hey, Lizzie. Your papers are ready."

I caught up to him in the mud room, and pointed at his boots. "You *are* going to take those off, right?"

"That's how you greet friends who do you weekend favours?"

"Hello, Cliff. Nice to see you. Thanks for coming by on a Sunday, and no doubt charging me double."

"Nice." With a smirk, he held up a manila envelope chock full of paper goodness. "We need to talk before you sign."

"I figured."

He sidled past me, headed straight for the couch where he flopped down and pointed at the cushion beside him.

I stood next to him, arms crossed, picking at the skin on my elbow.

"Sit."

"I'll stand."

"*Sit!*"

I did.

"You've got the whole town in an uproar. It's not every day someone as young as you insists I rush a will in a couple of days."

With a glare, I said, "So much for lawyer-client privilege."

"Most of the scuttlebutt points to cancer. Big-ass tumours, and with the diner, you've got no health insurance, right?"

"You've got a big mouth."

"I'm concerned about you. We all are." He sat back, crossed his left leg over his right knee, and stretched his right arm along the back of the couch. His attention skipped from the steering wheel of my first car, hung over the mantle like the antlers from a hunting trip, to my throw rug with the pattern of a *1967 Mustang* grill.

"You've got a nice home here, Lizzie."

"Thanks." I pointed at the papers beside him. "I appreciate your concern for me, and your need to spread the word that I might be in

164

trouble, might need some help. But I was counting on your *obligation* to keep my request confidential."

"You do realize," he said, his voice turning more serious than his usual over-confident bravado, "that the whole confidentiality thing is *moot* once you're dead."

And so the elephant appeared.

Cliff stared at me.

I stared back.

"So the rumour is cancer, huh?" I managed to ask.

He studied my face. "You're taking this awfully well. Better than I would." With a pause, he added, "Better than I *am*."

My voice softer, I admitted, "I don't think it's really sunk in, yet." I pointed at the papers again. "Can we get this over with, please?"

He switched to legal mode and started explaining. I checked my watch a few times, painfully aware of how much he was going to charge for this visit. At the same time, I'd likely be hanging with the Death dude before Cliff could send a bill. The diner was worth plenty. He'd find a way to retrieve his fees from my estate.

Clicking his pen, he pointed to the first sticky-arrow, and said, "Sign here."

I did.

Lather, rinse, repeat, more times than I wanted to count, with the occasional initials for good measure. Before my hand cramped, he clicked the pen closed, stuffed half the papers in the envelope and handed me the other half.

"Done." He extended his hand to shake. "Well, I hope this gives you some closure, love."

The *love* was a nice touch. I stared at his hand generating one of those awkward-silence moments, but when I looked into his soft brown eyes, I wondered if maybe he was being sincere. "Thanks. For being so quick." *Not unlike high school.* The thought brought a genuine smile to my face, and I slid my hand into his for the shake.

His touch felt warm. Not sweaty, or creepy. Warm. Comforting. A human kind of connection that reminded me I was still very much alive. I probably held on for a little too long, causing another awkward silence.

Finally, he said, "I'll show myself out."

As he left, I watched his well-formed ass saunter back and forth with his strides. With the self-reflection only the dying can truly muster, I wondered whether maybe Cliff had been more of a man than I'd given him credit for. That maybe he wasn't a regular in the diner because of the bacon.

Then the door closed and I felt truly alone.

For the first time in seven years, I didn't go into the diner on Sunday. After learning of the town's cancer-gossip, I decided to load up on cholesterol, stacking heart attack's chances. I defrosted smoked salmon in cold water in the sink, and while the pot came to a boil for poached eggs, I made hollandaise sauce, with extra butter and enough yolks that I should've picked up a defibrillator with the groceries.

My stomach was about to explode after four servings. Leaving the kitchen in a state that would normally drive me to drink, I chewed a few antacids, grabbed my car keys, and headed for the garage, feeling a need for speed.

Death was sitting in the driver's seat, with the window rolled down.

I swallowed, waiting for him to speak.

He picked at his nails, and yes, *ew*, licked whatever he scraped out.

My arms crossed over my chest, I demanded, "You said Wednesday."

"Yes."

"It's Sunday."

"You had four 'Eggs Montreal.'"

I hung my head in shame, then added, "Don't you have your own wheels?"

"I've always wanted to visit Niagara Falls. The Canadian side, naturally, since the views are more panoramic from their vantage points. And road trips are always more pleasant with company. Do you have a valid passport?"

I nodded. The thought of Death driving my car gave me a thousand different kinds of creep. But he seemed comfortable, and I wasn't about to give him a reason to be angry with me. I figured, what the heck? Why not spend my last Sunday with the dark dude on a road trip where I could spend time enjoying the scenery and pick the brains (if he had any in there) of a guy who had *literally* seen it all? Besides, I had intended to go for a drive, to feel the wind in my hair.

"Give me a minute."

"Take your time."

I returned with a bottle of water, my passport, and enough snacks for two. After the incident at the diner, I knew Death had an appetite, and I didn't want him sucking back all the beef jerky. When I stepped into the car, I expected it to stink like the booth had last Wednesday. This time, though, he smelled of old tires and blackened motor oil, as though he'd spent the last couple of days fixing all the cars in hell.

When I pulled my iPod out of my pocket, he blocked the USB port. "Driver picks the tunes," he said. From beneath his trench coat, he pulled out a CD, the kind you burn yourself, with the title, "Road Trip Mix," scribbled in red Sharpie across the top. "Do you have a GPS?" he asked.

I shook my head. "But I know the way."

"Lovely."

Death put my car in gear and before I could click the seatbelt into place, we were off.

***

By the time we had crossed the border into Canada, I had heard enough 1980s' hair bands for this plus a couple more lifetimes. Who knew Death had a thing for long-haired posers, distortion pedals, and Marshall stacks?

We found a fantastic parking space, directly across from the American Falls. "I don't think I've ever parked this close," I said.

Death yanked the parking brake, and shrugged. "It's a perk."

"Cool."

We slipped into the crowd and headed for one of the most recognizable railings from my childhood. The scrolls in the ironwork always reminded me of my grandparents. Nana had loved the falls, and dragged me here on more than one summer vacation while my mother ran the diner. My favourite picture of Nana and Grandpa was of the two of them, standing in front of the railing, him wearing those plaid pants with the white belt that advertised his job as a real estate agent. Her with her fine-as-a-wisp hair combed over, her white purse over her arm (to match his belt, of course), and her lips stained that deep pink-red she always wore on a bright, sunny day. I'm not sure what made them happier: being with each other, spending the day with me, or just the glory of a gorgeous day spent in misty gardens.

Death and I had lucked out with a perfect day of our own to gawk at nature's wonder. I inhaled a long, deep breath and tried to imagine what it must have felt like a few hundred years ago when the first white men, guided by the natives, saw the falls for the first time.

Turning my attention to my companion, if you could call him that, I watched Death as he studied the base of the American Falls.

"Penny for your thoughts," I said.

"I'm impressed."

"Wait 'til you stand at the brink of the Horseshoe Falls." I pointed toward the railing where a crowd of tourists jockeyed for positions at the edge.

Death lingered, grasping the railing like a bull rope. "Many die here each year. I understand, now, why they're drawn to the spectacle."

I leaned with my back to the railing, taking in the manicured gardens, the endless stream of cars circling for a place to park, and the countless phones raised to snap a dazzling selfie. Twice, I opened my mouth to respond, then changed my mind. Like Death, I was mesmerized by the power of this place. Somehow, in his presence, I felt the need to be profound. Otherwise, my words would waste in the wind, adding to the ever-present mist.

I asked, "Are you tempting me?"

"I've penciled you in for Wednesday."

"Shouldn't a guy like you be, you know, busy? All the time?"

"My services aren't required *every* time."

"Let the minions do the work, huh?"

"Precisely."

"I rate face time with the big boss?"

I looked at him when he didn't answer right away. He gazed at the water, lost in thought, or his duties, or whatever ran through his rotting mind.

"Am I special?" I asked.

"Everyone is unique, extraordinary in their own way."

I laughed out loud, catching the attention of a cluster of tourists. "Death waxes philosophical," I said, quiet enough that only the two of us could hear. I pointed at a young girl, the only one from the group still staring at the two of us, as though we were built of fear, and said, "You're scaring her."

"It's *you* she fears."

Staring back at the girl, flashing my best smile, I tried not to look like a psychopath with a pocket full of candy and a heart full of wicked intentions. She grabbed the hand of the nearest adult, probably her father, but continued to stare at me.

I asked, "Does she know what you are?"

He shrugged. "Only those in my agenda see beyond my humble attire." Gesturing, he held open his trench coat, revealing khaki shorts with zippered pockets and a plain white T-shirt. "What did you see in me, back in the diner, so that you recognized me straight away?"

"I don't know, exactly. I just *knew*."

For a moment, my heart skipped, as though a flash of something dire, like fur or scales, was about to erupt from beneath that trench coat.

The moment passed.

With a tug on the sleeve of his coat, I said, "Come on," and dragged him toward the Horseshoe Falls.

By the time we had walked along the railing to the brink—the spot where the water rushes over the edge to plunge and smash onto the rocks below—my clothes hung heavy on me, sodden by the mist. During one trip here with my grandparents, we had seen a movie about a family whose boat capsized in the river above the falls. The father swam to shore, the son was tossed over the falls with only a life jacket to protect him and he miraculously lived. The daughter was yanked out of the river in the nick of time by tourists who were milling around, right where Death and I stood now. The daughter's terror had felt so real to me, as though I had come within inches of being sucked over the edge to drop a zillion feet and break apart on the rocks below. Outside the theatre, on the way to our car, Nana and Grandpa had chatted about how real the experience had felt to them. All I could do was grip their hands, my Nana on my left and my Grandpa on my right, and try to swallow away the lump in my throat. For the first time in my nine years of life, I had realized that I could die, *would* die. That at any moment, I might close my eyes, fall asleep, and drift into oblivion. That day I had never felt so loved and yet also so alone.

Almost three decades later, everyone I loved had died, and I had filled in their gaps with nothing but loneliness and eggs. It struck me as grimly funny that I was spending one of my last days with Death instead of with the living.

"The precipice, or the *brink* as you call it," he said, "is definitely worth the walk."

Jolting back to reality, I smiled at Death. "Told you."

"You did."

I glanced around for the little girl, the one who had been more afraid of me than of my road-buddy, but the crowds were too thick to see her.

I asked, "You done?"

"Are you?"

I stuffed both my hands in my pockets, feeling cold shivers despite the warm day. "Yeah."

He tipped his hat, or at least pretended to, since he'd left the fedora in my car. I felt as though something had changed between us, like we were either making friends or sizing up our enemies. For the first time since his visit last Wednesday, I began to feel the weight of him, and the panic of time ticking louder than it had ever ticked before.

Without warning, my attention veered elsewhere. I remembered Cliff, drawing a crystal clear image of his face in my head, including his warm smile and the firm grasp he seemed to have of his own worth. Then my mind painted a rendition of his wonderfully formed ass.

When my focus returned to reality, Death was almost at the car. As I sprinted to catch up, I took one last look over my shoulder at the falls. The tourist girl was standing at the railing, her back to her family and their photo-documentation of the day. She crossed herself, made a series of scary hex-like gestures, and then spit in my direction.

Monday and Tuesday, I worked in the diner. My road trip adventure lingered so strongly in my mind that I could not bring myself to deviate from my routine for fear of losing even a minute's worth of my remaining life.

I wondered how many people in my position, those granted a week to chew through items on their bucket lists, would have chosen to spend their last moments doing what they had always done. Call it fear of living, maybe, since I hadn't really focused on adventure back when I thought I had all the time in the world. Or maybe I was simply clinging to the structure that made me feel safe.

Wearing my apron like a crown of thorns, I cooked burgers and fries, steak and eggs, and heaps of bacon while I convinced myself that Wednesday would never arrive.

Then, God damn it, Wednesday came.

I got to the diner at my usual 6:00 am, and Cliff was waiting by the door.

I smiled, before *and* after I looked him up and down. "Morning, counsellor."

"How are you?"

"Alive. You?"

"Same." He smiled back at me, like he knew what gutter my mind had been lying in. Or maybe he had followed my gaze and figured he was about to get lucky.

I shivered.

Imagined and anticipated every detail.

Doing the math in my head, I figured I could spare a good fifteen minutes with him in the back office and still have the grill fired up for my early regulars.

He grabbed a menu and chose a booth near the door. As I headed to the back to wake the kitchen, I yelled over my shoulder, "Be right with you."

"Take your time."

I haven't much left. I turned back to look at him, truly *notice* him. He was much more handsome now than he had been as a teenager, especially since he grew a beard. More distinguished, as though being a professional had made him a better person. Maybe it had. How did I miss it? Where had I been?

I winked and wiggled my hips a little, then sauntered through the swinging door, hoping Cliff might get the hint.

With one hand reaching for my apron, I caught sight of Death, sitting on my prep counter.

My heart skipped. I grabbed at my chest.

"You don't have time for Cliff." He paused, and added, "Or to take his order."

"I thought I had until eleven?"

Death reached into his trench coat and pulled out a small, black, leather-bound notebook. After flipping to the spot where the cloth marker held the page, he simply said, "No."

I sagged onto the stool I kept near the kitchen phone. "One last fling?"

"No."

"Not even a kiss? A good, solid kiss can be even better than the carnal act."

He ran his long, cold fingers down the open page in his notebook and shook his head.

Wondering what kinds of notes Death kept, I leaned in closer to have a look. My eyes began to water, as though they knew better than to allow me the chance to screw this pooch, or Cliff for that matter.

"Cliff!" I shouted through the order window. "I need you in the kitchen."

Without reacting to my cry for help, and without so much as a glance in my direction, Death opened the big walk-in fridge and stepped inside.

"Just a sec, Lizzie." Cliff called from the diner, sounding like a cross between confused and worried.

Death exited the fridge, carrying a full flat of eggs.

"*Someone's* hungry," I muttered under my breath.

The big guy held the flat with his left hand, balancing it like a pro, and with his right, he tipped his fedora at me. Then he flipped over the eggs. All thirty of them splattered across my floor. Everyone who's worked in a kitchen despises that sound.

Cliff's footsteps echoed on the tile. He was about to walk through the swinging door and flash me his handsome smile. All I wanted was to tell Death to come back tomorrow, or even in an hour, and give me one last chance to *live* instead of merely existing.

I didn't watch where I was stepping.

My shoe found the eggs and I flew through the air. My head hit the corner of the prep counter with a sickening crack-thud.

I closed my eyes tight against the pain, because we all know it hurts less when we can't see the blood. Funny thing about pain. Just when I thought it couldn't get any worse, that I couldn't take any more, that I was going to black out and it might be like falling asleep, and maybe I could see my mother again, and she would hug me, and I wouldn't even mention that time she borrowed my car and brought it back with a scratch on the driver's door, the pain intensified.

"Oh my God, Lizzie!"

Cliff was close. He sounded like he was in his own kind of despair. I wanted to look up, and see if he was standing over me, staring with longing as though he was anticipating a morning romp, too. But I couldn't open my eyes.

He shouted into a phone. Ordered paramedics.

My eyes still wouldn't open. My skull felt as though it was on fire. I was in a kitchen, so maybe fire was involved.

Cliff's lips found mine. I tried to kiss him back, savour the moment, but he was pressing down, pushing air into me. Into my lungs.

No! I thought. *We're supposed to kiss.*

Then the smell blindsided me.

Not attics and lanolin, not motor oil and old tires. This time, Death stunk of the job, of sewage, rot, and decomposing bodies. He must have been right next to Cliff, trying to figure out whether I'd stopped breathing so he could get on with his work. Judging from Cliff's continued attempts to keep me alive, I guessed the good lawyer didn't realize Death was in the room.

Or maybe he *did*.

When Cliff switched from blowing air into my lungs to pumping my chest, I used the air he'd gifted me to say, "You're...good..."

I needed another breath, if for no other reason than to scream out in pain, but Cliff was still pumping and counting to fifteen.

"Lizzie," Death whispered in my ear, full of comfort and pleasure. "Open your eyes."

The pain ends. Blissful, joyous, fantabulous cessation of the crushed-skull misery. I take in a breath. It doesn't feel the same, as though my lungs aren't part of the oxygen-equation any longer. Afraid to see what has happened to me, I slowly open my eyes.

Death stands over me, holding a set of car keys. Not mine, though. This set is the old-fashioned metal kind, no beeping car alarms or plastic fobs, or computer chip technology in sight.

"Where's Cliff?" I say. Looking around, I'm not in the diner. I'm lying on the pavement beside a red convertible. An absolutely mint condition *1967 Mustang*.

"I guess I earned a ticket on the up-elevator, huh?" I say.

"The car is merely a means of transportation."

I shake my head. "A *67 'Stang* is a hell of a lot more than a means of transportation."

He jingles the keys. "You'd best get going."

"Can I choose the destination?" I ask.

"It's your funeral."

A snort escapes me, right out my nose. For a moment, I wonder if Cliff saw my ungraceful reaction. Then I remember where I am. *What* I am. And sadness fills my insides.

He places the keys in my palm. I stare at them, then up at him, and ask, "How do I find my family?"

"The rules are different here. Finding love isn't about chance or destiny. It's a journey of conscious thought, of choices and consequences."

"You're waxing philosophic again," I say.

"And you're stalling." He points at the door. "Get in."

Moving with caution, I pull myself to standing, climb into the car, and put the keys in the ignition. Still unsure as to which direction to take, I turn over the engine but it doesn't catch.

Again and again, I try to start the Mustang, growing more frustrated by the minute, although time doesn't feel the same here. Convinced I've flooded the engine, I push the pedal all the way down, close my eyes, and remember that photograph of my grandparents by the railing.

The engine starts. I give the gas pedal a few pumps, feeling the exhilaration of the horsepower under my control. When I look up, Death is gone. I'm alone, stopped in the centre of a roundabout, with dozens of exits.

I recall a moment with my mother, on a night when her warm arms wrapped around me, tucking me in. I shift the car into gear and take the first exit that tugs at my soul.

GARLIC-STEAMED MUSSELS

Robert Smith

Working in a law firm is stressful. That's what people tell me. I don't feel it myself, but I understand how others could. Tight deadlines, belligerent bosses, and irate customers are the daily norm. You can literally see it grind people down throughout the day. New support staff don't last. The guys have pools guessing when the newbs will pop. Temps and newbies always burst in this pressure cooker. The lawyers get a kick out of detonating them, some pride themselves on it.

My boss is a lawyer named Ben Cane. He's a son of a bitch. He'll screw over a client, stab a fellow lawyer in the back, or hang a staffer out to dry. Nothing bothers him. He's clawing and scratching his way to the top. That's what barristers do.

"Frank," he barked at me today. "—where's that fucking file?"

"What file?" I asked.

"You fucking moron," he replied. "The Cassidy file. Get me the fucking Cassidy file—*now!*"

He hadn't asked for the file before that, but that's the way it's played. It's all a game to these guys. Sometimes he's like a rabid dog, but you can't let it get under your skin. You need a coping mechanism. If you don't have one, you won't survive. I deal with stress by slowing down. That's how *I* cope. I play it cool. If it's really bad, I take a long lunch by myself and chill. He brings the Ben, I bring the Zen. I don't let it get to me, and I never bring it home.

"Sir—" the waiter asked looking down at me, "—have you decided?"

Anthony, as was written on his nametag, dragged the back of his thumbnail over his eyebrow. He meant something by it. His black, beady eyes probed me, judging me. He critiqued what I wore, the way I sat, the fact I was alone. His lip almost curled up at one end, like I disgusted him.

Why does he think he's so much better than me? What gives him the right to criticize? Why is he demanding my order so quickly? I just sat down for fuck sake. Can't I have a little fucking time to think? Is this a test? I knew if I spoke, he would judge that too. There's a good chance he'd laugh.

Bristled by his arrogance, I looked back to my menu. I closed my eyes for a moment hoping the painful throbbing in my head would subside.

I wanted to jab, "Relax, Buddy—*I just got here.*"

I thought, *I should say: I'll tell you when I've decided.*

Maybe gashing him with a glare would let him know he's being pushy.

Perhaps I'll do both.

Before I got the chance, he mocked, "Come here to hide?"

"Excuse me?" I asked.

"You come here to hide like a little pussy-boy," he sneered. "You can't hack it at work, so you take your long lunches and you *hide* from your responsibilities."

I folded my menu and lowered it to the table. My hand drifted over the cutlery; I palmed a steak knife. Rising, I returned his glare, his curled lip, and his attitude. I held the knife so he couldn't see it, blade against the belly of my forearm. I gripped hard on the handle; blood fled the tense joints leaving my knuckles white. I took a step toward him.

The restaurant fell silent. Diners looked up from their lunches. They all stared.

They think I'm slow; I'm too dim-witted to comprehend the menu. They believe I'm too stupid to order my own food, too blunt to handle restaurant protocol. Maybe they think I'm a deranged knife wielding lunatic on a stabbing rampage. They're right. I will shred every one of these pompous mother-fuckers.

The waiter felt my malice, sensed my intent. All expression melted from his face and he turned to run. He wasn't going anywhere, not after slapping me with those insults. One can only stomach so much deprecation. Like a cat, I sprung and hit him before he'd taken a stride. My weight plowed him forward onto the next table and I rode him to the floor. Chairs fell with a crash, their occupants sent scrambling. Glasses shattered and silverware clattered. Hot brine from a large bowl of garlic steamed mussels splashed over us. The strong smelling liquid soaked through the waiter's shirt. Garlic burned my eyes. I grabbed a fistful of hair at the back of Anthony's head, squeezed the sopping clump, and rose to one knee. Free of their shells, several orange mollusks rolled from the server's back, heading for cover.

With my weight on his lower back, the waiter whimpered. Facedown in garlic butter and soaked in fish fluids, he was not so smug. I raised my arm and brandished the knife. A collective gasp escaped the lunch patrons. Their horrified eyes locked on me, transfixed on the scene.

My actions surely weren't the shocking events of this performance. They had heard the waiter's tone, his condescending questions, and his unprovoked verbal assault. They must have witnessed his forceful stance, his judgy glare, and his aggressive hand gestures. The scene in which I was starring featured the waiter as the villain—it had to.

I looked down at my prey. He pleaded. I glanced back to the shocked stares of our spectators. Their stares moved from my knife to my eyes. Their shock narrowed into anger.

One of them said, "Put the knife down, you fucking idiot. You can't do that."

Another one shouted, "Frank, settle down, you dumb fuck."

"Dumbass," someone barked.

"Look at him," another one chuckled. "He never knows what to do."

They all laughed.

"Fuck you," I yelled.

I bit down until my jaw muscles ached. Pressure built in my skull until I was sure it would explode. My anguish was their amusement. The squeak and grind of my teeth sounded loud in my head, but it did not drown out the mirth. I swallowed the hot ball that was growing in my throat, and plunged the blade deep into the waiter's right butt cheek. He screamed out in shock and pain. Shrieks sounded from the customers.

I drew the blade out slowly. Blood swelled up then spilled from the wound. The server's screams morphed. What had declared shock, changed to terror when I drove the knife down again—*harder*. Blood splashed from the first wound. I felt the splatter hit my face. I tugged the knife, but it didn't move. The blade had lodged into bone. Movement drew my eyes. A man rose from the closest table; he saw his opportunity. That's the way things work in this world. If you see an opportunity, you must act fast. This man saw one, and he acted on it. He made his way toward me, hostility in his eyes. I worked the knife hard until it popped free. The man retreated to his chair and sat.

With my arm, again ready to strike, I took aim at Anthony's ribs. In that moment, I took pause. The throbbing pressure in my head had subsided. I felt good; I felt free—*I felt alive.*

"Sir?" a voice from above asked.

The question startled me. My eyes popped open. I whipped my head up and shot him a look, an expression of surprise.

Anthony responded with a sheepish grin. "Are you ready to place your order?" he asked.

"No," I said, trying to gather myself. "Give me a few more minutes."

"Of course, Sir. Take your time."

The waiter spun on his heel and headed for the kitchen.

A couple enjoyed mussels at the next table. The woman smiled as her companion tried to fork one of the mollusks from its shell. Around the restaurant, patrons dined and chatted.

I blinked hard and returned to the menu in my hands.

"Frank," boomed Ben Cane, slapping me on the back. "This is where you've been hiding."

At once, from head to toe, my muscles tensed.

My hand drifted over the cutlery; I palmed the steak knife.

END GAME

A. Giacomi

immy hadn't been himself for a few days now. Tess and Benji were really starting to worry about him. I guess he hadn't adjusted as well to college life as we had. He wouldn't go to any parties, except the gamer parties he would throw in our very own dorm room. It was an exclusive group of the four of us and clearly, we were the only ones he showed any interest in hanging out with. His social status had been set as "dorm-dwelling dweeb without do-ability." Tess even offered to have the t-shirt made. Mostly we just laughed about the fact that Jim seemed to have no interest in getting laid, but when it became obvious that he had no interest in doing anything but attending class and playing his favourite video game, we began to think something more was going on. Tess thought it could be depression, Benji thought he was a bit OCD with his ever consistent routine, and as for myself, I maintained that James just needed to get laid. I didn't see a problem with playing video games all day, mainly because I was his roomie and my game addiction was satiated when he was around.

What good is a gamer without a gaming buddy?

As perfect strangers, we had hit it off all thanks to the game Satan's Lair. It had come out just days before our first semester. Jimmy had already set up his game system in the dorm when I arrived. He was very eager to begin playing and so we broke the seal off the game case on our very first day sharing the dorm room. It was our version of a toast to a great year ahead. I'll admit the game was creepy in nature; it was intended to scare the crap out of you within the first five minutes of play. There were demons and excessive blood, all the makings of a great game that one could become addicted to. I saw it in Jim's eyes that day, the addiction had begun. His eyes were glassy and filled with excitement, it was near impossible to break him away from the game when it was time for dinner. The grin on his face after playing for the first time said it all; this would be his conquest this year. First year was rarely taken seriously, so I didn't see a problem with Jim wasting away his days trying to beat the next level. It was his life to do with as he wished.

A few weeks after playing the game Jimmy realized that he would need more players to win a battle against a mega-demon so he recruited Tess and Benji a couple from one of his literature classes. They were a couple of nerds too and appreciated the game addiction just as much. Tess was a worshiper of wigs and had a new hair colour every day, whereas Benji looked quite normal, almost preppy until you spoke to him and you discovered his inner geek. They were an odd couple, but they sure knew how to game it down hard. It was strange to see such worship, and at times it was almost hard to participate in playing. They would seem a bit less human every time they came away from the game. I think it freaked people out since many who saw us exiting the dorm would avoid us like a skunk crossing their paths. That's when we realized we needed to blend in a little better, Jimmy was resistant of course, he liked the comfort of his dorm room and the people he had become accustomed to. Meeting new people was daunting.

Our first party was hosted off-site at a house Tess shared with a bunch of other girls. The amount of people there had Jim squirming with nervous knots in his gut. To be honest it was so full it teetered on the brink of claustrophobic in there. Even I had trouble managing my way through the crowds of drunken college kids and strung out strangers. Tess and Benji knew a bunch of people there and wandered off quite a bit. They seemed to fit in even though they embraced their nerdy ways. As for me, well, I was stuck with Jimmy. He looked about ready to hyperventilate when I mentioned I had to go take a piss. He begged me to stay; it was rather embarrassing to see a grown man beg so desperately, his eyes pleading and teary. Everyone was staring at him acting like a frightened child, some people even began to laugh hysterically at Jim, and that was the end, the final straw. He shoved people out of the way and made a run for it. I ran after him screaming for him to relax and get back to the party, but he never stopped running until he was back safely in his dorm room.

"What the hell was that lame exit?" I yelled at him.

Jim covers his ears as he slumps into a corner of the room shaking. I got to thinking perhaps he had some social anxiety and I should cut him some slack, so I stopped talking and turned on the game. It was the only thing that seemed to make him feel better, and over time it became his crutch.

After that party it was hard for Jimmy to leave the room, he spent four days playing that damn game and I stayed with him. Tess and Benji came knocking a few times but we pretended to be out. They knew better of course and gave Jim shit via text. In about three days he was ready to see people again, but he was starting to look a little worse for wear. That's when Tess started to look concerned.

"Jim? Have you been sleeping?" She asks in a worried tone as she shook her head toward Benji.

Jim shrugs. "A little yeah, guess I've just been caught up in this game."

"Maybe we should take a gaming break? Like, go away? There's Rock Fest next weekend, we could go to that. A friend said she'd get me tickets if I was interested..."

Jim shrugs again. "I don't know Tess, I don't think I'm fit to be out in public. Ever since I got here I just haven't felt myself, you know? It's like this place is a whole other planet."

Tess gave Jim a hug "I completely understand Jimmy, but you can't lock yourself away and hide from the world...okay? Just think about it, I think it would be good for you."

"So we going or what?" I ask Jim as Tess and Benji take their leave.

"Yeah fine..." Jim says in a less than excited tone.

I didn't push any further, as far as I was concerned that was a yes and that was good enough for me. I had been dying to get out and stretch my legs, socialize a bit, but I couldn't fight the feeling that something terrible would happen to Jim if I left him alone. Guilt made me stay; perhaps he was growing an unhealthy attachment to me as well as the game.

Bros don't ditch each other when times get tough.

The next weekend arrived quickly and Jim didn't look as vexed about it anymore. When he had heard that one of his favourite bands would be at Rock Fest, he perked up. Apparently, Jimmy had room in his skull for more than just a video game. On the drive over he went on and on about how The Razor Rebels rivaled some of the most influential metal bands of our time. He quoted lyrics and fanboyed all over the place. Tess and Benji looked about ready to barf. Jim was definitely killing the vibe in the car which was why we were so incredibly ready to get there already. If it wasn't for a much-needed pit stop Jim might not have made it to Rock Fest.

Benji pumps gas while Tess heads off to grab some snacks for the rest of the trip, Jim and I take the opportunity to visit the men's room. I didn't really have to use the bathroom, but Jim pretty much begged me to accompany him. This was definitely becoming an unhealthy relationship and I only had myself to blame. While in the bathroom he wouldn't shut up about The Razor Rebels and that's when I lost it. I snap. Something inside of me became violent and uncontrollable and terrifying. I shake off, zip up and find myself behind Jim, listening to him ramble on and on, but not actually hearing anything he's saying. What I see is red. Grabbing at Jim's curly brown hair I pull his head back and then smash it into the urinal in front of him. He gives a blood-curdling scream and it only makes me smile. I kick his legs out from under him so that he now lay bleeding on the floor, his eyebrow is split open and he might gain a black eye, but he wasn't nearly as hurt as I would have liked.

"What the hell man?" He shouts out at me as he presses against his open wound trying to pacify the pain. "I thought we were friends!"

"Jim you're really starting to annoy the shit out of me. Let's be honest here. I need this weekend. We've been cooped up in the dorm for so long that I'm starting to feel batshit crazy. I want to hurt you man, and that's not normal."

Jim stares at me with wide eyes. "So what? You don't want to be friends anymore?"

I rub my temples trying to find my sanity again. "Nah, I do...but I also want to get out more. So you need to shut up and let me get out more okay? You do that and we're cool."

"We're cool? You just beat the shit out of me!" He screams.

"Will you shut up!" I scream back. "If you tell anyone I did this, I'll fucking kill you, Jim. So keep your mouth shut, clean yourself up and let's get this show on the road."

Jim gets up but continues to stare at me in disbelief, I could see that he thought I was nuts, and to be honest I felt nuts. Pushing him out of the bathroom and back toward the car Tess spots him first and runs to his aid.

"Holy shit Jim! What happened?" She says as she examines the wound.

I wait patiently and stare Jim down as I await his imaginative answer.

"I... I... slipped. Damn bathroom floor in there is a death trap. Piss everywhere and I slipped and hit my head."

"Do you want to go to a hospital and have that looked at?" Tess asks still examining the gash.

I stare evilly at him, signaling that he better remember what I told him, or else he'd find himself in a much worse state.

"No, no, I'm fine Tess. I want to get to Rock Fest already! Let's go!" He tries to say enthusiastically and races toward the vehicle.

The rest of the drive is silent, I grin in victory, but Tess and Benji can't help checking the back every five seconds to see if Jim was okay. My blood boiled every time they looked back and it took everything I had not to smack them when they did. "He's fine" I mutter to myself, "not like he has a concussion or anything."

When we reach the festival the mood changes, everything felt lighter, even Jim gave me a brief smile and whispered the word "sorry". I guess he understood he could be really annoying at times. I felt a bit sorry myself, but I wasn't about to let him know that. I wanted him to keep in mind that things needed to change between us. We couldn't always do what he wanted because he was too terrified to leave his room.

Step one was acquiring our neon wristbands, allowing us access to all the stages, beer tent and even a discount at the merch booth. It wasn't long before Tess and Benji decided to venture off on their own; they asked Jim if he was okay half a dozen times before they ditched though and told him to call their cell if he needed to go to the med tent or anything. I rolled my eyes, they treated Jimmy boy like such a baby sometimes, maybe he'd man up if they treated him like one.

As promised Jim's band is the first spot we hit, and although The Razor Rebels were good, I couldn't help staring at the lovely blonde that kept looking over at us. She looked like something out of a magazine, drool worthy yet still adorable. I push Jim out of the way and begin to walk over to her when I realize I'm not the one she's grinning at, when I look back I find that she's looking at Jim. *Really?* I think in disbelief. She walks toward him as if I don't exist and starts talking to him about the band. Apparently, they had something in common; they were die hard Razor Rebel fans. She had noticed him mouthing all the words to every song and that's why she decided to pop over. Jim looked ready to shit his pants but somehow held it together and spoke to her. She twirled her hair and flirted with such obviousness that it nearly made me want to hit Jim again, but this time for a different reason.

"Get her number already!" I yell over to him.

He blushes but miraculously obeys. She very willingly writes the digits on his hand and kisses his cheek before heading back to her troop of ladies. Once she's gone I slap Jim on the back, "Nicely done son!" I smile at him. He smiles back quite proud of himself. It was about time Jim found himself a girl, and this one was quite the find. I guess she was into the whole nerd guy thing.

Jim and I check out a few more bands before meeting up with Tess and Benji who look a tad disheveled.

Jim laughs in their face, "So which bands did you guys see?"

To which they reply two different answers.

"Okay, you guys are really bad at hiding things." Jim continues to laugh to himself and he leads the way to the main stage where we would spend the rest of the evening.

It seemed like that little boost of confidence, and perhaps a quick beating from me was just what the doctor ordered. When we got back to school, Jim was a different guy. More confident, more outgoing, and less addicted to the video game Satan's Lair. Sure we still played, but it wasn't as much of an addiction anymore.

A month goes by and I'm impressed by the new Jim. The only thing that seems off is the fact that he doesn't really call Tess or Benji to come out anymore. My curiosity gets the best of me and I finally decide to ask what gives.

"Hey, Jim… what have Benji and Tess been up to?"

He shrugs, "How should I know?"

The tone in his voice screamed that he was hiding something. "Okay seriously, what's going on? They haven't called or shown their faces." We didn't exactly have any classes with them this term, but they usually would sneak into a few of our classes just to hang out.

Jim begins to sweat and I begin to grow angry.

"Answer me dammit!" I scream.

Jim shakes his head. "No," he says shyly.

Before he can shake his head again my hands are at his throat. "'No'? 'No' you won't tell me or 'no' you don't want to?" and then it strikes me. "Did you tell them that I hurt you? Is that why they won't come see us? Did you tell them?" I scream as my grip tightens and Jim begins to turn red. He tries to speak but can't utter a word, in my rage, I don't realize that I'm not only hurting him but cutting off his oxygen. Dropping my hands to my sides, Jim collapses, gasping for air.

"I'm sorry Jim, shit, something is seriously wrong with me," I say shaking.

Jim coughs trying to right himself. "No shit something's wrong with you!" He says with a wheeze. "They don't come around anymore because I told them not to."

Staring at Jim confounded I ask, "but why?"

"I don't need them anymore, that's all. I have you, we're best friends and really... I don't think they like you very much. So it got awkward, you know? I guess I pick you... even though you appear to be a psycho!"

I can't help it, I start laughing. "You choose me? Oh man, are you sure it was a good choice? I mean Tess and Benji never tried to kill you."

Jim finds his way over to his bed and sits on it. "Yeah okay, so you're crazy, but I'm not all that sane either. I guess we have that in common." He attempts a smile and pops in our game. Soon all is forgotten and behind us, as we attempt to beat the next level of the game. We had reached the part where we would have to sacrifice a teammate to continue in the game. The decision was hard especially since it had taken us so much time to build up our character's strength, but if we didn't sacrifice one, then Satan would be coming after us before we could complete our mission. Jim and I debate about who to toss into the pits of hell. Our mighty soldier, our sneaky ally, or our oracle? We rule out the oracle, knowing the future had its perks, and our mighty soldier had too much power invested in him to simply throw away. Jim pushes the button slowly as if our lives genuinely depended on this decision. Once the task is completed we high five and shut down the game satisfied with our advancement to the next level. A chill entered the room that day and it never left after.

The chill in the air followed us around. I know Jim and I both felt it, but we were too afraid to try and explain it. Something weird was happening.

On the way to class one day, we spot Tess looking a bit perturbed, almost as if she had seen a ghost. It takes her a moment to notice us standing in front of her, but when she does she turns and walks the other way. We both call after her, but she doesn't look back or reply.

"Well, that was messed up," I say to Jim.

"Told you man, she hates you," Jim says punching my shoulder lightly.

"Whatever," I snort. Slightly hurt by being brushed aside by our former crew, but it clearly didn't bother Jim so I decide to suck it up.

The hurt only makes me dive deeper into our game, which Jim didn't mind at all. We begin to skip classes again, stop mingling at parties and no one notices because no one cared. We weren't exactly popular or visible. Jim and I always did our own thing and without our foursome, it seemed less exciting to hang out anywhere else.

As the game intensifies we forget to eat. I notice Jim's clothes are fitting much looser and perhaps I mirrored his appearance a bit. There is a knock at the door while I examine our appearance and decide we might be decent enough to be seen.

"Should I get it?" I ask Jim.

He shakes his head, his eyes never leaving the game.

I don't bother to get up until the knocking comes again, this time accompanied by Tess's strained voice.

"Open up, please. Please!" she begs.

Jim, now more alert, races to the door and throws it open.

Tess stares at us as we stare back; it looked as though she hadn't slept in weeks. Something was clearly wrong, and my gut told me it had something to do with Benji since he wasn't with her.

"Tess, what's going on?" Jim asks, breaking the silence that desperately needed to be broken.

Tess simply begins to cry. "I don't know; it just seems like everyone is going nuts! Including me!" She paces the room a few times before noticing the game. What she does next neither of us could have predicted. Tess kicks the screen over smashing it to pieces.

"What the hell Tess?!" Jim and I scream in harmony.

Before we can stop her she takes the game out of the system and smashes it under her heel. The chill in the room grows colder. Tess' eyes grow wide when she can nearly see her breath from the cold surrounding us.

"I don't know what's going on, but that game... that game did something to Benji and it's going to hurt us too." She cries.

Jim goes over to comfort her. "What happened to Benji?" He asks gently.

"One day he just started talking a lot of nonsense. Something about his dreams feeling real. He kept talking about how he was being shoved into flames or something. Then the next day he was gone. I called; I went to his room, his classes. Spoke to his mom. No one has seen him. I filed a police report, but they don't have anything to go on, so they're going to shut down the case soon."

"Why didn't you say anything when I saw you in the hall? You ran... why?" Jim says curiously.

"I... I don't really know how to explain it... but I'm seeing things, they seem so real." Tess begins to rub her hands together, trying to dry the sweat from her shaking hands.

It was odd for her to seem hot in a room with a clear chill in it.

"What exactly are you seeing?" Jim asks concerned while I stare on baffled.

"That day I saw you and ran. I knew it was you, but I saw monsters eating you. I knew it couldn't be real, so I ran. I've been seeing monsters or demons. These terrifying creatures... it feels like they're coming after me."

Tess begins to sob uncontrollably and Jim hugs her tightly.

My brain races and then it hits me "Holy shit Jim! What if the game is doing this? It sounds like she's talking about the game! What was the last part we were playing?"

Jim searches his mind. "In the game, we killed off our sneaky ally and we just sacrificed our oracle to gain more points. You don't think the game did this? Do you? What are you saying Tess?"

Tess looks up from her tears, "You sacrificed my character and Benji's to gain points? Yeah... well, I'm doomed then... and Benji's already dead."

Jim furrows his brow, "Tess, that doesn't make any sense!" he yells as he shakes her shoulders.

"Yes, it does." She says wiping the tears away. "They'll come for me now and take me away. I'm next, don't you see?" Her eyes wide with panic as she clutches to Jim.

"Jim we have to do something man. I think we need to get her some help... like psychological help." I say blatantly.

"She's not crazy! I believe her!" Jim yells back at me.

Tess looks up, directing her eyes toward me. "Jim... who the hell are you talking to?"

Jim looks from Tess back to me and finally replies as he points, "Umm to him."

Tess stands up and starts to make her way toward the door. "Jim, there's no one there..."

He starts laughing as do I, the chick was crazy alright. She could see monsters but for some reason I was invisible?

"Jim are you doing this?" she says sounding terrified. "Did you lose your mind and decide to kill Benji? Did you slip me drugs? Are you trying to kill me too?"

"What the hell Tess! No! I'm not trying to hurt you. I don't know why you're seeing things and I have no clue where Benji is. We haven't seen him, honest!"

Tess slaps Jim, "Who's we? Snap out of it Jim, it's only you in here. You and me!"

Jim rubs his red cheek. "Jesus Tess that hurt. Is this some sort of joke? We've been a foursome since the year started, remember? Game dates with the four of us? Doesn't ring a bell? No? Nothing?"

"Jim… listen to me… there are only three players… there was only ever three players."

Jim begins to back away from her. "No you're lying!" he shouts.

She grabs something out of her purse and places it in Jim's hand, "Here look around with this, do you see anyone in here?"

Jim opens his hand to reveal a tiny mirror. He holds it up to himself and then up to Tess and then up to me. I have no reflection which leaves me baffled as well. Jim's hands shake as he views himself and an empty space next to him in the mirror. His terror causes him to drop the small mirror into a million pieces.

"That's going to be plenty of years of bad luck Jimmy boy," I say trying to crack a joke at this very tense moment. I knew I existed, but there was some clear evidence against that.

Tess comes up behind Jim and takes his hand. "Jim… come with me, we'll figure this out together. The game is gone, we survived it, now let's never play it again."

Jim nods. "Yeah I think I need to get out of here," he says, directing the response to me. "I thought you were real, I thought you were my friend, but all of this was in my head." He says as he knocks on his skull.

"Jim, don't leave like this man," I beg, "there's got to be some explanation. I'm here, I've been here, I'm real dammit!" My anger begins to take hold of me again, but this time instead of directing it at Jim, I find Tess to be my target.

Running over to her, I press my thumbs into her eyes and push with all my might. She screams, begging for Jim to help her. "I'm real now aren't I?" I yell as I push her eyeballs back into her skull.

"Stop!" Jim yells trying to grab a hold of me and realizing he can't. He continues to beg for his friend's life but I am far too desperate to prove my existence that I can't stop, I know it's wrong, but what I want more than anything is for Jim to stay with me, and if she lives, he'll leave. He'll believe anything she says.

When Tess stops moving I release my grip, her body hits the ground with a thud. Turning back to look at Jim I realize I have broken everything. He saw me, and perhaps he was the only one, but he now saw me as a monster, not as his friend. Things wouldn't be the same now; he would leave first chance he got.

"I'm sorry," I say to Jimmy who is now cowering in a corner of the room. "I didn't mean for any of this to happen. I was just so lonely. I needed you like you needed me. Friends... I missed having those..."

Jim looks up from his corner directly at me and asks "What exactly are you?"

Unfortunately, I didn't really have an answer for him; I was just as confused as he was. I couldn't remember anything before the dorm room, not a single detail of my life before Jim or how long I had been trapped in the dorm; I was just a lost spirit in need of a guide.

"I don't know... I might be a ghost, I might be a demon, or I might just be something that lives in your head, a figment of your imagination. As far as I'm concerned, I'm real... and I made a promise to myself that I would never leave you. Loneliness is a hard thing to live with. So like it or not I think you're stuck with me."

Jim doesn't look impressed, his eyes look distant, and then the screaming starts. His screams alert the other students and I can hear them all gathering in the hall, a few brave ones knock at the door, but when no one opens it I can hear someone dialing 911. Jim continues to scream through the clamor in the hall. Sliding down to have a seat next to him I realize that I was finally going to get out of this room for good. Crazy Jim was going to grant me a whole new view complete with a padded cell. At least I would be out of this place. I felt like I had been here too long already in some sort of limbo. I guess I had always felt that way but could never explain why I felt it.

As the door bursts open and police officers appear they find Tess's body first and then Jim cowering in the corner and of course they don't see me. I'm not real, I'm not here.

Feeling a tad guilty as Jim is dragged out of the room and thrown into a police car, I try to comfort him. "It's all going to be okay Jimmy. I'm here. They're going to find you guilty of all of it, but I'm here with you... always." I give him a little grin.

"Get him away from me!" he screams trying to get the cops attention by kicking the seat in front of him.

I guess it mattered very little to him now how crazy that sounded. There wasn't exactly anyone there to remove out of his sight. Slowly Jim exhausts himself and lays back in his seat the best he can in handcuffs. He glares at me as I sit beside him.

"Did you kill Benji too?" He whines.

Coming in a little closer, not that I needed to, I whisper maliciously: "maybe..."

I give him a knowing wink and we're silent the rest of the way. We would have years to talk this through, but right now seemed like a bad time to blab about it all. I wouldn't be a very good friend if I rubbed it all in his face.

Entering the facility, Jim pathetically begs one last time "Leave me alone."

I shake my head, "Sorry, but bros don't ditch each other when times get tough."

"I'm with you, forever..."

GRATITUDE

Danann Hawes

No clocks. No sun. Minutes like hours or hours like minutes? Time means nothing in the dark. Are my eyes open? I can't tell anymore. Living in a small enclosure or in the middle of a wide expanse of languid nothing feels the same. Then add crushing silence and the inability to move a muscle, but for the slight shift of my weight, a small pronation of an elbow, but not without considerable pain. When non-volitional, being cut off from your senses is the furthest thing from a meditative state one can imagine. If it has to, your mind will invent things to give you hope. Otherwise, it's like living an aware death, a floating angry consciousness eating itself like that mythical snake consuming its own tail.

I can make some noises, to be fair. Around the tight mouth gag, the muffled sounds are increasingly not my own, coming from something far more desperate, primal, and weak. I don't want to hear it. The rash on my stomach offers an unabated itch, courtesy of my feeding tube. My arms and legs are tied to bolts in a plywood board that doubles as my entire universe. The board and I lay flat, enclosed in a box with holes in it, similar to a pet carrier, except I'm not going anywhere.

And then there is the immense physical abuse but at least that's company.

I don't know if it's once a day, once a week, or once a month, but she does come visit me. I hear a key twist in a heavy lock, the screech of a thick metal door... then the sound of my box door as it's opened. My vision snaps back into me like magic, watching her silhouette against dim back lighting, her long curly hair, like vipers, streaming down her round face. She never removes my gag. Down here, we never exchange words. This is a one-way conversation, her own pirate radio show and I'm her sole listener.

She screams at me, often directly into my ears. She slaps and kicks me. Punches me, closed and open fisted. Eyes white-hot with anger, she calls me WEAK, a LIAR and a MONSTER. She tells me she will never let me respond. Never even let me beg. She tells me I have to take it. Forever. Sometimes, she defecates on me.

However, she always cleans me up; very carefully she unlocks one limb at a time, locking my bruised body into different positions, slowly shifting me around the board like a rotisserie chicken. I'm so weak, my body slowly atrophying, I doubt I could do her any damage, let alone with one limb at a time. Maybe when I was stronger, maybe at the beginning.

Different positions on regular intervals prevent bed sores. She fills my feeding tube with some sort of unknown liquid, ensures that the braces are tight, closes my box, then the door to my room. Then I await the next time my wife visits me.

We were both in our early thirties when we met. Young enough to still believe in love but old enough to be practical about it. She had come from a very poor family, was shy, somewhat insecure. I could sense a temper that belied her unaffected veneer, even then. We were both eager to love each other so it was not long before we were married and had Kelsey, our child. Our life was rolling along, solid, perhaps great. I know I have always had my demons, an imperfect upbringing, less than ideal genetics, but while I'm acquainted with my shadow, we are not friends and I'm always in the driver's seat. It was a good life and I was a good man. Not perfect but good.

One morning I woke up in this box and I've been here ever since. I've accepted I will never know why. All I know is she hates me. And that I'm about to escape.

Painstakingly, I have managed to chew away at the thick strands of cord in this gag. Grinding them between my teeth until they'd frayed, then broke. When I hear that key in the lock, with the cooperation of my lips and nose, I move the aerated piece of fabric on the gag slightly to the right, covering up the frayed and broken cords. Only a few left before the gag gives way. With my head free, if I wait until I'm put into a certain position—sideways, to my right—I should be able to bend my neck sufficiently to get at my right arm restraint. As long as I can bite through that in the span of a few days, I can free my arm, and the rest will follow. I don't know how I'm going to get the door to my box open, nor the door to my room, or anything after that, but I can't focus on anything that far ahead.

She opens the lid on my box and stares down at me in disgust. She calls me a "sick dickless piece of shit" and stomps on my genitals. She slaps me across the face, over and over, until I can feel my dehydrated brain knocking against my skull. I wonder whether the gag will break, ruining my plan of escape. Luckily, it holds. An even greater stroke of luck, in her fury, one of her earrings pops off and lands in my box. She doesn't notice, unaware that she has now offered me a better chance at those doors.

After another half hour of various humiliations, she cleans my wounds and starts the slow process of shifting my body on the board. I give her complete control, not an ounce of resistance as she straps my limbs into their new homes, the blessed side position I was looking for. Her breathing slows down, her countenance calms, as she moves through this familiar routine. Her touch almost starts to feel tender as her mouth and forehead relax and her eyes soften. By the time she finishes, my wife is almost with me and she can't look at me in the eyes anymore.

She closes my box lid and I sit quietly, sideways on my board, until I hear that familiar sound of the door lock. I bite down on the remaining cords of my gag. As I grind, my front teeth feel loose and I taste the blood from my damaged gums. It breaks and the gag falls from my mouth. I move my neck, shake my head, a joyous pain. I can speak freely but I don't utter a word, even under my breath. Not until I'm a free man. I don't want to hear that desperate tone, that pitiful version of me. Single minded, I rip and tear at my right arm restraint. Made of thick leather, I try to soften it with my saliva but can scarcely manage a drop. I persist and chew through the strap like a trapped wolf chewing through its leg.

I slide my arm out of the restraint. I free the rest of my limbs. This comparatively simple task takes on a surprising difficulty given how my hands shake, my basic coordination deeply compromised. I feel around for that earring, find it in a crease of my sweat soaked shirt. It's a diamond stud, one I had given her long ago. Of more immediate significance, it has a long sharp pin.

As it turns out, my box is secured with nothing but a cheap pad lock. A few stiff up-kicks and I am free. I can't worry that she might hear me. I need out. I feel for the walls and find that they are covered with strange foam panels, some sort of soundproofing. Where am I? Such effort and time has gone into this design. Who is she trying to keep the noise from? I don't have time to consider these questions. I have to get that thick metal door open.

Using the earring pin and a nail sourced from the box, along with the knowledge acquired through my misspent youth, I feel the heavy lock mechanism shift… until CLICK—it turns into place. I push the metal door open and step into a large musty room, a basement. My basement. I had set up a ping pong table in this very room last year. Or was it last month? My stomach drops as I turn to an even larger door between me and the stairs leading to the main floor. While I had installed the door, it looks different. Where are the bolt locks? Of course, she has reversed the door frame. Once designed to keep people out of the basement, a panic room of sorts, it's now repurposed to keep me in. I spend a moment to consider this irony until I'm interrupted by the sounds of faint murmurs from upstairs. I drag my broken body toward the sound, a vent leading up to our kitchen. I hear my wife's voice and can even make out a few short responses: "Yes," and "I see,"

Then I hear someone else. A man, the voice achingly familiar. I feel a surprising rush of jealousy. The truth becomes appallingly evident when he calls her "M," for Emily. Only I call her that. It was me up there.

This doesn't feel real. Had my time on the board stolen my sanity? Surely, but to this absurd extent? I listen to their discussion, a mere ten feet above me, playing the bizarre role of observer in my own domestic life. The other me dominates the discussion, Emily responding in that habitually meek manner I, at one time, been so accustomed to. The content of their discussion feels prosaic, increasingly one sided. I annoy myself, experiencing the benefits of a very singular type of self-awareness. Eventually, this interaction leads to awkward silence, then a desperate revert to current events. The version of me upstairs says:

"Did you hear about the recent arrests? More guys are facing life imprisonment for providing backroom jobs. Another great example of humanity not being able to uninvent its abominations. With the cloning technology available, all they need is one of those deep brain scans and some blood or hair and they are good to go. And it feels like everyone has had at least one of those scans these days. Did you ever get one?"

"No," she says.

"Yeah, well I did—when was it… two years ago? It will help detect early signs of disease, they said. Do you know that people have been busted for using their clones as fill-ins for them at work? Luckily, they don't ever come out fully right—always some physical differences that end up outing them."

An atomic bomb goes off in my mind as I look down at my own body, rubbing my hands over my legs and torso for the first time. I lift up my shirt to find a series of rashes, large red blotches across my chest. Lining my stomach is a strange series of irregular groves, clearly not the result of my injuries. I quietly move to a windowpane in the corner of the room and fearfully check my reflection. My face is pale, scratched, eyes bloodshot, deep lines across my forehead. I look terrible but at least my face still looks like me.

I stand idle in the basement, the truth struggling to set into my consciousness. If it had been two years since I underwent that scan, I am a cloned version of myself from two years ago. Welcome to your old life. Whatever I did to anger my wife was in the two years following the scan. I feel the deep burn of resentment and shame as I try to reconcile my feelings between being punished for something I have not yet done and the realization I must have done something very bad. But what?

I stop myself as this line of inquiry is enough to drive anyone insane, let alone someone already on the razor's edge. I'm weak, confused, and yet I may have an able-bodied ally up there if I can get his attention. I can't wait for her to come down here and hope to contain her and escape. I need him to be my intervenor, my rescuer. I need to help myself.

"HELP" I scream as loud as I can, my voice still carrying that desperate animal fervour. "I'm down here! I'm hurt! Emily has done it to you! She used your scan!"

There is commotion from upstairs and Bryan's booming voice: "What the hell is that?"

Rapid footsteps race down the stairs followed by the sounds of the bolts being removed from the door. It swings open and I come face to face with myself.

Bryan peers at me with horror, then sympathy, as his eyes scan my body, my wretched condition. This his face shakes with anger.

"Jesus Christ, what has she done?"

I stand there, huddled over, body broken, staring at him with pleading eyes. Then the sound of Emily as she trudges down the stairs, appears beside Bryan. She has fire in her eyes, the Emily that I know.

Bryan turns to her and screams "You did this?!"

Bryan's face begins a slow collapse, seeing his real wife for the first time. Emily sneers at me, grabs a nearby shovel. I stand there, vulnerable, at their mercy. Emily clinches her jaw, swings the shovel back. I brace for impact but watch as she slams the head of the shovel into Bryan's face.

I pour myself a glass of orange juice, sitting comfortably at the kitchen table. My face has healed. I'm clean shaven, wearing a button down long sleeve shirt. Across the table from me is Emily, applying some jam to a piece of toast. Also sitting with us is Kelsey, our daughter.

I turn to Kelsey and ask if she wants another piece of toast. She shakes her head without making eye contact. She asks if she can go play in her room. Emily offers her permission with a resigned nod. Emily looks up at me, mournfully, and takes a bite of her toast. I sit with this now familiar feeling of shame and regret. My demons had taken control. I am still trying to figure out how I could have done that to my daughter.

Emily studies me across the table. "Are you okay?"

I nod, averting her gaze.

Are my eyes open? I can't tell anymore, I think to myself.

"Can you tell me what you are feeling?" she asks.

I hold my wife's hand across the table.

"Gratitude."

SUBDERMAL

Brian F. H. Clement

Karen lay flat on her back as her tattoo artist worked on the inside of her forearm. They had chatted for the first half hour about the deathly cold weather, and Karen's favourite warm-weather vacation spots to escape the northern chill, but had settled into silence. Karen let her eyes stare into the ceiling pattern, and started listing things in her mind she might want to make for dinner. She preferred to distract herself from the rapid-fire dragging needle jabs and the monotonous buzzing of the tattoo gun. *Just a small piece today. She has to be almost done.* Karen lifted her head to look down. Cassie, the artist, had only finished a little over half of the shading, and hadn't yet started the colour. Karen scowled at her own sense of time and let her head drop back down. The pain had become nearly numb, like a bad sunburn someone kept poking at.

The tiny bell above the door chimed as someone entered. Karen was unable to see who it was even when she lifted her head up, due to the large barrier for privacy behind the front counter. The sound of boots stomping, and the patting of a jacket to brush off snow came to Karen's ears. She frowned. She had heard the familiar sounds before in an identical pattern, but they confused her now. *Those are office noises.* She heard muffled voices, the hint of a Haitian-Canadian accent. *There's no way he's...*

"You can go back and see her," the receptionist said.

Michaud walked around the corner and looked at Karen with a smile. She wasn't unhappy to see him—she liked being in his presence, and working with him—but it was her day off and she had made this appointment two months earlier.

"You're going to run out of skin, Wendleton," he said, and stood at her feet.

"I get one in a weird spot, it makes more weird blank spaces that need to be filled. It's like a never-ending game of Tetris, boss," Karen said.

"I see what you mean."

"You're not working today, are you?"

"I don't stop."

"Yeah, well I do," Karen said, and dropped her head back.

"My uncle's shop is around the corner, and I went to visit, but he's not in. Made a trip of it. Don't worry, I'll wait 'til you're done. We have to look at a crime scene."

"Ugh," Karen groaned. "Sorry, Cassie. This is my boss. Detective Benoit Michaud. I'm the stone he keeps trying to draw blood from."

Michaud peered in at Karen's arm. "Looks like you have plenty of blood left. What is that? A skull with legs? Sorry, I didn't realize they bleed that much."

"Skull with a hermit crab living in it. Sort of part-Japanese style, like me," Karen said, jokingly referring to her parentage. "Kind of wish I could crawl into a shell right now and drop to the bottom of the ocean."

"This'll be fun. It's not even a murder." Michaud turned to the tattoo artist. "How much longer will you be?"

Cassie stopped working and sat back. "Thirty minutes, give or take. Have to bandage it up and everything. You can pull up a chair if you like."

Michaud looked back and forth, and moved to a sea-green padded chair nearer Karen's head and sat in it.

"What should we get for lunch?" Cassie said, to no one in particular. Two of the other tattoo artists stopped their work and looked at her.

"Matsubuchi Burger," Michaud offered. "It's down the street."

The receptionist poked her head around the privacy barrier. "You should get burgers. You never get burgers."

"Burgers," a male tattooer across the room said. "We never get burgers." His wry smile suggested an in-joke Karen wasn't aware of.

Karen looked back and forth at them. "Are you guys joking? You really don't get burgers all the time? I didn't just happen into a tattoo shop sitcom?"

Cassie shook her head "no," and gestured to the receptionist. "Burgers."

Karen turned her head to look at Michaud. He shrugged and smirked.

Karen carefully adjusted her jacket over the spot on her arm where the tattoo was, protected by bandages and multiple layers of winter clothing. She pulled her seatbelt across and clicked it closed. "So if it's not a murder, why are we looking at it?"

Michaud drove south to Dundas and waited for an opening to turn left. Traffic moved slowly in the steady snowfall. "Crimes with supernatural overtones, not just murders. They don't just give me the weird ones, remember? I request them." He leaned over the steering wheel and squinted through the snow.

Karen turned to look at him. "So you going to keep me in suspense? What is it, terrorists? Extortion? Kidnapping?"

Michaud took an opening in traffic and carefully threaded his vehicle into the eastbound crawl on Dundas street. "Robbery. Bank job, in the business district. High visibility, but they controlled the exits, and waited for a day like this when they knew police would have a hard time responding with traffic like it is in the snow."

Karen raised an eyebrow and upturned her hands in a questioning gesture. "So what's the weird part?"

"There were seventeen patrons in the bank at the time. They're all in comas."

Karen sighed. "All right. That *is* odd. But you had to pull me in on my day off?"

"Need your eyes on it. You're good at picking up patterns, seeing organization. I've got my hunches but want to make sure I'm not just being crazy. Fresh crime scene. Plus the bank wants to reopen Monday morning, so they want us to finish going over the scene in the next thirty-six hours. Forensics is in there now in bunny-suits. We can observe from the second floor deck."

Bunny-suits. Karen shook her head. It was the colloquial term for the head-to-toe white coveralls forensic investigators wore while they worked in order to avoid tainting a crime scene with their own hair, shoe dirt, fibers, or any other debris. When dressed in them, they did bear a superficial resemblance to bad rabbit costumes, minus the ears.

"They'll let me in? It has to be restricted access," Karen asked.

"If you're with me it'll be fine."

Michaud pulled up and parked behind a city police cruiser to the side of the glass-walled bank. An officer approached and leaned in to look in their window, but Michaud held up his badge to ward off the uniform. The front of the bank had been sealed off behind police line tape, so after Karen and Michaud exited his car, they moved to a side entrance. The flashing red and blue of police lights cast beams through the falling snow, which was beginning to taper off. A uniformed officer in a dark winter jacket and fur cap stood questioning a shivering security guard. Michaud waved at the officer and stepped inside with Karen.

"Where was security during all this?" Karen asked.

Michaud shook his head. "We'll need to ask the supervising officer here. From what I gathered already though, it sounds like they were hit with stun guns by members of the group who took over the bank. I'm going to go chat with the officer. Can you take a look at the security footage?" Michaud pointed to the glass-walled office in which a dazed-looking security officer gathered the relevant video files for playback.

Karen yawned and nodded. "Uh huh."

"You're not fading on me, are you Wendleton?"

Karen shook her head "no."

"Sorry, boss. Always feel exhausted after a tattoo."

Michaud smirked and patted her on the shoulder. She turned to the security booth and knocked on the glass, then stepped inside.

"Hey, need to get a look at the footage from during the robbery today please."

The security officer nodded and queued up four different monitors to the same time code and started playback. Karen leaned in, the bright glow of the screens illuminating her face. Across the different monitors she watched as the customers in the bank went about their business: filling out forms, chatting with tellers, looking at their phones as they waited in line. Suddenly, from two different entrances, people in grey hooded sweatshirts, sweatpants, and balaclavas swarmed into the bank brandishing machetes. They moved immediately to the security guards, and as Michaud mentioned, hit them all with stun weapons. At each entrance, two of the invaders stood guard while several others waved their blades at the terrified patrons and bank workers. After gathering the staff together and asserting their control with threats of dismemberment, the masked people moved from customer to customer, tearing open each one's shirt in teams of two. One held a bucket filled with a thick, black liquid, while the other dipped the machete in and used it to carve symbols into their victim's chest. Once this was accomplished, the person who had been cut fell to the ground and fainted. At first the attackers looked confused, as if expecting something to happen. Only after the attack was finished, and every customer lay unconscious on the floor, did the robbers actually take any money from the staff. One of them, Karen assumed the leader, looked back and forth, and directed his cohorts to gather money, almost as if improvising on the spot. The invaders then fled on foot, and the staff lowered their hands and rushed to the aid of the unconscious customers.

"That's it," the security guard said.

"Hmm. All done in under three minutes. Must've had it rehearsed pretty

carefully. Doesn't even look like they care that much about the money either," Karen said.

The guard shook his head and ran a hand over his dark, curly hair. "Been robbed here, once before. Never seen anything like this though. Fucking machetes. Jesus."

Karen took a deep breath. "Could all be bullshit too. Just trying to distract us with the symbol-carving. Might really just be about the money. Had a case I helped the Detective with last year. Stalker kept hounding this singer, leaving her creepy notes about sacrifices, sending her emails, messages over social media, using occult symbols. Started painting them up in venues she was scheduled to perform in. We looked into it. Wasn't a cultist at all. Guy was just an asshole trying to scare her."

"Did it work?"

"Yeah, it did. He mixed so many different things together it was easy to tell he was full of shit."

"That stuff, it smelled bad."

"What?"

"Sorry, when you said 'full of shit' it reminded me of the stink. The black goo they dipped the machetes in. Stunk. Smelled like moldy potatoes."

"I'll have to tell Michaud that. We'll need copies of all the video files, from every camera angle," Karen said. "Not how I wanted to spend my weekend."

"You got it officer," the guard replied.

Karen chuckled. "I'm not a police officer. I'm just a research assistant."

Michaud walked up and looked into the booth. "Anything? I'm going to stay here for a while and question the staff."

"Great footage of the whole thing. I'm surprised."

Michaud nodded, thinking. "Would you mind taking it and going over it in the station's video room? Make hard copies of anything important. If we have time we can visit the victims in the hospital. Otherwise we can continue tomorrow."

"Can do. Weird thing. They made no attempt to obscure the cameras or even avoid them."

Michaud shrugged. "The age we live in. Everybody wants to be seen. Maybe they wanted the footage to go viral after we release it."

Karen sat hunched over, her winter coat still on, and shivered as she stared into the monitors in the police video analysis room. The heat was set to a barely tolerable level, and to ward it off, she rubbed her hands up and down her arms, and only darted a hand out to adjust the settings on the playback unit. She sighed, set the video files to replay again, and took a sip from a mug of hot tea. She let the footage play again, and held the mug, letting it warm her hands. The attackers, seven of them, looked young. By their appearance, and in relation to the other people in the bank, they appeared to all be young men, late teens to early twenties, mostly pale complexions. Karen thought about what Michaud had said. *Did they want this to go viral? Did they want to be seen?* She paused a clip and expanded the video image, zooming in on the increasingly grainy monochrome image of a victim's chest as the robber attacked. She moved the clip forward frame by frame. At the distance from the camera, it was impossible to tell what was being carved into the person's skin, but she saw a pattern in the movement. *They're not just hacking and slashing. Every carving is the same.*

Karen sat back and folded her arms, then took another sip of her tea as she looked at the paused image. She shook her head and tapped the keyboard for printouts of several of the images. The pattern of the carving drew her attention. Something in the movement. *Too fluid. Practiced. The looks on the faces of the victims.* They didn't try to fight back, or run. They screamed, they flailed, but it looked contrived. Something about it felt rehearsed. And the way the attackers acted as if they expected something to happen, and then were almost surprised when they had to settle for robbing the bank. Something about it was all wrong...

"Hey, you almost done? It's been over an hour. We need to go look at the comatose victims before it gets too late," Michaud said. His voice snapped her attention back and she turned to look at him. Karen blinked and took a deep breath. Her eyes felt dry. Her tea sat, still half-full, on the desk next to the keyboard. There was no steam wafting off of it any longer. She felt the mug. It was cold, like the room.

"Sorry, I guess I must have dozed off. Not sure what happened there," Karen said.

"You were staring right into that monitor when I walked in here."

"Probably startled me awake. Should've said something first."

"I stood at the door and I said your name. Twice."

Karen frowned. She shook her head. "Weird." She stood up from the desk. Her legs were numb, and she stretched before she walked. She grabbed the printed sheets from the nearby printer and handed them to Michaud.

Karen and Michaud donned the required smocks, masks, and hairnets as handed to them by the nurse in the hospital. Despite the increasingly late hour, the ward contained a flurry of activity, most of which was the staff trying to keep multiple police officers from disturbing the patients. Aside from the expected winter accident trips to the emergency room, they had seventeen comatose bank patrons with gouges in their chests.

The harried nurse turned to Michaud and Karen. "I can give you brief access only. Your photographers are already taking pictures of the victims. We need to keep this short because we're still not entirely certain what happened to them, and we want to restrict this area to essential medical personnel only."

Michaud nodded, and Karen followed as they entered the ward. As the nurse had mentioned, a pair of police photographers, similarly attired to everyone else in smocks and masks, were in the process of shooting photos of every chest wound. Karen stepped closer to one of the beds, and immediately raised the back of her hand to her mask. The modly potato smell that the security guard mentioned was still evident. It was a foul, subtle reek that crept into her nostrils and hung stubbornly there. *If there was a full bucket of that stuff I'd probably throw up.* Karen looked around the room at the victims who had their wounds uncovered. She frowned. *All of them are in the same place. All the same shape. Like I thought.* The black substance had apparently spread out from around the wound, making subtle grey patches beneath the skin.

Michaud turned to another officer, who had been chatting with a doctor. "Kehoe. We're going to need to get some of the black liquid the attackers smeared their machetes with. Was there enough in the wounds to gather a sample?"

"Yes, detective. I've already taken some in sample jars and sent it in. We're getting photos of all the wounds, which are all the same shape and placement. There was no sign of resistance on the part of the victims. It's as if they just stood there and barely flinched."

Michaud nodded, looking around the room. "Probably more to this than a crazy robbery, but that hardly needs saying."

Karen turned and watched the staff as they worked on one of the victims, evidently the last who required treatment. The wounds had been cleaned already, and the police photographers quickly snapped additional photos from the end of the bed, and moved back. Karen stared into the pattern of the cuts. It resembled a down-turned crescent, with a pair of crescents below it facing outward, arranged in a triangular configuration. It looked like an inverted pyramid, or maybe the stylized head of an ox...

"What's the matter?" Michaud said, with the tap of his hand on her shoulder.

Karen turned to him. "What do you mean? Just looking at the wound."

"You didn't hear me? I said your name. Where'd you go off to, Wendleton? Spacing out on me?"

"What?" Karen laughed nervously. *I guess I was getting distracted, absorbed by staring at it. Why didn't I hear him?*

Suddenly, screams erupted behind them. Karen and Michaud spun around and were confronted with a scene of chaos. One of the victims had leapt off her bed, grabbed a food serving tray, and was swinging it wildly at everyone within reach. She wailed shrieks of rage as she slammed the tray into a nurse's arm, and swung it around at another. The police in the room, including Michaud, rushed to restrain her. As they grabbed hold of her wrists and disarmed her, Karen saw that the woman's eyes were covered over with black liquid, like what the attackers smeared their machetes with. It ran from her ears, eyes, nose and mouth. Karen was momentarily stunned, staring in disbelief at the bizarre situation. Her heart raced and she was frozen, unsure of what to do. *I'm just a civilian. They don't need my help. But do something!* Michaud and the others had pulled the raging woman back down onto the bed. All Karen could think of to do was draw out her phone and snap photos of the woman's face running with the repulsive black ichor.

The police held the woman down against the bed, and a doctor ran over with a syringe and injected her. The sedative acted quickly, and the screams became a low groan, and then finally a sigh into unconsciousness.

Michaud stepped back toward Karen, breathing heavily. He bent over to catch his breath with his hands on his knees, then drew himself back up. "Care to take a guess what that was?"

Karen was shocked into being speechless. She swallowed and took a breath, looked back and forth as if to search for her words, then spat out a stream of rapid thoughts. "Something in the substance on the machetes maybe. Looks just like what's running from her face. Maybe they were in on it with the attackers. Maybe it's the black ooze, causes psychotic violence. I mean... I don't know. Could just be that she woke up and freaked out because she didn't know where she was."

Michaud chuckled and took a deep breath. He put his hand on Karen's shoulder. "Go home and get some sleep. Need you refreshed for tomorrow. I'll pay for a cab. I've got to stay here for a bit and lock this down." He approached the other officers, who were equally stunned by what had happened. "I want all these attack victims restrained and sedatives ready on all of them in case what happened with her happens with any of the others. We don't want to take any chances."

Karen tossed and turned for an hour. The ancient radiator in her room blazed heat she couldn't control, a side effect of living in an older building. When she threw her bed covers back, the radiator cooled down, and she pulled the sheets back up. The image of the symbol carved by the attackers stuck in her mind, like someone had scrawled it on the inside of her eyelids and the streetlight outside her window illuminated it so she couldn't ignore it. Karen blinked, rubbed her eyes, and tried to control her breathing. Her mind went to strange places, made connections between the events of the day. Michaud's voice drifted through. *Everybody wants to be seen.*

She was warm. Too warm. She looked up from her hiding spot in the alley behind an overturned and smashed washing machine. The light from nearby fires turned the storefronts across the street into a dance of orange and yellow light fighting with shadow. Corpses littered the alley and into the street. Six, seven, eight of them. Men in vests screamed, laughed, and cheered maniacally as they fired rifles from behind their barricade of crashed cars. Karen couldn't see who they were shooting at. At once, all of the wild-eyed men turned on another in their midst and shot at him, pushed him back from their barricade, and riddled his body with bullets. They laughed and screamed. There was no reason that Karen could see. They were mad with bloodlust. She looked up at the wall of the alley, lit fleetingly by the fires in the street. The symbol from the chests of the bank robbery victims was painted up on the building, an enormous mural of blood.

Karen blinked, and she was on the roof of a warehouse. Two had pursued her to the far corner. They were streaked with blood, clothes torn and all semblance of civilization gone from their faces. They tried to balance on the peak of the roof, but both fell, one after the other, and tumbled off the side of the building with dull, meaty thuds as they hit the pavement below. Karen sat and looked out over the city. Fires raged. Plumes of smoke billowed, and explosions shot columns of flame into the air. Across it all, sirens, screams, and crashes echoed. She looked down at her hands, normal one moment, then in an instant she held her own hands, as if split into two bodies. Her other self was a mirror image. Her, but not her. The other Karen's hands were webbed, black, with splotches of orange. Other Karen handed her something, and she looked up into the face of her other self. Stripes of orange.

"You'll need this," she said.

Karen awoke with a gasp. She looked around her room, still dark but with the blue-grey light of pre-dawn. There were no killers, no screams, no blood. "What the fuck was that?" she whispered to herself. She looked at her hands. They were empty. The dream was still clear in her mind, more vivid than most she had. Something in it stuck with her. The symbol on the wall, in blood. It reminded Karen of the feeling of her skin crawling when disgusted, but this was if something were crawling inside her brain, a thought she couldn't shirk. She took a deep breath through her nose and slowly exhaled, then shuddered. *Hot room, dreamed about fire, and that stupid symbol. Breakfast will shake that off.* She swung her legs around out of the bed and sat up.

The station staff was still filtering in for the day shift as Karen arrived. She raced to the floor of Michaud's office and unzipped her winter coat as she moved. Her brisk pace had warmed her up within her insulated jacket and the itch of sweat formed on her back. The hall outside Michaud's office was empty, and his lights were on as Karen entered. The blinds were open, but the stark winter light barely filtered through enough to illuminate the walls lined with framed photos and his corkboard, covered with clippings of supposed supernatural occurences. She wasn't surprised to see Michaud at his desk, poring over papers and photographs from the bank robbery. She dropped her jacket on the table she used for work, and opened her laptop. The ideas that had come to her as she awoke still swirled in her mind.

Without looking up at her, Michaud spoke. "Two more of the victims woke up during the night and tried to attack their nurses. Good thing we had them restrained and sedatives ready." He held up a printout of the phone photos she had taken and sent him of the crazed woman at the hospital.

Karen stopped for a moment, but immediately went to work on her computer. She loaded images she had drawn to resemble the carved symbol from the attack, and fed them into an online reverse image search. Rows of similar picture files lit up Karen's screen. Many were cartoon images of ox heads, one a sign from a cattle ranch, and a few were geometry instruction diagrams. One stood out to her though: an image that was digitally drawn, of the same curved lines she recognized, drawn in black against a yellow background. Karen clicked the link and found herself on the public profile photo of someone named "ShroomBloom" on the social networking site Budsie. She clicked the profile photo, bringing up a description that read, "The Bloom begins soon, kids. Event info coming. It'll be big. It'll be famous. And no one will know what we're up to until it's over."

"Hmm," Karen said to herself as she looked over the page.

Michaud spoke up behind her. "Got the toxicology report back, by the way. The black goo on the machete is the same substance that oozed out of their faces. It had a significant fungal component to it. Live fungal spores. Gestation period of the spores propagating in the body was about three hours. Lab analyst thought they, uh... had an effect on the brain. Shuts down higher reasoning, increases aggression. Her theory anyway. Needs more time for a detailed analysis."

"ShroomBloom," Karen muttered to herself.

"No chance it'll become airborne based on what she said. We're lucky we had masks on though. Lab analyst said there's a fifty-fifty chance the black liquid from the face could infect someone else if introduced into a wound. I mean, I guess it's a good thing the stuff has to be concentrated to have any effect. Means they can't put it in the water supply or spray it over the city."

Karen didn't turn around. She began typing again, and searched through the site for more instances of the symbol and ShroomBloom's posts. A public group popped up called "Shroomies" and Karen looked through event postings and gatherings. The final post, which had been deleted, was for a "flashmob"-style event. It was to be located at the bank. She looked through group members, event attendees, and cross-referenced them with all the names of the bank attack victims, looking for similarities. She searched hashtags for "shroomies" and "thebloom." Everything was public with no attempt at secrecy.

"What the fuck?" Karen said. "Hey boss, what you make of this?"

Michaud was silent. Karen blinked away the dryness in her eyes from staring at the computer screen. She turned around.

"Boss?"

Michaud stared into the photos across his desk. He usually had an intense scowl when scrutinizing evidence or crime scene photos. This was different. He looked blank, emotionless.

"Detective Michaud," Karen said, more forcefully.

Michaud widened his eyes, blinked, and turned to Karen. "Yeah?"

"You didn't hear me? I was calling your name."

"I was just looking at this photo of the symbol carved into this person's skin," Michaud said, and pointed at it.

Karen frowned and walked over. "Same thing happened to me. I spaced out, remember? Staring at the symbol."

"I wonder," Michaud said, and pulled over the magnifying lamp he had attached to his desk. He lowered it and switched it on, then looked into the lens. "Yeah, take a close look at the edges of the wound." He backed away to let Karen in. She leaned over and saw what it was he had seen: the hint of blue-black outlines on the skin by where the cut marks were made, smaller than the grey spots she had noticed already. "Remind you of anything?" he asked.

"Yeah," she said, and leaned in closer to the magnifying lamp's lens. "Looks like a tattoo. Maybe a shitty stick-and-poke job done at home with a handheld needle, some ink, and a bottle of alcohol. Faded, like it didn't heal properly."

"It's not visible on the security footage, is it? Before the attackers started cutting, I mean."

"No, it's too far back and too grainy. The staff in the bank wouldn't have seen it either. Even if they did, they were probably too shocked to remember."

"So what if the attackers and the victims were all in on it together? They had the symbol tattooed on them, as a guideline for the cuts. Or maybe they didn't know what exactly was going to happen. But it looks more and more like all these people knew each other before the incident."

Karen stepped back and looked at Michaud. "That sounds like what I just found online. I think they knew each other, and met through a social media site or app. They were organizing events, totally in the open. Like you said, they wanted to be seen. And the symbol. It affected you and I both. What if it's not just a coincidence? What if it acts like some kind of visual hypnotic device, inducing a distracted mental state? Maybe one that makes the viewer vulnerable to suggestion."

"Now you're using your thinking cap, Wendleton," Michaud said with a smile.

"God, what if they wanted that symbol plastered up everywhere?"

Michaud's smile drooped back into a look of dead seriousness. "Shit. Did the news get a look at it?"

"They would have if everyone at the bank died, but no one did. They were bandaged and taken to the hospital too quickly."

Karen pulled her chair over and sat facing Michaud. "Okay, I know we're going far down this rabbit hole of 'what ifs' but try this one: the whole plan was to use the black goo to make everyone in the bank go on a killing spree right there. What I saw on those sites and event listings wasn't violent. It was all about having fun doing 'the bloom' like they were going to a party. Maybe the victims just thought it was going to be a fun prank, or a political protest, where they'd get hallucinogenic mushrooms. The symbol dulled their thinking over time, they got the tattoos from the leaders, the attackers, and the substance was meant to make them start killing people right there. But the guys with the machetes messed up. In the footage they stop for a second, like they're surprised. They didn't expect everyone to just black out. Maybe the dosage wasn't high enough. Maybe they didn't breed the fungus right. And instead everyone went comatose, and the murder impulse didn't kick in until hours later."

"Would've made more sense for them to go kill-crazy at the bank. More public victims, bright lights, more visible than the hospital, and guarantee the symbol winds up on the news and going viral online."

"Maybe the bank was just a trial run. The organizers, the guys with the machetes, they could be going for a second try right now. Getting more recruits, or using another batch we don't know about. They're tweaking the recipe. They didn't care about being secretive, remember? Maybe they thought they'd go out at the end in a blaze of destruction and finish their ritual."

"...or maybe they just want chaos. Maybe there's no reason for it. Maybe they just want to hurt people."

Karen shook her head. "So what do we do?"

Michaud took a deep breath. "No chance we can trace those machetes, or the outfits. Too generic. Not enough DNA evidence at the scene, and that would take too long, plus I doubt these guys are in the database. We'll have to work through the ingredients in the black goo. Where they would've got the spores, who would have had access to designer strains of biological materials, and how they got the equipment to handle it all without ingesting any of it themselves."

Michaud, being a police officer, had the credentials to look into purchases of equipment used for fungal cultivation on a broad scale. He searched through academic databases of people in biological science, mycology, and plant cultivation. Karen was limited to public news articles and social media posts. Outside Michaud's office windows, the grey winter skies made it dark despite the noon hour. The snow had ceased and it was quiet, for a Monday afternoon in the city.

Karen sat back and away from the screen. She stretched, and held her hands over her beleaguered eyes as she took a deep breath. "I need a nap."

"Most of this job is paperwork and research, Wendleton. I can count on both hands the number of times I've had to draw my weapon, in over a decade of police work. Hell, you don't even get to carry a weapon. You're a civilian. If you were hoping for a crazy rooftop chase today, you're probably out of luck."

Karen looked at her screen from between her fingers. Something stood out, as she saw all the reference lists and photos all at once, from a distance. "We're overthinking this," she said.

"What was that?" Michaud asked from his desk.

"You're looking for the same thing I'm looking for, right? Angry people, dismissed from a job, axe to grind, that sort of thing. Maybe they dabbled in conspiracy theories, the occult, all that. But we know from the video that they're a group of young men, late teens to early twenties. How about if it's just internet trolls taking it out of the online world and into real life? Maybe pissed at the world because girls won't date them. Or maybe they're just doing it for a laugh. They think it's funny that people will die."

"That's fucked up."

"Last year I read a book about the effect that repeated and intensive use of the internet has on the human brain. It makes distracted thinking the norm. Slow, methodical thinking atrophies. The cults that you and I have seen are all about years of devotion, sacrifice, pain, with little chance of reward, until their elder gods, or great apocalypse, or whatever happens. But these guys, the machete attackers, wanted instant gratification. So did the people who got cut, who were probably in it with them. The leaders probably just found out about something they could use and figured out a way to run with it. I don't think they came up with it all themselves. They might not even be smart enough."

Michaud nodded, and picked up his desk phone. He punched numbers and waited, tapping his hand against his desk. "Yeah, this is Detective Michaud. I need a list of recently reported missing persons between the ages of," he waved his hand in the air, trying to think of a range of ages. "…thirteen to twenty-nine. Excellent. Can you have it sent to my departmental email please? Thanks." He hung up the phone and turned to Karen. "I'm going to need you to cross-reference the names with any names that stuck out to you from the lists you have. If we're lucky we can find someone who was maybe in school for some of this stuff, was in that mushroom group, had any connection to the victims, and hasn't been seen for a couple days, or longer."

Driving north through the city was slow going in the slush. While the weather had abated, plows had only completed the major arteries, with smaller residential streets still deep with snow. Michaud drove while Karen rode beside him, reading over a set of notes that accompanied photographs she had printed out of the various people they sought. They had agreed their most promising person-of-interest was a twenty year old university student by the name of Connor Wilfred. He fit their profile perfectly: he had studied mycology, spent hours online arguing on message boards, had no girlfriend and few other friends of any kind, and had the financial resources to organize the concoction of the substance from the attacks. He had also not shown up for any of his classes or school group activities in over a week.

Karen held Wilfred's photo up in the waning later-afternoon light. "What's up with the bad Hitler Youth haircut?" The young man in the photo had a light dusting of mustache that looked like it belonged to someone several years younger desperate to appear older.

"No idea. Maybe he's obsessed with studying the military but would never join it. One of those guys."

Karen looked out the window and up at the passing streetlights. "Had a bad dream last night. One of those ones I had to reassure myself a few times after that I was awake and everything was all right."

Michaud kept his eyes on the road. "What was it about?"

"City was on fire. People killing each other. Everyone had gone crazy. I was just hiding. That symbol was painted up on a wall in blood."

Michaud chuckled. "You were just looking at it too long. The security camera footage too. No wonder you had nightmares. It gets easier the longer you're on the job. But yeah, that woman in the hospital scared the shit out of me too."

Karen shook her head disapprovingly. "No, it was more than that. It felt like a memory, but one that hadn't happened yet. Like I was trying to warn myself about something that's going to happen."

Michaud raised his eyebrows and shrugged as he drove. "Well I guess we better catch these guys before they have a bunch of people go on a rampage then."

"You get to catch them, boss. I just get to help you find them."

Michaud pulled up to the side of the Forest Hill road and parked. He looked at the imposing structure they sat in front of, a brownstone mansion the front door of which was flanked by columns. The wide front yard was a slightly rumpled, soft white blanket of snow. Michaud turned back to Karen after a few moments.

"What do you see?"

Karen leaned forward to get a better look at the house. "Lights are off. No movement. No tiretracks on the driveway. No footprints to the front door. Looks like no one's been in or out for at least a day."

Michaud nodded. "Good job, Wendleton. I'm going to head up there and knock on the door, ask questions of anyone who might actually be in there." He checked his sidearm and re-holstered it as he spoke, then attached a body cam to the front of his coat. He looked at his hand taser, then replaced it in the pocket on his belt. He pulled out a mini computer and handed it to Karen. "Monitor me on this. I'll have my earpiece and mic on so you can hear me and I can hear you. If you see anything while I'm at the door, or if I head around the back, call for backup. Got that?"

Karen nodded. "You don't have to worry about me coming to rescue you. I'm not even armed."

"Don't forget it. You're a civilian. I hate filling out paperwork on civilians who die on my watch," Michaud said with a mischievous smile.

Karen smirked and rolled her eyes. "Yeah, yeah. Get moving."

Michaud checked over the camera and switched it on, then stepped out of the vehicle, and shut the door behind him. He trudged through the snow directly toward the front door. Karen flipped open the computer monitor and switched it on, and went to the feed for Michaud's camera. She fumbled with the wires for the headset, but managed to get it on just as Michaud reached the door. He appeared to already be speaking.

"...hear me yet? I'm just at the door now."

"Sorry, just got the mic on. I can see your feed fine."

Michaud knocked on the door. Karen looked at the monitor image of his hand using the brass door-knocker, and then up at the distant sight of him at the building through the car window. She began recording the video feed.

"No answer at the door. I'm checking the front window."

Michaud moved over and peered inside, allowing the camera to view the interior as well. Karen squinted at the dimly lit room. The furniture was antique, or designed to look like it, and all the trappings inside the house gave off the air of years of high-priced collecting. Past the front room, little else was visible, and nothing stirred. Michaud panned down. Two human bodies lay on the floor, motionless.

"Holy shit!" he said, and backed away. "I'm uh, going to get a better image of the two bodies in the living room. I can't tell if they're dead, or unconscious." He moved the camera to get a better view, and knocked on the window as loud as possible without breaking the glass. Karen was able to see the pair were a man and a woman, who looked to be in their fifties or sixties, greying hair and both in sweaters. There were no obvious signs of a struggle, nor blood or trauma to the two people. "I'm going to have to check on them. They might still be alive. Call it in, get someone else out here as soon as possible."

Karen looked around the car for Michaud's backup radio, and saw on the monitor that he was working on the front door with his police-issue lock gun, a small device used to pick locks.

"Okay, I'm proceeding inside now to assess the condition of the two individuals who appear to be unconscious or possibly deceased," Michaud said, for the benefit of the recording. "If they're dead, I'll exit immediately to avoid further tainting the possible crime scene."

Karen pulled the radio out of the glove compartment, switched it on, and worked the frequency tuner. She looked up again. Michaud was in the front room, standing near the window. One of the upstairs windows had a light on in it. Something stirred, a fleeting silhouette that was at the corner of the window, then was gone.

"What the hell?" Karen muttered. The light switched off, and the upstairs window was again dark. "Detective, I think there's someone in the house with you. Upstairs. Can you hear them?"

"What? No, don't hear anything here."

"I saw a light on upstairs. Someone just shut it off. I saw a shadow of a person, I think."

"Shit."

Karen looked at the monitor. Michaud had drawn his handgun and held it out in front of him, braced by his flashlight. The beam lit up a circular spot across the room as Michaud scanned toward the stairs.

"This is the Toronto Police! If you're upstairs I need you to come down immediately with your hands in the air."

Karen looked up at the house again. She could see Michaud's back as he moved away from the window and toward the stairs. The two people who were unconscious on the living room floor stood up behind him.

Karen shouted in a panic. "Michaud! Behind you!"

She turned to the monitor as Michaud spun around and the camera view revealed the faces of the two people as they rushed toward him, screaming. Their eyes, noses, and mouths ran with the black liquid she had seen at the hospital on the attack victims. Michaud yelped as both of them grabbed at him. The body cam was knocked off and to the ground. Karen's view on the monitor became a static image along the hardwood floor as Michaud's feet shuffled by. *I have to get in there! I don't care what he told me to do.*

Karen fumbled with the radio as she ran toward the house. "This is Karen Wendleton assisting Detective Michaud at 383 Ravensdale road, he's in serious danger and needs backup and an ambulance immediately!" she said as she took leaping strides through the snow. All Karen heard was the pounding of her pulse in her ears and her own gasping breaths as she reached the porch. *No gunshots. Is that good?*

She raced to the open door and looked inside. Michaud stood, panting, over the two who had attacked him. They both lay motionless on the floor again. Michaud, with only one set of handcuffs, had cuffed them to each other. He held his taser in one hand. He turned to look at Karen.

"Damn it, Wendleton. Did you at least call for backup?"

Karen nodded, wide-eyed. "Uh-huh."

Michaud holstered his sidearm as he shook his head at her. He turned at the sound of running footsteps. Someone raced from the stairs toward the back of the house. Michaud groaned and gave chase. Karen heard the sound of a back door being thrown open. She stepped back from the front door of the house, unsure of what to do. She turned at the sound of Michaud's yelling, an incoherent mass of sound she guessed was along the lines of "stop right there, you're under arrest." A thin, pale young man ran from the back of the house around to the front yard, clad only in a thin dress shirt. Karen was certain it was the student they were looking for. She kept her eye on him as she bent to gather snow, compacting it into a hard ball. Michaud was trying to keep pace with him, but they both stumbled in the deep snow. Karen stepped off the porch and set her feet. *Summer softball, don't fail me now.* She wound her arm back and threw the snowball. It hit the young man in the side of the head with a hard "paff." He jerked to his side and fell in the snow, just long enough for Michaud to reach him and tackle him as he tried to get back to his feet.

"I don't like running in the snow," Michaud said. The man was pinned under Michaud's considerably bulkier mass.

Karen walked toward both of them. As she saw his face more clearly, she knew that it was indeed Connor Wildred. He held his arms up. They shook with nervousness as he stuttered. "I'm sorry! I didn't, I didn't..." The wails of sirens approached, and an ambulance followed by a patrol car rolled up, lights flashing. The red and blue strobes lit up Connor's face. His eyes were watering and his nose ran with snot. "Oh God! I don't want to go to jail!"

Michaud rolled his eyes. "Then tell us where your friends are. We want ShroomBloom and all the other creeps with the machetes. Did you do that to your parents inside? Did you put that fungus shit in them?" Two paramedics and two uniformed officers approached. Michaud pulled his badge off his belt to show them and pointed them toward the house.

"I, we, I didn't, it was just a joke!" Connor spat out. "I mean, yeah, they deserved it. We had to be sure we got the batch right this time."

"You were going to do it again? Another attack?"

Connor's face squished into a pitiful pre-cry. "Please don't hurt me. I'll tell you where they are." Michaud sighed and hauled the youth up by his forearm.

The trio drove into the downtown core, with Connor sulking in the back seat. Once he had given up the location where he believed the rest of the attackers were, he crumpled into a moping sack. Karen turned around and looked at him. He looked out the window, either unable or unwilling to make eye contact. His breath formed a circle of condensation on the glass that matched the colour of the clouds.

"Did you kill your parents?" she asked.

"They're not dead," he snapped back, suddenly looking at her. "The fungus, it can be removed from their systems. We don't have the anti-toxin but I know it can be synthesized. I shouldn't even talk to you without a lawyer."

"I'm not a police officer. I just want to know why you did it. Off the record."

Connor shook his head. " I thought I'd make money. It was an investment. I thought I'd make a lot of money."

This information was something entirely unexpected by Karen, and not something she had considered. "How? How do you make money off making people indiscriminately violent?"

Connor looked down at his lap. " I didn't want it to go so far and be so violent. That wasn't my idea."

"But you went along with it."

"I had the capital. I bankrolled most of it. We started off trying to make a fast-growing mycoprotein strain, as a food substitute. But then we stumbled on the Kuro fungus. It has psychoactive properties but then they bred it and worked it until it caused the violent outbursts." Connor held his hands palms up. "They thought we could release it, and then sell the cure. Jack up the price. My investment, my profit. Simple as that."

"Your 'shroomies' group?"

"Just a way to get people interested. We mostly got ravers. Didn't think anyone would notice if they O.D.'d."

"That symbol, the one you carved into everyone's chests, was that your idea?"

Connor sighed. "No, that was Steve. He's the one who thought this was all part of some higher purpose. He pushed for increasing the violence-inducing properties of the fungus." Karen flipped through the photos in her files for anyone named Steve. He had huge round glasses, bad skin, and a ratty ponytail, and wouldn't have looked out of place in a bad 90's alt-rock band. Connor continued, "The rest of us thought it was a good marketing tactic. Perfect clickbait, right? Like a fishing lure. People see the symbol, click the ad while they're online, buy the black goop. Boom, profit. The first attack videos would go viral and we'd monetize them to make even more money. The symbol would be like a brand inside their brain." His excitement was palpable and Karen found it disgusting.

"Just that easy, huh?" Michaud said without looking away from the road. "Great business model."

Connor looked back and forth at Karen and Michaud. "You're not taking me to the condo building now, are you? I mean if they see me with you they'll know I talked."

"You afraid?" Michaud said.

"Well, they have machetes."

"We're taking you to be booked first. And it doesn't matter, we would've found your friends eventually. You guys weren't exactly secretive about any of it."

"The more obvious we were, the better. Didn't think the police would track us down so quickly though."

Karen was nonplused. "You wanted to be caught?"

"Eventually, sure. We'd be like celebrities. Can you imagine our follower count?"

Michaud shook his head. Karen could tell he was restraining himself. She knew the Detective had a history of drinking before he sobered up, and this was probably a moment he wished he'd be able to take a swig of whiskey and then wallop Connor with the bottle.

Michaud drove the car to the side of the road in front of the Crystal Tower condominium building. Like many other condo buildings that had recently gone up in the southern part of the downtown core, it was an immense, glass-coated structure that featured some intentionally asymmetrical outcroppings, which helped distinguish it from the other myriad nearby skyscrapers. From the street, Karen was able to see the fourth floor gym, in which spandex and tanktop-clad denizens went about workout routines and rode stationary bikes. Three patrol cars pulled up behind them and the uniformed officers gathered around Michaud for instructions.

"Don't think these guys have any firearms," Michaud said. They've got machetes, maybe stun guns, but they probably won't come at us with them. They're mostly just dumb kids who wanted attention. They'll probably knuckle under as soon as they see us. Be ready for anything though. Worst case scenario, they've gotten poisoned by the substance they cooked up and will go apeshit when they see us." He handed each officer a dust mask and set of goggles. "In the event they try to hit us with the black liquid they were using, we should put these on before we we enter the unit. There's a slight chance the substance can enter our bodies through our mouths or nostrils and infect us. It's unlikely unless it's introduced directly into the bloodstream, but don't take any chances."

After a few brief words with the concierge, Michaud, the other officers, and Karen were accompanied by a security guard to the forty-sixth floor. The elevator ride was tense but quick. Karen stood in the back, unable to see the door through the wide-shouldered forms of the uniformed police. The only one she was able to see over was a redheaded woman officer whose hair was tied up into a tight braid under her cap.

The elevator doors opened with a swift "whoosh." No one moved. Karen was unable to see what was the matter. The smell, however, hit her immediately. It was the noxious, pungent stench she had smelled at the hospital, like rotten potatoes magnified a thousand times.

"Masks and goggles," was all Michaud said.

Karen did as instructed, as did all the officers. They all slowly filed out, and Karen was able to see what had surprised them. The hallway, floor to ceiling, was coated in foul, dark green tendrils of creeping mold, sprouting out from the doorframe of the unit they had come to investigate, 4619. The door was ajar. Michaud and one of the uniformed officers moved forward and drew out their flashlights. Michaud lightly tapped the door with his foot to open it all the way and shone his light inside. From behind the officers, Karen saw a scene of nightmarish carnage. Bodies, five of them, lay splayed out across the floor and draped over furniture. Each had deep knife wounds. In the hands of most were machetes, with a pair lying on the ground amongst puddles of blood. Crimson streaks were splashed everywhere. The mold grew onto everything: across tables and chairs, up the walls, over the corpses, and covering the windows. Michaud shone his flashlight up onto the far wall. Amongst the random splatters of blood and encroaching trails of mold was a message written hastily in blood: "I got under your skin."

"Jesus Christ," one of the officers whispered. The silence was only broken by the sound of wind rustling the gore-stained white curtain as it hung across the half-open balcony door.

An ear-splitting shriek tore through the air. Michaud and the other officer shone their flashlights toward it, and saw the red-soaked form of a young man running toward them. Two officers drew their handguns and aimed. One yelled, "Freeze! Hands up! Do it now!" Other officers chimed in, barking orders at the crazed assailant.

In the chaos and bobbing light of the flashlights, Karen saw that the young man's skin and clothes, amongst the blood, was covered in drawings of the hypnotic symbol. He stopped and held the machete in front of him with both hands, eyes fixed on the blade. It was Steve from the photo Karen had seen, but his glasses were missing and his hair had been cut short. There was no black liquid running from his face like the others.

"Put the knife down now! Put it down!" Michaud yelled.

The blood-drenched man stood shaking for a moment. His eyes darted back and forth, and they welled up with tears. He dropped the machete to the ground with a clatter. He looked at Michaud and the other officers, and shook his head in denial, as if just for a moment he realized what had happened. As the officers moved toward him, he screamed again, then turned and ran for the open balcony door.

"No!" Michaud shouted. The assembled officers jumped toward him, but it was too late. Steve leapt over the guard rail and into the cold darkness. Michaud and another officer looked over the railing just as they heard the distant crash of Steve's body hitting the building's glass atrium roof forty-six floors below. Michaud was speechless for a moment, until his sense of duty took over. He turned around and stepped back inside the living room. "Call forensics. Call someone about this mold. We might have to quarantine this floor, or the whole building. We're probably all going to need to be decontaminated. Holy fuck," he said, and shook his head.

The officer with the flashlight spoke up. "Did he do all this, or did they do this to each other?"

Michaud looked around at the bodies. "Each other. I think he just rode it out. Knew we were coming and got them all to kill each other."

Karen's mind flashed back to her nightmare. The mutilated corpses in front of her made her cringe backward as she recalled the world she had seen in her dream. She spoke up from the doorway. "All this for some attention. They wanted to be noticed. I guess it worked."

"I can think of more productive ways to make people want to look at you," Michaud said with a terse grumble.

"Get the feeling this won't be the last time we see something like this."

Michaud looked at her. "I hope you're wrong, Wendleton."

HOUSE OF DANDRIDGE

Jason White

The house stood like a blackened tooth in an otherwise clean mouth. A rotten fang that stabbed Samuel Dandridge's memory and chewed his brain raw. The last time he'd seen the house had been from the back of a police cruiser. He'd strained his much younger body in his seatbelt to watch the house slowly disappear through the rear window. Aside from nightmares, he had never set eyes on the black-painted monstrosity again.

Until now.

Today, the house was his.

He looked up at the black shutters, the black flower beds hanging from the bottom-floor windows. Had Aunt Aldornia ever planted black daisies in there? Maybe her leaving the house to him in her will was a cruel joke.

Fucking bitch.

But he was here, wasn't he? He didn't have to be. He could have left the house in the past where it belonged. Instead, he had come to its threshold like some penitent servant. But he had nothing to repent. If anything, the house needed to repent to him.

Samuel laughed and shook his head. As if this house would ever apologize to him, even if it were possible.

So why was he here? Could it be so simple to close a painful chapter in his life and move on?

Maybe.

Better yet, there was money to be made here.

Although he had not seen Aunt Aldornia since he'd been taken away, he had hoped she'd at least painted the house a different color. Aldornia was too much like her brother, Samuel's father. They'd loved that black. And they had the same midnight black hair, identical thick eyebrows which peaked mischievously, making them both look like the Devil's children. His father's pointed goatee added to the demonic appearance.

Samuel climbed the steps to the front door. He stopped his finger from ringing the bell. He owned the house now. He could enter and leave as he pleased.

The dark, cavernous interior reminded him of a funeral home or some ancient Gothic mansion. It smelled of dust and antique wood. Nothing had changed from when he'd lived here. The place had been frozen in a time capsule during the past seventeen years. He turned around, inspecting the wood-paneled walls and high ceiling and, when he had come full circle, his heart nearly stopped.

An old and wrinkled face stared down at him. Her eyes and mouth formed three straight lines holding no emotion, though Samuel saw the spark of recognition.

Even the Dandridge servants hadn't changed.

"Coral, it's been years," he said, his heart now pounding at the surprise.

She nodded. He'd forgotten her height. He felt like a ten-year-old, standing before her. It made him lightheaded.

"You have grown much, Samuel." she said, her voice a sharp knife cutting through the ether. "Your room is ready. Follow me."

"But… I didn't even phone to let you know I'd be coming."

She turned her back to him, heading toward the massive staircase. She laughed, a sound he had never heard come from her before.

"I did not doubt that you'd return, Samuel," she said. "I didn't doubt it at all."

Two servants shuffled in and out of Samuel's old bedroom as he and Coral entered. They carried extra pillows and blankets to the bed, their eyes staring at the floor as they passed, as though he were a prince rather than a simple heir. He didn't mind. They were the first difference he'd come across in the old house. And they were young with firm breasts. Samuel stiffened below the belt as he turned to admire how their light blue uniforms exaggerated the flow of their bodies.

Oh, the possibilities. He chuckled. *If only I weren't selling the damned place.*

"You can play later," Coral said, calling his attention back to her own tall and bulky shape. Behind him, the maids giggled as they came back into the room.

Had he heard the old woman, right? The stiffness in his pants loosened under that constant frown of hers. As though her words held a magical effect, he followed her back into the hall. He glanced back at the women working on the bed, and this time they returned his stare. Both smiled and blushed. That Coral wanted him to play with the maids later made him feel… repulsed.

He turned and followed Coral down the hall, trying to keep his voice calm as he talked.

"I don't plan on staying the night. I booked a room at the Marriot downtown."

Coral laughed. Again, the high-pitched, witchlike sound surprised him.

"Don't be stupid," she said. "You'll stay here tonight, where you belong. Marvell can collect your luggage later."

"I don't think you understand," he said. "I don't want to stay here. I don't even plan on keeping the place."

She stopped and turned. He almost rammed right into her. Her eyes danced over his face before finally resting on his own eyes. When she smiled, her teeth yellow with gaps between each tooth, it didn't seem real. It looked mean.

"No, I don't think you will," she said. "You've inherited too much just to give it up."

Samuel frowned. The way Coral spoke those last words seemed as though she meant something else. Something darker. And now her eyes sparkled with some hidden joy. It turned Samuel's blood to ice.

Still, he followed her back down the stairs. As promised, an old man Samuel also recognized hauled in his luggage. He, too, was tall with salt and pepper hair that wrapped around a shiny dome. He sported a goatee.

Coral turned and smiled. "You can take Mr. Dandridge's luggage up to his room, Marvell," she said, without taking her eyes off Samuel.

"My suitcases were locked in my trunk," Samuel said, returning her stare while patting his pockets, looking for his keys. "I don't remember giving anyone the keys, never mind the permission to go through my car!"

Marvell stepped by Samuel as though he hadn't even spoken. This close, the man looked much older, his face skeletal and absent of life. His eyes were sunken back into their sockets, giving the appearance of caves resting above the rocky cliffs of his cheekbones.

"You put your keys where your father used to put his," Coral said, motioning. "Right on the hook beside the front door."

He wanted to argue that he'd done no such thing. It was useless to waste energy on it. Let the old woman think whatever she wants. Soon, she'd be unemployed, looking to spook some other unfortunate family. The thought warmed him, gave him power. Power he directed at Coral as he looked back up at her. But she was no longer staring at him. Instead, her gaze followed Marvell as he shuffled zombielike up the stairs, one of Samuel's two suitcases in each hand. Her smile evolved from sinister joy to hunger.

And something else, something that rescinded whatever power Samuel thought he had gained over her. How silly to expect a simple thought could beat this creature! The sparkle had returned to her eyes, now awed and ecstatic. Filled with worship.

"I've been looking forward to this day ever since you left," Coral said. With that, she composed herself. Her smile faded, letting the frown lines return.

After chasing the maids away from his bedroom, Samuel crossed to the table next to the fireplace. There he found a decanter half-filled with what he assumed was scotch. He poured himself a couple fingers and sniffed the bronze liquid. He was satisfied to find he was right. It burned like heaven going down, and within seconds, it coursed through his blood stream. He hadn't eaten in at least twelve hours, and the alcohol soothed his aching muscles, distracted his mind from nonsense.

He decided to stay; not because of his old caretaker, Coral, nor her prostitute underlings. No, he'd stay because his suitcases were already here, his eyelids hung heavily from the long journey, and he'd save money in doing so. The thought joined ranks with the alcohol, and he smiled as he sat down in the plush chair beside the table and decanter. Perhaps he'd get the fireplace working and sit here until he fell asleep, drinking glass after glass of this liquid gold.

As though summoned, Marvell came in carrying a silver tray covered in a massive dome. He smelled the greasy meats and steamed vegetables within. The old man placed the tray on the table beside the decanter. From there, he headed to the fireplace and pulled a lighter from his pocket. Kneeling, the old man flicked the lighter until flames caught. With that done, and without once having acknowledged Samuel's presence, the old man turned and sauntered out of the room.

Just like my childhood, he thought.

The flames licked the air, warming his face. He was at peace, so comfortable that if he just closed his eyes, he'd drift away. He hadn't felt this calm in days. Not since learning that he'd inherited this ancient manor. Eventually, he did let his eyes close. What was the harm? For good or ill, he was here for the night. He might as well just let himself relax... and slip away...

There came a knocking, like a giant's footsteps stomping around downstairs. It shook the foundations of the house, and Samuel sat up, the bed sheets covered in his sweat. Wide-eyed, he looked around the dark room and heard a new sound; voices echoed in the night, providing background music to the infernal pounding.

The voices chanted words he knew to his very core. He swung his legs from under the sheets. He was terrified of touching the floor with his bare feet, as if doing so would cause the chanting and pounding to reach up through the floor and grab him.

But he had to. If he stayed here, he'd go insane.

The cold hardwood floor stung the soles of his feet. He noticed the bed was much higher than he remembered, coming up to his stomach. All the furniture was bigger, as if someone had snuck in while he slept and switched it all. He looked down at the pajamas he wore. Cowboys and horses. They covered his child-sized body.

He shook his head to clear the dream.

He stepped into the hallway. A breeze swirled around his body, cold fingertips dancing upon his skin. Whispers flooded his ears, speaking languages he'd never heard. They momentarily drowned out the cacophony from the lower floors, and he knew they urged him onward.

The chanting and pounding were louder as he headed down the staircase. Pictures bounced against the walls. One of the pictures, a photographic portrait of his father, shattered on the floor. Samuel barely noticed these, barely noticed the broken shards of glass piercing his feet and the bloody footprints he left behind.

On the bottom floor, he turned the around the bend and headed for the kitchen. Then the basement's entrance. The pounding was a rhythm that reverberated through him, becoming one with his racing heart.

Allor Allor Manatis Satanis. Allor Allor Manatis Satanis. Allor Allor Manatis Satanis.

He knew it by heart.

It haunted his past and future. And yet...

...and yet...

Why fight it? Why make this a negative experience?

The smoothness of the hardwood floor turned rough and splintered as Samuel stepped into the cold, damp stairwell leading down, down, down...

Allor Allor Manatis Satanis! Allor Allor Manatis Satanis! Allor Allor Manatis Satanis!

His skin itched. It burned. His muscles ached all the way to the bone, as though some unseen force twisted and stretched his flesh beyond its limitations. The sensations summoned a flood of memory. Memory of

—Allor Allor Manatis Satanis Allor Allor Manatis Satanis Allor Allor Manatis Satanis—

great transformation. Of pain and wonder and great terror.

ALLOR ALLOR MANATIS SATANIS ALLOR ALLOR MANATIS SATANIS ALLOR ALLOR MANATIS SATANIS!

In the basement now, surrounded by pitch black darkness. Wait! A light flickered in the almost liquid motion of candles in sync with their atmosphere and Samuel's intrusion. It came from a room across the vast field of darkness.

The sounds made his ears ring, and they too came from the room. He crossed the cement floor.

ALLOR ALLOR MANATIS SATANIS ALLOR ALLOR MANATIS SATANIS ALLOR ALLOR MANATIS SATANIS!

Did he want to enter? Did he truly want to know what was in that room?

He stepped in. Expectant, exultant faces lit by soft light waited for him. They were so much shorter than Samuel, as though he had grown on the journey down the stairs. They wore black robes. A circle hung on the wall behind them, a star lined throughout the center. Within the star was the face of a goat; its chin the bottom point, its ears the left and right points, its horns to two upper points.

The chanting stopped.

The pounding morphed completely into Samuel's heartbeat.

Congregants and interloper stared at each other for what felt like forever, until the closest robed figure—his mother, Samuel realized—raised her hands and screamed:

"He has come!"

He looked down. Newly formed muscles bulged from beneath the tatters of his pajamas.

No longer did he feel the coldness of the cement floor beneath his feet, nor did he feel small and insignificant. His legs, no longer human, resembled an animal's, covered in black fur and bending in two separate places, with hooves instead of feet. The black fur also covered his stomach. His chest, once skin and bone, now supported two medium breasts, like a woman's.

His goatish screams filled the underground cavern. They echoed off the walls. The people down here with him joined in his fury. He swiped his powerful hands at them; their crimson innards flowed, splattering, soaking...

Samuel awoke, his heart pounding, the bed sheets covered in his sweat. The only light came from the dying flames of the fireplace. He sat up, his head still spinning from the alcohol. It was unlikely someone had stripped and carried him to his bed while he slept. A light sleeper, he usually woke if someone merely entered the same room as he. Unless he had stumbled here all on his own? Had he drunk so much he'd forgotten how he had fallen into his old, childhood bed?

He sat up and looked across the room, to the fireplace, where he'd sipped whiskey. The bottle of bronze liquid was still nearly full, so he hadn't blacked out. He hadn't even gotten drunk. Still, his head hurt, and his tongue and throat felt like they were made of sandpaper.

As he rubbed his eyes he noticed the movement within the murky shadows. On the other side of the room, opposite the fireplace, a woman moved gracefully as though guided by a breeze. There was something inhuman about her. A green glint to her eyes caught the light of the fire. When she smiled, her teeth were like that of a great white shark, pointed triangles capable of tearing through flesh with ease.

"Welcome home," she said, her voice a snake's hiss. She bent toward him, fluid and hypnotizing. Her smile grew, and thick strains of drool dripped from her teeth. "I've waited so long."

Samuel grew hard despite the mere vision of her turning his blood to ice. He recognized something about her.

She laughed as though reading his mind. She leaned in closer, closer, closer...

Samuel closed his eyes, but nothing happened.

When he opened them again, he was alone. The woman had disappeared into the ether from where she had come.

Sleep would not come for the remainder of the night. Hours stretched into centuries. The glowing embers of the fireplace cast playful shadows onto the ceiling. As the shadows slowly died, Samuel puzzled over his experience. Were the dreams actual memory? Was the strange woman a part of that dream?

He debated whether he should leave or stay. This time yesterday, he'd had no intentions of staying at all. Yet here he was. Perhaps his unconscious mind forced him to stay here, to confront old demons that had followed him throughout the years. Upon reflection, Samuel realized he had spent his entire adult life running from this very house and the memories it held. He had travelled the world with the funds his parents had left him, never letting anyone get too close.

Tonight, that aloneness had turned to loneliness. Exhaustion. In all his life, he had never felt this empty. He had also never craved the company of another person as he did right now. It was almost enough to drive him out of his bed, to pack his clothes and escape. But he remained staring at the ceiling, the dancing orange and black fading to complete darkness.

He would stay.

Either that or sell the place—closing permanently the gate for finding peace with his ancient, child self.

The sun rose, a blinding spotlight that shined through the massive windows. He dressed and showered. When he left his chambers, the smells of cooked eggs, bacon, and the aroma of brewing coffee permeated his nostrils. He felt made of the hardest metal.

The feeling died when he entered the kitchen, sat down at the table, and looked into Coral's eyes.

"You saw her, didn't you?" she said. And there was that smile of hers again. That goddamned fucking smile.

He spent the day in stale offices—with lawyers and bankers—and then the funeral home and real estate agency. He told the latter to hold any advances on selling his new property; he was undecided as to what he would do with the manor just yet. The concerns of death and how it had benefited him sucked his day away.

Death, he thought while eating a Big Mac in his rented Ford, *is a full-time job.*

He could count the times he had met Aunt Aldornia on one hand, so the business of arranging her burial was cold. He was already a rich between his own ventures and what his parents had left him, but his aunt's death quadrupled his wealth. That should have made him feel satisfied, at least. But he felt nothing for his newly found wealth, felt nothing for Aldornia who was found dead by the entrance of her bedroom, her hands clutching at her chest, her face blue and eyes wide.

Samuel couldn't shake that image. Had she seen the same things as he had: the woman with the sharp teeth and glowing, green eyes.

The thought made him smile, almost vengefully. It was her brother, after all, who had called forth the dark gods in his childhood, staining the fabric of his reality, separating him from the herd of humanity.

But why regard this as such a bad thing? Perhaps he'd simply been born into it. Genetics. Learned behavior. It didn't matter. There was power in all this, somewhere. The dream last night where he had turned into a devil-goat standing ten feet tall on two powerful legs proved it.

As the day progressed, he felt better and better. He'd almost ignored the whole situation, but now was glad he had decided to come. In fact, he couldn't wait to get back to the manor. He wanted to investigate. He had other worlds to explore.

That night, Samuel ate his dinner downstairs amongst the hustle and bustle of the two young maids, Coral, and a wandering Marvell. The young maids fussed over his food and kept his drink filled, all the while bending over to show off ample cleavage. Life returned to his nether regions as they worked around him. The fantasy of taking advantage of them no longer seemed so disgusting.

He was returning to his old self. His old self, but now with acceptance of the power that had haunted his past.

He had to find a way to harness that power. And he had to do it on his own. He couldn't just call up his parents' old devil worshiping friends and suggest a ritual for old times' sake. He chuckled. Coral glared at him as she passed through the dining room.

The first of his plans he began once he had dismissed the young maids from his bedchambers and the rest of the house had grown silent. Wearing nothing but a robe and the stench of sweat and sex, Samuel headed into the corridor outside. The carpeted floor caressed his bare feet. A crop of goose bumps blossomed along his arms and shoulders. He considered going back into his room and fetch some clothes, if not a sweater, but decided against it. He went down the twisting stairs onto the main floor. The kitchen was dark and still smelled of roast beef from dinner.

The basement door, made of solid wood, looked identical to the one in last night's dream. The steps were freezing. They groaned beneath his bare feet, only getting colder as he went. and he cursed himself at not slipping into his Nikes. Yet, if he got his shoes now, he might decide to stay in the warmth and safety of his room. No, he had come too far to turn around.

He swiped at the sweat on his forehead with the sleeve of his robe before it had the chance to blind him. Not that he could see in this inky blackness. And was the silence humming in his ears a blessing or a curse? Finally, he reached the bottom and hit the light switch. Horrid, orange light filled the room.

Nothing lay in wait. Not even the ghosts of his memories.

What had he expected? To change physical form once the light was on? Did he feel that the descent into darkness was a symbolic death, and the light a sort of rebirth into power?

Insanity!

He laughed, the sound of his voice echoing through the empty chambers of the underground world.

So empty down here! Weren't most basements cluttered with storage? He stumbled around, careful not to step on any nails or glass shards. The Baphomet pentagram he remembered stenciled at the center of the floor was also gone. Yet, if he listened carefully, he could almost hear the chanting of long ago...

Allor Allor Manatis Satanis

...but it was less than a whisper. More like the sigh of his thoughts, a wind blowing through dimensions, dying as fast as it came.

He checked the other rooms, where he finally found the usual boxes full of nothing but knickknacks, old and broken clocks, moth-eaten clothing. The wine cellar he found stocked with vintage wines from the 1990s and early 2000s. From these, he selected a bottle of Chateau Lafite Rothschild Pauillac from 1996, perhaps the most expensive here, and returned to his room.

He sat by the table, near the whiskey and fireplace. He watched the flames die while sipping the wine. His eyelids grew heavier by the minute. He thought about heading to the bed, where he could stretch out and drift away, but he couldn't move. He sat paralyzed with drowsiness. Paralyzed with his imaginings of power having been swept right out from under his feet.

Self-pity nearly swallowed him. Did he really think he would change into the devil and inherit all the power of the world?

A nice dream, he thought, closing his eyes. Devilish power. Satanic yearnings he never knew he had.

But it was all bullshit. Nothing but some fragment from his fucked-up childhood coming back to haunt him. Was it really a surprise, considering he now slept in the room of the house he had tried to forget for so long?

He again considered selling the place and leaving it in the past, where it belonged. But before he could come up with a conclusion, his head began to bob, his eyes closing on their own. His body relaxed and the glass of wine slipped from his fingers. He didn't stir when it shattered on the floor beneath him.

Sometime later, Samuel sat up straight and rubbed at his eyes. He had fallen asleep again, but if he had dreamed, he had already forgotten.

He was not alone.

She stood before the fireplace. Someone, presumably her, had rekindled the flames, and their light turned her hourglass figure into a silhouette of curves. This was the same woman from last night.

She approached, her hair a thick black curtain around her shoulders and naked breasts. She arched her back and opened her mouth. So many sharp teeth. Was she smiling or coming at him to bite? It didn't matter. No matter how much he struggled, he couldn't move.

The woman reached out and bent over so that when she fell to her knees, her hands landed on Samuel's upper thighs.

The jagged sharpness of her teeth had changed. When she smiled at him, her mouth was normal.

"Welcome home," she said. "Now it's time for you to claim your kingdom."

The air in the hallway sent a welcome chill up and down his spine. The woman turned to make sure he was still following. She reached back and took his hand into hers. Her grip was hard, her skin cold. Together, they headed down the stairs, and Samuel was immediately reminded of his dreams. Or, what he had considered as nightmares until today. They entered the kitchen and from there they entered the basement entrance.

He heard them chanting…

Allor Allor Manatis Satanis

…and now it filled him with joy.

Pain immediately crushed the emotion. Agony shot through his legs and arms, his jaw and skull. He screamed. He tried to stop his trembling limbs from taking one step farther, but the woman tightened her grip and pulled him forward. She caught him when he stumbled.

He barely heard the chanting for the grunts that came through his gritted teeth. This process was much less painful in his dreams, therefore proving that right now, in this moment, he was awake. His feet twisted, bones snapping. His screams morphed into something ... inhuman.

Samuel towered over the woman when they reached the landing. This stranger, this Lilith, he thought. Awe glimmered in her eyes.

Love.

Devotion.

Lust.

Her smile was human and hungry. She took his hand—now covered in fur—and led him into the dancing light of the ritual chamber.

It was as he remembered: the Baphomet pentagram on the middle of the floor, the large, six-foot candle holders at each point. Fat flames danced, reaching for the ceiling.

Coral and the young maids stood on the pentacle. Coral's skin was smooth, her breasts perky despite her age. Marvell stood off to the left, robed, his arms crossed before him. Everyone looked to him as they would a king, a god. Their god. One of little pity or mercy. One of little love.

But those he did love, he loved with all his heart. He even loved Coral. She was more a mother to him than his real one.

He loved the maids for entirely different reasons.

"You must kill them to become whole."

It was the woman, the stranger he thought of as Lilith. She rounded into his vision, her eyes catching the light and glowing as green as a cat's. Her teeth grew sharp and massive.

He closed his eyes. He breathed deeply, but his heart raced. A thick sheet of sweat covered his body. He wanted to run up the stairs—away from this madness. The joy that tickled his soul horrified him. Joy at the transformation made complete—made forever—only to evolve further as he aged.

He didn't want this.

It was all he ever wanted.

He opened his eyes. Coral and the maids were watching him.

I can do this, he thought. *I can do this.*

Again he closed his eyes, and visions of blood filled the blackened screen there. Of bodies being torn to pieces. And a sound permeated everything: deafening, exotic, inhuman and lustful. It seemed like hours passed before he recognized it as his own laughter.

He awoke on the cement floor with the taste of metallic blood on his tongue. He was naked and once more in human form. His head pounded. The hangover of a lifetime.

Coral, the maids and the pentagram had all vanished. As had the Lilith woman. Marvell, however, stood up from his seat beside Samuel. The old man's knees popped as he struggled to get up, but once he was on two feet, he looked as solid as stone. He held out his hand to Samuel, and his expression was that of a proud father's.

"Welcome to your home, my son," he said.

Samuel shook his head. He wanted to ask Marvell where the women had gone. He remembered doing... terrible things to them. But he knew that the old man had taken care of it. How, exactly, he wasn't sure. He no longer believed that the Marvell was entirely human.

But then, neither was he.

He kept his mouth shut and grabbed Marvell's rough and calloused hand.

"Are... Are you who I think you are?" Samuel asked.

Red glimmered there in Marvell's irises. For a moment, he looked twenty years younger with a head full of black hair, a pointy goatee. When he nodded, his hair transformed back into white, a dome of skin at the top of his head.

"The others will be here soon," Marvell said. "We've been waiting a long time for this."

Samuel nodded. Power surged through him, and he knew at that moment he could move mountains with a thrust of his hand. He could destroy his enemies with a glance. And his dark journey had only just begun.

He thought of his childhood self—the scared little boy he had been—and wished he could go back and shake him. Yet, things had worked out just fine. Just fine indeed.

"Well then," he said. "We'd better prepare for their arrival."

Marvell smiled. His teeth were sharp and triangular. And then both the old and the young headed up the stairs to the surface.

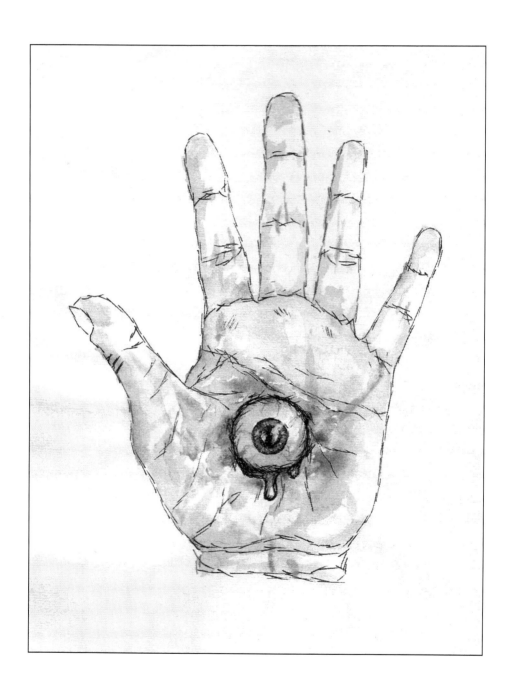

DEAD FLOWERS BY A ROADSIDE

Kelley Armstrong

The house is damnably silent.

I sit in the middle of the living room, furniture shoved out of the way, one chair tipped over where it fell, pushed too hard in my haste. Shards from a broken vase litter the floor. One is inches from my hand.

Amy would panic if she saw it. I close my eyes and imagine it. Her gasp from the doorway. The patter of her stockinged feet. The soft click of the piece against the hardwood as she snatches it up. Her voice as she tells me not to move, she'll clean the mess, I need to be more careful—really, I need to be more careful. What if I'd cut myself? What if Clara had run in?

In my mind, her voice is not quite right. The cadence, the tone are fading already. Amy's voice. Clara's voice. How much longer before they slide from memory altogether? Before I'm reduced to playing old videos that don't sound like them, not really, and telling myself they do, just so I can still hear their voices in my head.

I open my eyes and look at the ancient book lying open in front of me. Spidery writing, water-smeared ink, barely legible. The air smells faintly of acacia. That's critical, the book says. The dead will not speak without the scent of acacia to pull them through the ether.

Not true.

I know it is not true because I have seen the dead. Heard the dead. All my life they've been there, flitting past, whispering in my ear. Never once have they needed acacia.

Yet for three months, I've been trying to contact them. My wife. My child. I beg, I plead, I rage and shout for a sign, any sign. Comfort, any comfort. In desperation I turn to the books, to the acacia. But I hear only silence. Damnable silence.

I look down at the shard of glass by my hand.

Daydreaming again, weren't you? Amy laughs. *Always dreaming. Always distracted. One of these days, you're going to hurt yourself.*

I run my finger along the edge of the shard. As sharp as her ceramic knives, the ones I bought for her birthday, kept in the cupboard so Clara wouldn't mistake the white blades for plastic.

And don't you use them either, she'd said to me. *Please.*

Worried about me. About us. That was her nature. Double-checking door locks. Double-checking the stove. Double-checking Clara's car seat. Even if she'd done it herself, she always double-checked. If Clara or I so much as stubbed our toes and yelped, Amy would come running.

She'd always come running.

I take the shard, pinch it tight between thumb and forefinger. Drag the edge along my arm. Blood wells up.

"Amy?"

I cut deeper. Blood drips onto the dirty pages of the useless book.

"Amy? I need you."

Damnable silence. Always silence.

***

Crouched at their graves. Talking until I realize I'm only speaking to fill the silence, and I stop. I touch the marble. Cold. Always cold, even now with the late winter sun beating down.

No flowers. I took them away as soon as they started to wither. Dead flowers by a grave seems wrong. Left and forgotten. Nothing here should be forgotten.

I bring new mementos every week. Something small. Something meaningful. A franc from our honeymoon. A seashell from our last vacation. A button from Clara's first communion dress. A cat's-eye marble from Amy's childhood collection. Indestructible. As memories should be.

I come here twice a week to talk to them. I know they won't hear me, but I hope others will. Other ghosts. I can see them flitting past the graves. Wandering, endlessly wandering, looking for someone to take their message to the world beyond.

That someone used to be me. I couldn't set foot in a cemetery without being besieged by the dead. Now they give me wide berth. They know I come with a plea of my own. Find my wife. Find my daughter. Tell them I need to see them. Need to speak to them.

I want something from the ghosts, so they'll have nothing to do with me. I sit here and I talk to my wife and child, and I pray my words will thaw the hearts of those shades. I pray one will finally approach and say "I'll do this." They don't. They keep their distance and they wander in silence. Always silence.

The doorbell rings. I hear it through the garage walls. Someone on the front porch. Someone come to call. I ignore it and keep working on the car.

Three months, and it's almost finished. The windshield replaced. The engine repaired. The dents pulled out.

There's one thing I can't fix. The blood on the passenger's seat. No longer red. Faded to rust brown. But still blood. Undeniably blood.

The insurance company didn't want me to have the car. Too badly damaged, they said. We've paid you, now let us dispose of it. I'd pulled out my contract and showed them the clause where I could buy back the wreck for a few hundred dollars. At least let us remove the seat, they said. No one needs to see that. But I do.

"Hello!" a voice calls.

I stay crouched by the front of the car, replacing the cracked headlight. The door opens.

"Hello?"

It isn't anyone I know. I can tell by the voice. I consider staying where I am, but that's childish. I stand and wipe my hands on my jeans.

"Can I help you?"

It's a portly man, smiling that desperate, too-hearty smile of the salesman. I let him talk. I have no idea what he's saying, what he's selling. Just words, fluttering past.

"I'm not interested," I say.

He sizes me up. I wonder how I look to him. Unshaven. Bleary-eyed. Worn blue jeans. Grease-stained T-shirt. A drunk? An addict? Can't hold a job? Explains why I'd be home in the middle of the day. Still, it's a decent house, and he's desperate.

He sidles around the front of the vehicle.

"Nice car," he says.

It isn't. Even before the accident, it was a serviceable car, nothing more. Amy had wanted something newer.

Not fancier, she said. *Just safer, you know. For Clara.*

I hear BMWs are safe, I said. *You're a lawyer's wife now, not a law student's. You need a BMW.*

She laughed at that. Said I could buy her one when I made partner. I played along, but secretly made phone calls, visited dealers, planned to buy her a BMW or a Mercedes, whichever would make her feel safer. It was to be a Christmas gift.

Christmas.

That's what we'd been doing three months ago. Christmas shopping. The mall busy, the shoppers cranky, we'd left later than we expected, past dark. Cars were still streaming into the lot, circling for spots. A woman saw me putting bags in our trunk. She asked if we were leaving and I said we were. When I got in the car, Amy was still standing by the open rear door, trying to cheer up Clara, fussing, her nap missed.

Hon, there's a lady waiting for our spot.

Whoops. Sorry.

She fastened Clara's chair and climbed into the passenger seat. I started backing out.

Wait! I need to double-check the—She glanced back at the car waiting for our spot. *Never mind. I'm sure it's fine.*

"You restoring it?" the salesman's voice jerks me from the memory and I glower at him. I don't mean to. But for a second, I'd heard Amy's voice, clearly heard it. Now it was gone.

"Yes," I say. "I'm restoring it."

"Huh."

He struggles for a way to prolong the conversation. I bend and continue tinkering with the light. He stands there a moment. Then the silence becomes too much and he leaves.

A week later, the car is roadworthy. Barely. But it will make it where I want to go, all the bits and pieces intact, no chance of being pulled over.

The roadside.

I pull to the shoulder. It's dark here, just outside the city. An empty snow-laced cornfield to my right, a bare strip of two-lane highway to my left. In front of the car, a crooked cross covered in dead flowers. More dead flowers stuck in a toppled tin can. I didn't put them there. I don't know who did. Strangers, I suppose. Heard of the tragedy and wanted to mark the place. I'd rather they hadn't.

I didn't need that wretched memorial to remind me where it happened. I would know the exact spot without any marker, the image burned into my memory.

Coming back from Christmas shopping. Dark country road. The car quiet. A good silence. A peaceful silence. Clara asleep, Amy and me being careful not to wake her. Snow falling. First snow. Amy smiling as she watches the flakes dance past.

A pickup ahead of us. A renovation company. Boards and poles and a ladder piled haphazardly in the back.

Oh, Amy said. *That doesn't look safe. Could you...?*

My foot was already off the gas, our car falling behind the truck until all we could see was its rear lights through the swirling snow.

She smiled. *Thanks.*

I know the drill.

She reached over to squeeze my leg, then settled back to snow-watching silence.

Another mile. I'd crept up on the truck, but was still far enough back, and she said nothing. Then I saw it. A figure walking down the other side of the road. A woman in a long, red jacket.

I looked over. Ghost, I told myself, and I was quite certain it was, but I'd hate to be wrong and leave someone stranded. I squinted through the side window as we passed and—

Watch—!

That was all she said. My head whipped forward. I saw the ladder fly at us. I swerved to avoid it. The car slid, the road wet with snow. An oncoming car. I saw the lights. I heard the crunch of impact. Then... silence.

Now, three months later, I sit by the side of the road and I hear her voice.

Always dreaming. Always distracted. One of these days, you're going to hurt yourself.

Yes, I hurt myself. More than I could have ever imagined possible.

I get out of the car. The tube is in the trunk. I fit it over the exhaust pipe, and run it through the passenger window. Then I get inside and start the engine.

Does it take long? I don't know. I'm lost in the silence. There's a momentary break as a car slows beside me. The driver peers in, thinks I'm dozing, revs the engine, keeps going. The silence returns. Then I begin to drift...

I wake up. The car has stopped running. I check the fuel gauge. Half-full. I try to start the car, but the engine won't turn over. I slump onto the dashboard, defeated.

Then I hear... something. A bird call? I look out the windshield. Fog, so thick I can't see anything else.

I get out of the car. The hinges squeak. I leave the door open behind me and walk around the front. The memorial cross is there, but it's been replaced, the flowers fresh and white, the can beneath them upright and filled with daisies.

Clara loves daisies. I smile in spite of myself and walk to the flowers. More scattered around it. Still more trailing off toward the field.

As I follow them, I stumble through the fog. That's all there is. Fog. Rolling across the field. I look down at the flowers, crushing beneath my feet. I keep going, following them.

Another noise. Not a bird call. It sounds like...

"Amy?" I call. "Clara?"

A voice answers. Then another.

The silence ends.

PEN

Monica S. Kuebler

Sometimes a pen is just a pen.

Just a plastic tube

filled with ink,

guided by gravity,

until there is no ink.

Sometimes a pen is just a pen,

and what I need is not a blue stain

on white sheets – poetry.

What I need is a shovel

to dig my way out of this

or a hammer

to bring down hard on your skull

to beat the red ink out of you.

to beat the anger out of me

to beat you to the punch line

before you make me bleed.

Sometimes a pen is just a pen.

Too narrow to shove down your throat

to stop the screaming.

Not sharp enough to break through skin

and bone to stop the breathing.

Sometimes a pen is just a pen

and I've stopped believing in my own words.

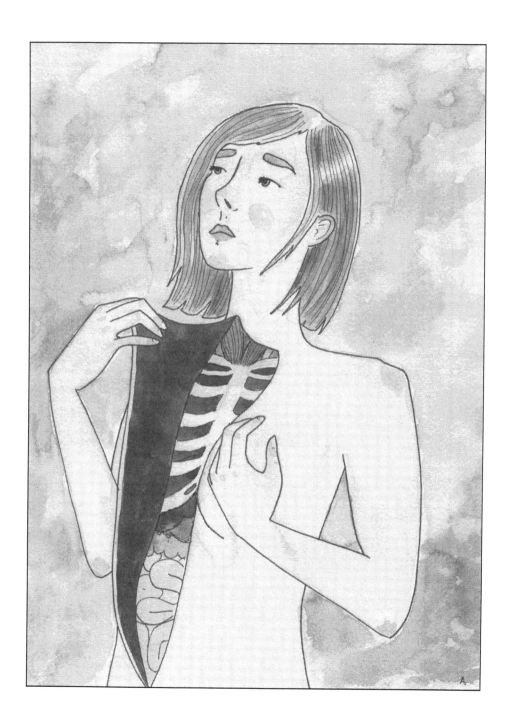

THE SLOW HAUNTING

John R. Little

"You didn't kill me, Timmy."

"Don't call me Timmy. You know that. It's Tim... but I *did* kill you."

"It was an accident."

"Why are you here?"

"You know."

"I can't see you. Turn on the light."

"Can't do that. I can't touch anything. My fingers go right through. It's pretty weird."

"Does it hurt?"

"No."

"Why aren't you in heaven?"

"You know."

"I'm turning the light on."

Tim climbed out from under the covers and walked to his bedroom door. He blinked as he snapped the light on. He hadn't been sure where Dennis was. His voice seemed to come from everywhere.

"Here," said Dennis. "Right where I belong."

Tim looked up at the top bunk bed, and sure enough, there he was. He looked the same as he always did, sitting cross-legged in the middle of the mattress, arms back as if supporting himself.

Would that work if he can't touch anything?

Looking at Dennis was like looking in the mirror. Same dirty blond hair, same round face and blue eyes, same small mole on the right cheek.

Dennis smiled. "You don't seem surprised to see me."

"I never felt you leave."

Dennis floated down to the rug and stood face to face with his identical twin. "We've been together since we were born. Can't change that now."

Tim moved to hug Dennis, but his arms fell through thin air and he jumped back in surprise.

"You look real."

"I am real. To you. But things work differently now."

"How long can you stay?

"As long as you want me, Timmy."

"It's Tim."

Three months earlier, Timmy's mom sat on his bed, beside him.

"Timmy? It's time to get up."

She swept the hair out of his eyes and touched his cheek.

"We all miss him, but we have to carry on. Today's the big birthday for you. Moving your age into double digits. It'd be a good time to—"

"He would have been ten, too."

"Yes, and we'll always remember him on your birthday. And on Christmas and on summer holidays, when you two would be out throwing your baseball around, and on the first day of school, and on every other day of the year."

"It's my fault."

"Don't ever say that, Timmy. We know it was an accident. You were both curious about the gun. We should never have had it in the house."

Her eyes watered, but she kept her voice firm, not wanting to cry again in front of him. "If it's anybody's fault it's mine. I should have told your father to take the gun with him when he left."

Silence covered the room like a blanket of snow. She heard the tick-tock of the Spider-Man wall clock and the swoosh of a car as it drove through the wet streets outside.

"Timmy?"

"I think I should be called Tim now."

"Okay."

"We stopped calling him Denny last year. I should have done the same. Timmy is for little kids."

She saw a forced smile on his face and stood back so he could climb out of bed. The frame creaked. The noise had never bothered her before, but without the constant chatter between the two boys, every sound seemed out of place.

Tim didn't play any baseball that summer or any of the summers following. Eleven years old... twelve... thirteen... somehow it wouldn't be the same. The twins had played ball together since they got their first T-Ball set when they were five. They graduated to Coach Pitch at seven and spent most of their waking time in summers playing.

But now Dennis wasn't there to catch Tim's pitches, and Tim couldn't be Dennis's fielder when he'd hit fungos in the park.

271

Their fifteenth birthday was on March 15.

"Beware the Ides of March, Timmy," whispered Dennis just before daylight.

"You say that every year."

Dennis didn't answer for a few moments. Tim yawned and rubbed his eyes, waiting for a bit of sunlight to start the day.

"Let's play some baseball this year."

"You can't play."

"Sure I can. I'll have just as much fun as you will."

Dennis had aged along with Tim. They were still mirror images.

That Saturday in late May Tim picked up his glove, went to the ball field, and joined a pick-up game. He played second base and standing right beside him was Dennis, as he always was. Dennis wore his own glove and smacked his fist into it as they both set their stance for the batter.

Tim never talked out loud to Dennis when anybody was around, but he could still talk to him in his mind. Maybe that's where Dennis talked, too. Tim never really understood how it all worked that he could hear Dennis but nobody else could see or hear him.

In the third inning, the batter smacked a grounder up the middle. It was bouncing between Tim and Dennis, and both of them moved to the middle to try to get the ball. It went right through Dennis's mitt and into Tim's. Things like that still surprised him and he dropped the ball.

"Darn."

"Don't worry," Dennis said. "You still stopped it from going to the outfield."

At the end of the game Tim asked Dennis, without moving his mouth, "How'd you get the glove?"

His twin shrugged. "I get whatever I need. That's just the way it works."

They walked side by side down the street toward home. They ducked into a 7-Eleven and Tim bought a Coke. He knew Dennis would find a way to have one in his hand when he next looked.

The sun was hot, but Tim didn't feel like rushing home. Burbank might have hot weather, but it was nothing like the heat in their apartment. Mom always promised to find a bigger place with air conditioning, but it never worked out. She worked in a nearby bookstore, but money was always tight since Dad left.

The boys walked through Valley Park and found a cool spot sitting at the base of a shade tree. They drank their Cokes and watched people walk by.

"You ever wish things were different?" asked Tim.

Dennis had never hesitated in answering Tim, and so he was surprised that he didn't hear the answer rumble around his head.

"Dennis?"

"Oh, well, sure. I wish I was still alive. Who wouldn't?"

"It was an accident."

Again Dennis didn't reply. He just finished his Coke and then tossed the empty can into the air. It disappeared.

"You know that, right?"

"Yeah, Timmy. I know what happened."

"It's Tim."

"You need to ask Lisa out."

"What?"

"She's just waiting for you to ask. I listened to her talk to that new girl the other day. You know, the fat thing. Lisa told her you're cute."

"*What?*"

"Just trust me. Lisa's hot. Ask her to a movie or something. We'll all like that."

Tim didn't know what to say. *Lisa?* Did Dennis really hear her say something?

But then, why not? A bunch of other kids were dating. He picked up his glove and smacked it.

"We should get home. Mom's making macaroni casserole."

"Again."

"Again."

The next day, Tim saw Lisa at the water fountain outside home room. She was wearing a light blue skirt that showed her long legs. To avoid staring at them, he wondered what it would be like to touch her dark, curly hair.

"Go on."

Tim moved a step closer but froze when Lisa finished her drink and looked up at him. When she smiled, it felt like his guts were going to fall out.

"Hi," she said.

"Hi."

"Did you want some water?"

"Jesus, Timmy, just ask her."

"Keep quiet."

He nodded to Lisa. "Hot day." He started to turn the water on and when he was looking down, he asked, "Would you like to go to a movie sometime? Or something?"

A million years passed in silence. The water ran down the drain while he watched with a parched throat.

"Sure," she said. "That sounds like fun."

Six weeks later, she kissed him. They were holding hands and walking home after the last day of school. She stopped walking, turned to him, and out of the blue leaned to him and kissed him.

"Wow, that was nice," he said when she pulled back.

For once, Dennis kept quiet.

That night, Tim woke in the middle of the night. He'd dreamed of Lisa again, and he had a huge erection. He wasn't surprised. He often woke this way after dreaming of her, and he started to stroke himself, thinking of the day when they would be together. He knew it would happen one day, thought she wanted it as much as he did, but he also knew he was too afraid of screwing things up to try anything.

He thought of feeling her boobs and touching her between her legs, wanting her to touch him as he was doing to himself.

"You should move faster with her."

Tim jumped and pulled his hand back. He pulled the blanket back on top of him that he'd moved aside earlier. "Jesus, you shouldn't be spying on me."

"You know she wants you to."

"Shut up."

"I see it in her eyes."

"What do you know? You died five years ago. You never had a girlfriend. You don't have a clue what it feels like."

Silence filled the room, and Tim felt terrible. He'd never wanted to bring up Dennis's death. His erection wilted away.

"Dennis? I'm sorry. I shouldn't have said that."

Still nothing. Tim climbed out of bed and flipped the light on. The top bunk was empty.

In the years since Dennis was killed, they'd lived together with their secret friendship. The bond between them was stronger than between any other friends Tim knew of, and he would never endanger it.

"Dennis? Come back. Please."

He pulled out the chair from his desk and sat, staring at the bunk beds. After a moment, he noticed the tick-tock of the clock and glanced at it. 4:42 a.m.

The gun was supposed to have been locked up in the cabinet near the bathroom, but the whole apartment had been turned upside down. Dad was leaving, and neither Tim nor Dennis knew why. Mom spent all her time in her bedroom crying. She only came out to go to work, and when she arrived back home, she brought fast food for the twins' dinner. For two weeks, they lived on burgers, pizza, tacos, and wings.

Then Mom started to be okay. She never did talk about why Dad left, and he never came to visit them. Tim only saw him the one time, at Dennis's funeral. Even then, they didn't even find a way to say "hi" to each other. Dad sat at the back of the church with a woman Tim didn't recognize.

The cabinet wasn't locked.

It must have been due to the rush of Dad moving out. He'd been grabbing things all over the place, throwing them inside two ratty suitcases, glaring at the boys, and yelling at Mom who yelled right back.

The twins mostly tried to sit on the couch, holding hands, hoping the fight would just end.

Dad yelled one more time at Mom, and then he stormed out and slammed the door. After crying for an hour, Mom washed her face and left too. Tim knew she was going to the bar down the street. He hoped Dad would be there, too, but that seemed like a slim possibility.

"What a mess."

"Yeah."

There were clothes scattered through the apartment, some of Dad's, some Mom's, and even some of the boys. They picked up their own clothes and took them to their room. There was broken glass in the kitchen and papers covered much of the hall floor.

"I think they're bills or something," said Dennis.

"Hey, look."

The cabinet door was ajar. Through the glass window, they could see the gun.

"Wow. I'll get it," Dennis said as he swung the door open and grabbed the gun.

"Let me have it. I saw it first!"

"No, I've got to—"

"Damnit, Dennis, you can't have everything and—"

Tim pulled his mind back from that awful day and focused again on the top bunk.

For the first time in his life, he felt alone. The invisible elastic band that always connected him to Dennis had snapped, and he was adrift, as if sailing off on a lifeboat by himself.

He opened the top drawer of his desk and pulled out his scrapbook. Inside were photos of him and Dennis, several from the last year before the accident. He touched Dennis's pictures and tried to smile, but nothing felt right.

Tears fell down his cheeks. He blew his nose and wiped his face before flicking the light back off and heading back under the covers. All thoughts of Lisa were gone. He just replayed memories of Dennis and himself in his mind for about thirty minutes. Finally he drifted off to sleep.

"Hey, sleepyhead. Time to wake up."

"Dennis?"

"Who else?"

"You're back!"

"I couldn't stay away. I missed you."

Tim stood beside the bed and stared up at Dennis. "It's Saturday. Wanna hit a movie this aft?"

"Sure."

Tim got dressed and they went down for breakfast. As always, Dennis paced around the kitchen and living room, waiting for Tim to eat his cereal. Mom read the newspaper and drank a black coffee.

"You should try a coffee sometime," called Dennis. "We're getting old enough."

Tim shrugged and answered silently, "Doesn't smell very good."

"Lisa'll like you better. Make you look grown up."

He finished off the Rice Krispies and rinsed his bowl in the sink.

"She wants you to grow up faster. Wants you to fuck her."

"What did you say?"

"Tim?" Mom looked over at him. "I didn't say anything."

"No, it's okay. Sorry, Mom. I was just…"

"Talking to Dennis again? I thought you'd stopped that."

Dennis started laughing.

"Do you ever feel that he's still here?" asked Tim.

Mom put her paper down. Dennis stared at her and then back to Tim.

"I feel him every day. I'll always have him."

"Bullshit," Dennis said. "She's got nothing."

"Yeah," said Tim. "It just feels like he's right beside us sometimes." He looked over at Dennis, who now was wearing his spring jacket.

"Oh, aren't you the funny one."

"We'll never forget him." Mom picked up her paper again.

Tim grabbed a lacrosse ball and his baseball glove and walked over to the schoolyard. The back of the school was solid, no windows, and he tossed the ball at the wall. It bounced back just as hard as he threw it, and it smacked hard into his mitt.

For thirty minutes, Tim threw the ball over and over. Dennis dodged in front of him, trying to block Tim's view. The normal game they played.

"I meant it," Dennis said. "She wants to fuck you."

"Don't say that. She's nice. She wouldn't talk like that."

"Sez you. Just go for it. She's waiting for you to find a way."

The next day, Tim met Lisa in the afternoon and suggested they go for a walk through the woods in the park. Almost nobody ever did that, because there weren't any normal walking paths. You had to pick your way among thick trees.

As they moved into the forested area, Tim clenched his mouth and took hold of Lisa's hand. She didn't shake him off, just smiled.

"That's nice," she said.

"See," said Dennis. "Told ya."

They found a clearing in the middle of the woods, sat down, and talked about school. They laughed, and Dennis just watched. At one point he rolled his hand in a circle. *Get a move on.*

During a lull in the talk, Tim leaned over and kissed Lisa. They kissed for a long time, and Tim felt unbelievable. Lisa placed her hands behind his head and he tried to copy her.

Go for it.

She was driving him crazy and that gave him courage. He moved his hand under the front of her T-shirt and lifted up to cup her breast. He couldn't believe he had the nerve to do it.

"Hey!" Lisa slapped his arm away. "What do you think you're doing?"

"I— I thought..."

"I'm not that kind of girl. Besides, we're only fifteen, for God's sake. I thought you liked me."

"I do. I *really* like you."

She stood up and crossed her arms. "I'm going home."

"I'm sorry."

"You can come with me if you want or you can stay, but I'm going."

He rushed to keep up with her as they headed back out through the trees to the street.

"Lisa, I'm really sorry. I was just being stupid."

She slowed her walk a bit and looked at him. "C'mon, let's get home."

Dennis laughed on the way out of the woods and all the way home.

Later, Tim asked him, "Why'd you lie to me?"

"Just trying to help. I thought she wanted it."

"You said you *knew*."

"Yeah, well. I was wrong. But at least you got to feel her boob."

Lisa and Tim were eighteen when they made love for the first time. It happened in the back of Tim's ten-year-old, second-hand Taurus, and this time it was Lisa who engineered things.

Dennis sat in the front seat and didn't make a sound.

They were twenty-one when they got married. Dennis was Tim's unofficial best man, standing right there along with the rest of the wedding party. He wore a matching tuxedo.

Lisa's parents were happy to splurge for a huge ceremony. "As long as you understand we won't pay for another one," her father whispered to her that morning. "So, make this work."

Tim's dad wasn't invited.

Lisa's father walked her down the aisle. She was the most beautiful bride in the world, and even after all these years, Tim couldn't believe how lucky he was to be with her.

Every day is devoted to you, my love. He would never tell Dennis but for the first time ever, Dennis was not the closest person to him and never would be again.

Tim's voice cracked when he said, "I do." His hand shook as he slipped the ring onto her finger, not caring one whit that he'd be paying for the diamond for the next three years. She was worth every penny.

Through their courtship, they'd talked about everything to do with their future. Career aspirations, kids, houses, even what they wanted to do when they retired, though that was an unimaginable time in the distant future. She wanted to be *sure* he was the right man for her.

Their entire lives were mapped away in her mind, and he loved her all the more for it.

Dennis helped answer all Lisa's questions, which was fine with Tim. After all, they were one, and what mattered to Dennis mattered to Tim. Sometimes he just figured it out faster.

The newlyweds wanted three children, spaced over eight years. Not too close together, not too far apart. They planned to conceive their first child a year after their marriage.

Sixteen months passed.

"Tim? Look!"

She held the little plastic stick up to his face. "Positive!"

"Hey!"

He picked her up and twirled her around their apartment. When he put her back down, he stared at the test. "You're sure?"

"Well, these things are never 100 percent, but I'm as sure as I can be."

"Get her a glass of wine to celebrate," called Dennis. "Piss her up!"

Tim ignored him. "We need to get you to the doctor to double check."

They kissed. The elastic bond between Tim and Dennis was definitely weakening as the bond grew stronger with his own family.

Seven months later, Lisa delivered a perfect set of identical twin girls. They named them Patricia and Denise.

Patricia was Lisa's mother's name. Tim said he wanted to name their other daughter Denise, to honor his long-dead brother. Lisa thought that odd, but she liked the sound of the name.

"Denise is the pretty one," said Dennis. "Of course."

Tim laughed. "Just like I'm the more handsome of us."

Dennis spoke more somberly, "I feel like I'm their father as much as you."

Tim just nodded and smiled. *Not a fucking chance*, he thought.

Having his brother's ghost around was second nature, and he could always carry on separate conversations with him and with Lisa whenever he needed to. Some things, though, were better left unsaid.

Lisa never suspected he was talking to a dead man.

Tim could never imagine how his life changed after the girls were born. They became his first thought every morning and his last thought at night. He held them in his arms every evening, waiting for them to fall asleep. And when they learned to smile, he knew he was totally sunk. His whole life was devoted to the girls.

Lisa didn't mind. She never felt ignored or neglected, and she appreciated all the time Tim spent taking care of them. It gave her a chance to escape after being with them all day while Tim was at work.

Even Dennis didn't mind. He seemed to love the girls just as much as Tim.

"I wish I could hold them," he said one night.

Lisa was out picking up a couple of groceries, so Tim talked out loud. "We're awfully lucky. Everyone says so."

Dennis reached his hand to Denise and pretended to pat her hair. Tim thought he felt more involved in the family when he acted out like this.

"Just don't leave any guns around," Dennis whispered.

Tim didn't answer. He was shocked that Dennis would even bring up such a possibility.

They heard Lisa's car door slam and the ghost pulled his hand back, as if he'd been caught doing something he shouldn't.

Tim automatically switched to talking to Dennis in his mind. "I wish she'd met you when you were alive."

"Well, she kinda did, since we're identical, right down to the last cell."

"We only look the same. We don't think the same at all."

Dennis shrugged and floated to the other side of the room, knowing Lisa would rush in and sit down where he'd been sitting.

"No, we don't," he said after a moment.

By the time the girls hit their ninth birthday, Lisa's long-term plan for their lives was scattered to the winds. They never conceived another child and probably never would. Neither of them wanted to go to the doctor to see whose plumbing was at fault. They were happy with Denise and Patricia.

The bigger house she had hoped for didn't work out, either. Living in Burbank wasn't cheap, and they'd only been able to afford to rent a basement apartment. Both of them worked full-time, she in the local Starbucks, and he at an auto body shop. They weren't rich, and sometimes he wondered about the end-game of Lisa's plan—retirement. He'd already passed his thirty-first birthday, and he could see tiny tufts of gray hair on the back of Dennis's head. He refused to look that closely in the mirror, but he knew what he'd see.

"Hard to believe it's their birthday again," said Dennis. He'd been missing for the past half hour, which had worried Tim.

"Where've you been?"

"Just reminiscing."

"What do you mean?"

"Sometimes, I just get sad." He walked to the window and looked outside. "Do you ever think about that day?"

Tim moved to stand beside him. The girls were in their room, napping, and Lisa was out picking up party supplies. It was still a few hours until the guests arrived.

"Sure. I still think of it all the time."

"We were nine. Just like Denise."

"And Patricia. Why do you always leave her out?"

"You shouldn't have tried to grab the gun."

Tim took a long breath and watched a car roll down the street.

"It was an accident."

Dennis said, "It's hot. I'm going to open the window."

And he did.

Tim took a step backward. *What the fuck?*

His first thought was that he'd just had some kind of daydream—imagined what he'd seen. But, no. He replayed it in his mind. Dennis had leaned down and turned the rusty lever at the top of the window, lifting the screen and pushing the window open.

"You can't do that."

"Apparently I can."

"What the fuck's going on, Dennis? How long have you been able to do that?"

Dennis stared at him. "Since you fucking well killed me." He took a step toward Tim, who stumbled back and found himself in his easy chair. "You can touch things. Why wouldn't you tell me?"

"Let me show you something," Dennis said. He moved to Tim and grabbed his left arm.

"Jesus, what are you doing?"

Dennis's fingernails were sharp. He scratched deep into Tim's arm, leaving three bright scars.

Tim stared, speechless.

"You *killed* me."

"It was a fucking accident, and you goddamn well know it."

"I remember the pain. I didn't die right away. Remember that? You shot me in the gut."

Dennis lifted his T-shirt and rubbed his stomach and chest.

"You burst my left lung and fragments of the bullet bounced around everywhere. My heart started to leak, and I couldn't get enough breath. I guess Mom never bothered you with all the gruesome details."

Tim couldn't say anything.

"You don't remember? I suppose you don't remember me drowning in my own blood, spitting up painful red vomit and looking at you for help. And I'm sure you don't remember how you just froze, didn't move a muscle to help, didn't call 911, didn't do a goddamned thing."

"I was only a little kid."

"A little murderer, you mean."

"You always told me you couldn't touch things."

"I lied."

"What's going on? Why are you doing this?"

"Because it's Denise's ninth birthday. She's lived as long as I did, and that's long enough."

Tim stood up. "You touch her and I'll—"

Dennis laughed. "What? You'll kill me?"

"It's time for you to go."

"Actually, on that, I agree. I've just been waiting for today. Waiting a long time. I've already killed her. That's where I was earlier."

"You shit. I don't believe you."

Tim pushed past Dennis to go toward the kids' room, but Dennis grabbed him. He had more strength than seemed possible, and he used it to throw Tim down into his chair.

"And I called the police to confess. They should be here any minute."

"They wouldn't be able to hear you…"

"Sure, they heard me. Probably recorded me. And my voice is identical to yours."

"Let me get to her."

Again he stood, and again Dennis threw him down, rougher this time.

In the distance, Tim heard a siren, and in his heart he knew that Dennis was telling the truth, that Denise was dead.

"How did you…?"

"I strangled her. She was sleeping and I used every ounce of my strength to squeeze the life out of her. She tried to fight, but there wasn't much she could do. She didn't understand why her daddy was doing that."

Tears rolled down Tim's face.

"They'll find my DNA on the skin beneath her fingernails. Defensive wounds. Just for good measure I spit in her face."

Tim closed his eyes and lowered his face into his hands.

"Of course, the DNA they find will match yours. We're identical twins, after all. Even our scratches match."

Dennis rolled up his sleeve to show identical scars to those he'd given Tim.

The sirens screamed as two patrol cars pulled up in front of the house.

"OPEN UP!"

"Not yet, brother." Dennis kept Tim a prisoner in his seat.

After a moment, the police broke down the door and found Tim alone in his living room, staring with guilt into his hands.

MEMORIES

Sèphera Girón

"Come on, then," Laurie pleaded playfully as he held out his hand toward Morena. Long slender fingers wiggled invitingly toward her. Morena stared at his hand and then looked up into his dark eyes that glowed like shiny black buttons in the sunset. "You know you have to do it."

Morena took a deep breath and clasped her hand into his, following him into the bar. The glare of sunset descended into a dim smoky haze of tavern even though cigarette smoking had been banned for years.

Instantly, the memories came flooding back. They ebbed and flowed through her mind, pulling in and out of focus through a kaleidoscope of pain and distrust, echoing that stabbed-in-the-gut feeling that warned *something isn't right* as logic kept demanding proof. Then the ensuing anger and grief of the pointless arguments that inevitably followed.

The musky scent of stale beer and B.O. slammed back nights of endless talking and squabbling, tears and pleas for revealing the elusive invisible elephant in the room. It was there but what was *it*?

Morena stared at the clumps of people gathered around tables, hunched over pints of beer. The drone and buzz of drunken revelry accented by the blaring music from the jukebox mirrored the events unfolding in her mind.

"Don't be afraid," Laurie said softly.

As they stood waiting for their beer to be poured by the old wiry-haired bartender, Laurie firmly grasped Morena's hand. He stared earnestly into her eyes. She wanted to fall into their dark bottomless depths, tossing the painful shards of the past away.

"Remember, we are to here to make good memories," he said solemnly.

"Yes, good memories. I must forget about the bad ones," she said feeling as though the words came out as automatic pilot. Logic told her he spoke the truth.

"Yes. Always forget."

Morena closed her eyes for a moment, concentrating on the comforting warmth of Laurie's hand.

They'd met through a friend of a friend some months before at a writer's conference and had connected through email and Messenger. It was difficult to maintain contact because they lived in different cities but their common interests kept them taking advantage of social networking opportunities. Morena shed her bitterness and sorrow when she spoke with him. He made her laugh and forget her grief and her age and she blossomed forth into fresh new hope. His youthful *joie de vivre* was infectious and she forgot the nearly two decades that spanned between them. After weeks of more intense connection by phone, they decided to meet in person once more. Morena invited Laurie to Toronto and he accepted.

They planned their weekend together around taking a trip down Morena's most horrific memory lanes to create new memories. Release the baggage of the past so only light and love remained. Several phone calls had evolved around the concept of reinventing one's self through the realigning of neurological connections. From failed relationships, from familiar and distasteful haunts, from memories.

No drugs, just the euphoria of a positive experience implanting a new memory into the archives to replace the old. Retrain the homunculus.

Tickle the god spot. Delete the fragmented connections and replace with lightening-speed wonderment.

She wasn't quite sure what the "wonderment" would consist of, but she hoped she had the right idea in mind.

The previous night of Laurie's arrival, Morena tucked him into an air mattress in the living room. His bus was three hours late so it was the middle of the night by the time they made it back to her apartment. She stared at him fumbling with his suitcase and toiletries, so exhausted he couldn't form a sentence. Although his eyes had shone with joy when he spotted her, the ache of his tired body was clearly winning his attention. She knew it wasn't the time to suggest a joint shower and left him alone to do what he had to do.

She tossed and turned, hugging her pillow, unable to sleep well. She thought of him lying out there on the air mattress, and why? He could be beside her, his firm strong body nestled against hers, the warmth of human contact cuddling against her in anticipatory desire. She had slept platonically with many men, including her husbands, and wished she hadn't been so shy about suggesting contact they likely both craved.

A shudder, a very tiny one, had buzzed through her when she shook his hand at their very first meeting. It was a spark of interest but nothing more than meeting a nice looking man who was a writer as well as she. At the time, she had been happily married and not looking for anyone. They passed each other on social networking sites now and again and she considered him one of her thousands of friends that actually communicated once in a while. But nothing more.

And as far as she knew, he considered her a peer as well. The more one posted on other people's walls, the more friends of friends are garnered and therefore, potential fans. That's why it was called social networking.

When her marriage died, Morena and Laurie connected at a conference. Although they only saw each other briefly over coffee for a few bleary-eyed minutes, Morena sensed it again. An electric chemistry between them; a rumble in her belly, an anticipatory echo that indicated a connection that needed to be explored.

When at last fitful sleep claimed her, the clawing talons of nightmares tore through her subconscious. Her gut roared and rumbled. Her shrink had said to trust her gut. She only saw the doctor a few times after the marriage breakdown. The sessions were her mostly reliving the past when in fact, in daily life, she'd already had moved on. And as she lay sleepless, her guts were rumbling up a storm. It wasn't the hungry rumble. Just a painful lurching of discontent. The nightmares wove in and out of her discomfort. Her torso shredded by sharp instruments, her vision impaired from repeated beatings. She saw ghosts and demons, all dancing an eternal dance, luring her soul from one eternity to another. And none looked good to her.

Her screaming woke herself but amazingly, when she peeked out into the living room, Laurie was still lightly snoring under the covers on an air mattress.

A trip to the bathroom solved some of her problems but the nightmares haunted her until well after dawn.

Morena opened her eyes as the bartender placed their beers down. Laurie threw the bartender a bill and gave Morena a pint. He raised his glass to hers.

"To creating new memories," he grinned, his smile wide and friendly, his eyes sparkling with secret delight.

Morena clicked her glass to his and tried not to wince as the jukebox blasted, "Shook Me All Night Long," one of *their* songs. A song that needed to be transitioned from where it had sunken to painful back up to its rightful spot under pleasurable. The small parquet dance floor swelled as people swarmed to gyrate and play air guitar to AC/DC. Morena glanced at Laurie who was eyeing the pool table.

"That song... it's one of them," she said softly. Laurie nodded.

"One of your songs?"

"Yes, and I don't want to remember that anymore," Morena said.

"Then you won't," Laurie said as he led Morena to the dance floor. She followed his lead as they danced to the song. Morena worked at creating new dance steps to erase the old ones. Every now and again she would look up to find Laurie intensely watching her.

It was refreshing to be with a man that watched her instead of always looking around for something better. Her last couple of exes had been notorious for girl-watching and her self-esteem had slid to a negative capacity over the past decade. However, it was nice to notice that she was the one being eyed this time; by Laurie and by other men in the bar as well. It wasn't as if she was dressed any different than usual. T-shirt and leggings, her sneakers and loose long hair were the same casual look she'd had for years. Maybe too many years of that too.

Laurie danced closer to her and took her hands, spinning her in a rock 'n' roll fox trot.

"Did he dance like this with you to this song?" he asked.

Morena shook her head.

"No, not at all," she laughed.

"Then we're creating a new memory," Laurie whispered as he spun her around the room. She followed his lead, feeling like Scarlett O'Hara dancing for the soldiers. Only she was the soldier.

Morena followed him, looking up at his pale face, his strong jaw and dark eyes. He had shaggy black hair that made him appear artistically rebellious, mad yet intelligent at the same time. He had an odd patience with her and she wondered how much of it was courting purposes and what his true tolerance level was when the mask was off. Some of her exes had been uber-charming when they met, but once they had her commitment, they used their cunning manipulative tactics to create lives that didn't mesh with their chosen committed lives and made her pay for their inner unhappiness.

When the chorus rocked out for the last time, Laurie twirled Morena with one hand and flipped her back over his arm so that she was staring up at him. He froze, gazing down at her. He drew his face near to hers as he gently lifted her with his strong firm arm. His strength melted into her and she rose up, wrapping her arms around his neck as he lifted her. They kissed and he gently spun her, pressing her pelvis against his until her feet rose lightly from the floor. She was giddy when he set her down, and girlishly cast her eyes down as she avoided his keen-eyed stare.

The song melded into Metallica and they continued to dance. Morena watched him under her bangs, studying his face with intensity, as if sifting for clues. She had to be cautious these days. She had to make sure that she didn't repeat the mistakes that led her down the destructive path where now she needed closure.

One way to do that would be to create new memories. As they ordered another drink at the bar, Morena looked around at the people.

"It's like a throwback to ten years ago or so." She sighed. "Things just never change, do they?"

"Only if you want them to," he said, sipping his beer.

"We have no real control over some events. Such as what another person feels or what they're doing behind your back?"

"But you can," Laurie said as he led her over to a stool in the corner. It was slightly quieter there and he leaned over to tell her.

"You trust your gut. You listen very hard. Be an animal. It's all about instinct."

Morena put her hand over her solar plexus. She closed her eyes and listened for a sign.

There was nothing. Her guts had been emptied in the night. There was nothing to rumble or even sense, just an aching hollow sensation.

She opened her eyes.

"You are blocking, Morena. You can start to unblock by letting me in." Laurie took her hand and pressed it against his heart.

"Close your eyes, Morena," he said. He leaned forward and kissed her.

The touch of his lips against hers was warm and soothing. She trembled in his arms, thinking about hours of conversation that she never considered would end in a simple kiss.

However, in that instant, in that warm brush of lip upon lip, she knew. That tiny spark she had initially felt glowed hotter, an orange-red flush lined her cheeks.

"New memories," she whispered to him. Her head spun. She smelled the slight hint of a musky cologne mingled with a strong soap. She captured the moment in her heart to retrieve in times of sadness. No matter where their path would lead, she could always remember this moment unlike any other moment. And that moment was good.

"Yes," he said. They danced some more and then it was time to move on.

"Where are we going?" he asked.

"You'll know," he responded, hurrying along the sidewalk. He led her down the street until they reached a small park.

"Is this the one?" he asked. She nodded.

"How did you know?" she asked, staring at the familiar park with its maze of walkways and gardens.

"I did my research before I came over, don't you worry," he said.

"You researched my bad moments."

"Just from what you've told me on Messenger. I looked up a couple of your old haunts so that I knew what to expect."

Morena nodded.

"Sure."

For a slight instant, the spark in her stung and her empty gut rumbled.

Research.

But he was a writer. That's what writers *do.*

In the park, the moon was partly obscured by a cluster of trees. Morena followed Laurie into the one of the gardens. There was a cobblestone path that wove through a variety of foliage until emptying into the *piece de resistance*, a mermaid fountain surrounded by marble fish. There was a stone bench by the fountain and several small trees in gardens beyond.

Morena stared at the bench. Tears welled in her eyes as visions of her painful break-up with Hank flashed through her mind.

"It doesn't have to be that way anymore," Laurie said as he led her toward the bench. They sat down together. The stone was hard beneath her bottom. Laurie held her hands in the familiar position, near his heart, looking earnestly into her eyes.

"You weren't meant to be together. You know that. So what if he told you here or anywhere else."

"He'd been cheating on me for years. It hurts to think you were the special one, when in fact you were less than second best."

"But you don't have to think about that anymore. Now you can think of new things," Laurie said.

"I know and I do."

"Re-imprint the painful memories into charming new memories," he said, kissing her hands. "You had no part in his inner discontent."

"I suppose you're right."

"So tell me, Morena, what memory do you wish to create with this garden, this bench? What would wash away the tears?"

Morena looked down at her lap and contemplated his words.

"Well, what's that?" he asked after a moment of silence, pointing toward a tree. It was rather dim in the garden but Morena spotted something shiny reflecting in the glow of the rising full moon.

"I'm not sure," Morena said as she walked over to it. "Looks like a ghetto blaster."

Laurie walked over to the rectangular object and picked it up.

"Sure is. Wonder if it works."

Laurie twirled the dials. The radio was fuzzy. He popped open the top.

"Looks like a DVD in there. Soundtrack from *Footloose*." He smiled.

"Footloose? Jesus."

"Some good songs on there. Listen."

He pressed the button and the CD started. He pushed the tracking button until he found what he was looking for.

"Somebody's eyes are watching you." He crooned to her making sinister gestures with his hands.

"I've never really thought of that song that way before. Creepy."

He reached for her and pulled her into him, holding her firmly around the waist with one hand, the other clutched hers. Her breasts pressed into him, and she lay her head against his chest. She thought she would hear his heart beating but maybe her own blood rushing through her ears blocked the sound.

"What else is on there?" Morena asked. "What other songs are from that show?"

"How about "Hero"? That's a catchy one." He grinned.

Before she could respond, Laurie was dancing in front of her, miming the girl singer as if he was a big Motown star. When the chorus busted out, he started to do push-ups on the cobblestone path. Morena laughed at him and urged him to get up before he cut himself on something.

"More. One more!" he pleaded. He was out of breath, his bangs sticky from sweat hanging down just over the top of his eyes.

"All right."

He clicked on "Let's Hear it for the Boy" and did more goofy dancing for her. Morena was impressed by his outrageousness as well as his natural grace and style. She applauded when the song was over.

He put the ghetto blaster back under the tree.

"So tell me, how will you feel about this beautiful garden now?" he asked.

"I'll never forget you," she said. "Never."

"One day you may want to forget me too but for now, the memory of this laughter far outweighs the sadness you carried for years. Dontcha think?"

"This is true," she said. "Thank you." She kissed him on the lips, full and hard. She was breathless when she broke away.

He held her hand tightly as he led her from the garden. She walked along swinging his hand and staring up at the full moon in pleasure. Their bond was cementing. It would only be natural to enjoy each other once back at her apartment. She was impatient with anticipation and nearly missed his next words.

"I need you to help me," he said. He stopped walking.

"Help you with a memory? Here in Toronto?" she asked.

"Yes. I had a memory here once. It was in a small hotel on Spadina. Perhaps we can find it," he said.

"Sure." Morena nodded.

They walked a few blocks, past the University and the big old houses that lined the loop. Where there were residential century homes now loomed old buildings housing stores and other commercial venues along the Spadina strip just before the garish lights of Chinatown began.

"It was this one..." Laurie said as they stood underneath a lethargic neon sign that sporadically blinked. The old crumbling building had housed hotels and boarding houses for more than a century and though it should have been torn down decades ago, it still stood.

"This is where you had a memory?" Morena asked, staring with trepidation at the faded neon. "I've heard that this place is haunted."

"What old building isn't?" Laurie joked. Morena laughed, the sound pinched as her throat squeezed tight. Laurie raised his dark eyebrows. His flesh was so pale, the rays of the full moon splashed along his face in translucent streaks. His eyes glinted red for a moment from the flash of the sign.

"I'll tell you my story once we're inside," he said.

As Morena followed Laurie up the rickety stairs toward the glass stores that reminded her more of a grocery store than any hotel, her guts rumbled and churned. She had heard all kinds of horrible stories about this place over the years. The hotel for lost souls. The dead end of humanity.

The sense of his urgency was disturbing her. The pleasant vibrations he had set off in her earlier were gone. Now there was panicked feel to his movements and she wondered why he was so agitated.

"I want the key to room six," he said with a sigh. Morena noticed that he didn't have to check in. The whole dimness of the hotel was setting her radar into overdrive.

What was she doing here?

She watched him put the key in the door and gasped as it swung open. He hurriedly ushered her inside and shut it with a click of the deadbolt behind her.

And then another.

In the middle of the room there was a circle of women seated in chairs. As Morena stared, she realized that they were bound and gagged. Five of them. Five women who looked just like herself.

And there was an empty chair for one more.

"What is this?" Morena asked but the slam of camphor-fuelled cloth against distracted flesh rendered her limp enough to seat her at her proper place at the table.

As Morena returned to consciousness, she was aware of the women staring at her in silence. She tried to speak but realized her mouth was taped shut. She studied the others carefully and realized they were all duct-taped closed as well.

Her head spun. Was she dreaming or awake? A strong chemical odor permeated her senses and she tried to suck in more oxygen through her nose. Dizziness was overriding her reality and she struggled to focus on what was happening.

The women around the table swam in and out of focus in a hazy blur. Long dark hair framed pale faces. Dark eyes watched her, a fearful reflection of her own.

Who are you and why do we all look the same?

Morena stared into the eyes of the woman nearest to her. They were wide, her tightly taped mouth revealing no secrets. Morena's gaze lighted on the next woman; another muted doe trapped in the headlights of dark pain and torment.

Laurie stood at the head of the table, a proud smug grin on his face.

"Oh the stories are the same. We all are the same. In the cycle of earth it truly doesn't matter in the end. All that matters is that balance is restored. Pain gathered up and disposed of in a meaningful fashion is pain that has been worth the sacrifice."

Laurie walked over to Morena.

"The others have heard my song before. Some of them many times. But you are the final one. Six beautiful chances to save my soul."

Laurie brushed his hair from his eyes and walked over to the girl across from Morena. He played with her hair as she shuddered and recoiled from his touch. Laurie's eyes met Morena as he tormented the woman with slow nuzzle of his scruffy face against her smooth pale one.

Morena's stomach painfully rumbled. Her hands were tightly tied to the arms of her chair with an itchy twine.

Morena pleaded with Laurie in a moaning wail, her taped mouth rendering her unable to form little but the cadence of her cries. He mocked her with his eyes and kissed the top of the head of the next girl. The trembling woman closed her eyes in fear as his hot breath grazed the L of her shoulder.

Morena's stomach lurched and a bitter acid taste flooded her mouth. She swallowed it down.

Laurie laughed as he watched the women squirming in revulsion.

"How it must feel to be on the other side? Oh, yes, but I wait. I was." He sniffed the hair of another woman and kissed her along her arms.

"I was the pawn in everyone's game." He licked the ear of the last woman and stuck his tongue in it. Playfully he swirled it around as she leaned away from him.

"You broke me most of all, Tina," he said to the air. He flickered as if his essence was shifting. A blinking haze undulated through the air and he shook his head.

"Very well," he said. "The time has come."

Laurie turned from the table and went over to a sideboard covered in dust and debris. Morena craned her neck to see what he was doing. Laurie lifted a freshly polished sword from the table. The blade that was easily over a foot glinted in the dim light cast by the swinging light bulb above the table. Morena noticed a golden urn studded with red gemstones and a large golden goblet covered in raised ornate symbols and more polished rubies.

He held the sword, glinting in his hands. He ran his fingers along the blade, stroking it lovingly.

"Six, six, six..." Laurie muttered. "There are six. The last time. Then I will be free."

Morena shook her head in protest and in doing so, noticed the other women doing the same.

Laurie approached the first girl. He shifted her chair around, his strength surprising as stronglong fingers grasped the wood and moved it. The woman tried to protest through her taped mouth as she roughly spun around. Her eyes dripped tears, whatever makeup she may have once wore, long sobbed away.

Laurie studied the woman, "Tina", his dark eyes glassy. His tipped the sword so that it pointed at the top of her T-shirt. Slowly he drew it down, the blade catching on her skin, leaving a streak of blood in its wake. He watched the beads of blood swell up through the shirt and ooze from the fresh wound.

Her face grimaced as her flesh parted beneath her t-shirt. Soon her torso was split, her large breasts splayed to either side, leaking from her t-shirt. She gasped through her nose, snot bubbles impeding her breathing.

Her muffled cries weakened as blood flowed in branching pathways along her body. Morena shivered.

"When I was here," he proclaimed, "I was a teenager. Eighteen and a half to be exact. That was an awkward age of manhood and child."

Morena nodded her head, though once again he wasn't addressing her specifically anymore.

"I came to this hotel room under ridiculous circumstances. But of course, six years, six months, and six days makes a lot of difference in perspective." Laurie held the wounded woman up by her hair and looked into her dull glazed eyes before tossing it down in disgust. "You learn what is real pain and what is emotional pain. You learn that some people are evil and need to be stopped."

Morena widened her eyes. *Evil?* What had she done that was evil? Truly evil?

Had she?

Was she in denial too?

"Everybody lies. Some lie to hurt, some lie to escape, some lie to be selfish, some lie to protect. Stories are lies. The news is lies. Not one person can say they go through life without a lie."

Laurie stood before the second woman. He held the sword up and a large glob of "Tina's" blood dripped onto him. He wiped the blade theatrically and carefully onto the backs of his pants before raising it toward her again.

"Yes, Tina. The lies are what the game is. But when the game causes true pain, it isn't a game anymore. Games are for laughter and freedom, not to hurt and torture."

Laurie wound her hair around his fist and pulled her head back. He held the sword at her throat.

"When a young boy secures a hotel room for a low-rent hooker, the least you can do is give him a blow job." Laurie sneered. Tina Two's eyes bulged as he pulled her hair, straining her neck backward.

"You don't scam the kid out of his money and leave him tied up naked in a chair." He lowered the sword and roughly pushed her head forward so that it hit the table. Morena flinched at the sound of Tina Two's head cracking. When Tina Two raised her head again, blood oozed from the gaping wound where her flesh and bone were splintered.

Laurie ripped at the T-shirt of Tina Two with one of his hands, tearing away her bra. The other slapped at her chest until her flesh was flushed and welted. Blood from her forehead spilled across his hands in a crimson Rorschach splatter. He laughed.

"Ah, Tina. How much fun we could have had. But you were a common thief. And worse than that, you lead me to my demise. Imagine that? A troubled teen, not one of your scum bag cheating husbands or cracked-out junkies, but just a young kid wanting to get laid without fear of rejection. And you couldn't do that."

Laurie pulled at one of Tina Two's large round breasts and clamped his teeth around it. He chewed roughly and she squawked in pain though the tape. He spit out her tit and slapped her across the breasts.

"Whatever, you whore. You had to make sure I remembered this fucking shithole of a night for eternity."

Laurie drew the blade across her neck and giggled as blood spilled forth from the slit. A strange gargling sound came from the wound and Tina Two was still.

"You want some of that, whore?" Laurie asked Morena as he approached her. He grabbed her jaw and forced her face up to meet his. "What are you looking at? You never seen a ghost before?"

He dropped his hand.

"A ghost, a demon, a haunting...I'm stuck here reliving that night forever." His voice softened and for a moment, Morena recognized the man she had enjoyed earlier that day. "But I found a way out. And I have to take it."

Morena shook her head.

"What does it matter? I'm already dead. Even hell would be better than this. This likely is hell. I don't know. But to see myself die every year. To see those cracked-out addicts kicking in the door and robbing me before slicing off my cock and disemboweling me over and over again. And for what? 'Cos i was a horny kid? How is that so evil? So wrong?"

He sobbed for a moment then looked over at Morena with clear dark eyes.

"If I were still alive, I'd probably like to date you. You seemed like a nice lady."

Morena trembled.

He stood up, clutching the sword in his hand.

"However, I've played this game too long to stop now because of one woman who will likely break my heart. I'm probably just 'transition' guy anyways, and we all know how those guys do." He sneered. "Besides, I'm already dead."

Laurie drew the sword across Morena's face quickly and forcefully. The bottom half of her head hung in a ruined mess. She looked up at him, her disbelieving mind fizzling out. She wanted to say something to him but could only think that she needed to think before the blade came down again. All thoughts were gone.

For a while.

Morena didn't know how long it had been since the night she had been slain by Laurie. She was adjusting to her new ghostly life, as were the other women. They had each other for company and that made the time pass.

In her new ghostly form, Morena never had to worry about her gut feelings anymore. As time wore on, the ghosts found themselves able to turn into human form for longer than a flicker or two to scare guests.

Before long, they were able to adapt to their human forms for days at a time. And could teleport to any human they desired while that human slept.

Morena often visited her exes and saw how despite all their promises and boohooing, nothing had truly changed. *She* just wasn't there anymore.

The other women too had similar explorations. They too discovered that their past loves had gone on to destroy more people.

Soon enough, talk began to turn to leaving the purgatory of the hotel and the endless anniversary slaughter when Laurie took their lives.

"What was it Laurie said?" Tina Five asked.

"Six, six, six…"

"Well there are six of us now. We each get one three times, and we're free."

"What if it's per person?"

"I doubt it. I bet it's the sacrificial number and it matters not who benefits. Six of us should make it extra special."

"I suppose…"

And so the ghosts began their hunt.

It was time to create new memories.

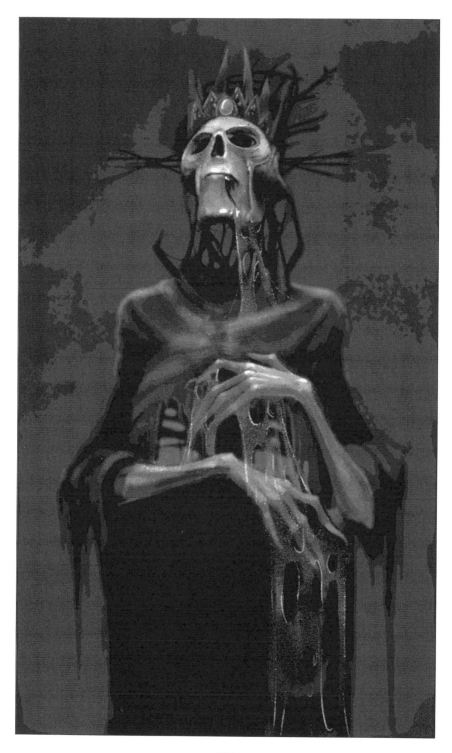

THE LAST STRAW

Lou Rera

"Go on Gary. Touch it. It's not alive, asshole."

"No way, man," said Gary. "There's something creepy 'bout this thing. It looks like that scarecrow in Jeepers Creepers."

"That's a freakin' movie, ya dipshit," said Bill. "Some farmer wanted to scare the fuck out of some crows—why not use a sinister scarecrow? Now go on, ya wuss, touch it!"

Bill McCaferty and Gary Koch looked at each other, then at me. They were both drunk. They'd spent the better part of the late afternoon and early evening draining their pay envelopes at the Double Dip Inn with T. Rice and a crusty old bastard named, Crim. All of them were haggard miners, not long for this world. If Black lung didn't get them, the booze and smokes would.

Bill whispered into Gary's shriveled ear. Gary raised his right eyebrow, looked around as if expecting someone to tap him on the shoulder. He snorted, then hawked out a slimy ball of phlegm. Gary whipped it out, and with the pissing strength of a sick old horse, did his best to arc a stream on my leg. He missed. He hit Bill's tattered steel-toed work boots.

"What the fuck, asshole?"

"Chill dude, ya told me to do it, ya dickweed!"

Gary zipped himself up, and did this weird thing with his tongue. He protruded his lower lip like it was packed with snuff. He looked left then right, then said, "I know it was only a movie, but that scarecrow in Jeepers Creepers could fly off the pole he's stuck on 'en kill people. Fly away with 'em—suck out their eyes!"

In a high-pitched squeaky voice Bill mocked, "Please Mr. Jeepers Creepers sir, don't keel me, oh pleeeease." They both chortled again in their drunken haze. Gary pulled a Bic lighter from his jacket, doused my face with moonshine, then lit it on fire. A charred blackened hole remained where my scarecrow's face had been.

In fiction, reincarnation has been a staple in dozens of stories from the X-Files to Chucky. In those tales, someone is executed, then reborn as something else. In past lives, I *was* the homicidal maniac from Haddonfield, butchering sex crazed teens as I wore my signature overalls and white William Shatner mask.

Bill and Gary have had a good laugh, burning away most of my face. My temporary blindness forces me to crawl. I can fix my scarecrow face, but it's my recollection of my past as a killer that incites my rage. I ache with murderous thoughts. I dream of gutting some bastard from groin to sternum.

I swear to the demons that devour the souls in hell, I will murder those sluts and studs in Haddonfield on Halloween. I will rip that town a new one. Until then, I need to kill someone. A trial run. Practice.

I pat the ground for scraps to rebuild my face. A few strips of burlap, black buttons and some other odds and ends will make me whole again.

In a cornfield near town, I am tethered to a laundry pole to frighten crows. An unknown force rides the cross breezes over the plains. A gust of wind wiggles my hat. I concentrate and I twitch my thumb and move my finger. The annoyed crows fly away. Two crows stay behind to test my skill as a floppy man of straw. I snap the neck of one. The remaining bird hops, then plucks out his brother's eye. I jump, he drops it. His beak is empty. The crow tries again.

Caw caw.

I laugh then chop the air with my arm. The crow jumps. It's lost its savage grip on the stingy remains of snapping tendons and collapsed veins. Flecks of straw and mouse shit-pellets rain from my coat. I am in a state of suspended decay, a desiccated effigy of a man of straw, whose purpose is to frighten.

It's October, and Halloween will soon be upon us. I've learned townsfolk are the same everywhere. I am the different one. I will be the intruder in the store, cradling cans of soup on top of scraggly arms, losing bits of myself here and there. I'll carry food I'll never eat. That I can't possibly eat.

Groceries will be a prop in a play where I'll star as the leading flimflam man in the destruction of other people's lives. My simple looks with button eyes and a cross-stitched mouth will allay their fears. I am the jester in the room, dancing my way into the warmth of their hearts.

I'm in Curtisville, on my way to the ground zero of Haddonfield. A nowhere place with pickup trucks rusting near the Double Dip Inn, where the friends of Bill McCaferty and Gary Koch fortify their day with rotgut moonshine. T. Rice and Crim slug it back next to the grease pit and rusted barrels behind the bar. T. Rice wipes his bearded mouth on his filthy sleeve as a crow swoops down from a utility pole and whisks away some discarded jerky. Crim sees me. I find it humorous, even amazing, that a walking scarecrow does not seem out of place to him. It's October. He nods in my direction, like we're old friends, and shrugs. Crim and the rest of the town will never remember seeing me.

I walk over to a life-size wooden Indian at Miller's Country Store. With one hand, the painted warrior shields his eyes, as he scouts an invisible enemy. The other hand holds a sign, "Cigars Sold Here." The Indian and I are effigies—comical stand-ins to serve at the pleasure of bullet-headed white Americans.

The day is crisp. I'm comfortable in the chill. Fresh produce is stacked high on the weathered wooden racks. On a rusted metal milk can from the 1950's, a glass jar is half filled with coins. The jar serves as a paperweight. A few torn notes read, IOU. I can smell the sweetness of apples. Fall is everywhere. Death is sooner than later for someone here.

I walk through the double screen doors. The hundred-year-old oak plank floor groans with every step I take, but it's the simple *jing-a-ling* of the entry bell that announces my presence. An extremely large young woman waddles out from the storeroom. A mixture of fear and uncertainty washes over her face. She looks over her shoulder and I imagine she wonders, *"Are there more like him?"*

My patched hobo sack hangs from my shoulder on a strap made of rope. It's worn and smells acrid from nights of sleeping in the mud and rain. But the odor is no worse than the subtle stink of this small town fear.

The cashier trundles up to the register. She places her greasy half-eaten pizza on a piece of ripped brown paper, the oil stain spreads like blood on a carpet. She straightens her nametag. *Dottie.* Of course her name is Dottie. A name from another era, from a time when innocence didn't equal ignorance.

She has a nose ring in the center of her moon shaped face. She drops her keys, bends over and I can see her tramp stamp hovering over the crack in her ass. Dottie's hair is matted in clumps as she rests her flabby arm on the plastic bag carousel. Skin oozes through the grate, waffling like Silly Putty. Dottie rams gossip into the ear of a leather-faced woman buying a carton of Kools. A cigarette smolders from her lips. The sting of the smoke scrunches her eye, as a curl of ash crumbles onto the counter. She glances over her shoulder and pretends to ignore me. The smoker wheezes as she shambles through the double-screened doors. She tiptoes over a sign taped to the window to get a better look at me.

I can sense that Dottie doesn't like strangers. I am the unknown. I am a manifestation of all of her fear. She will learn a valuable lesson today: That all is not as it seems. Love thy neighbor, but never trust him.

I am here to show this woman that all hell can break loose when you least expect it, and I will bath in the fire that will ignite her demise.

"Got a party to go to, mister?" she asks.

I remain silent.

"Do ya?"

"Nope. Just me being me."

Her perplexed look borders on controlled anxiety.

"Are you for real?" Then she catches her own attempt at a joke and in a moment of cockiness—chuckles to herself. She cranes her neck in search for a patch of skin anywhere on what she thinks is my costume.

"Well Halloween ain't fer a few weeks yet, mister. So what cha doing?"

"Well *DOTTIE*, you could say I'm rehearsing. It's sort of a practice run. Like my ol' self Michael. Remember the murdering man in the mask from Haddonfield, Dottie? The deranged killer of sluts and studs?"

"How's that mister?" she asks, with a trace of nervousness in her voice. "I don't g—"

"Are you really that fucking clueless, Dottie? Is it really any of your fucking business *why* I do what I do? I *can* call you DOTTIE now, right? After all, *tonight* you'll get to know me like no one else you've ever met."

I can imagine the wheels "a turning" in that sludge riddled brain of hers. She is searching her memory for some prankster from her past, capable of joking with her this way.

"Rory, is that you behind all that stuff?" she asks. "Golly, you had me going for a minute. So what gives, Rory? What's with the scarecrow getup? Got any weed?"

"It would be much better for you if I *were* Rory, wouldn't it? But I'm not. Think hard, Dottie. Put that fucked-up little brain of yours into overdrive. You don't know me, do you? And that's what frightens the fuckin' shit out of you. Am I right?"

Her eyes flick back and forth like one of those cat clocks from the 1950s. With the tick-tock of the seconds, her fear heightens, then bubbles into pure panic. Unconsciously, she twists her hair, and bites her lip. She marches in place like a five-year old needing to pee.

For Dottie, those seconds must have felt like a microwave ticking down to the beeps, signaling that her Hot Pockets are ready. I imagine she thought, *"Mind your language mister. Believe in the Lord and Jesus will save you. Oh GOD, please help me Jesus! Aw Fuck'n hell. He's going to rob the place, or worse!"*

Dottie is a victim of the butterfly effect. I'd explain that concept to her, but I'm just not in the mood to rattle off all of the possible things that needed to happen to bring both of us to this juncture.

I sense her apprehension. Her deodorant has failed her in a moment of budding tension, and I take a deep breath of her steamy rank. Her lip curls as she wipes the beads of sweat with her apron. The terror she feels is like the realization that a piece of meat has caught in her throat. I've always wondered how panic manifests itself, at the moment when a lion clamps down on the throat of a gazelle. Does instinct convert to pure resignation? Is there such a thing as the Kübler-Ross five stages of dying in the quick moments during a violent death?

"Just wondrin' if I knew you, is all," she says. "Just being friendly, mister."

"Well if you must know, DOTTIE, you don't know me. You may have seen some of my earlier performances on Demand. You know, the murdering maniac in the white mask? But here's the kicker. You will get to know me in a very BIG way. And when we're done here, maybe I'll stick around for a while to see the rest of the town. Kick up my feet a little and see the shit storm hit the fan."

"I'm closin' soon, mister. Um, I don't know what you had in mind, but I'm kind of busy." Her fear is effervescent. "Clyde Fretwell is in *fact...*" Dottie looks at her watch, and adds, "...on his way *right* now." Her features make her look as though she's drowning in confusion. "Well, not many strangers stay fer long, the town bein' so small 'en all. Heck, there ain't nothin' going on after seven, unless listenin' to that drunk 'ol fool, Red Stillwell, hoot and howl like a dog in the streets, does it for ya."

She's nervous. Her tension thrills and excites me. I feel alive. Exuberant. I feel the power of adrenaline for the first time in my new skin. My journey from a scarecrow in a cornfield, to a threatening stranger in Miller's Country Store has been a long one. I have yet to raise a hand to this woman. Her mounting terror is based solely on our discussion. I have said things simply to fuck with Dottie's head.

I watch her squirm as she looks at the mud on my jacket and the smirk stretched across my burlap face. The jagged stitching of my mouth, separates. It reveals to Dottie a cavernous indefinable blackness of the interior of my scarecrow's mouth. My stuffing has been augmented with urine and pellets of shit from rodents. Ticks burrow into the mice that are sickened in my brain. Unable to move, they steep in the horror of my thoughts.

I can see the trance of uncertainty well up in her eyes. I am the stone in her shoe and the gnat buzzing in her ear. I am her worst fucking nightmare delivered into her humdrum life. I'll save her from another useless Saturday night of cheap beer and bumbling sex.

She looks at my groceries. "Mister, will that be all?" I detect the quaver beneath her stern tone. She still has a modicum of control, or at the very least, her own perception of control. She's nervous and this makes me grin. No one else is here with us. She does not look up. The chain-smoking customer has long departed but I can still smell her lingering tobacco stink. I know Dottie realizes she's alone.

"Eat your pizza, Dottie," I say.

I let my arms fall—groceries tumble everywhere. Two cans of creamed corn roll in opposite directions. They sound like the low rumble of thunder on the hallow oak floor.

She can't speak. Dottie looks toward the door and must realize it's too far to run. Before she can take a step back, I am on her. I grab her by the neck and press my gloved thumb deep into the indentation above her collarbone. I push so hard I can feel her spine. I know I have just crushed her trachea. Her tongue juts out like a frog flicking flies. With my free hand, I ram the half-eaten slice of pizza into her face, breaking the bridge of her nose. I slam her head into the edge of the cash register with such force, her head cleaves like a melon. She's dead before she hits the floor.

I tilt my head with the quizzical look of a dog trying to make sense of an unfathomable scene. I notice the paint spattered CD player spewing a Zeppelin song near the microwave and donuts. What I see before me is a spontaneous art installation conceived by a madman. The steady drip, drip, drip of her blood is in its slow motion journey to the crimson pool blooming on the floor. I have succeeded at what I'd set out to do.

Headlights flash on, then off. A truck lumbers into the parking lot, doing a zig-zag around the potholes. I walk to the end of aisle two. I freeze like a decoration for the Halloween season. Little Debbies on my left side and Spam on my right. Behind me, there are rows and rows of candy and chips. A hand scrawled sign is taped to a shopping cart. It reads: "10 bags of chips for 10 bucks!"

A dude in a filthy John Deere cap, with grease up to his elbows, walks through the door. He gasps, but doesn't scream. The guy bolts, then pauses at the door. He pokes his head up like a meerkat. John Deere man walks swiftly around me down the aisle to the cooler and grabs two cases of Bud. He tiptoes around the body and snatches two cartons of Pall Malls. He exits in a flash. Even as I savor my evening of ultra-violence, I am not surprised by the beer thief's callousness. These people deserve me.

I consider this experience my scarecrow clan's version of Rumspringa—my Bar Mitzvah in hell—my confirmation into the church of Satan. I have consecrated my reincarnated soul upon the bloodied earth of damnation. Not in a grandiose Biblical way, but in the simplistic brutal way I ended Dottie's life. Plain, uneventful, and as simple as blowing out a match.

I have released her from her from her piggy ways.

"Hey Rory, got any weed?"

Yet, all the energy I've expended makes me wonder if her destruction was worth the effort? I think back to my rebirth—a time of swirling winds and the sounds of rustling leaves in acre after acre of cornstalks. That kind of solitude requires only a flick of the wrist or a nod of my head. For that little effort, the crows disappear.

In the hours that follow, the town is abuzz with the horror of Dottie's murder. In small town quickie-marts across the freedom plains, robberies, muggings, and scattered murders are as common as a sixty-four-ounce orange Slurpee. The news has given the town a collective brain-freeze. As it must, life will go on. Mice fuck, eat, piss, and then skitter on with their day.

Officer William "Bud" Hammister, of the two-man police force in Curtisville, calls in the State Police. My hideous crime is too big for the locals. The State boys find few clues. Hammister tells his partner, "The perps wanted to throw us off. Those bits of straw and dirt came from a cornfield. Dottie was decoratin' for Halloween 'zall."

In the dozens of crime scene photos on Hammister's desk, two should have caught his attention. In one photo, taken shortly after the murder, there is a scarecrow propped up at the front of aisle two. In the photo from the next morning, numbered JC1978, the scarecrow is gone.

ABOUT THE AUTHORS

D. J. Adadjii
fb.me/djadadjii

D. J. Adadjii is an emerging voice in horror and dark fantasy fiction. Although somewhat of a neo-luddite, Adadjii can be reached at fb.me/djadadjii.

Kelley Armstrong
kelleyarmstrong.com

Kelley Armstrong is the author of the Cainsville modern gothic series and the Rockton crime thrillers. Past works include Otherworld urban fantasy series, the Darkest Powers & Darkness Rising teen paranormal trilogies, the Age of Legends fantasy YA series and the Nadia Stafford crime trilogy. Armstrong lives in Ontario, Canada with her family. You can find her online at www.KelleyArmstrong.com

Dead Flowers by a Roadside originally appeared in The Mammoth Book of Ghost Stories by Women, edited by Marie O'Regan (2012).

Suzanne Church

suzannechurch.com

Suzanne Church grew up in Toronto, moved to Waterloo to pursue mathematics, and never left town. Her award-winning fiction has appeared in Clarkesworld, Cicada, On Spec, and her 2014 collection Elements. Her favourite place to write is a lakefront cabin, but she'll settle for any coffee shop with WiFi and an electrical outlet. Soul Larcenist, book one in the Dagger of Sacrados trilogy set in The Ed Greenwood Group's #Hellmaw Universe, is now available in multiple formats from the usual portals.

Death Over Easy originally appeared in Danse Macabre: Close Encounters with the Reaper, edited by Nancy Kilpatrick, Published by Edge Science Fiction & Fantasy Publishing (2012).

Brian F. H. Clement

brianclement.com

Brian F.H. Clement was born in Kelowna, British Columbia, Canada. He took up independent film in the late 90's, writing and directing 7 features in Victoria, BC, which were distributed by small labels around the world during the DVD boom of the early 2000s, and received screenings at film fests from Germany to Brazil, Australia to Argentina, as well as all over North America. One of these films, *Dark Paradox*, served as inspiration and background for his first novel, *The Final Transmission*. His most recent novel, *Assimilation Protocol*, is a sequel to *The Final Transmission*, and is coming soon from Damnation Books/Caliburn Press. Currently he writes for the web and print comic series Ghost Cats. Brian is the recipient of several film-related awards and currently resides in Toronto, Ontario, Canada where he works in film and television distribution, and continues to write and direct when time allows.

Subdermal is an original short story which features two of the main characters from, and takes place before the events of the novel The Final Transmission.

Derek Clendening

derekclendening.com

Derek Clendening lives in Fort Erie, Ontario where he writes and is also an artist. Recent books include The Vampire Way and Taken. Visit him online at derekclendening.com.

A. Giacomi

A.Giacomi is a writer, artist, and educator from Toronto, Canada. She is the mother of two tiny humans who inspire her to create weird and wonderful works that are both giggle worthy, bizarre, and unique. She is the author of The Zombie Girl Saga published by CHBB Publishing. A four-part series told from the zombie's perspective. She is deeply influenced by her fangirl tendencies and loves to throw lots of pop culture into whatever she creates. Other works include, Poveglia -The Island of The Dead available in the Beautiful Nightmares women in horror anthology, Slumber Games available in the Man Behind the Mask 80's themed horror anthology, and Hell on Earth in the And The World Will Burn dystopian anthology. To find out more about A. Giacomi and her works, visit www.poeticzombie.com

Sèphera Girón

sepheragiron.ca

Sèphera has been writing creepy tales since she could hold a pencil. Her book career began in 2000 with the publication of *Eternal Sunset* (Darktales Publishing, 2000), followed by *House of Pain* (Leisure Books, 2001) and *House Magic: The Good Witch's Guide to Bringing Grace to Your Space* by Ariana (Conari Books, 2001). Over twenty-three published books later, she's still working hard at scaring and delighting her readers. When she's not writing, she is a freelance editor, an actress, a tarot reader, and the Canadian Chapter Head of the Horror Writers Association. Sèphera is one of the contributors to The Great Lakes Horror Podcast, which is enjoying success on iTunes. Sèphera currently resides in Toronto.

Danann Hawes

@Hawesman
https://www.facebook.com/danann.hawes

Danann Hawes is a Toronto based horror writer. The author of 5 screenplays, he also enjoys writing short horror fiction. He is currently working on his 6th screenplay, a genre mix of horror, comedy and romance. Danann is also working on a short film and is in the early stages of co-writing a sci-fi feature. During the weekly nine to five, Danann is a Publisher for a small legal publishing house. He is interested in collaboration and enjoys interaction with his readers so please feel free to reach out.

Repo Kempt

Repo Kempt spent over ten years living and working in the remote communities of the Canadian Arctic. His short story *Left and Leaving* recently appeared in Pantheon Magazine. He is a regular columnist for Litreactor.com and when he's not writing, he's trying to do everything else all at once. He lives with his wife and his little dog, Galactus, on a cricket farm in rural Nova Scotia. You can find him on Instagram at @repokempt.

Nancy Kilpatrick

facebook.com/nancy.kilpatrick.31

Nancy is an award-winning author and editor, with 18 novels, 220 short stories, 6 collections, and 15 edited anthologies to her credit. She has also written 1 non-fiction book and 2 graphic novels.

Base of a Triangle was previously published in Horrors! 365 Scary Stories (1998), and reprinted in Cold Comfort (2001).

Monica S. Kuebler

blood-magic.net
wattpad.com/deathofcool

Monica S. Kuebler is a contributing editor at Rue Morgue magazine, author of Rue Morgue Library #3: Weird Stats and Morbid Facts, co-producer of the Great Lakes Horror Company podcast, and founder of LibraryoftheDamned.com. She also writes monster stories, and has spent the last half decade serializing her young adult vampire series, which kicked off in 2012 with Bleeder (Blood Magic, Book 1), at blood-magic.net. For more about Monica, visit monicaskuebler.com.

Shebat Legion

@shebatlegion

Shebat Legion's quirky tales include; *I Am Anastasia's Bracelet,* and *Just Like an Angel*, published in the shared-universe anthologies, *Sha'Daa: Facets,* and *Sha'Daa Inked*. Her stories, *Ophie and Undertaker*, and *Undertaker's Holiday* appear in the award-winning *Heroes in Hell* series, created by Janet Morris. Miss Legion is the creator of *Vampire Therapy: Chronicles of The Cat's Ass Boutique*. She is also the author of *Vampire Therapy: Jackson and Eva*, and is presently at work on book two of the *Vampire Therapy* series, *Elizabetta*. Recent stories in anthologies include: *Saltwater*, and *A Bird in Hand*, both for *Tales of the Fairy*; *Sasha Brook* for *Darklight Four*, *Father's Day* for *Slice Girls*; *The Apple* for *Group Hex Vol. 1*; *The Highway* for *Dark Corners*; *Pop, Goes The Zombi*, for *Twisted*; *Whatever Lola Wants* for *UnCommonMinds*, and *Silicon Oar* for *UnCommonLands*. Shebat Legion's newest release is her very first children's book, (ages 4-6) called *The Fork Tree* and is illustrated by Erika Szabo.

John R. Little

johnrlittle.com

John R. Little has been publishing horror and dark fantasy stories for more than two decades. With his 17 books to date, he's been nominated for the Bram Stoker Award four times and has won once. His most recent novels are DarkNet and Soul Mates, and he is hard at work on his next novel. John loves to hear from his readers, either on Facebook or at his web site, www.johnrlittle.com

The Slow Haunting was originally published in the anthology *Dark Delicacies 3* (2009).

Stephen B. Pearl

stephenpearl.com

Stephen B. Pearl's works range from post-apocalyptic science fiction, The Tinker's World Series, to his Norse inspired high fantasy, Horn of the Kraken, based on the Fate of the Norns Ragnarok RPG. His other works encompass paranormal, Nukekubi, Pagan centric paranormal romance, Worlds Apart, The Hollow Curse and the Samhain and Yule anthologies, military SF erotica, War of the Worlds 2030 and SF detective erotica, Slaves of Love, and straight erotica, the Happy MILF and DILF day anthologies. His writings incorporate real places and focus on the logical consequences of the worlds he crafts. For more, visit his website: www.stephenpearl.com or his Amazon page: www.amazon.com/author/stephenpearl

Mary Rajotte

maryrajotte.com

Toronto-native Mary Rajotte has a penchant for penning nightmarish tales that haunt and terrify. Her work has been published in Shroud Magazine, and in anthologies from the Library of Horror Press and Shroud Publishing. Sometimes camera-elusive but always coffee-fueled, you can find Mary at her website www.maryrajotte.com.

Lou Rera
lourera.com

Lou is a member of the Horror Writers Association, Just Buffalo Literary Center, and the Short Fiction Writers Guild. His work includes award-winning flash fiction and short stories. His first novel, *SIGN*, was published by Netherworld Books in June 2014. Lou Rera is an Associate Professor in Communication at SUNY Buffalo State.

Andrew Robertson
@AndrewAwesome76

Andrew Robertson is an award-winning queer writer and journalist. He has published articles in *Xtra!, fab magazine, ICON, Gasoline, Samaritan Magazine, neksis* and *Shameless*. His fiction has appeared in literary magazines and quarterlies such as *The Sirens Call, Undertow, Deadman's Tome, katalogue, Feeling Better Yet?*, and in several anthologies including *Gone With the Dead, Group Hex Volumes 1 and 2, First Hand Accounts, DILF, MILF: Happy Mother's Day* and *Abandon* among others. He is the founder and co-host of The Great Lakes Horror Company podcast, official podcast to Library of the Damned, and a member of the Horror Writer's Association.

Douglas Smith
smithwriter.com

Douglas Smith is an award-winning Canadian author described by Library Journal as "one of Canada's most original writers of speculative fiction." His fiction has been published in twenty-six languages and thirty-two countries. His work includes the urban fantasy novel, The Wolf at the End of the World, and the collections Chimerascope, Impossibilia, and La Danse des Esprits. His non-fiction guide for writers, Playing the Short Game: How to Market & Sell Short Fiction, is a must read for any short story writer. Doug is a three-time winner of Canada's Aurora Award, and has been a finalist for the John W. Campbell Award, CBC's Bookies

Award, Canada's juried Sunburst Award, and France's juried Prix Masterton and Prix Bob Morane. A short film based on Doug's story "By Her Hand, She Draws You Down" won several awards at film festivals around the world. His website is www.smithwriter.com and he tweets at @smithwritr

Fiddleheads was been previously published in Chilling Tales 2 (2013).

Robert Smith
RobertSmithThrillers.ca

Robert Smith hails from Prince Edward Island (off Canada's east coast). On this small island, ocean waves drive hard against red cliffs. So, with fears that the sandstone island might soon melt into the Atlantic, Robert finished his studies in Information Technology and moved to Canada's capital. Robert has worked in network design, administration and security. He also flipped burgers, waited tables, and blended drinks for an orange guy named Julius (not that any of that matters). Now, he manages a digital forensics team, supporting investigations (during the day), and writes. This author writes thrillers (psychological, suspense, crime and horror). Pick one up if you like that sort of thing. And visit www.RobertSmithThrillers.ca for the latest news.

Julianne Snow
@CdnZmbiRytr
juliannesnow.com

Julianne Snow is the author of the *Days with the Undead* series and *Glimpses of the Undead*. She is the founder of Zombieholics Anonymous and the Co-Founder and Publicist at Sirens Call Publications. Writing in the realms of speculative fiction, Julianne has roots that go deep into horror and is a member of the Horror Writers Association. With pieces of short fiction in various publications, Julianne always has a few surprises up her sleeves.

Jessie Turk

twistedtalesstudio.com

Jessie Turk is a VFX production coordinator by day, and writer by night. Most of her published work to date have been articles and blog posts about an industry she is intimately familiar with: film. Somewhere along the way, she decided it was time to tell her own horror stories, rather than just talk about them. Jessie is a newly emerging author, and EVIDENCE is her first short story published in print as part of Group Hex Vol 2. For updates, articles, and the occasional scary story, visit Jessie's blog at www.twistedtalesstudio.com.

Jason White

Jason White is a writer and podcaster. He has published 18 short stories in various magazines and anthologies. Look for his story, Dweller Messiah, coming soon in the C.H.U.D. Lives tribute anthology from Crystal Lake Publishing.

ABOUT THE ARTISTS

Dinis Freitas (Cover Artist)
facebook.com/thedinisf

Toronto-born and raised, Dinis discovered his love of design while avoiding the curriculum of his University degree. This led him to work with Pride Toronto, Canadian musical artist Esthero, US based textile/home furnishing studios, and Canadian designer Ami McKay. He is self-taught and currently curates an Instagram account that caters to discarded toilets which has been featured in Toronto zine Crapnation! Now a designer for Fabricland he maintains his youthful creativity through his love of Transformers.

Brett Bakker
brettbakker.com

A lifelong horror fan, Brett spent his childhood jumping from couch to couch in a vampire cape his mother made him and later when he got old enough, cut his teeth in the world of graphic design laying out issues #47 - #70 of Rue Morgue Magazine. He later went on to design and illustrate Fangoria's 300th issue anniversary cover where he rebuilt and reintroduced the classic Fangoria logo which had not been used since the magazine's early heydays and now continues to be widely used to this day. Still an avid fan of the genre, these days you can find him working on new ghastly designs on his account at redbubble.com as well doing a wide variety of design and illustration work spanning different genres and industries.

Aramika Kliavin

zorachk.wixsite.com/aramika

Aramika completed traning in Europe and Canada, and received a Bachelor of Fine Arts (BFA) at OCAD University in 2012. She creates conceptual, at times surrealistic artwork that captures the essence of her imagination, combining traditional european techniques in new and innovative ways.

Johnny Larocque

johnnylarocque.com/

Johnny lives to make things, mostly messes, but also comics at totalrando.com

Izzy McCoy

izzymccoy.com

Painter and illustrator Izzy McCoy hails from the former mining town of Marmora, Ontario. Her formative years saw the young Izzy learning to paint by peering intently over her mother's shoulder as she crafted whimsical Dutch folk art scenes on wood. By igniting Izzy's imagination, these early influences informed her use of cross-cultural themes and imagery, which appeared throughout her scholarship at OCAD. To date, such elements continue to impact upon her art. Izzy's work has appeared in animation form on MTV Canada and she has contributed art to publications such as The Walrus Magazine.

Monstermatt Patterson
monster-matt.com

Monstermatt Patterson, The Man of a Thousand Bad Monster Jokes, is the award-winning author and artist of *Ha-Ha! Horror* and *Bride of Ha-Ha! Horror*. He writes for several websites, appears in Troma films and other low budget fare. He also appears regularly on the Six Foot Plus (6FtPlus) podcast.

Jen Rec
facebook.com/jenrec75

Jen Rec is a transplanted Torontonian now living a simpler life in Waterloo Region. As a lifelong fan of the Horror genre, her work is often of a dark theme. Usually working in her preferred black ink, she lists classic Science Fiction, Horror Comic books and Tattoo Art as her inspiration. Currently, Jen Rec is part of a collective of local Toronto artists who have recently launched an adult colouring book titled "PunkPourri" and is currently working on a second edition. Stay tuned for her next big project "Monsters Are Real": A Study of Serial Killers. You can find Jen Rec online at Jen Rec Art on Facebook, and jen_rec_art on Instagram.

Jordan E. Smith
eshelledesigns.weebly.com/

Originally from Prince Edward Island, before settling in Constance Bay, Ontario. Jordan studied Horticultural Industries at Algonquin College and interested in illustration, tattoos, reading, rock music, Tarot, Sacred Geometry, the Occult, spirituality, sleeping, eating, sleeping, collecting vinyl, pool, cats, collecting everything, Photoshop design, snowboarding, writing, stones, horror movies, and more illustration

Arinn Westendorf

arinn.com

Arinn is your average art dork. She's really into ghosts, reading, learning new things, telling jokes, and taking photos. She spends most of my free time either hunched over her art desk or shoving my camera in people's faces. Arinn is interested in photographing people more than things or places, and loves drawing animals, ghosts, and weird spooky people. She loves drawing ghosts so much that she has teamed up with author Brian Clement for a new comic called Ghost Cats- find them at ghostcats.ca.

Listen to the Great Lakes Horror Company Podcast on iTunes and at the
Library of the Damned at http://libraryofthedamned.com/